Mirren Jones is the pseudonym of the
collaborative writing partnership of
Marion Duffy and Elaine Atkins.

Eight of Cups is their first novel.

Visit their website:
www.mirrenjones.co.uk

Also by these authors

Non-fiction

Facilitating Groups in Primary Care

Facilitating Organisational Change in Primary Care

EIGHT OF CUPS

Mirren Jones

A catalogue record for this record is available from the British Library.

ISBN 978-0-9560841-0-1

First published in Great Britain 2008 by EM People
Crathie Bridge, Meigle, Blairgowrie, Perthshire, PH12 8QZ

Cover designed by Ann Landrock

Typeset by The Windfall Press, Isle of Lewis

Printed and bound in Great Britain by Gomer Press, Llandysul

Dedicated to Auntie Tessa and Doris

Women of indomitable spirit

Little girl blue

Picture me then at eight years old. Red shorts, a white button-through blouse with little puff sleeves, and a pair of blue and white striped canvas gym shoes. Two kirby grips to hold back my unruly shoulder length dark hair, one on each side of a ragged middle parting. Rosy cheeks from a summer spent in the local park. A little breathless from pushing that swing higher and higher then running right underneath it and out of reach, before it swung straight back down again.

Then come with me to a cheap hotel in Glasgow. We're all there for the weekend for a treat while Dad's at a Local Government conference. It's about 10pm. Norma and Campbell are fast asleep, I'm reading 'Five on Kirrin Island Again' with a torch under the bedcovers. Mum's crying softly into the pillow and I can sense a problem. Dad is 'in a mood.'

Feel my fear.

He comes back into our room, slams the door and launches into a fierce interrogation – 'Why didn't you come to meet me after the dinner? What did you get up to? Why is *she* still awake? Why did you pick this lousy guest house anyway?'

And know that you'll need to comfort the younger two when they wake up, put a consoling arm around Mum's shoulders and hold back your own wobbly tears. Everything must stay calm.

And still feel that fear – almost forty years on. Only now, for the *very first time*, recognise what it is and where it all started. And – what's worse – the effect it has had every day of your life from that day on.

**

What the world saw was Diane, eldest child of Ken and Isobel Steven. Lively, tall for her age, a fast runner when she wasn't falling over her own oversized feet, happy out of doors, head in a book otherwise. A bright child who does well as she moves into Forfar Academy, developing real talent as an artist, and with a strong sense of right and wrong, manifesting itself in support for all underdogs.

But indoors, I was someone different. I was 'the watcher.' Six pm and no sign of Dad – better listen out for his key. Back door pushed open roughly – maybe he's angry. Mum fidgety and fragile – is she expecting trouble? Dad's voice roughening up – will he go for Mum or will it be one of us? Not that he ever raised a hand – his look, tone, accusations and overpowering body language had the ability to reduce us all to quivering wrecks.

I watched for us all. And when they came, these black days, I stayed strong for the others and minimised any possible triggers. It became what I did; it became who I was; the knot in my stomach a permanent feature. I could breathe really quietly if I had to and never caused any trouble at home. If necessary, I could distract the other two and move them out of range. And I became Mum's best friend. Just so that everything could be calm.

No-one else knew. Not even Bruce.

Dad struggled from time to time with his moods but we never talked about that. Mum was either queen of the walk or little girl lost depending on how Dad was. Oh we had some good times – holidays at Dunoon, trips to the Lammas Fair in St Andrews, an odd Saturday night at the Palace Theatre in Dundee to see Francie and Josie. The reality of it was that despite his depressive episodes, Dad was often in good humour, Mum could be apparently carefree and the other two were just silly kids having fun. But I always had to watch.

My honed observation skills served me well in the old folks' home that year between leaving school and leaving home. Not a stray chin hair escaped my notice. Every tearful sigh at the end of visiting hour was consoled with a kind word or a stroking of the wizened old arm. That carer, coper, rescuer side of me given every opportunity to grow long and clinging tendrils, squeezing the life out of other aspects of my personality.

Perhaps the weight of it all only struck me for the first time when at 18 years of age I arrived in Edinburgh for Freshers' Week with an oversized suitcase, and a bag of books for pre-course reading which frightened the life out of me with their intellectual titles. What on earth was 'Structure, Culture and Function?'

Leaving home doesn't mean leaving it all behind, however. Even Dad's death twenty four years later didn't put an end to it.

Francka took me back through those long years when safe,

warm, relaxed and comfortable in her cream leather recliner, I began to unravel the cord.

The routine had become quite familiar. A warm greeting from the small white-haired German lady, after the brisk walk uphill to her Victorian villa with the view over Perth. A cup of tea in her cosy sitting room with its curious juxtaposition of Christian and Buddhist artefacts. Then the magic words delivered in her heavily accented voice:

'Ten, nine, eight – more and more relaxed.

'Seven, six, five – deeper and deeper you go.

'Four, three, two, one – now you are totally relaxed and comfortable.'

By session six, she had learned much of my story, and took me a stage further towards some kind of resolution.

'Diane, look for the child coming down the road towards you. You know how old she is and what life has been like for her. Now welcome her, give her a hug and ask her to sit with you for a while. Tell her you love her and that you know how hard it has been for her to be a good and kind daughter and sister. Tell her you will always remember and value what she did and that she should be proud of herself.

'Sit for a while with her, and then let her know the time is now right for her to go and play and put the sadness and worry away for ever. You will be there for her if she ever needs you. When you are ready, give her a final goodbye cuddle and kiss and wave her off back down the road.'

* *

I've had to bring back the young child that was me several times over the years, sit her on my knee and deal with some difficult memories from the past. No more burying them. No more pretending to be Miss Perfect, Miss Super Coper.

Remember in detail, feel the feelings again, comfort, protect, release the child from all responsibility – and then let go. Cut the cord. That was the idea. That was the theory anyway.

Knowing me, knowing you

All I'd thought about that last summer had been getting away to Uni. Starting a new life. Having a good reason for not being there. That was it – not being there. Because if I *was* there, I could never move on, never change, never blossom. Never be anyone other than that caring, coping Diane. My role in the family might as well have been set in Rubislaw granite.

My first day in Edinburgh had been like a wedding day. Something to look forward to for months. Visualising it, anticipating the excitement. Imagining myself dancing. Dreading it and dying for it all at the same time.

Then the next day was like the first day of married life, when you'd never thought beyond the wedding. Suddenly it's *what now?* And *is this it?*

And then it dawns on you and excites you. No-one knows you here. You've proved yourself by getting in. You can reinvent yourself. Make up your own history. Be who you want to be.

So you try. Try to be like the others, the in-crowd. That casual air of confidence. That knowing how to do everything perfectly. Having all the right hallmarks.

'Yes, I'm in Social Science. Want to work for the UN eventually. World poverty maybe. That was my special for Modern Studies. Got an A for it. Amazing considering the wild social life I was having at the time. Had to keep all that hush-hush from the parents though. They would have had a fit.'

Maybe you even start to believe you're a new person.

But then that old shadow moves back into view and threatens everything. You're face to face with that old familiar you. And all the things that worry you, cause you grief, hold you back. The things you hate about yourself.

Meeting Nancy hastened the shadow's return. She was everything I would have loved to be – and wasn't. Or so it seemed.

Nancy's first version of her life story had *silver spoon* and *the world's my oyster* written all over it.

Name: Nancy Thorpe, loving and much loved gentleman farmer's daughter, sister of Peter. Mother's family owns a famous emporium in Skipton.

Home address: Highwood End Farm, Netherby, Skipton, in Yorkshire. Education: private girls' school where she played first violin in the orchestra and excelled at sports. Qualifications: three good A levels. Pets: pony called Ginger, dog named Molly. Hobbies: music, hockey, hunting, show jumping

Relationships: currently available and with a wealth of knowledge to share. Experience with men: lost her virginity at 17 to Nigel, twenty-two, drop-dead gorgeous, tall, dark and handsome with the bonus of a car! The village girls hadn't seen the like of him before. Thereafter sampled some of the delights of the local Agricultural College and the Bramham Moor Hunt.

Ambition – short term to have a ball in Edinburgh for five years before leaving with a degree in Vet Medicine. And long term to add a house in the country, a sexy loving husband, several children, a couple of retrievers and a stable full of thoroughbreds.

The truth was a little less glittery. It came out over a few halves of cider in Jinglin' Geordies one wet Monday night. We were huddled near the coal fire, moaning about the weather. Putting off getting down to some essay or other that was due in soon. I was feeling a mite sorry for myself and indulging in a spot of the old 'I'll never get a decent degree here. I'm not bright enough' and so on.

Nancy's retort of 'try having to get As for everything and then you can moan' opened the door to the realities of being Nancy.

It seemed the gracious Mr and Mrs Thorpe were struggling to make a living out of Highwood End Farm, niggling at each other constantly in the day to day grind. Brother Peter had been designated black sheep of the family after daring to choose a life as a motor mechanic down south, over his heritage on the farm. Nancy was leaving the area to get as far away as possible from the parochial, busybody, nosey neighbour existence where you were a 'slag' if you had more than one boyfriend in a year, and a 'hussy' if you dared wear a short skirt out on a Saturday afternoon. And as far away as possible from her parents with their provincial expectations and traditional values.

Losing her virginity in the woods hadn't been the earth shattering experience she'd expected either. She'd got a bird's nest in the back of her long, permed hair, which had been really difficult to comb out. Her mother had seen it and guessed what she'd been up to and from that day on, had disapproved of each and every boyfriend. And in truth, there hadn't been all that many.

Three good A-levels was short of the mark for acceptance into Veterinary Medicine. So she was in Biology through clearing with a vague promise of a possible transfer to Vet if she excelled in the first two years of the BSc.

And as for having a ball for the next five years – well maybe – but at the same time taking care not to aggravate a back injury which had kept her off her beloved horses for many months and curtailed her activities both in and out of the saddle.

So – she wasn't just as together as she'd made out. But she didn't dwell on it, tell others about it or let it colour her day. She had a vision of her future and it would motivate and spur her on till she achieved it – regardless. With her beautiful long dark hair, boundless vitality and a knock-out smile, she launched into every day with confidence, determination and optimism.

She was blunt too.

'Tosh, utter tosh Diane. You can be whatever you want to be. Do whatever you want to do. You've got loads of talents and skills. Don't be such a sap. Life is for grabbing by the balls and making it work for you. I'm not listening to any more crap about *can't or don't feel up to it, or not good enough*. When it comes to jobs, if you want to do more than wipe old biddies' arses for a living, you'll have to project ability and confidence, and stop worrying about the rest of humanity. And if you want a man you'll *need* to stop all that or he'll think you're a right wet lettuce. You can choose you know. You can choose you – and what you want. And you'll only be restricted by your own lack of belief.'

'Well. .... It's not that easy Nancy.'

'Stop it. There you go again. Now think positive. Look, there's a guy in a dark blue jumper over there looking at us. See if you can get him over here.'

'Maybe I'll just watch you this time Nance. Pick up a few lessons from the expert.'

In the space of ten minutes she'd got his name (Chris), his life story, a round of drinks and an invite to a party the next night in Mylne's Court.

'Now, wasn't that easy?'

It was if you were Nancy.

Friends will be friends

Unlike Nancy, who'd arrived in Edinburgh not knowing a single soul, I had the security of an old friend from schooldays. We'd met a couple of years before at the 1970 Midlands Girls Hockey training week. On that dreamy summer day, on a pristine hockey pitch untouched since the previous season, the line up had me at centre half and Patricia at centre forward – on opposite sides. We all knew the form – no sticks above the shoulder, no backsticks, no feet unless you were in goal, eye on the ball, look for a space, run into it and keep your marker in view. The first few games I was all gangly legs and out of puff, unco-ordinated and caught flat footed on numerous occasions. Things got better though – on and off the pitch.

It was in the days before the teachers' strike when the local schools played regularly on Saturday mornings, Forfar Academy umpired by the formidable Miss Mudie (Ma Mud) in her track suit bottoms and woolly hat, no longer able or likely to run far but *miraculously* capable of seeing all at a considerable distance from the play.

I had met Patricia on a number of occasions during secondary school – first year tennis matches, junior athletic games, first eleven hockey leagues and now Midlands' trials. We were usually in direct competition with each other, grudging in defeat and smug in success. Hockey camp gave us a chance to get to know each other in a more personal and less competitive way – at least off the pitch.

There were four to a room in the camp dormitory at Belmont – two sets of bunks. Patricia insisted on the bottom bunk. Apparently you couldn't be sure that the bedding was always clean on the top bunks – or so the story went. So I quickly bagged the other bottom one, wishing the best of British to the other two, whoever they turned out to be. There were other myths around about mice in the kitchens, mouldy bread in the syrup pudding and a dishy local lad behind the bar at the village pub. What they didn't know, they made up.

We must have looked an odd couple. Patricia was wiry, dark haired (in a perfect bob), slim faced with angular features, small and neat in every way. I had outgrown all my classmates by the end of first year and they never quite caught up with me. I was best described as 'lanky'. It was just as well Birrells' stocked plenty size 7s or I'd have struggled to find a pair of shoes to fit. My hair had an unfortunate kink in it which rendered it unpredicable at best. And my nose might have been a throwback to the Roman march through nearby Alyth. However, we shared a determination to win at the beautiful game and by the end of that week, made arrangements to stay in touch.

I was fascinated by Patricia's home life. There isn't a religious divide on the East Coast, but the truth was that I had never even been in a Catholic household. Statues on painted shelves, crucifixes above the beds, disturbing pictures of bleeding hearts in the sitting room and a little receptacle of holy water at the front door. I didn't know whether it would offend them more to ignore it or make the cross the wrong way round the first time I went to visit the Foley family in Johnstone Avenue.

Their story was similar to many. Michael Foley of Irish descent had met Anne Mitchell, Dundonian through and through, at a dance at the Dundee Palais. Anne took instruction at St Joseph's Church with Father McBride to prepare for nuptial mass in July 1951. In the next five years Patricia arrived second after the unfortunate Paul, and before Mary-Margaret and Martin. The others were red haired but Patricia took after the Mitchell side.

We took to meeting once a month or so after hockey camp so that Patricia could supposedly keep me up to date with the hockey news. We could chat for hours over a couple of cokes in Green's cafe without having to spend much. What I really liked about her was the way in which she had her life mapped out and clear in her head. You worked hard, you focussed on what you wanted to achieve, you didn't waste energy on people or things that would get in the way and you always remembered the *poor wee mites in Tullynaught* where your Granny would still be now if she hadn't had a plan to better herself.

For the most part it seemed to work. Patricia (never 'Pat') occupied the top right hand desk in every classroom in St Joseph's Primary School, won the Leng Medal for singing *Ae Fond Kiss* so sweetly, ran faster than anyone her size or bigger under the age of 12 in Dundee and was a good help with the younger ones for her harassed Mother. She had set her mind on being a primary school teacher early on. It was a vocation after all and one of the most important jobs to be done in this or any town.

I looked on with admiration at Patricia's single mindedness. But there was one thing about her – she got quite agitated if you touched any of her stuff. The books on her bookshelf were in order of size, the shoes under her bed in pairs and facing in the same direction, the ornaments on her windowsill in some specific pattern not immediately obvious to an observer but instantly noticed by her if moved. She would make reference to the 'clumsiness of the wee ones' and how she wanted a lock on her bedroom door. I suspected there might be more to it than that, and wondered how she would manage in halls at Craiglockart if she had to share a room. She'd better get in there first and pick the bed with the least stains on it.

New kids in town

September 1972 – Edinburgh – Freshers' Week Year 1

Maybe I was born with 'should', 'must' and 'better not' hard wired into my brain. I never considered what I, just me, would really like. The result was that even pleasant experiences presented me with imponderable questions:

Can I really justify buying that new jumper which I don't need, when half the world is starving?

How can I be sad when I've got everything I want, and more?

For me there was no such thing as free choice, or even a free lunch. My internal critic always imposed limitations or conditions. The Ten Commandments could have been written just for me with their emphasis on *Thou shalt not.* Years later, I would consider the Dalai Llama's view that the purpose of life is to be happy – but even then, after all that I'd been through, I wasn't entirely convinced.

So it was then, that I first met Carys. We were standing side by side in the long winding queue inside Wilkie House to complete our first major rite de passage during Freshers' Week 1972 – matriculation. Without the benefits of the digital age it was a tortuous business of forms, flashes, photographs and all manner of information about course options, directors of study, grant awards and vaccination status.

I noticed firstly that Carys was looking a bit wan, and secondly that she was carrying a copy of *The Existence of Mind.* Maybe the girl was lonely. Catching her eye and pointing to the book, I remember asking, 'Well, does it exist?'

Carys (hung-over as it happened) hadn't actually read the book, rather it was an accessory to her blue stocking image – long black skirt, black tights, dangling ear-rings, multi-coloured patchwork style cardigan and black woollen pull on hat. Her reply 'Well now, give me at least until week two and then I'll tell you,' would later become part of the Dalmeny Street Girls' vocabulary.

The queue inched forward so slowly that we had plenty of time to correct and improve first impressions and go much further.

I was conscious of the possibility of gaining a new and clearly intelligent friend, and to make myself appear rather more of a highbrow than I felt inside, I expounded on my interest in society and how it organised itself to support and protect its weaker members. Carys, ever keen to emphasise her intellectual prowess, focussed on her plans to get a PhD and then study and work abroad on a suitable theological topic.

I told her about my work in the old people's home, describing it as a mind expanding, life changing experience. Carys described her music as an expression of 'an inner searching', which had begun with her first tentative solo steps on the piano.

Amazing what a few days at University can do for you.

We moved on to first impressions of Edinburgh – The Athens of the North, Auld Reekie, The Windy City – how it was endlessly fascinating, offering beckoning glimpses of the Castle, the Crags, the sea and the hills at every turn. How its old stone tenements, seven or eight stories high and hundreds of years old, had retained their air of antiquity and domesticity despite the invasion of tourist-trapping exhibitions and guided tours. We both loved the solidity, the elegance, the stoicism and the dependability of the capital city with its imposing situation on seven hills and its history disappearing back into the mists of time.

She moaned that I had landed lucky getting into Pollock Halls – rooms cleaned regularly (if you were out of bed of course), central heating, a proper desk to work at, an anglepoise lamp even, breakfast provided (with scope to sneak out a boiled egg and a buttered roll to keep for lunch) and dinner where you had a daily opportunity to view at your leisure the available 'talent' which was otherwise holed up in the science departments at Kings' Buildings or in the Medical School. Compare that with Mrs MacDonald's B&B where spartan was king.

Celts together although oceans apart in the way we looked then. I wore what you might call *functional* clothing – a navy reefer jacket, navy cords, and a yellow Aertex tee-shirt. Carys, with the pointed features, black black hair and petite build characteristic of her Welsh origins, was dressed like the intellectual she believed herself to be.

Neither of us had ever travelled far from home, living a largely local based life, pre-occupied with parochial concerns. We were both keen to savour the variety, taste the freedom and grasp the opportunities that were all around us. I was amazed at the assortment of people I had met in these first few days – Khalid, a Libyan mature student who was under pressure to get married so that his younger brothers could then do the same, Suzanne who had got pregnant in fifth year at school, had the baby and left it behind with her mother in Newcastle, Heather who had freakily followed the same path as me by leaving school early and going to work in an old people's home in Larkhall and was now studying Social Science. Carys had obviously used a different conversational strategy with her new acquaintances – Mike who had six straight As at Higher from Dollar Academy and wanted to be a brain surgeon (no kidding), Helen who had a passion for Mary Queen of Scots and intended to become the national expert on the topic, and Taavi who was into documenting the oral history of shamans in Finland.

After an hour queuing to endure the rigmarole of matriculating, we recovered with coffee and apple turnovers in the Women's Union in Chambers Street. The only spare chairs were at a table where an athletic looking girl with long dark hair and a healthy country glow was sitting reading The Horse and Hound magazine. I asked if we could join her and then felt obliged of course, to exchange a few words. It was my first encounter with Nancy.

'We've just matriculated. Laborious business. What about you?'

'Flippin' 'eck. It took me ages. Thank God my photo turned out okay. Couldn't bear to carry my matric card around all year with me looking a dog's dinner. How are the turnovers? I had parkin – just to see if they could make it the way we do in Yorkshire. Not bad though.'

'They make a change from bridies! That's our local delicacy,' I replied.

The chat wandered easily and seamlessly through mid Wales, the Yorkshire Dales, the Vale of Strathmore and back again. We backtracked with a laugh into formal introductions:

'I'm Diane Steven, born and bred in but glad to leave Forfar. Studying Social Sciences.'

'And I'm Carys Lloyd-Jones, escaped from the isolation of West Wales, and signed up for Religious Studies.'

'I'm Nancy Thorpe, from the Skipton area of Yorkshire, here to study Biological Sciences but hoping to get into Vet Medicine.'

We indulged in the standard freshers' chat – how hard it was to find your way round the huge library in George Square, why you bothered signing up for all sorts of weird and wonderful clubs and societies at the Freshers' Fair when you'd never have time to get round them all, and what a brilliant range of shops there were in the city, from Jenners posh department store in Princes Street (only looking) to the wee shop on Victoria Street which sold only brushes (again, only looking!).

Freshers' Week ended with The Freshers' Dance in the Assembly Rooms in George Street. It was somewhere between a ball and a disco with live music, DJs, and party decorations, but a casual dress code and hot dogs and stovies for supper. We decided we might as well go together now that we knew each other.

Two thousand students were matriculating over the space of a week. Chance or fate would decide who stood in which particular queue on which day and whether or not they might start chatting. Having a coffee and finding a common interest or an easy familiarity might transform that initial social chat into a developing friendship.

Nancy joined the hockey trials in week two. She and I met at hockey practice most weeks from then on. Even when Nancy's old riding injury was playing up, she'd go along for the beer afterwards.

As fate would have it, Carys and I had both elected to take a short course in academic writing, Carys to stay ahead of her group, and me to overcome my performance anxiety. We would meet at the end of East Preston Street to walk the short distance to Appleton Tower every Thursday night for the following six weeks. Carys apparently noted in her next weekly letter home that she now had four new friends – Lesley, Alix, Nancy and Diane. I felt a small glow inside when she told me.

Ain't no sunshine

October 1972 – Mrs Mac's – first term, first year

'I don't know whether I'm going to be able to stand it, Lesley, living here for a whole year.' Carys was looking quite dejected, sitting cross-legged on her bed.

'Well, there's plenty wrong with it, I know; Mrs Macdonald's attitude really gets me – she's so old-fashioned, and there's all the rules and regulations we're supposed to abide by. A curfew at midnight, that's too early when you're supposed to be a student; 'no visitors except by prior arrangement', and so they go *on* and *on*, I can't even remember them all. But we've got to make the most of it and not let it get to us because there's nowhere else to go for now, unless some of the other students drop out of halls and free up some places. How would we know if that happened anyhow Carys? There's probably hundreds of first-years like us trying to get out of their digs.'

'We could make friends with someone in the accommodation office, act as if we're really unsettled, miserable beyond, us being so far away from home, and then they'll feel sorry for us and put us higher up the waiting list maybe.'

'Mmm, I think they'd look after their own first, but it's worth a try.'

'Okay then, I'll go over tomorrow and start sweet-talking someone and see how far I get. If that doesn't work we'll go again the next day, together, and put some more pressure on. Eventually they might get sick of us complaining and find us somewhere else just to shut us up!'

Carys and Lesley had been in Mr and Mrs Macdonald's B & B establishment in Lutton Place for one month. They were already fed-up of the small room they were sharing, the luke-warm bath-water and the mundane daily breakfast which *always* consisted of Cornflakes *or* Weetabix, plus toast with marmalade or jam, and tea or coffee. Bacon and eggs were a special treat on Saturday mornings, but *only* if the girls confirmed by Friday morning that they would definitely be there to eat it.

Mrs Macdonald didn't like to waste any food – in fact, she didn't like to waste anything at all. Not the slivers of soap that should have been long consigned to the waste bin. Not the bread that was almost (but not quite) past it and ready for the birds. Not the bottom layer in the jam and marmalade pots, even though it might have lots of old buttery bits and crumbs. Not newspapers, which were piled up in the porch, ready for lighting the coal fire in the TV lounge. Not putting on a wash unless the machine was full. Not altering the setting on the gas fire in the bedroom unless given permission (if one of them was brave enough to ask).

Not left-over food from anyone's plates, which Mrs Macdonald would neatly scrape straight into the dog's bowl. The girls used to bet that she made a mental note of how much each set of left-overs weighed, and then adjusted Hamish's dinner accordingly, giving him more, but preferably fewer, dog biscuits. The one thing they *liked* about the place was Hamish, a West Highland terrier who was actually more dirty-grey than white. Unlike his owners he was a friendly character.

'You know the jokes about the Scots always being tight with their money? I think they've been based on our landlady, what do you reckon?' Lesley giggled at her own wit.

'Absolutely! But not all Scots are like her thank God or we'd have been forced to go back home before now I think.' Carys joined in the giggling.

At the thought of going back home, Lesley's mood changed. Her pretty face, covered with freckles, looked slightly crestfallen. She pulled herself up in the bed a little and pushed her long auburn hair back off her shoulders, tucking it behind her ears, an action Carys noted that Lesley performed whenever she was feeling anxious. Her large green eyes were moist.

'Are you really happy up here Carys? Do you regret choosing Edinburgh University over Lampeter now?'

'I'm fine, Lesley, other than having to live in this dump.'

'Aren't you homesick at all? Because I am.'

'Not yet, not quite. There are things I miss of course, like my mother's cooking – I could murder some Welsh lamb stew – nobody makes it quite like she does – always heaps of big, tasty, lamb meat, fresh off the mountains, the lambs having been bathed in soft rain, and having eaten bountiful herbs and wild flowers.' Carys fancied herself as a bit of a poet, she'd won a number of prizes for her poems and creative writing in the Urdd eisteddfod over the years, including at national level once, two years ago.

'Your Mum's Welsh cakes are brilliant Carys! Have you got any left in the tin from the last lot she sent up?'

'They're all gone bar one which is a bit stale by now, but if you're desperate I could sell it to you for *5p*.'

They both laughed at the absurdity of the conversation, then quickly became a little anxious they'd get told off like last week for making a noise again. It was 11.15pm after all.

'So what are you homesick for then?' Carys asked.

Lesley didn't even think about her response, the words just came tumbling out in a long, unstructured list.

'My own bed. All the family sitting down to Sunday roast dinner together. We fill that table you know. We've all got our own places. Baby John next to me. Dad at one end. Mam at the other. Annette and Mary squabbling over something. Tommy and Mark kicking each other under the table. Maureen and Rose whispering and giggling.

'And seeing Nana and Bampa on a Saturday, they're really sweet, and very good for their age – they're in their late 70s now. Oh and chatting with my mum after my sisters have gone to bed. Even going to mass at St Teilo's. I miss that, isn't that a bit weird? Well, maybe it's not because I've been going there all my life and know everybody. The church here is different, not half so friendly, I just sit in the back pew on my own as I don't like to ask other people to squeeze up in the pews nearer the front. Then there's my best friend, Bernadette. We live in the same street, she's three doors down from me and I miss her a lot. She says she's definitely going to come up and stay for a few days once I've found somewhere else to live. Oh, and China, the cat, he's a Siamese we got from the animal shelter where I used to work as a volunteer every Saturday. He ended up there after his owner – an old lady – died. I never thought I'd hear myself say this, because normally it drives me to distraction, but I'd love to hear him meowing at me for food right now.'

Lesley's voice had began to wobble a bit and she stopped adding to her list, going completely quiet.

'Oh, poor you, that's a lot of things to miss. But it won't be long until Christmas and then you'll be home again, seeing everyone, and going to your own church. Was it St Teilo's you said?'

'Yes, that's right next door to my old primary school. I've always lived in the same house in my part of Cardiff. I must have been nuts to think it would be the best thing for me to move so far away to go to University, but deep down I know I had to come to Edinburgh, because it's the right course for me.'

'You'll just have to give being in Scotland more time, get used to the differences up here.' Carys tried to be helpful, whilst at the same time steering Lesley off the subject of being homesick as she didn't like it when people cried in front of her. When that happened she never really knew what to do about it; whether to just leave them, or put her arm around them. Whichever she chose to do, inevitably it resulted in her feeling awkward.

'Are you sure *you're* not homesick other than for your Mam's cooking?' Despite the growing darkness, Carys knew that Lesley had turned to face her and could imagine the earnest look on her face.

'In Welsh there's a word for homesickness, its "hiraeth", have you heard of it?' Carys replied.

'No.'

'Hiraeth is homesickness that the Welsh are supposed to get when they're away from Wales. It's an awful thing to suffer if you do get it, because there really is no substitute for being in Wales, and having all things Welsh around you. Thankfully I don't have it yet, maybe because I've not been away long enough, and also because I'm enjoying being in the big city too much. It's a lot more exciting than Aberystwyth I can tell you!'

'Colder though,' Carys added as an afterthought.

Lesley's mood seemed to have lifted a little now. 'I think it's funny that we've ended up together in the same digs, us both coming from Wales, don't you? What are the chances of that happening? A pity I don't speak Welsh though, like you, Carys, otherwise we could talk away anywhere and no-one would have a clue what we were talking about, would they? I hated our Welsh teacher in school, Mr James, he was weird, very tall and thin, always wore the same old brown tweed jacket. We were all really surprised when we discovered he was married and had children. We thought he was an old bachelor. What used to annoy me a lot about him was that it was so obvious he had his favourites – Bethan and Nia – the only ones who spoke fluent Welsh. I never tried very hard in Welsh lessons and gave it up at the end of form 3, so I don't even have it as an 'O' level. I can't even sing all the words of the national anthem, isn't that terrible?'

Carys thought it most definitely *was* terrible, although she didn't want to make Lesley feel guilty about it so she said nothing. All the while Lesley had been telling her story she had wanted to set the record straight regarding Bethan and Nia. She'd developed a burning need to defend Mr James and the two Welsh-speaking girls she'd never met, even if it risked upsetting Lesley in the process.

'Maybe it wasn't favouritism, Lesley. For native Welsh speakers like me, it's more natural to speak in Welsh, and if *their* first language was Welsh as well, they were just doing what came naturally; they wouldn't even have thought about it offending anyone, why would they?'

Lesley was quiet for a few moments then said, 'Yeh, maybe you're right. I hadn't thought of it like that. Perhaps we were just jealous of Bethan and Nia. They always got top marks in Welsh without *any* work, or so it seemed, whereas we all struggled; some of my friends couldn't make head nor tail of the language, even though they'd always lived in Wales. You see, in some parts of Cardiff you won't *ever* hear Welsh being spoken, and most people living there have got a *Cardiff* accent, even the Pakis have. Some people are even anti-Welsh language altogether. I did once try to get onto the Urdd school trip to Llangranog; but my mother went bonkers when I asked her if I could go – she said the Urdd was like the "Welsh Hitler youth" and no way was I being allowed to join it or go anywhere where "nationalism was going to be stuffed down my throat" and that's the polite version of what she actually said ...'

'Lesley that's ridiculous. The Urdd is a great organisation. It's respected internationally for what it does. I was a member all through primary and secondary school and had loads of fun in it and met lots of lovely boys. I can tell you that you've definitely missed out, and if ever I get to meet your mother I *will* put her right about it. Urdd Gobaith Cymru *is* a League of Youth, she was correct about that, but it was formed to encourage young Welsh people keep the Welsh language alive and develop as good citizens, not for any sinister reasons for God's sake!'

Lesley thought it best to pretend she was feeling sleepy by now, because the conversation was getting far too heavy for the time of night, and Carys was off again, waxing lyrical as she was prone to do (especially after a few drinks), Lesley had discovered. It had been a long month, this month they'd been forced to share the same room, usually trying to go to sleep at the same time. Lesley hoped they could be good friends long term, but it wasn't easy getting to know Carys because she seemed to be a bit secretive. It felt like hard work sometimes trying to find out more about her, whilst Carys herself was very good at finding out about other people, Lesley had learned.

Carys then recited the Urdd motto with fervour and hoped Lesley had been listening carefully to what she had been saying. She didn't like the sound of Lesley's mother at all; hopefully she would *never* have to meet her.

'Byddaf ffyddlon i Gymru a theilwng ohoni,
'Byddaf ffyddlon i'm cyd-ddyn, pwy bynnag y bo;
'Byddaf ffyddlon i Grist a'i gariad ef.'

Lesley's voice was soft and sleepy. 'That sounds lovely Carys, but you'll have to translate it for me 'cos I don't understand a word except for *Gymru*.'

'Okay, that's easy.'

'I will be faithful to Wales and be worthy of her,
'I will be faithful to my fellow man, whoever he may be;
'I will be faithful to Christ and to his love.'

'See, that's what the Urdd is really all about. Now remember to tell your mother that at Christmas. Set the record straight.'

'I will. Sleep tight.'

Lesley turned over and tried to drift off to sleep, thinking she might ask Carys to teach her some Welsh; she'd do that in the morning over breakfast, perhaps. She doubted that her roommate would give a 'No' for an answer, given Carys's obvious passion for it, although she wasn't the most patient person Lesley had met …

Carys had already moved on to thinking about her first assignment – The Early Christian Church in Scotland. Pity Diane and Alix weren't into religion at all. She could have discussed it with them. You would have more chance of a tryst with the devil if you relied on Alix!

Let me live

October 1972 Edinburgh

Just to keep her memory in top form and if she was a bit bored, or even to add a touch of colour to her impersonations of the typical Aberdeen quine, Alix would recite the cakes on the Mackay's Bakery order form:

In alphabetical order: almond slice, apple tart, apple turnover, chocolate donut, chocolate éclair, coconut haystack, coconut iced finger, cream donut, Eccles cake, Eiffel tower, fern cake, fondant, fruit slice, iced donut, iced finger, jam donut, lunch tart, meringue, pineapple tart, rhubarb tart, snowball.

Not that she intended, *ever again*, to be packing boards or ticking off orders. That was all in the past.

Aberdeen, the all-girls' school, cold and miserable weather, what the neighbours might think, Asti Spumanté, rowies, sensible shoes, shopping with Mother in E & M's, bible class. Every last one of them could rot in hell for all she cared. She might once have tussled with her conscience when Dad was short in the bakery and asked for her help; or when Mum needed a second opinion on some hideous outfit with black patent shoes and matching bag, for a Ladies Circle outing. But – thank God – these days were gone. It was up with the hemline, down with the neckline, out with the cigarette, polish up the high heeled boots, emphasise the sparkling green eyes – and party!!

She'd well and truly served her time as the precious late baby of Rab and Olive Mackay, curtailed her basic instincts in case the neighbours *did* find out, simulated academic effort at St Margaret's School and dutifully practised her tennis and swimming. Now it was time to keep only the best from the past and create a fun-filled, carefree future.

God (or maybe the Devil) was smiling down when he allocated her a place in Argyll Student House – a cross between halls and a flat, where the rent included all bills, some cleaning and the watchful eye of an offsite warden. The rules were minimal and the comfort levels surprisingly high. Her five housemates were Georgina, Emily, Annabel, Hilary and Grace – all ex public school, all well heeled like herself, and all primed for parties. Alix was a neat fit – posh, pretty and a bit reckless. The others were Law students which didn't make for stimulating conversation – had she been looking for it. But so what? Studies were only a small part of first year university life.

Alix made a couple of friends early on – Carys from Wales on the Arabic course and Brenda from Edinburgh itself in her French class, both suitably intellectual and achievement orientated. She could always trawl them out if Mum and Dad visited. What they didn't know wouldn't harm them. They would go home happy in the knowledge that not only was their pride and joy so clever but didn't she just sparkle and shine next to the small Welsh girl and the rather plain but nice lass from Edinburgh.

Life was going to be just great.

Further on up the road

1973 – June – end of first year

Patricia and I were playing in the all Edinburgh students' hockey tournament. I was still occupying a small, basic room in Pollock Halls with enough space to swing a very small kitten, and a bed barely wide enough for a 19th century chimney sweep. I didn't even have a view of The Crags. Patricia was living and studying on the Craiglockart campus and finding it all a mite claustrophobic after a full year surrounded by holy willies, even worse than herself, a Dundonian born and bred in the Irish enclave of Lochee. Nancy was on the sidelines, the old riding injury acting up, but still able to shout like a fishwife in support of the Edinburgh Uni team. The match was at Peffermill, not too far from her Suffolk Road hall.

The chat after the match was of summer holidays, seeing old friends again, exam results, plans for next academic year, and the joys of having a bit of cash for a change. I can't remember later how Dalmeny Street came up, but it was probably something to do with my friend Kirsty Mary from Stornoway who regaled us all in the pub afterwards with her tales of island life. She added a further dimension to An Tir, an Canan 's na Daoine (The Land, the Language, the People) – the word was unpronounceable but the meaning was clear – The Shagging. However, she was intending to settle down to some *serious* studying come October – final year for her and her flatmate Maggie who was a bit on the strait-laced side anyway. The other three flatmates were in the process of moving out, back to halls for the last lap. Kirsty Mary and Maggie would be looking for three girls to take the vacant rooms after the summer visitors had departed the city with their tartan hankies and their whisky miniatures.

Flashing a look at Patricia and Nancy, I got in first – 'we'll take the rooms – if you've no objection of course.'

The flat was on the top floor of an old stone-built Edinburgh tenement just off Leith Walk. There were a couple of attic rooms, making it the biggest flat in the close. Strictly speaking there were three bedrooms, one large lounge with bay window and curtains which were several inches short, an eating kitchen and a bathroom. The large lounge had been partitioned to give two more opportunities for the landlord to sit on his ample backside and collect rent while investing very little in the comfort of his tenants. That meant one room didn't have a proper window. We'd agreed to take it in turns to sleep there. However, Patricia went first and decided to stay, making do with the borrowed light from the hall, while delighting in the biggest cupboard in the flat – just brilliant for organizing all her books into size order and her clothes into neat, perfectly pressed piles – jumpers, tee shirts, shorts, tracksuit bottoms, jeans, pants, bras, socks. We tended to congregate in the kitchen where an assortment of old chairs and a Formica-covered table soon became the focus of the chat and gossip.

True to her word, Kirsty Mary adopted the life of a nun for nine months – well, that might be stretching it just a bit – and worked hard for a 2.1 in History. She hoped to go back home in time to help with preserving the memory of a way of life disappearing like snow off a dyke in an island better known for its emigration than its local culture. Maggie kept a low profile, but we all knew better than to kick up a hooley on a Sunday when she was around. Some things were still sacred it seemed.

Being new to the flat, the three of us took our time to see how things were done before we volunteered a few suggestions. Patricia would gladly take on the job of cleaning the kitchen (she had seen the grime behind the cooker, and the out-of-date packets in the larder). I wondered if we might not have a rota for baths so that the water wouldn't always run cold just when I felt like one.

Nancy suggested a kitty for household items since it hacked her right off when someone used the last of her cotton wool when she needed it to take off her nail polish. Yes! Yes! and Yes! were the answers. And while we were at it – would Nancy mind not bringing boys home on a Sunday night as that was the night Kirsty Mary did her hair, and would I please remember to take my key whenever I was going to be late as Patricia was fed up getting out of bed to let me in?

Just a few minor niggles, easily sorted. But oh! – the freedom. To sit up all night if you wanted, talking about every subject under the sun from ban the bomb, to the rights and wrongs of abortion.

To fry up an onion, a few rashers of bacon, some sliced carrots, a handful of sultanas, a tin of chopped ham and a cupful of rice, add a liberal dose of seasoning salt and end up with enough savoury rice to line our stomachs before a few halves of draft cider in The Edinburgh Folk Club. It was a world away from halls; a taste of grown-up living, and included, of course, the ubiquitous party.

When we reminisced – and we did that often, particularly in our final year in the flat – that first party always featured in our stories. Alix would start it with, 'Remember Simon dancing to Maggie May, shirt off and looking gorgeous. You should have hung on to him, Nancy.'

'Yes, maybe,' she'd reply. 'I don't know what *you* saw, but you seemed to be very busy chatting up that Roger guy, until his girlfriend caught you out. And what about later, when Alastair thumped that guy I knew from the Central Bar who called him a Weegee bastard? I thought all hell was going to break loose. Just as well Kirsty Mary chased the Edinburgh lads or heavens know how it might have ended.'

'As it was the police arrived, and the ambulance men!' Lesley might chip in. 'Don't forget about Kirsty Mary breaking her leg when the stair light went out.'

'Or about me sweet-talking that big copper. I put my best teacher's voice on that night and told you all the party was over.' Patricia had kept us all right, even then.

'It didn't stop Alix,' I would remind them all. 'She just went over and took big Pat by the hand. I've never seen him look more like a puppy dog than he did that night.'

It was a running joke between us – big Pat and Alix. I had fancied him myself.

But always we came round to the climax of the evening.

Nancy had suggested a game of cards. Simon had offered to teach her to play poker. Tom'd had the bright idea of adding another dimension to it. Carys had been wise to that one and made sure she put on an extra cardigan, a scarf and a pair of socks under her boots when she sidled out to the loo. Strip poker commenced. There is no doubt the two boys would have cheated had Carys not been there. In the end it hadn't been necessary as Nancy had found herself down to a single silver chain while the others still had a couple of essentials to go. The sanded floor was a cold place to sit. Nancy had laughed off her embarrassment when the boys scarpered at the sound of Patricia welcoming Lesley and Kirsty Mary back from Casualty. We never let her forget it.

I say goodbye, and you say hello

September 1974 – start of third year.

Lesley and Carys had been regular visitors to the flat after the party. Maybe it was something to do with the Celtic connection. Maybe it was because Lesley had been so caring towards Kirsty Mary over her broken ankle. Whatever the reason, when it came to the time for Kirsty Mary and Maggie to graduate and return to the islands, Patricia and Nancy agreed with me that it made sense to ask the two Welsh girls to fill the spaces. Anyway, we couldn't be too careful about taking in complete strangers – they might not be willing to bunk up if one of the other girls brought a fellah home and wanted the only double bed in the flat for the night. One might be vegetarian and need an extra shelf in the fridge for all those sprouting things. The other one might burn smelly candles and play weird Eastern music and Patricia would never have stood for that. And anyway, the three of us who were left all liked Lesley and Carys and knew them as well as you can do without living together day and night.

The Welsh girls were delighted. They had managed to move out of Mrs Mac's B&B into halls after a while, but now that Carys was looking for a bit of a life having proved herself on the study front, and might, if she got lucky, want to bring a man back to her room, it was definitely time to move on. Lesley was keen to inhabit a different area of the city, following her fright with Paul. No way did she want to risk bumping into him if he was still around.

So that was it all set up for the end of September, until Alix phoned me in a panic the last week of the holidays. Newly flown in from Jersey, having spent an obligatory few days with the parents on their late summer holiday, she had expected to move into a new flat with Georgina & Co from Argyll House. Emily and Annabel had been in charge of finding a flat for six, *near the Meadows if possible, single room each of course and for God's sake, a decent shower.*

It seems flats for five were easier to come by.

'Christ, Diane. I'm really stuck. You wouldn't see me homeless would you? Surely you can fit me in somewhere at least for a while. Patricia's away a lot on teaching practice. Maybe I could share her room. I'll even pay the lion's share of the rent for it – Dad would never know. It would mean a regular supply of cakes if that helps. Just think of it – iced donuts for life! Mum always brings a load when she visits. Honestly, I'll be no bother. *And* I do know a bunch of good looking lads. So it's a deal then?'

'The lads' would have to be my selling point to the others. No question of sharing with Patricia though. Even I, her long term buddy, wouldn't consider it. 'Too messy!' would be Patricia's judgement of anyone who entered her perfect domain. Carys and Lesley would just have to share. That would be easiest all round. Alix could have the boxroom – and the rest of us would take great delight in watching six foot rugby players cope with the narrow bed.

I thought it possible that Nancy might object. She wasn't over keen on Carys as it was – too much of an intellectual (and an achiever, if it came to that). Alix might be a bit of competition on the male front. Or maybe Nancy planned on keeping her head down for the next year, given recent events.

Judgement Day

Highwood End Farm, 5th July 1974

The postman always arrived about the same time each morning – 9.00am. He would come tearing down the rutted drive in his red van far too fast to ensure the safety of the various animals to be found in the vicinity of the farmyard. It was a miracle none of them had been killed over the years, although there had been a few near-misses, most notably Mr Thorpe's favourite sheepdog, Laddie, who had been lucky to emerge from a collision with only a broken leg. If Mr Thorpe had seen it then he would have given Jim a busted nose for his trouble over the incident, but the postie had alerted Mrs Thorpe to the dog's plight, then driven off before the farmer could vent his fury.

Ever since, the Thorpes and their postman had been at a permanent standoff. Mrs Thorpe had complained on several occasions to the Post Office about what she viewed as reckless driving, but to no avail, since the response was that the *mail* was being delivered safely. The Thorpes refused to keep their animals out of the yard, which, after all, they argued, was where farmyard animals belonged. Jim refused to slow down because the farm was always the last call on his round and he wanted to be away quickly and finish his shift. To get back to his house for breakfast, he said, but if the rumours in the village shop were to be believed, it was to have his bacon butties with the woman who lived in Beech Cottage, her with the reputation for soliciting postmen, ever since the dairy had stopped its door-to-door deliveries.

On this particular bright and sunny morning, the only person waiting anxiously for Jim's arrival was Nancy. She was on tenter-hooks, unable to settle to anything since the previous night. Ever since 8.30 when she'd finished a piece of toast her mother had insisted she ate, she had been pacing up and down the kitchen like a caged tiger in the zoo. Now she was feeling quite sick.

Sleep had come only fitfully to Nancy the previous night. She had tossed and turned in her bed, finally succumbing around midnight, only to dream a few hours later of being sucked down into a swirling, bubbling whirlpool from which there appeared to be no escape. She had fallen into the pool feet first for some reason, and had felt her legs being pulled down, then her body, arms and shoulders, until only her head was above the water. Just before the water reached the level of her mouth, she had woken with a start, drenched in a cold sweat, with a sense of foreboding coursing through her whole body.

After that she had lain awake for four hours till 7.30 when she had forced herself out of bed, feeling hung over, a sensation with which she was quite familiar. Except that on this occasion she had not even experienced the pleasure of being drunk the night before. *What a bummer.*

D-day had arrived and it was bringing the moment of truth. Once Jim's van came round that corner it would be less than a minute until she could retrieve the mail from the porch. Nancy's heart started to beat faster at the thought of opening the envelope containing the results of her second year exams. The more she thought about it, the more any trace of optimism she might have had evaporated. She couldn't stand much more of this waiting. She looked at the clock for the umpteenth time that morning – 9.05. He was late; today of all days, he was bloody well late.

As that thought passed through her mind, the van came whirring into the yard, skidding as it did so, then turning around very fast to face back the way it had come. This was Jim's usual manoeuvre, setting up the vehicle for a quick getaway. If he'd had a better one, he could have burnt rubber from the tyres the way he drove. The door swung open to reveal a short, wiry-looking man carrying a bundle of envelopes held together in an elastic band. Jim was about to push the bundle through the letter box when Nancy yanked open the porch door saying 'I'll take those, thanks,' then turned quickly and shut the door in his face before he could utter a word.

Even before Jim had slammed his van door and driven off, Nancy was already sorting through the pile to find the particular envelope she was searching for – the one with an Edinburgh postmark. And here it was now, right in front of her eyes.

'Go on then, open it for goodness sake!' Nancy's mother shouted from her position at the stove.

'I'm trying to, Mum,' her daughter replied nervously, being careful not to rip the contents in her hurry to get the slip of paper out.

Her second year exam results were printed on horrible, thin, flimsy paper. Mrs Thorpe was peering over Nancy's shoulder. 'That's great, love, isn't it? You've passed them all, and one of them with a credit. Well, done! I'll give your father a shout to come and see.'

'No, Mum, don't bother. It's not great. They're no good at all,' whispered Nancy, in a voice that was uncharacteristically subdued.

Nancy looked at the print-out again. Four passes and a credit. Four big failures as far as she was concerned, and five failures in terms of University regulations: the results were not good enough to permit transfer to the Veterinary science degree. Not good enough by a long shot. She would require a minimum of five credits, Nancy had been told at the start of second year, and now, here she was, ten months later, holding the proof that she couldn't cut it – again.

'I don't understand, Nancy, what on earth do you mean they're no good?' her mother interrupted Nancy's thoughts.

Nancy wanted to get out of the kitchen, but knew she wouldn't get rid of her mother unless she offered her some kind of explanation.

'Well it's simple. All black and white. I can't transfer courses now. I needed five credits and I've only got one. I'm going to have to stay doing biology. Let's face it, Mum, I'm never going to be a vet.'

At that point Nancy ran out of the kitchen, up to her bedroom, locking the door behind her. Utterly dejected, she slumped wearily backwards onto the bed, covering her face with her hands and letting the tears flow.

Nancy's angst was acute. The tears might have stopped after five minutes, but the anguish and guilt lasted for weeks afterwards. In fact, she had barely come to terms with it by the time she returned to Edinburgh in September. Two years before, after failing to get high enough grades at A levels, she had promised herself she would pull her socks up and work harder, in order to meet the standard for the Vet Science course. She had been given a chance by the University to show she could do it, she had been given the backing of her parents, and she had made a deal with herself. Now, it was obvious to all, Nancy thought - she had let everyone down, hadn't she? Why had she? Why hadn't she achieved high enough grades?

It was easy to rationalise. Too much partying, too much drinking, not enough reading, not enough library hours, too much time spent on men. She had gone over and over it in her head, ever since the results arrived. Why had she behaved like that when she knew, deep down, that time was running out and this was her last chance? Then she would take the other tack and convince herself that she *had* worked hard. She had spent hours in the library, looking up original references for essays. She had swotted hard for the exams, calling a halt on the partying weeks beforehand. But, if she was being really honest with herself, she had found some of the work complex, harder than she had expected, and she *knew* she hadn't answered some of the exam questions well. So what was the real reason then? When Nancy asked herself this question she wasn't at all confident that she knew.

Shortly after Nancy returned to Edinburgh still somewhat upset about her future plans being dashed, she took Diane into her confidence, asking what she thought about it all. Diane could always be relied upon to speak her mind, in the nicest possible sense. They spent a couple of hours sitting in Nancy's room with a bottle of red and a very large bag of peanuts, listening to Simon and Garfunkel gently harmonising away in the background. Whatever Diane said to Nancy must have had a profound effect, because after some quiet reflection, she reverted to her old, cheerful, energetic self, finding a balance between her studies and her social life, just the way she liked it to be.

So what happened to bring about a return to Nancy's usual joie de vivre? Nancy visited a place she hadn't been to very often in her twenty years of life so far – that part of the subconscious that speaks the absolute truth. The bit that prods us every now and again, asking us to open our eyes and acknowledge the world as it actually is, which is not necessarily how we perceive it to be. The part that shows us who we really are, warts and all. And the answer that Nancy knew to be the truth was that she wasn't academically bright enough to be a vet, no matter how hard she worked. She wasn't a Carys, and she didn't ever want to be one. She was herself, and she would make the most of her personality and her abilities without beating herself up any more. So Biological Sciences it was then. Second Class honours no doubt, but also a whole lot of fun along the way. She might not become a vet but the rest of her vision could still become a reality.

Take that you bastards

October 1974 – Dalmeny Street.

By the middle of October the six of us third years had finally sorted out the sleeping arrangements in the flat, and after two weeks of settling in, had come to an acceptable system for the use of the double bed in Nancy's room. We'd agreed a rota for flat cleaning duties, and a kitty for household essentials. The new girls (Alix, Carys and Lesley) were generally accommodating and suitably deferential to Patricia when she was on her high horse. They learned how to manage her, just as Nancy and I had done the previous year. It was worth it to have Patricia keep everything under control in the flat. That way you would never run out of toilet paper or find hairy mould growing in the fridge. She did draw the line at condoms (used) under the beds though, and told Nancy and Alix as much.

Sunday tea-time we tended to congregate for a chat. In week three, Alix presented her now legendary 'Book of Bastards'.

One of the definitions of 'bastard' in The Concise Oxford Dictionary is 'a disliked or unfortunate person or thing'. In Alix's infamous book that would be far too pale a description. The preface of her big, red 'Book of Bastards', which was written in large, bold, black ink by Alix's own fair hand read thus:

"I have compiled this Book of Bastards to vilify those men who have, by virtue of thought, word, or deed, caused severe emotional or physical pain to myself or other members of the sisterhood. All new entries of individual Bastards in this book will be publicised widely by the sisterhood, immediately the Bastard and his heinous crime is listed. The sisterhood considers this its solemn duty in order to ensure that the Bastard does not cause distress to any more women. Once entered into this book, the Bastard remains there for life. No dispensation for subsequent good behaviour, saintly actions or persistent grovelling can be given under any circumstances. Bastards beware! You have been warned."

Alix (On behalf of good women everywhere)

Alix didn't do anything by halves. And as the preface made clear, she meant business. The idea for the book came from the first man Alix met at university who warranted the description. Poor Julian, he didn't know what had hit him. He surely could not have been thinking straight when he ended up having a one-night stand with the buxom blonde behind the Men's Union Bar, three weeks into his relationship with Alix.

Firstly, Alix did what might have been expected in the circumstances – bawled him out in private, delivering an ear-bashing of which an Aberdonian fishwife would have been proud. Secondly, she poured a pint of beer all over him the following week when they just happened to be at the same party. Thirdly, and causing him the most damage by far, no doubt, she told any female student who would care to listen that he was absolutely lousy in bed, largely as a result of possessing a rather small cock, she said, gleefully. This remark was reinforced to good effect by Alix holding apart her index fingers in front of her face to show the dismal distance between them, at the same time wrinkling her nose up to form a suitably distasteful expression. She was a good actress, you had to hand it to her. The fact that she was distorting the truth in that Julian had a perfectly normal length member didn't bother Alix's conscience one little bit. She was seeking revenge and boy did she get it! He had a hard time afterwards finding anyone who would go out with him until the next crop of first years arrived.

His entry in the Book set the standard for the string that was to follow.

Date April 1974: The First Bastard

Name Julian Barker

Qualifications for entry: Blatant and pre-meditated two-timing.

Detail of offence: Causing public humiliation to Alix Mackay and damaging her previously unblemished reputation of being the dumper, not the dumped.

Bastard Rating: 4*

The BOB, as it was affectionately known thereafter, became something of an institution. At least once a month, and usually after a few bottles of wine, contenders for entry were the subject of animated discussions, followed by Alix leading a ceremonious voting procedure (one vote each, 'Yes', 'No', or 'Abstain'). There had to be a majority in favour of entry for a Bastard-elect to be confirmed, and his place awarded for posterity. It wasn't often that there was disagreement, although occasionally Nancy thought Alix was being over-zealous with her accusations, particularly if it was someone else's bastard. If it had been up to Lesley, half the male population of Edinburgh University could have been consigned to the BOB. By contrast, and probably just to be contentious, Carys often argued for the other side; she did so enjoy the challenge of a debate, whatever the topic.

Whenever a 'Yes' decision was made, Alix would announce, in sombre tones, 'John Smith (or whoever it happened to be), you have been found guilty of causing grave upset to the sisterhood and thus have been consigned to the Book of Bastards for eternity,' and then we would all cheer lustily.

All except Patricia, who refused to have anything to do with this ceremony. She simply could not bring herself to see it as just a bit of fun. What bothered her was that there was no potential for forgiveness. Had it been possible, for example, to gain exit from the BOB for good behaviour (equating to the chaps having done some penance, in a manner of speaking), then she might have reconsidered. But no, Patricia! The sisters were adamant – once a Bastard, *always* a Bastard.

Love Hurts

February 1974

Not even Patricia would have forgiven Paul, not that Lesley would ever have told her the details. He'd been a bastard all right – book or no book. And there had been no book eight months previously

There were still some beautiful traditional old swimming pools in Edinburgh. Lesley and Carys often went to Warriston Baths, where after a taxing 30 length swim, they would spend the rest of a wintry Wednesday afternoon in the Turkish baths getting thoroughly warmed up and chilled out. It was the nearest thing to heaven – wrapped in big white fluffy towels, talking in whispers, relaxing between the hot rooms, cooling down with a tingling arctic plunge, even going for a sleep in one of the private cubicles.

Lesley would have done well if she had stuck to Warriston. However, she sometimes fancied a quick dip before tea and The Commonwealth Pool was just round the corner from Pollock Halls. It had none of the charm of Warriston but for simple length bashing it was fine. You could have a decent shower too; so often, on a Monday night, she'd pop in about five o'clock.

She normally kept her head down and her mind focussed on reciting the rosary while she swam. A decade of the rosary, followed by an Our Father and a Glory Be fitted nicely into the 50 metres and stopped her from becoming bored. It also salved her conscience about performing her daily duties which had tended to slip ever since she'd come to Edinburgh. She could more readily recite the bones of the skeleton, starting from the feet and working all the way up to the cranium.

One particular Monday in February, she was just at the bit in the Lord's Prayer where the Catholics say 'trespasses', and the Protestants prefer 'debts' when a child got into difficulties in the pool. The young male life guard proved he hadn't been sitting in a total dream by plunging straight in and pulling wee Margaret out. She spluttered, coughed, cried a bit and was soon smiling again after the Greek God wrapped her up warm in a big towel and found her Mum. It was all over in a very short time – and no lasting harm done. Well, at least to Margaret.

Lesley treaded water and watched. All thoughts of Glory Be and Mother of God disappeared as she watched the life guard patrol round, before sitting in the high chair next to the diving pool. He was about six feet tall, with very dark hair, light blue eyes, a straight slim nose, a toned but not overly muscled body and a crinkly smile. He was perfect.

She spent the next twenty lengths wondering how to attract his attention and whether or not he had a girlfriend. She decided not to go down the dramatic line – she wouldn't fake drowning. She also knew she was more attractive dry than wet. He was probably a student earning some pocket money and would be working some kind of shift pattern. Best to bump into him when fully dressed.

Carys might have been able to help her with a strategy, but Lesley wanted to keep him to herself at this stage. So she decided to go for a swim at the same time the following week to check if this was a regular shift. Maybe she could find out where he lived and loiter there in the hope of seeing him one day after lectures.

The next Monday he was on duty again. She was too nervous to complete the full thirty lengths so left the pool after twenty, with a few token Hail Marys, to get dressed and go up to the 'Shivery Bite'. Fortunately the hair drier was working so she did the best she could with her long red hair, put on some Nivea to counteract the dry patches on her cheeks, applied petroleum jelly to her lips for a bit of a shine and attempted to look casual and confident, on the outside at least. Two slowly sipped cups of Nescafe and a lemon Danish later, she spotted him striding to the exit, black leather jacket collar turned up in anticipation of the cold wind, kit bag slung over his left shoulder, skin smooth and gleaming. She breathed in deeply, checked the glass door for her side view, and followed him out. He walked down Dalkeith Road, headed past Pollock Halls, and turned left into East Mayfield. Without a backward glance, he disappeared into number four.

On her next visit, she went straight from payment kiosk to café, happy to skip the swim on this occasion in favour of looking her best. What to wear had been a tricky one. Brown suited her. A bit of eye shadow and a spot of colour on her pale cheeks helped brighten a winter complexion. She took the chair right by the door of the cafe. This time he stopped for a box of matches – pity, she would have preferred a non-smoker. She smiled at him as he passed to go out. He smiled back. *A fine pair of tits..*

Monday the 10th, he sat down at her table, with a broad smile and a 'Hi.' His name was Paul. He was from Doncaster, played football, had a life saving qualification, two brothers, a dog called Snap, and was in final year of a surveying degree. She stuttered her way through being Welsh, having seven brothers and sisters, liking animals, and studying to be a nurse, before she brought up the night he had saved the little girl. He was quite blasé about it – it broke the monotony of the four hour shift. She couldn't see past his blue eyes and his perfect profile. When she couldn't think of another thing to say to prolong the conversation she smiled and said 'see you next week then?'

'Well, hang on. How about a drink maybe?'

They left the building together.

'I've got some wine in the flat actually.'

'Oh ...okay then.'

'It's just down the road a bit.'

'Oh, really? Not far then?'

'We're just about there now.'

'Handy for the pool isn't it?'

'Here, take my hand, the stairs are a bit dark.'

'It's quiet here. Are your flatmates in?'

'Just one and she's out on a Monday. Red or white? – we've got both.'

'I don't mind really – white maybe then.'

'So tell me a bit more about yourself, Linda.'

'Lesley it is.'

'Sorry, of course – carry on.'

'Not much to say really. You know I'm from Wales but I love Edinburgh now and I'm really looking forward to my placement at the Sick Kids. How about you?'

'Why don't I show you my room and you can see my collections.'

'Collections?'

'You know – rosettes for swimming competitions, Bob Dylan records, football programmes. Get to know the real me!'

She wasn't sure if he was joking or not. In fact she wasn't sure how she felt now that she was here with him. His breath smelled of cigarettes, there was a photo of the so-called flatmate with her arm around his neck on the sideboard, and he was ladling into the wine with a vengeance.

With their glasses topped up yet again, he led her by the hand and they sat down on the bed in his room. He turned her face to his and kissed her long and hard on the lips. What now? It was fair to say that Lesley was something of a novice at the dating game.

What was it that Anna Raeburn woman had advised? Keep your legs together or keep your head together?

It was all just a bit confusing and he seemed to be moving faster than she expected.

He expertly unhooked her bra from behind and caressed her. All the time, his breathing was getting faster. He wasn't talking at all now. If she attempted to say anything he kissed her quiet. When his hand moved up and under her skirt she began to panic.

God, help me please. How can I stop him? I didn't mean it to go this far, honest. He's not that nice really. I don't really like him now that I know him. Help me out please.

She tried to move his hand away, looked for her wine glass, began to sit up, smoothed her skirt down. He was persistent and rough with her. Pushed her head down onto the pillow, pinned her shoulders to the bed with his upper body, pulled her skirt right up above her waist and yanked her pants down. She contracted every muscle in her body in an attempt to push him away.

'Stop it, stop it, please.' Her voice was shaking, the tears leaking from her eyes..

'Prick teaser, that's what you are. Nothing but.'

He turned her over and pressed himself against her back. Up and down, up and down he moved on her. She squeezed her thighs tightly together and kept them like that, just in case. She whimpered when she heard him moan and felt the warm stickiness on her skin.

Each step of the way home she was tormented by guilt and self loathing.

Oh God, oh God, I'm so sorry, please hear me. I can't tell Mam.

She's got enough to do with all the kids, and Dad. It's my own stupid fault anyway. I don't deserve any sympathy from you. It'll serve me right if I never get another man. Will I be punished for this? I know it goes against everything we've been taught in church. God, please forgive me. I'll make sure I keep my head down and concentrate on my work now, I promise you. I won't go back to that pool again either. Never, ever. Please forgive me, God.

Lesley cried herself to sleep that night, but from that day onwards, set her mind on other things. She vowed never to speak of the incident to anyone, so no Paul appeared in the Book of Bastards.

It was as if she believed that she could eradicate the memory simply by an act of will.

Picture me

March 1975

'Hey Diane. Here Diane. What have you got in that box Diane?'

'Can I carry your bag for you Diane?'

'Where were you last week Diane at half term? Did you go home Diane?'

'Did you eat any of those big Forfar bridies?'

'Did you bring any for us?'

'What are we doing tonight Diane? Can we do hand prints again soon – that was brilliant last time.'

They were all around me, jostling and talking over one another, each one vying to be closest or to have the honour of being equipment bearer. A ragged looking bunch; grubby, clothed in an assortment of hand-me-downs or badly fitting cheap trousers and jumpers. Some of them hadn't seen a hairbrush in weeks.

The art room in the community centre wore the same neglected look. Regulation grey paint cracking and peeling, orange plastic chairs chipped and wobbly, ageing notices about baby clothes, swap shops or sponsored walks long overdue for binning.

I joked and laughed with them as I fought my way through the swing doors. 'Give me time to get in boys. We've got all evening you know. And next Monday, and the Monday after.'

'Yeh, but we want to get started. I've had a great idea for the posters for the May Day parade. You know those black face things we did a few weeks ago – what did you call them again?'

'Silhouettes?'

'Yeh, that's the word.'

'Well Darren?'

'Well, we thought we could do a silhouette picture of each of the committee – you know, all in black. And then a big coloured picture of each of us kids. We could put a row of the committee faces on one side of the lorry and a row of our faces on the other, with 'Kids Rule' on the flags we'll be waving and on the tee shirts if you can get some.'

'And how will you draw the silhouettes without the committee members being here?'

'Easy Diane. We've got those pictures from the Christmas party. We can copy them or even trace some of them. And then we can draw each other for our portraits. I know we're not all that good yet but we can make it really obvious who it is. You know – a huge big nose on Michael's, and sticky out ears on Jim's.'

'Shut up Darren. Take a look in the mirror and see your own scabby spots.'

'Okay, okay boys. Sounds like a good idea to me. How many weeks have we got?'

Forget landscapes. This was stretching my skills beyond the comfort zone. And not just in the artwork.

These were disadvantaged kids from one of Edinburgh's deprived areas, carefully hidden from tourists' view in the outer suburbs of the city. Most of the city's 'fung students' would never even have had cause to enter the area. It was known only by its reputation which stretched as far as the European parliament and back.

The City Council had acquired some EEC funds for child social development – not enough to do much more than buy materials and room space for a couple of years for an art class. The University Volunteer Bureau promised to find a tutor – or was it playleader – for the group of ten to thirteen year olds showing a glimmer of interest in the idea of a Monday night art class.

It made a change from wiping aged bums, plucking out chin hairs and settling disputes over who was sitting in auld Jeanie's chair. The residential home experience was useful though. As were some tips from the local community education officer Jean.

'Keep it simple. Don't let the cupboard key out of your possession. Make them clear up every week or ban them. And don't give them an audience if anyone is acting up. Take them to one side. They're not a bad bunch but they'll know how to wind you up if you don't get it right.'

The girls weren't slow to offer me advice either.

'Bloody sit on them if they don't behave,' from Carys.

'Heavens above, Diane. What are you wasting your time with that lot for?' from Alix.

'Well I think that's great what you're doing Diane. With all my crowd at home, I've had enough of kids. I prefer cats myself but at least you're giving something back. University should be about giving, as well as having fun in your spare time. Don't you agree Nancy?'

'Quite right, Lesley. You'll be keeping your arty skills up, Diane, and that volunteer co-ordinator isn't half gorgeous too. No wonder you signed up, you dark horse.'

I looked at her quizzically. 'I never even noticed. I just feel so privileged to have this kind of life that I can't ignore the fact that there's real poverty and hopelessness just up the road from this flat, and do nothing to help. Believe me, this isn't much but it's something. And I really enjoy it now that I've stopped being scared of them!'

'Scared of a bunch of 12 year olds? Get a grip Diane. Just as well they aren't looking for History lessons or I'd soon sort them out.'

'Lucky for you Carys, there isn't much call for that down there. So you're spared.'

'And so are they,' I added under my breath.

Already I was protective of them, trying to make up in small ways for any perceived lack in their lives. A hairbrush here, a hug there. A lot of praise where a little would have normally sufficed. A blind eye when a telling off was deserved and expected. Remembering brothers' and sisters' names, asking after sick pets or invalid grannies. Acting like big sister, using humour and gentle teasing to win them over. Fighting their corner when the idea of an all kids' float in the May Day parade was vetoed by the committee. And finally, dressing up in a gown and mortar board with a giant ruler to front the decorated lorry on the 1st May.

God it felt good.

Who do you think you are?

May 1975 – final term, third year

Ambition was a word that had always been in Carys's vocabulary. As a very young child, she might not have known, consciously, that she was ambitious, but she knew that she always wanted to be the best, to be first, and to be famous. She could always find a way to get what she wanted. When she *was* older and famous, she would put her fiercely competitive nature down to having been brought up as the middle child, with a brother either side.

Once she reached grammar school, Carys's ambition couldn't have been more explicit. She made no secret of the fact that she enjoyed being considered very clever. The staff-room consensus in the third week of the first term was that Carys was most definitely destined for University. So here was this precocious eleven year-old, the teachers' pet, telling everyone that she was 'going to University to study Classics', or so she had thought back then.

Unusually for a child who was always top of the class and clearly gifted academically, she wasn't ostracised by the majority of her schoolmates as a 'snob' or 'brain box', although there were the odd jealous few, who avoided her whenever possible.

Carys was not only academically bright she was also aware enough to realise that if she wanted to be 'in' with her school friends, then she would have to make a pretence of needing to swot hard, like everyone else had to, in order to get through tests and exams. They weren't to know she was blessed with a photographic memory and found it all rather easy. When they fussed and worried themselves to a frenzy on the way to school about a test, or whilst waiting outside the exam hall, she would join in enthusiastically, saying things like 'Oh my God – I haven't revised *that* bit!'; then promptly come top of the class with a minimum of 80% anyway. Somehow she got away with it, her popularity rising exponentially the day she showed the girls the maths formulae she had scribbled all over her thigh – upwards of her skirt hem that is. They wouldn't have dared do that for fear of being caught, but Carys dared.

She often took risks because she had confidence in abundance, based on experience covering up naughtiness at home with elaborate lies if necessary. That was preferable to telling the truth and getting a full-on row for it. Her father was not a patient man, and her mother could go into sulks for days and lay on the guilt trip if she was upset. Carys loved her parents of course, but she didn't relate much to her mother's housewife role and her father was a bit of a distant figure – a respected Head teacher who was almost Victorian in his manner, like his parents before him.

She was much admired for her sports prowess. Carys was good at hockey. Very good indeed. She played Left Wing where she could fly up and down the whole length of the pitch, taking a long shot and banging the ball into the net whenever she could, much to the chagrin of the Inside Half whose job it really was to score the goals. It was that desire to win coming through again, for which she was willing to walk over others on the way up, if she had to.

Carys's parents had provided a home environment for their three children which ensured schoolwork and serious activities were highly valued. The latter were defined as reading, music and religious adherence. There were piano lessons for Carys from the age of five. The peripatetic teacher came to the house every Tuesday after school, when they would sit at the grand piano in the drawing room and go through the pieces given to practise the week before. Carys liked playing the piano, but she didn't much like the scales; too boring, she felt, although she understood the reasoning behind practising them. By the age of seventeen she had passed all the exams of the Associated Board of the Royal Schools of Music, gaining a merit or distinction in every one. She also played the church organ at service on occasion, when her parents would beam at her from the front row. They never offered much praise, but she knew they were quietly proud of her achievements.

'Success breeds success,' is an oft-quoted phrase which could have been written just for Carys. She never failed at anything, or perhaps she only engaged in spheres where she was certain to excel. But that is the sort of thing only the jealous few might say. Typically sweeping the board each year at the school eisteddfod competitions in poetry recitation and essay-writing, Carys gained the occasional second place, instead of first, but that only served to make her even more determined to win the next time.

And so it was that without any self-doubt or reservations, Carys was the first third-year Edinburgh University student to have the arrogance to enter the Theological Society's annual open essay competition for the Selwyn Harold Smith Award; a venerated prize which ordinarily attracted entries purely from established academics and the clergy, most of whom were already distinguished in their fields.

Locking herself away for the Easter holidays, either in her room or in the library reference area, Carys read voraciously, from a wide source of literature, making copious notes as she went. She phoned her father and picked his brains about Strata Florida Abbey, and asked him to retrieve and copy some Welsh language documents for her from the National Library of Wales in Aberystwyth. Then she theorised, critiqued, analysed and expounded upon her theme of 'The case for the canonisation of Meredith of Pontrhydfendigaid', until she felt she had a product worthy of the attention of the Head of Department, who had offered to review it on his return from holiday, prior to its submission.

'It's good,' he said, smiling benevolently at her. 'I would just strengthen the middle section by including some extra evidence, if you can find any. Otherwise, go for it, and good luck. Don't be disappointed if you don't win, because you'll be up against some very stiff competition. But we'll find an outlet for your essay somewhere else if you don't get lucky.'

His secretary kindly typed it up for Carys and off it went, well before the closing date, by which time Carys's focus was onto some light relief – pop concerts and poetry readings.

The judges were astounded when they discovered that their winning essay had been submitted by a *twenty year old* student of Religious Studies at Edinburgh University. Their critique was published in the subsequent edition of the Society Journal and therefore had world-wide circulation. A summary of the Journal report was published in the University's magazine, much to Carys's delight:

'This year's winner, Carys Lloyd-Jones, produced an exemplar of scholarship with her rigorous treatise on 'The case for the canonisation of Meredith of Pontrhydfendigaid.' Written with cornucopian flair and style, her essay tackled the different eschatologies, yielding surprising

connections to Meredith's life and work with the Cistercian monks of the Strata Florida Abbey. It is to be hoped, in the light of this meticulously researched work, that the Roman Catholic church will now re-examine its 1968 decision not to beatify Meredith.'

The *Scotsman* newspaper of the day also ran a small feature on Carys's success, under the banner 'Edinburgh University student scoops prestigious international prize', along with a photograph of her beaming and holding her certificate. The Head of Department was delighted with Carys, but even more delighted with the publicity it attracted for the Department.

She lost count of the number of people who stopped her the week the article had appeared in the *Scotsman* and offered their congratulations.

'I always told you I'd be famous one day,' Carys said to her parents. To the girls in the flat she said, 'Yes! I'm famous at last,' as she gave the victory salute. And so she was. And didn't they know it.

Firstly, she got outrageously drunk on a celebratory bottle of champagne, and then within an hour of sinking it was sick all over herself and the living room but couldn't clean it up because she was legless. That did not go down very well with Patricia, as one might imagine.

Secondly, over the next few weeks she developed an inflated opinion of herself as an intellectual, decrying the girls' reading choices as 'lightweight,' or 'badly written,' 'inconsequential', or 'an inaccurate sociological portrayal of our times.' It got that they were almost afraid to leave any book or magazine hanging around in case it attracted a comment.

Initially they put up with it, letting her bask in the post-publicity glory, but the evening she picked up Nancy's 'Day of the Jackal' and said 'I don't know why you waste your time reading this junk when there is so much good literature to be had,' was the straw that broke the camel's back, given that Nancy had just got a D for an assignment and was going to have to resubmit.

'Look Carys,' Nancy retorted, turning on her irritably, 'just keep your fucking intelligentsia opinions to yourself will you? If *I* want to read popularist stuff for plebs then that is just what I'm gonna do. If *you* want to read clever crap instead, then bog off and just go do it and give us all a break.'

As usual it was Diane who soothed ruffled feathers and calmed everyone down, engineering a consensus agreement for them all that it was okay to disagree about their choice of reading as long as it was done *silently*. And, coming up with the brilliant idea of a penalty fine for those who broke the rule, to be put in an old coffee tin, which would be emptied once a term and the proceeds used to buy the Sunday papers until the money ran out.

They all rallied round Carys later that year though, when she had news of a different sort.

Useless regrets

Christmas holidays final year – Tregaron, Wales

The clock was ticking away as usual in the sitting room. It was a miserable night outside – cold, frosty, dark and windy. Mrs Lloyd-Jones made cocoa for everyone before her husband closed his study door and began catching up on some report or other to be completed by the start of the school term.

It was hard to feel anything other than low and a bit flat after the Christmas festivities. Dafydd was bored. The Subbuteo game had taken a bashing over the past few days and he was looking for something else to do. He might go and find Huw and see if he wanted a game of cards or something if he wasn't taking his bike apart and putting it back together again.

Mam was twittering away to herself as she took down the Christmas cards, not the slightest bit bothered that no-one was listening, let alone responding.

'That was kind of Auntie Peg to send you that postal order, Carys. She's only got her pension. I wonder if Beti and Evan got up to Yorkshire to visit Mary this year, with the roads being so bad.'

Carys was head down in a book as usual: 'The Son of God: The Origins of Christology and the History of the Jewish-Hellenistic Religion' by Martin Hengel. It wasn't exactly holiday reading but she was hardly in festive mood with finals in sight and a programme of study and revision to follow. In fact her dedication to work had been a source of some grumblings over the holidays. Mam and Dad had thought she ought to go with them to visit all the Aunties and join in with the carol singing to raise funds for the chapel roof.

'I can't believe you can be so selfish, Carys. It makes me wonder what type of girl we've raised in this house,' from Dad.

A while later, Dad popped his head round the door and said he was going up a bit early as he had a touch of heartburn. Probably the last of the mince pies they'd eaten with the cocoa. Better off in bed on a night like this anyway. Carys barely acknowledged his good-night.

It was a few chapters later when Carys heard the commotion.

‘Carys, oh Carys love. Come up quickly. *Please*, now love.’ It was Mam’s voice disturbing her concentration. At first she shut her ears in exasperation, but when Huw burst into the room white-faced and trembling she was forced to take some notice.

‘Carys! He’s white, he’s not moving, he’s just lying there. I think he’s dead. I think he’s dead!’

‘Who’s dead?’

‘Dad, it’s Dad. Oh God, what will we do? Quick Carys!’

Mam had gone up to bed sometime after Dad and found him still and not breathing. Carys stifled her rising panic as she ran upstairs. He was lying across the bed, half dressed, not moving. Huw tried to revive him.

‘Come on Dad. Breathe! Breathe! Please breathe for me. Breathe for Mam. Don’t go! Stay with us!’

Carys dialled 999. Huw could hear her speaking as he worked on Dad.

‘Yes, that’s right. The house is at the end of the lane. It’s very dark. But I’ll put all the lights on. Please, please ask the men to hurry as fast as they can.’

After an apparent eternity, the ambulance finally arrived, the men’s boots covered in snow and their breath visible in the cold night air.

‘Now just show us where your father is, lovely. Don’t worry. We’ll do everything we can.’

The ambulance men worked on him, thumping his chest, trying to get him to breathe, for what seemed like ages, before they took him away. Mam went with him in the ambulance, shivering and weeping quietly. Carys and the boys followed behind, Huw driving their father’s car. John Lloyd-Jones was pronounced dead on arrival at hospital and transferred straight to the morgue.

Mam was bereft and inconsolable. Dafydd wailed like a baby. Huw and Carys supported each other, staying strong while making all the formal arrangements. Huw took on the role of head of the family, and Carys suppressed her grief for reasons of expediency. She had only another ten days before term started.

The funeral took place five days later. Dad had left his instructions in an envelope marked ‘in the event of my death’ – not that he had had any sense of foreboding but just because he was like that – organised, systematic and meticulous about detail. For other decisions – flowers, food and drink for the mourners, donation to the chapel and so on – Carys thought it best to give her Mother two options in each case. As you do with a child so that they think they have chosen.

'I thought chrysanths or lilies Mam for the wreath? Which would you prefer?'

'Dad wanted a simple coffin, Mam. Here are two that the undertakers have – which would you like to choose?'

The Deputy Head, Mr Pugh, insisted that the school choir would sing and that the hymn would be 'Crug y bar', apparently one of Dad's favourites for school assemblies, although that was news to Carys. She hadn't discussed school with Dad for a long time come to think of it.

There was a big turnout as you would expect. John Lloyd-Jones had been headmaster of the big school for twenty years, but had also grown up locally and was well known for his beautiful baritone voice, his love of the language, his upright and honest character and his dedication to the education of young people fit for the modern world but with a firm Welsh stamp. Mrs Thomas traced a familiar path on the chapel organ – Rock of Ages, Abide with Me, Cwm Rhondda. You could have heard a pin drop when the senior boys sang their Crug y bar. Mam's tears were overflowing and running down her powdered cheeks.

The Minister asked Mr Pugh to say a few words on behalf of the school. He must have stood on tiptoe at the lectern, or worn shoes with big heels as he looked taller that day than Carys had ever seen him. Normally she would have switched off from his pompous voice and his platitudes but this was her father he was describing and she attended to every word.

'Well now, he was a wonderful man, was John Lloyd-Jones, as I'm sure everyone here would agree. I have known him for more than 30 years as a friend and colleague and never once doubted his commitment to his job, his family or his country.'

There was a lot of nodding and a few smiles too as he recounted a life of hard work and dedication.

'He was able to marry up the best of the new ideas with the strong traditions of a Welsh education for all. And he took his staff with him, inspiring them to work equally hard for our young people. His family were his pride and joy. He simply glowed when they did well at school and in competitions. He wasn't boastful though. Just let us know in a quiet way what they had done.

'It is a tragedy for all of us that he is no longer with us to realise his hopes for the future – a better future for this area and for each and every one of us, as our young people develop into upright, hard working and creative individuals, with a love of country and of God.'

And with a slight bow to the grieving widow, 'I ask you to remember his family at this time. Whatever loss we colleagues and pupils feel, it is nothing compared to losing such a husband and father.'

Mr Lloyd-Jones would have been proud of the send-off they gave him.

When it was all over the family had time to wonder why he had died so young, whether or not it was the stress of the job – 'Yes,' said Mam, 'he never stopped working.'

'No,' said Huw, 'he loved what he did.'

Or maybe genetics – Uncle Owen and Tain Huw had both died around the same age from heart problems. Had he been upset about anything? 'Well, he did miss you a lot Carys and you barely gave him the time of day when you were home,' according to Mother.

'That's nonsense Mam. Don't say that!' Carys couldn't believe her mother could be so harsh at a time like this.

It was hard for her mother to pick up the threads, easier to sit by the fire and sob a little; look in the mirror and see a face aged overnight and cry for her lost self; walk into his study and look for some sign that he might still be around.

January was advancing. Term started on the 12th, but by the 9th Mam was still wandering around as if in a trance. Could Carys leave her like this? She had tried once to broach the subject and backed off immediately Mam had started sobbing and clinging to her. She had to find a way though – she simply needed to get back – to gain some sense of normality.

Carys had phoned Lesley the day after her father died, dreading her tears and sympathies, and had been very matter of fact about what had happened. Lesley had taken on the job of informing all the girls. They had sent flowers of course – a group wreath – and individual cards. Patricia had organised a Mass to be said. (Carys didn't pass that bit of information on to her mother, although she took care to write a note to Patricia expressing her gratitude on behalf of the whole family). They all phoned to express their sympathies and were just a little surprised that Carys was much as usual. Perhaps just a shade more serious in tone. Or maybe she was just putting a brave face on it.

She finally got away on the 14th, after Auntie Beti had agreed to come and stay for a week or two. Hopefully Mam would get back to normal soon. Life really did have to go on.

She flopped into her reserved seat on the train, suddenly very weary and glad of some quiet time. The compartment was empty save for an older man. He smiled as he took out his sandwiches. She was mildly irritated by the chomping sound he made as he worked his way through salmon paste on white bread, two slices of fruit loaf and an apple, but kept her mind focussed on her book. He suddenly sneezed. Apologising, he pulled out a brown edged white handkerchief from his coat pocket.

Dad had one like that. Oh Dad …

She ran to the ladies, opened the door and fell into the tiny compartment where she wept and wept till her chest ached and her head thumped. Her Dad was gone. She'd never see him again. She hadn't kissed him goodbye. She'd never told him she loved him. Now she never would.

There was a queue forming when she finally opened the door. She could hear them as she squeezed past:

'Come on love. We thought you'd fallen asleep in there.'

'Thank goodness for that – or I'd have been mopping the floor soon.'

'I was nearly going in the men's toilet; that shows how desperate I am.'

That would be the last of the tears, she vowed. Dad would be better served by her getting a First Class Honours degree. She would discourage any sentimentality from the girls in the flat. Some things you just have to keep to yourself.

From Russia with love

April 1976 – spring term, final year. Dalmeny Street

'Blast, bugger, shit!! Oh fuck!!!' Even by Alix's standards this was an outburst. That straight road to a glittering future, with regular party stops and racy, fun-loving companions had taken a sharp left turn. The test was positive.

Okay girl, no need to panic. This is easily sorted.

The Edinburgh Phone Book indicated a choice – The Brook Advisory Centre or The Student Health Service. Best go for maximum anonymity. No need to tell anyone else. Just turn on the tears and up the little girl lost, or if absolutely necessary, threaten to do something silly.

To give the Brook Doctor her due, she did try to engage Alix in a full discussion on the various options and their possible consequences.

'Miss Mackay, or may I call you Alix? I wonder if you are aware of the different ways in which we can help here?'

'Yes, yes, I am, but I know what I need to do. It's really quite simple.'

'Well, yes, I can see where you are coming from, Alix. But we do find that many of the girls have another think about things when they hear more about the range of options on offer – adoption for example.'

'Out of the question. Just not possible. My mother's very ill you know. This would just about finish her off.'

'Well can I give you this material to take away and read at home? I'll make you another appointment for Monday – we've got some time on our side – no need to rush into things.'

'No really, my mind is made up. It was just an unfortunate chain of events and it can all be stopped now if you organise the op for me. How long will that take?'

What seemed to clinch it was the fact that the prospective 'father' would definitely not be around to be of assistance, having last been spotted staggering along the banks of the Volga with more vodka than blood in his veins and a surname which would have challenged even Alix's fluency in Russian, had she bothered to ask what it was.

She could have contacted Gerald in Moscow of course but preferred to keep his opinion of her rather more rose-coloured in the meantime. He might have a significant role to play in her future employment. No point in jeopardising all of that. So with little further discussion, and with the offer of post-op counselling, Alix had a bed booked for the following week at the local women's hospital. She wouldn't actually miss any classes either since the Easter break was still on. Well, that was that sorted.

Actually it did go smoothly. She slipped out of the flat before 8.30 on the Friday morning, presented herself at the ward, was given a pre-med by 10.00 and it was all over by 12 noon. She might have been sobbing when she came round from the anaesthetic but she put that down to the effects of the drug. The care was perfunctory but adequate, the nurses seeing a stream of girls in and out every week, each no doubt with her own reasons. She was discharged with a pack of pads after the doctors' rounds next morning and ordered a taxi to take her back to the flat. She would report only a simple D&C if asked.

She bled for a few days but otherwise observed no cause for concern. She thought she might give sex a miss for a week or two though. Didn't really fancy it for some reason.

No-one might ever have known had the girls not been sitting around in the kitchen a couple of Saturdays later chit-chatting, catching up on their news and drinking cups of coffee to go with Lesley's latest baked offering – deep tin chocolate cake.

'Fab cake as always Lesley.'

'Thanks Carys. We Welsh know how to bake don't we!'

'Rubbish,' replied Nancy. 'Yorkshire lasses are the best bakers in the country.'

'Pity you broke the mould then,' from Carys.

Not much one for idle gossip, she tried to elevate the content of the conversation somewhat by quoting from The Methodist Conference Statement of 1976.

'Listen to this girls. "Abortion is always an evil, to be avoided if at all possible by offering care to single mothers during pregnancy."'

Without thinking, Alix exclaimed: 'That's reactionary rubbish. Just as well no-one tried that on me when I went to the Brook …'

There was stunned silence. Lesley was in a state of shock. She had strong views on the morality of abortion, particularly having worked in the gynae ward at The Western General and seen a fully formed 19 week foetus in a bowl in the treatment room one evening. Carys buried her head in the offending ecclesiastical report.

Nancy blurted out what everyone else was thinking: 'Do you mean that you've had an abortion Alix?'

Diane tried to recover the situation: 'Stop! This is Alix's own business and nobody else's.'

Alix for once was struck dumb. She realised there was no way back from her slip though and, choosing her words carefully, made a short statement in a clipped tone, before leaving the room with her emotions still in check. 'I had intended to keep this whole matter private, for obvious reasons, but now that you've put me on the spot Nancy, I will just say briefly, that yes, I did require a termination of pregnancy. This was through no fault of my own. I am now fully recovered and would be grateful if you did not mention the topic again, particularly in my parents' – or Patricia's – hearing.'

The front door slammed shut shortly afterwards. Nancy reported Alix in full flight striding along towards Leith Walk.

'Well, what do you make of that then? said Nancy.

'You might have been a bit more cautious,' said Diane

'Don't see why. She let it out. What does she think we are here? We would have helped her out if she'd asked. And for God's sake, Lesley, stop looking so shell shocked. She isn't the first, and she won't be the last. Time you grew up.'

'But abortion is such a sin,' said Lesley. ' Just as well Patricia is away. She wouldn't have let Alix off without a piece of her mind.'

'Just as well she *is* away then,' said Carys from behind the report. 'And you don't need to be the one to tell her either when she gets back.'

'You should keep your head down, Carys. You started all of this. We were just enjoying a nice chat when you had to bring the subject up. You're supposed to have respect for different religious beliefs anyway.' Lesley was uncharacteristically rattled.

'There's no point in all falling out over this,' said Diane.

'There'll be a time and a place to discuss it with Alix, but it's obviously not now. I suggest we just keep an eye out for her and see that she's okay. Patricia probably *would* go mad so why don't we just keep it to ourselves?'

Diane had a quiet word in Alix's ear over croissants next morning. That would be the end of it, but if she did need anything, she knew where to come.

Alix wasn't daft. Although the abortion had been easy enough to arrange, she didn't want to go through that again. After the recommended six weeks, she went back to the Brook Centre and got herself fitted with a coil. You can't sick that up and then get pregnant. That was one worry out of the way.

Now to concentrate on her finals. The party girl knew when to stop – then.

This is the last time

Summer 1976 – 30th June

The five of us from Edinburgh University had all graduated the previous day and had the numbness to prove it from four hours on McEwan Hall seats, but it was the parents' payback time and we all smiled for the camera. Patricia, already a Bachelor of Education, by virtue of an equally boring graduation ceremony at Craiglockart College the day before, took the photos and made sure we all received copies later.

We had planned one last evening together in Dalmeny Street before clean up day on the 1st and my wedding to Willie on the 3rd. Concentrating on organising the evening displaced any melancholy about the 'adjournment' of the group – for the moment anyway.

The plan was that all six of us would invite a partner to have a proper dinner in the flat and then selected friends would join us for drinks and a bit of a party. Actually that made it all sound rather simple. What really happened was that Alix and Carys battled it out over several weeks to design the perfect evening before Patricia suggested, after tea one Sunday night, that we all sat down round the table, and had a fair exchange of ideas so that we could come to a proper agreement. Lesley was quick to show her support for that idea; I was glad to have the conflict levels reduced and Nancy was out with Michael and couldn't give a toss as long as his wife didn't find out about the party.

'Prawn cocktail,' said Lesley.

'Not that again,' from Alix.

'Smoked salmon?' suggested Carys.

'For God's sake, it's end of term,' said Lesley.

I remember suggesting that vegetable soup would be cheaper.

'It *is* a party after all,' retorted Carys.

'How about pâté then?' said Alix.

'Okay, let's go with that. Smoked trout pâté from the deli in Stockbridge it is.'

So much for a fair exchange of ideas and a proper agreement. Discussion over the rest of the menu followed much the same pattern – upmarket ideas from Alix, predictable ones from Lesley, forceful and uncompromising from Carys, and I suppose mine were cheap and cheerful – until Patricia heard one she agreed with and pronounced it fixed. We missed Nancy's usual creative input. But it did mean Patricia could land her with one of the rotten jobs when it came to who did what.

She of the organising mind made copious notes in her ring bound jotter which then formed the basis for her detailed plan. This took a few days to compile. Meanwhile the rest of us girls waited for our orders with the customary dread.

'Alix! You're always telling us how you can charm your way out of any situation, so I suggest you sweet talk the neighbours about the possibility of a little noise on the night. You can also make any apologies afterwards.'

'Christ, Patricia. I don't even know most of them, apart from that dishy big Pat downstairs. I'll certainly give him another good talking to if I get the chance! But I'm not sure about the others. How about Lesley doing that? She looks like butter wouldn't melt.'

'No, I've got other jobs lined up for her. And one more thing you can do is go to the off-licence and order the wine, sale or return, along with some free glasses. You spend enough money in there most weeks. I'm sure you can work the old boy easily enough. Now, for the food … Lesley, would you go to the deli and buy the pâté? You can always pick up some of that lovely dark chocolate at the same time, for your chocolate orange bread pudding.'

'Okay then. What about the ingredients for the spaghetti carbonara?'

'Nancy's making that, so I thought she could organise it. No problem with that Nancy? And while you're out, see if you can pick up some paper plates and napkins from Woolworth's, would you? You can co-ordinate them with whatever it is you and Diane are doing to decorate this place.'

'I don't mind doing the cooking, but I hope someone else is on the washing up. You know I like to keep my nails nice.'

'Trust you Nancy. I did have you down for it but see if you can negotiate with Carys maybe. Just make sure you let me know so that I can amend the plan.'

'What else is Carys doing? I can swap something for the

washing up.'

'I've got Carys down for organising the sound system and the records.'

'I'll do that,' said Alix, not usually known for volunteering for anything that wasn't bottle or man shaped.

'Wait a minute; you're messing up all my plans. Let's just take stock now. Carys, would you take over the table setting and dish washing? I'll do all the cleaning up, since I'll be the sober one, and I'll see to the bins. Diane, you did agree to work with Nancy on making this place look presentable. Are we all clear now?'

I faked enthusiasm. 'Yes, Patricia. You can remind us all again nearer the time, too. Or post that action plan up in the kitchen and we can all sign it.' Patricia was oblivious to the 'yes, miss' tone which was creeping in to the discussion.

Once it began to take shape and we could begin to see how it could work, we enjoyed a cosy togetherness getting everything ready. Nancy and I were to combine my so-called artistic skills with her resourcefulness to turn the flat from a close relation of Greyfriars flea market into something a bit more sophisticated for the evening. But in the end we opted for a historical theme – overlaid with pure nostalgia – *The Dalmeny Street Girls – past, present and future.*

Using secrecy and subterfuge to amass the accessories, we sneaked Patricia's PVC coat, Alix's pink platform boots, and Lesley's vintage long velvet skirt from their wardrobes. We made an album of photos of us all at various student parties and events from the Freshers' Ball 1972 in the Assembly Rooms to Alix's 21st in The Bistro. Nancy constructed a collage of cards we'd sent each other which had kicked around behind the old radio for ages. I typed up everyone's favourite recipes and had them enlarged and framed in cheap plastic from Woolworth's – lemon pudding, fish pie, sausage casserole, Black Forest gateau, and pineapple upside-down-cake. I even contacted the various parents and asked them to bring a few old childhood snaps of their darlings in secret to the graduation for a 'name the baby' competition. Nancy excelled herself by writing a poem about the group – The Dalmeny Street Girls – charting the beginnings, the bondings, the break ups, the fun, the farce and the fantastic times we'd had. All was set and we would keep any tears in check till after the others went home.

The 'boys' arrived in dribs and drabs. Willie was already sporting his wedding day haircut and had scrubbed up well after a dirty job replacing some of the wiring in Thomas Carlyle's birthplace, in Ecclefechan. By that stage he knew Lesley's Nick and Patricia's Trevor well enough to have found a common interest in football. Rangers winning the treble joined them together in holy vitriol. Trevor had gone to the pub first – it had become a habit as a way of de-stressing after a day's teaching practice at Broughton. Nancy's Michael had made a real effort not to look conventional and country. He wore a pair of flared jeans and a pink shirt. The ten-year age gap was forgotten when he produced a crate of Newcastle Brown Ale.

Fortunately Alix had had the good sense not to invite any of her 'yah' friends from the Home Counties, hitching up *for this week only* with Mark, the 1st XV rugby captain. His thighs kept the rest of us girls enthralled for most of the night and the boys hanging on his every last word about his experiences behind the scenes at the last Scotland v England derby. That left Carys's man. We could never be sure what type she went for. But on this occasion she roped in one of the boys from downstairs who had wandered in and out of the flat in various guises over the past three years – boy next door borrowing cup of sugar while eyeing up the talent, first aider when Lesley tripped while washing the stairs and took a tumble, local handyman when the sink choked – almost one of the family. In his moleskin trousers, checked shirt and cowboy hat he could have passed for a young Clint Eastwood – had he possessed the looks to match. At least he wasn't an ethics student musing on whether or not enjoyment via the five senses was a legitimate use of the short time God has given us on this earth. Kenny would do fine on this occasion.

We made some rather stilted small talk until the punch started to take effect and then Alix lit up the party with a few impressions – of weird and wonderful friends we had made over the years, of boyfriends who had tried to muffle our orgasmic moans through the paper thin walls, of Aunties who had come to stay for a few days and had turned a blind eye to some of the goings-on once fortified with a light refreshment, and of neighbours who had either washed the close almost to extinction or had left smelly bin bags to fester in the Thursday summer sun while waiting for the

Friday collection. That started the reminiscing and we girls must have bored the boys almost to sleep with our stories. Patricia of course did not take much in the way of alcohol and in her crystal clear mental state was insistent that Alix had strayed from the facts.

Whatever the truth, we all agreed we'd lived life to the full at university. Read widely, debated, developed our intellects. Dallied with interesting men. Honed our conversational skills. Learned how to share with others, live in groups.

Were we ready to go forth and create our futures? Some of us knew what we wanted – a PhD and a job abroad for Carys. Some of us fantasised about the joys of married life and children – I was one of them. Others had a vision of service to the community – Lesley certainly. But we'd always be The Dalmeny Street Girls. We'd stay in touch. We'd always be there for each other. We left the flat on the day of my wedding to Willie – a happy event. No place for tears fears or regrets. These would come later.

NANCY'S STORY

Forbidden Love

"Mr and Mrs Kenneth Steven request the presence of Miss Nancy Thorpe on the occasion of the marriage of their daughter, Diane to Mr William McDonald on July 3rd, 1976."

There you have it – the Diane Steven that Nancy and the girls knew became 'Mrs Diane McDonald' when she married Willie in Leith St. Andrews church, Edinburgh. It had been no surprise that Diane was the first of them to walk down the aisle; she and Willie were so well suited. Diane had always seemed to be the marrying kind, with her natural way of caring and nurturing, and had made no secret of the fact she wanted children ('I want at least three,' she'd said, whenever asked), whilst everyone else, other than Lesley, was more circumspect on that score.

The bride had worn a simple white dress and summer flowers in her hair. Her white shoes would 'dye well later,' she'd joked. Nancy mentally awarded full marks for practicality. However, full marks also for the booze afterwards at the low-key reception – a meal in a private room at the Covenanters followed by a 'few' drinks.

'Those Forfar loons can fairly put it away,' Alix had remarked.

Carys had suffered a headache for three days afterwards to prove it!

Why Diane had chosen to get married to Willie in Edinburgh and not at home in Forfar remained a secret between her and Nancy.

Patricia's wedding to Trevor later that year, the Saturday before Christmas, saw the second 'Mrs' created, this time a Mrs Baker, at St Joseph's Catholic Church Dundee. They'd all had a private joke about it, in the nicest possible way, since everything had gone entirely to a meticulous plan, which was so perfectly in keeping with the student girl they'd lived with. This time Nancy had awarded full marks for convention and some more for pomp and ceremony. Minus a few for the priest's boring and very long sermon. A+ though for the reception. The Irish sure knew how to party. And Trevor's family showed that the English could sometimes match them.

A wave of emotion had overtaken Nancy at Patricia's wedding, catching her completely off-guard. There had been nothing like that during Diane's ceremony. Perhaps, she thought, it had been something to do with the choir's singing during the nuptial mass, or the scale of the whole event, all those gorgeous flowers, candles and incense – so very atmospheric. Whatever it was, it had touched a raw nerve somewhere.

As the minutes passed, Nancy struggled to identify the nature of this unexpected feeling that seemed to be coming from her stomach, spreading out inside her chest, threatening to well up to a crescendo. Then it became clear, and she could give it a name – envy. She didn't *ever* remember feeling envious of Patricia before, but she certainly was then, there in the church, seeing her friend standing at the altar with Trevor, husband-to-be. An unlikely image of herself, with Michael standing quietly beside her, putting a ring on her finger, had flashed into Nancy's head. Squeezing her eyes tight under the broad-brimmed felt hat, she'd had to work very hard to stem the flow of tears. She ended up with deep nail marks in one of her palms, using her other hand on it to produce some pain in an effort to gain control of herself. She tried to keep focused on Patricia, but it was too late, the idea of the impossibility of that image ever becoming reality had taken hold, so that all through the remainder of the service she continued to struggle with her emotions.

Thank God for my long fringe and this ridiculous hat, and that I'm not the only member of the congregation snuffling into my handkerchief; they'll just think I'm being soppy over Patricia, I hope.

But the floodgate had opened, and refused to close again on the conflicting thoughts that tormented her for the larger part of the next day.

So is this what I really want? She asked herself over and over afterwards, once she was safely home. A union for life? A marriage with Michael? That wasn't how it was supposed to go, was it? We had agreed, right from the start, that we'd keep it light-hearted, keep it fun; the subtext being that there would be no expectation of commitment, of anything long term, let's just enjoy it for what it is, right?

Wrong.

You are so very wrong, Nancy girl, she finally admitted, to the mirror.

By the August, just after she'd left University, and moved into a tiny flat in Dalkeith near her workplace, it was obvious she was falling deeply in love with Michael, and the emotional distress was racking up, notch by notch, day by day, making her feel almost ill with its intensity, and the hopelessness of it all. In September, after a particularly long, luxurious love-making session, Michael admitted he felt the same about her, taking their relationship to a new level. It was now out of control.

Sometimes she used to wish she'd never met Michael in the first place, and then she would have been spared all the anguish the relationship brought in its wake. Yet, when she was with him, it felt so right, so very real. Fated even, she believed. Why else would they have bumped into each other that November Saturday in 1975 on her Auntie's farm in the depths of the Borders?

* *

That day had created vivid memories, engrained forever in her mind. She remembered the baler twine was cutting into her shoulder on the last hundred yards' walk back to the game cart. Hardly surprising, given the weight of the two plump cock pheasants tied one-either-end and dangling by their necks. The picking-up team was two handlers and dogs down due to the fluey bug doing the rounds, so the remaining two men and dogs were working extra hard, gathering all the shot birds for eight guns. Nancy had been asked to help with Tam's load. It was heavy work, though thankfully the last drive before lunch, so a welcome break was soon to come.

When Nancy peered into the old cart there was a large pile of pheasants already there, so she placed her two birds carefully down, starting a new row, and as she did so, had a certain feeling, not quite hair on the back of the neck standing up, but a definite knowledge, that someone was behind her, watching her actions intently.

'Is one of those the runner that I winged? I saw him coming down in the mill field, then legging it towards the burn. I hoped Tam's lab would find him. Damn nuisance Portia not being here today to fetch my own birds for me.'

The voice was male, well-spoken, and quite typical of the 'guns' on the syndicate although today's shoot was a 'let' day for a corporate client. She turned around to face whoever it was, answering, 'Yes, I think it is, at least, I got him from Tam, who had too many birds to carry on his own.'

'Oh, that's good; I don't like losing injured birds, not good sport.'

'No, it's not,' she agreed.

Their eyes had locked during this brief exchange. She felt her feet become rooted to the spot. She had no idea whether he was going to say anything else, or indeed, whether she ought to add to the conversation, find a way to continue it. She had tried to look natural, as if he were just another well-heeled gun, and she just a lowly beater, simply doing her duty.

He broke the silence with 'I was here a month ago, as a guest of the syndicate. Didn't I see you then with your boyfriend?'

'Yes,' she replied, following up rapidly with 'No! – Well, I was here, but Thomas isn't my boyfriend; he's just someone I know from University, he comes along sometimes if he's free and Jock's short of beaters.'

The lie just came out. Later Nancy remembered how strange her voice must have sounded, slightly strangled perhaps. She hated herself when she lied, which didn't happen often, she reassured herself; yet she suffered pangs of guilt for weeks after that big one – a denial of poor Thomas, her current squeeze, relegating him to the status of a passing acquaintance.

'Not quite as bad as Judas,' Carys had teased, when the tale had been told.

'I'm Michael by the way, Michael Robertson.' He didn't offer her his hand to shake. 'Portia, my lab, is having a phantom pregnancy, frantically digging up the house and carrying things to her basket all the time. She's quite distracted, wouldn't have had her mind on the job at all today, so I left her at home.'

Nancy laughed at his description of the poor bitch with her hormones all awry.

'No, I suppose not, in the circumstances.'

They were still gazing at each other intently. He was about six foot tall, with a full head of black hair, clean shaven, slightly tanned, with, in anybody's book – not least of all Nancy's – gorgeous deep brown sparkling eyes. As he smiled at her, he showed his even white teeth between full, rich lips. She felt it was time she looked away, but didn't want to.

'I'm Nancy, Nancy Thorpe.' Now what else could she say? 'I'm a final year student at Edinburgh University, studying biology.'

'Jolly good. I'm in Edinburgh too, working in Forsyth and McKenzie, you'll have heard of them, no doubt. William over there's a colleague. We're here with some of our clients.' He turned and pointed to a short, podgy, ruddy-faced man wearing an expensive-looking tweed shooting suit. She looked at William politely, only very briefly, whilst he returned his gun to its case. She was far keener to turn back to the prettier sight facing her.

They gazed at each other for another few seconds, although to Nancy it felt like minutes. For her, this was lust at first sight, with no doubt about it. She didn't usually go for older men, but she could easily rationalise why this was different. He could only have been ten years older at most, and *very* tall, dark and handsome. *And* from his appearance, clearly loaded. She recognised his gun as a Purdey, confirmation indeed.

A nearby shout diverted her attention from Michael for a moment.

'Nancy, come on, Jock's told us lunch is ready in the bothy, and he wants us to get going.'

'Ah, that time of the day already,' Michael did not look away as he flashed another smile at her, 'but hopefully the best sport is yet to come.'

She felt weak. Was he flirting with her? She very much hoped so. 'With any luck,' was all the reply she could manage.

She offered a silent prayer that her lipstick was still on and her mascara hadn't run after the morning's exertions; all that hard beating through the woods and game crops. With a heart rate faster than normal she turned and walked over to join the other beaters who were climbing into the wagon. Michael on the other hand, got into a Landrover Discovery with William and went off for lunch to the Farmhouse, where Auntie Jane would have put on a sumptuous spread for the party of guns and their guests.

It had been one of those seminal moments in life. The sort that isn't expected but just happens, leaving one with a feeling that some kind of pleasant electric shock has been transmitted, whose after-waves reverberate for days.

She wanted him, and she had a pretty good idea the feeling was mutual. But it could only be wishful thinking, surely? For all she knew he was married with children, worked away from home a lot and already had a mistress. Probably also filthy rich. Why on earth would he be interested in a student? She had an uncomfortable hunch he was maybe one of those men who flirted with women all the time, on some kind of power trip, using their good looks and charm to impress, knowing they had the ability to make women go weak-kneed.

'Chocolate boys' Lesley called them.

Nancy could mimic the South Wales accent with ease. 'They think they're chocolate!'

Unless he came as a guest of the syndicate another time before the season was out, she wasn't going to see him again anyway.

Forget it, she warned herself. *Just forget it for once, okay?*

* *

Later that day, during the afternoon drives, she watched the guns with unusually keen interest, whilst trying to pretend that she wasn't watching them anymore than usual. Which peg was *he* shooting from? Did *he* look her way at all? Not that she could make out much, but – she did see him drive away at the end in a new black Range Rover with a personalised number plate, MR1. It was the car she'd seen first thing that morning, as the beaters were standing around waiting to be called to the wagon.

Davy had remarked in a low voice, 'Just look at the bloody state of that, some of these folk have more money than sense.'

They'd noticed the back bumper with a large dent in it, and a deep scratch all down one side through the front and back doors and along to the bumper. There were muddy wellies in the passenger side, fingerprints all over the rear side window, and dog nose marks right around the boot window. The car was filthy and didn't look as if it had been cleaned since new. But worst of all,

Nancy remembered, there had been coats, bags and toys piled up in the back seat, either side of a baby seat secured in the middle. There could be no denying it, Michael Robertson's Range Rover was most definitely a *family* car, a fact that she clearly chose to put completely out of her mind when she agreed, at the New Year shoot, to meet Michael for a lunchtime drink in Edinburgh.

Caught in a moment

If asked to defend her behaviour, then Nancy would say, with a convenient degree of self-delusion, that she'd never intended, in any kind of a pre-meditated sense, to become involved with a married man; someone ten years older than herself, and with a young child. Yes, she freely admitted she had felt a huge sexual attraction to him, from the word go, but, she would protest, she also thought he would be an attractive companion. Honestly – she agreed to go for an initial drink just to find out more about him, believing she could keep her feelings in check.

So much for good intentions. The drink turned into lunch. The second lunch resulted in an invitation to dinner, in Prestonfield House, no less. Expensive, classy; they tucked themselves away in a corner for privacy, 'but if anyone recognises me, I'll introduce you as a client,' Michael had warned. The deceit had well and truly begun.

Diane asked her several times was she sure she knew what she was getting into? And what about his family? How would she deal with the thought of that?

Nancy had been fairly flippant with her responses. 'I'm not sleeping with him, Diane; in fact I'm not doing anything with him other than socialising,' (*and a bit of kissing*).

'Yes, I know he's married, he hasn't tried to hide the fact; but he's not happily married. He loves his little girl, he's not suddenly going to leave his wife for a student he's having some meals out with, is he? Besides, I've no intention of becoming a scarlet woman!'

Diane would shrug her shoulders, give Nancy a knowing look and reply 'Mmm, we'll see.'

Nancy was initially somewhat overawed during the dinner, being in those surroundings, listening to Michael's stories of his business dealings. Obviously he moved in very different circles to the student and family ones with which she was familiar. He was self-assured, but not in an arrogant way. They disclosed more information about their backgrounds. She hadn't realised he was quite so upper class, so well connected. If she was truthful, she found this aspect slightly intimidating, but would never have admitted it. Their mutual love of the countryside – country pursuits, dogs, horses, walking, agriculture was a great talking point.

They stayed at table, locked in animated conversation for hours, until their coffee cups were quite cold and empty, the periodic genteel interruptions of the waiter being the only thing disturbing the growing bubble around them. By the end of the evening Nancy felt as if she'd known Michael for an age, as opposed to a period of three months and only three meetings. She was perfectly clear, in her own mind, that she had never met anyone her own age who held such a fascination for her, to the extent he did; she was also adamant, now, that she wanted more of him, her stated intention of never becoming a 'scarlet woman' receding conveniently into a cabinet somewhere in the dark depths of her mind.

Naturally, when he said she was interesting and enjoyable company she wanted to believe him. When he admitted he also found her irresistibly attractive, she knew they were getting onto dangerous ground, but by then she didn't care. She just wanted him to kiss her, imagining his lips on hers, the electric shivers that would produce, hardly able to contain herself until the end of the evening before they went their separate ways, knowing that the goodnight parting would be all the excuse they needed to cross the line.

She hadn't appreciated, at the time, just how much of a risk Michael was taking by meeting her for those lunches and the dinner; by telling her about his background, the problems in his marriage. But she did know that he trusted her, right from the start.

'There's something about you Nancy,' he'd said, 'you seem older than your years, in some way, yet still with such a positive attitude to life that the young have. It's so refreshing. I feel I can tell you anything and you'll understand.'

He certainly knew how to flatter; not overtly, or brashly, or with sexual innuendo, in the unpractised manner of boys, but gently, starting at a safe distance away, then homing in by ever-decreasing circles, with the consummate accomplishment of a bird of prey. She felt an intense hit, every time, and *extremely pleasurable it was too,* she thought.

Michael wasn't the only one taking a risk There were risks for Nancy as well – with her exams looming in May she should have kept her head down and not been gallivanting with a desirable man in March, looking for adventure. The thought had not escaped her attention; she felt confused, conflicted. Hadn't she had enough exam failures already? Yet how could she settle down to swotting with all that lust and excitement swirling around inside?

Consultation with the girls about her dilemma did little to reduce any doubts Nancy might have had about the desirability of the relationship.

Lesley took the moral high ground and issued a lucid warning in an uncharacteristically stern tone. 'You're being absolutely daft messing around with someone ten years older than you. It will all end in tears, mark my words, and you won't be the only one crying – there's other people involved here too, Nancy.'

Patricia said nothing; she didn't have to – her aura of disapproval was strong enough.

All Alix wanted to know was, 'Just how much money does he have then?'

Whilst Carys's take on it was typically academic. 'It raises some interesting societal issues. The age and class divide, and the possible effects of adultery on the nuclear family, of course.'

But of course.

Nancy felt completely alone with her predicament. *Should she? Or shouldn't she?* That was the question. She hadn't brought him to the flat, not yet, for good reasons. She didn't want the girls to put him off, since he wasn't guaranteed a friendly reception, and it was never empty, so they wouldn't have got privacy.

In the end, her dilemma was resolved fairly quickly. Two weeks later Michael telephoned her (it was most annoying, she felt, that she always had to wait for him to contact, not the other way around, but then a developing affair is bound to have restrictions, isn't it?), and suggested she accompany him on a viewing, to an old farmhouse ripe for conversion, down the coast towards Dunbar.

'It'll be fun Nancy. I'll pack a picnic; you bring a few things as well, including your Wellingtons, but keep your fingers crossed for fine weather.'

How good she felt, sitting up high, in the passenger seat of his Range Rover, chatting away about this, that and the other. He smiled at her all the way down, chipping in with snippets about Portia, the office, his daughter Lucinda's latest exploits – but sensibly, didn't mention his wife – an off-limits subject as far as Nancy was concerned now.

They approached the farmhouse up a long, winding, private road, pulling over as they reached the circular drive in front of the house.

'Wow, impressive,' she said, looking up at the wide Georgian façade and huge doorway. 'Is there anyone living here?'

'No, the owner died last Autumn. Now his son has put it up for sale. By the end of today I need to have done a full survey for a potential buyer, who has an idea to convert it into flats. I'll do the full report tomorrow morning in the office.'

'Lunch now or later?' she asked.

'Let me make a good start first, then we can have lunch a bit later on – there's a nice orchard around the back – we could spread the picnic out there if the rain holds off.'

Nancy poked around the rooms in the manner of an inquisitive child, peering into crannies and opening every door.

'It must have been fabulous in its heyday,' she shouted to Michael, who was busy measuring up along the hallway. 'Look, come and see!'

Standing in front of the end bedroom window it was possible to take in the view all the way to the sea. The garden led into the orchard, which was surrounded by fields, until they disappeared into a mass of bluey-grey water. It was stunning.

'How lovely it all is here,' she exclaimed, as Michael came and stood behind her, peering out over the top of her head.

'It's not as lovely as you,' he murmured into her hair, twirling her around to face him, taking her face into his hands and kissing her lips tenderly at first, then more firmly. She let her body respond naturally, nestling into him, finding where she fitted.

She could have pulled him down on her then, but a warning kicked in, reminding her she shouldn't be seen as a push-over, not just yet.

'Hey,' she said, coming up for air, 'you'll never finish the work at this rate.'

'You interrupted me, remember?' he smiled, gazing at her intently. She felt weak again, just as she had at the game cart, the very first time she'd experienced this intense look.

'Next room then!' she teased, breaking out of his grip and trotting along the corridor, buying some time to get her emotions in check.

* *

The orchard was lovely. Long-established apple trees with knobbly trunks and branches bearing the first buds, stretched out in rows through the grass.

Michael drove the car to the orchard gate and lifted the large wicker basket from the boot. They dined like kings on fine crackers and pate, cold chicken legs and salad, followed by cheese and fruit, and a bottle of Chablis, which he'd put into a cold bucket of water earlier.

'This is the life,' she said lazily, leaning back, putting her hands under her head to gaze up at the sky. 'Beats studying any day.'

Michael moved closer, mirroring her pose. 'And the weather's kept fine for us too – I put in a special request.'

'You think of everything, don't you?' She turned to him, smiling dreamily, her fingers tracing round his collar in a lazy circle, the tips touching his skin, ever so lightly, provocatively, sensuously. She was losing herself in his smell, knowing for certain now that she was, like a boat being pulled by a strong current, moving inexorably into deep water, to wherever the flow might take her.

'Perhaps,' he whispered into her ear, 'we'll have to see.'

He bowed his head and began to kiss the top of her throat, pulling down the zip of her jacket just a little, before pressing her closer, kissing her lips passionately, but gently, as if asking her a question.

Yes, her body screamed, yes, now Michael.

She kissed back enthusiastically, burrowing into him even closer. They both knew what was about to happen was inevitable; if there had ever been a hidden agenda for the trip in either of their minds it was now going straight onto the table. Fondling, frantic reaching for body parts hitherto untouched, clothes coming off only where necessary to give better access, urgent sex on the cold, hard ground. Both of them were getting it out of their system at last; willingly, thankfully.

They didn't speak until they'd finished, until they were lying apart again, covered by a blanket, defence against the weather, or perhaps against some embarrassment. Michael spoke first.

'I'm so sorry, Nancy, what must you think of me? I just couldn't help myself once we started kissing like that. I should have asked you if it was safe.'

'Michael – you don't need to feel sorry about it – I'm not a silly young girl you know, I wanted to do it as much as you did and enjoyed every minute.'

Safe? Christ! I bloody hope so.

Later, when the surveying was done, they sat in the car drinking coffee, some unspoken words between them, which surfaced just before they left the property. Michael looked pained.

'I can't give you what you want, Nancy. I'm not free to do so. It could never be more than snatched moments in the overall scheme of things.'

She felt a flash of anger. 'How do you know what I want?' she'd replied petulantly. 'This is fine by me; I've got my own life to lead as well. Let's just be grown-up about it, shall we?' But in truth, back then, fighting to keep conflicting emotions under control, she hadn't felt particularly grown-up at all.

Deeper and deeper

Snatched moments, he'd said, which turned out to be a very apt description of their torrid, very part-time affair over the next three months. Some more lunches, a few dinners, the odd short trip. She brassed it out back at the flat and took Michael there for coffee. Whenever possible, usually over a lunchtime, when there was more likelihood of everyone being out, they would make love in her bed. Not that they spoke of making love, or ever said *I love you*, because that wasn't supposed to be in the script.

Once the girls had met Michael, their concerns mostly evaporated.

'He's charming,' said Diane, 'I can understand your attraction.'

'What a handsome hunk!' she got from Alix.

'Not one for the BOB yet then?' was Carys's offering.

He'd even come to the flat-leaving party, fitting in better than Nancy ever imagined he could. She'd felt so good, that night, introducing Michael as 'my boyfriend.' Then afterwards she'd thought about it and felt sad, self-delusional even, because he wasn't that at all really was he? To the rest of the world he was her secret lover, the one it wasn't supposed to know about, the one she wasn't supposed to mention.

Because she didn't get to see Michael every week, Nancy managed to swot hard enough to pass her exams, ending up with a creditable 2:2, enough to secure a job as a research technician in a scientific lab near Penicuik. She spent two weeks at home in Skipton after Diane's wedding, before returning to her new flat. It had seemed strange with the girls gone, being on her own in Edinburgh. But not quite on her own. Michael would arrive, usually on a Thursday evening, and stay a few hours.

Their friendship endured, despite the restrictions. Over time they grew closer to each other, in an emotional sense, no doubt helped by the cosiness and privacy the flat afforded. She couldn't imagine Michael not being part of her life. When he said 'I love you', in the throes of a particularly tender session in September, she cried, letting the tears flow, not caring about hiding them.

'I love you too,' she'd responded.

They made love over and over again then, until they were exhausted, and their feelings had become deeper and more meaningful than ever before.

'I don't want you to go,' she'd told him, from under the duvet, watching him getting dressed to go home.

'Believe me, I don't want to go either, Nancy,' he'd said, his voice low and quiet, 'but I must.'

That night changed everything. She hadn't intended emotional involvement with a married man, but now it had happened; slowly, almost imperceptibly, and there was no going back. Some days she felt elated, full of hope for a joint future together, at other times depressed with the futility of the relationship, angry about how unfair it was that she couldn't have the man of her dreams, just a small part of him. She kept reminding herself it was nobody's fault but her own, other than Michael's, quite obviously. They'd been just two consenting adults having some fun; they should have kept it like that, or got out while the going was good. Now it was complicated by feelings; deep, strong ones, that hurt, and pulled her in opposite directions. Love was supposed to strengthen, that's what she'd been led to believe. The reality felt different. She could feel herself becoming weaker, compliant, complacent in what, she refused to acknowledge tacitly, was a game of love. By December, with Christmas looming, she had grown increasingly unsettled.

She took herself to Skipton for Christmas – traditionally a time for families, and Michael was with his. She conjured up image after image, tormenting herself over his supposed idyllic setting.

Was he sleeping with his wife again or was he thinking about her, wishing he were with her instead? Was he thinking about her at all?

He phoned to wish her Happy New Year on January 1st, after a week's silence.

Her mother wanted to know, 'Who was that, Nancy?'

'Just a friend,' she'd said, 'an old friend from Edinburgh.'

She couldn't concentrate on anything after that phone call. As the day went on she became more and more upset. She needed to talk with someone, someone who could listen, give impartial advice, give her a hug, tell her it would all work out for the best in the end.

She phoned Diane. 'Can I pop in and see you on the way back up tomorrow?'

'Great!' Diane had said. 'I'll be here waiting for you. Bring some of your Mum's treacle toffee if you can!'

Nancy's story was all prepared, she had gone over and over it in her mind on the journey up, the questions she wanted to ask Diane. By the time she reached Carlisle she was pretty wobbly. When she saw Diane she almost burst into tears.

'Mum been driving you mad then? Christmas is a nightmare time for families. They say that more people contact The Marriage Guidance Council during January than at any other time of the year. We had the usual here. I tried everything possible to make it a perfect day for Mum and Dad, steak pie not turkey for Dad, gravy made with the giblets to satisfy Mum. Then I had to factor in Willie's Mum and Dad too and his Gran. So that meant opening presents on Christmas Eve instead of Christmas morning, trifle as well as Christmas pudding, charades in the evening instead of dozing in the chair, no derisory comments during the Queen's speech. It was supposed to be our first Christmas in our own home but Willie and I barely exchanged a word. Stay single Nancy – I'm telling you. Do your own thing. Be your own person. All this compromise is exhausting.' A rare outburst from Diane.

The day took a different turn then. Diane was keen to go for a long walk, talk over the old days in the flat. Look back on the times when they'd done silly things and had a good laugh. She was a talker not a listener that day.

The cottage was freezing, the coal fire barely removing the chill in the living room. A hotch-potch of wedding presents, given in the limbo of no fixed home to furnish, was dotted around in opportune spots – the stripy cotton rug livening up the fireplace, the set of three blue vases in a line on the window sill, hiding the flaking paint, the quilted orange bedspread taking the eye away from the tired old brown carpet in the bedroom.

'How long have you got this place for? Can you decorate it if you want?'

'A year in the first instance. But Willie's keen to move on with his job. So who knows? It's not exactly a love nest, is it? And I'm so cold here most of the time. And then when I'm at work it's baking hot for all the old folk. I've got chilblains for the first time in my whole life. Maybe when spring comes I'll have the energy to freshen it up. I'm tired all the time these days.'

Nancy tried on several occasions to bring the conversation round to Michael and herself. When the girls were discussing what they'd had for Christmas, Diane had laughed at Nancy's cashmere cardigan.

'What? You in cashmere? All you'll need is the pearls now and you'll be a real county type!'

New Year resolutions failed to provide a hook – 'Well if you will take up with a married man, you're sure to be on your own when everyone else is out in cosy couples, aren't you?'

After a few glasses of mulled wine Diane mellowed a bit and was recounting the summer evenings when she and Willie had been up in the hills, lying in the heather to get their breath back and then savouring some lazy lovemaking. They'd taken one or two chances, leaving the Dutch cap behind and crossing fingers instead. 'You can't do that of course. That's the problem with affairs. At the end of the day you have to deny the essence of sex. There's no getting pregnant for you, is there?'

Nancy gave up on the idea of spilling her grief, sobbing on her friend's shoulder, being mothered. Diane had told her all she needed to know without being asked. Nothing would change while Michael was married. No point in grieving over birthdays spent alone. Nothing to be gained by torturing herself with images of his day-to-day family life, however imperfect he might say it was. There was nowhere to hide now. She either got out or he had to commit himself to her – and only her.

Next day they had time for a wander round the shops in Dumfries, before Nancy's train back to Edinburgh, Diane apparently refreshed after allowing herself to moan about life, Nancy resigned and resolved.

'There's a fine Hermes scarf for you Nance. Might as well go the whole hog!'

'This isn't a bloody joke Di. Give it a drink will you? I came here for a bit of sympathy and you just find it all a big laugh.' She started off in the direction of the station.

Brought up short, Diane made to pull her back. Nancy shrugged her off.

' But don't you worry, I'll sort this out for myself. No, no, it's too late now. It's time for my train. I'll phone you when I know what I'm doing. Thank Willie's Mum for the jam will you.'

Now for an exit strategy. No man had got the better of Nancy Thorpe yet.

Exit strategy

In contrast to her usual long list of New Year's resolutions (which were almost always broken by January 7th each year – and then shelved for the next), in January 1977 Nancy had only one on her list, but it was singularly big.

She'd made her decision about Michael, now she was determined that he would make his, one way or the other. She had a 'speech' all prepared, having rehearsed it so often after leaving Diane's house, that it should have been word perfect.

Michael, we have to talk. I've given our relationship a great deal of thought over Christmas, and I've come to the conclusion that it is precisely because I love you so very much that I can't carry on like this any longer. It's too painful for me. I've decided, for the sake of my sanity, that if you can't commit to me properly, then I can't continue to see you. We'll have to call it a day.

She prayed that when the time came, she would find the strength to say it without breaking down.

He rushed through the open door, enveloping her in a massive bear hug, almost squashing the breath right out of her body. Holding her face up to his he leant down and kissed her tenderly, saying, 'Nancy, Nancy, Nancy, I've missed you so much my darling girl, where have you been all my life?'

She tried to stay calm. 'Missed you too. Skipton, of course. Let me get you a drink. How was Christmas?' Wriggling out of his grip she made for the kitchen, listening all the while.

'Christmas? Awful, bloody awful, apart from watching Lucinda. This year she didn't just play with all the wrapping paper and empty boxes, she actually looked at each present in turn, holding it up in the air delightedly, babbling on and on excitedly, trying them out, saying their names, you know, "dolly", "horsey", "teddy", that sort of thing. I've taken some lovely photos. Oh – and the Boxing Day shoot went brilliantly – you should have been there! Jock put on a grand show of birds and old Portia surpassed herself – she must have fetched at least two out of three on every drive.'

'None of that sounds awful,' she shouted back, 'so what actually *was* awful, then?' She bided her time returning, feeling a need, despite all the rehearsals, for some fuel to stoke a fire under the speech. A mention of 'the wife' – that would do it, in fact, anything provocative to give her an entrée.

'The in-laws,' Michael said, as if he had a bad taste in his mouth. 'We had them over for dinner, and to stay a few days – Annabel's stupid idea – not mine – along with her great-aunt Phillipa. She's a testy old bird to cope with at the best of times, but put her together with Phoebe and then it's double the trouble. They're simply dreadful; miserable, whining, old biddies: this isn't right, that's not right, the state of the country today, *everything* warrants a complaint, it seems. And I always feel like I'm being interrogated whenever they ask me a question.'

'Maybe you are,' volunteered Nancy, walking back through. 'Do you get on with your father-in-law?'

'On a superficial level, yes, I suppose. But he's not really my type of man. Very brisk, proper, typical ex-military top brass, likes discipline, routines, things to be done properly. Don't think he had much experience of his own children when they were young – he seemed to find Lucinda a bit challenging, which of course if one's only used to peace and quiet and perfect order then one would do, because like every other two-year old that I know she's noisy, messy and completely unpredictable. You should have seen his face when she crawled up on him, all sticky fingers, and then proceeded to push her chocolate bar into his mouth – she refused to take no for an answer and it ended up all over his damn moustache!'

He laughed heartily then, that rich, throaty laugh that never failed to make Nancy smile, want to hug him, pinch his cheeks even. Touch him. She could feel her resolve beginning to drain away, like water trickling slowly down a sink. Now it was flowing out through the soles of her feet, too fast for comfort. Unless she said something quickly it was going to be too late, all resolve would be completely gone. She handed him the coffee and sat down in the chair opposite.

'Michael, we have to talk.'

He smiled. 'Of course we do, but later on; there's something more urgent required first.'

He leaned across the space between them, pulling her up from her chair and over to the sofa in one swift, strong movement, in the manner of a parent dragging a child to come and sit next to him. Before she could utter any protest he held her face firmly between his hands and started to kiss her, slipping his tongue between her lips and flicking his tongue all around the inside of her mouth. She couldn't help but respond, instinctively allowing her body to press against his, melting into him as they fell sideways onto the cushions. He quickly rolled her over onto her back, started to kiss her neck whilst at the same time lifting up her jumper, pulling the right cup of her bra away to expose her. With his mouth on her nipple and the growing hardness of him on her thighs she felt weak; powerless to stop him. The familiar surge of longing flooded her body, coming in waves, drumming out all reason, and the remainder of the words she had planned to say completely disappeared from her mind.

Afterwards, when they lay in a dishevelled, sticky pile, her head stuck uncomfortably against the arm of the sofa, she became more aware of the full weight of his body, and felt a sudden urge to push him out of her, as a spike of anger rose up inside. Before he'd arrived she'd been so firm in her resolve *not* to do this, not to be a push-over, yet once again the minute he held her she'd succumbed without resisting.

How weak I am really. So pathetic. Get a grip! Now!

'You're squashing the breath out of me,' she groaned, 'get off please!'

'Sorry.' He pushed up, locking his elbows and looked down on her. 'That better M'lady?

'See, told you I'd missed you,' he then said playfully as he rolled off, squeezing his back between her body and the sofa's edge. He ruffled her hair and kissed her forehead gently.

'My turn to get *you* a drink now.' Grinning, he jumped off the sofa, pulling his pants and trousers on hurriedly. She watched him buckle his belt, feeling sick with the knowledge of what she'd promised herself she would do tonight.

'What would you like?'

'A whisky, please,' she replied.

'At this time of the day?' he made a face at her, feigning a frown of disapproval.

She took a deep breath, attempting a smile. 'It's still the holidays for me,' and silently, *God knows I need some Dutch courage.*

By the time he returned Nancy was dressed again, more composed, but only just.

He held the glass out to her before sitting down.

'Okay, Nancy, now what was it you wanted to talk about earlier?'

'Us,' she said, and then it all came pouring out in a torrent, before she could change her mind. The words not in the rehearsed order, but the intent was clear enough.

Here they were, hanging in the air, too late to retract, even if she'd wanted to stuff them all right back from where they'd come. She wasn't sure what she'd expected him to say, neither did she have a picture of how he would react, but she certainly wasn't expecting total silence, which is what she got, for what seemed an age, but in reality was only a minute or two. Nancy bit her lip and tried not to cry, not to say anymore, to sit it out, wait for him to reply first.

Eventually he spoke, quietly, earnestly. 'I suppose this was going to happen sooner or later, wasn't it Nancy? I, I just don't know what to say. I don't have any answers for you just now. To be honest, I'd not given the long-term future any thought. I've just been living for the present. Loving you. Wanting you. Willing us to carry on.'

'But Michael ...' she started to interrupt, stopping when he waved a hand at her.

'Please, let me finish. This is difficult enough as it is. I haven't told you any lies about my marriage – it's dead, dead as a dodo, just like I've told you before. I *don't* sleep with Annabel, I *don't want* to sleep with her ever again. I've slept with no-one but you, Nancy, not since our first time.' His eyes burned with intensity as he spoke, his face fixed firmly on hers.

'But it's not as clear-cut as you're making out, not for me. It's not a simple choice. I have Lucinda, and I don't want to lose her – Annabel is vindictive enough as it is. If she found out about us, then I'd surely have a battle on my hands for access.'

He was looking more pained now, running his hands through his hair nervously, sighing heavily as he did so.

'My parents, Nancy – they're old – they would hate any scandal, plus financially I'm indebted to them. If they withdrew that support, then I'd be in a lot of difficulty. I love you; you mean the world to me, but please, please don't ask me to choose, not like this, not just yet.'

He was struggling to maintain a sense of composure by then. 'We need time, time to work this through. It's come as rather a shock, that's all.'

She could see that he was genuinely upset, and that he was pleading with her, yet still she couldn't suppress her anger; an indignant, rising anger, that had grown with every word he'd spoken. She'd focussed on all the 'buts', heard the excuses loud and clear. His child. His wife. His parents. His money. It seemed all about *him*; where was *she* in all of this? Nancy felt sick to the pit of her stomach, not wishing to hear any more words.

'Michael, I want you to go now,' she said, as firmly as she was capable. 'I'm tired, and I'm upset. I don't think I can talk any more today.'

A response that Michael considered irrational, given the circumstances.

'Nancy, you said you wanted to talk, so let's talk. This should be the beginning of talking, not the end. You can't start this and then suddenly stop it again. How do you think I feel?' said with an air of indignation.

Her tone was false, bitter. 'Yes I can, Michael. I can do anything I like. I'm free, and you are not, that much is obvious.'

Nancy was sounding like a truculent child, but she didn't regret the retort. If she wasn't to fall back into his arms then she *had* to stay hard. She was cross, sad, empty of words, but full of conflicting emotions; they were swirling around in her head, in her stomach, taking her way beyond her range of control. She didn't trust herself to be sensible or coherent any longer, as the sobs began, involuntarily, from deep inside.

'Nancy, please don't cry, it will be all right, it *will*.'

He tried to put his arms around her but she pushed him away sharply.

'It's not *all right*, Michael,' she screamed. 'This is not *all right*! Just go home will you?'

The look he gave her then stayed with her for months afterwards.

'Okay, just as you wish,' he mumbled. 'It's probably best I do go now. I'll phone you in a couple of days.'

She didn't answer him because there was nothing to say; she had no suitable words to express the way she felt.

After he'd closed the door behind him Nancy went to lie down on her bed and she wept; all the words they'd spoken repeating over and over in her head in random fashion, completely out of sequence. She couldn't take them in. Hours later, she went over them again, trying to make better sense of them, but she wasn't entirely sure that it made any sense at all. She could have been in a play, acting out a scene; the lines so carefully learned suddenly going haywire in the face of the other actor's response. And all the while that terrible quandary in her mind.

What have I done? Precipitated a crisis that needed to happen? Or just ruined the best relationship I've ever had?

A hard rain's gonna fall

He couldn't have said how long, exactly, he'd been sitting, huddled awkwardly between the wheel of the stationary car and the sea. It would be futile, given Nancy's mood, he thought, to go back to the flat tonight; yet neither did he have any desire to head home. Nancy's ultimatum had shaken him to the core. He felt stuck in time and space, his mind retracing her words, and then his own, over and over again; and now, he had no sense of what to do next, or even what he might say when he spoke to her again, so he had just sat there, waiting for some inspiration to move.

His body shivered involuntarily, bringing his focus back to the car. It was freezing outside and he had not turned the heater on. The first flakes of the long predicted snow had started to fall, looking deceptively pretty, illuminated by the street lamps, swirling downwards, pooling together to form a thin, white carpet on the road. He noticed how quickly a layer of snow was collecting on the bonnet of the Range Rover, warning him that he must leave immediately, before the snow got any heavier. Pulling himself up straight, Michael looked at the clock – 20:35. It was likely to take another hour in these conditions before he would reach home, where right now, he knew his wife would be getting more anxious and agitated with each passing minute, just as she always did when he was out late and it began to snow.

'My wife,' Michael spoke out-loud, as if testing the sound of the words in the air for verification. 'Oh God ...'

He slid the gear stick into the 'Drive' position and pulled away smoothly, aiming for the A701 and into a certain interrogation from a stony Annabel, thirty miles ahead.

* *

He slept only fitfully. An eerie stillness had descended on the room following Annabel's outburst – anger at his lateness, tinged with relief at his eventual arrival. He had feigned extreme tiredness. The meeting had been long and difficult, he had said. The drive had been arduous given the conditions. He was very sorry, but now he needed to sleep – he had a busy day again tomorrow.

In truth he was indeed fatigued, but for reasons best kept to himself. He felt exhausted from the after-effects of too much adrenalin, from the strain of keeping his emotions inside, from holding that awful sinking feeling deep in his stomach where no-one would be able to see it.

The bed felt hard against his back, the mattress buttons dug into his skin. Annabel was sleeping on her side, facing away from him, her heavy nightdress wrapped tightly around her thin body; her snores rising and falling softly, in precise rhythm, as if she was orchestrating them from her subconscious, in time to an unseen pendulum. It had always irritated him hugely, this snoring; it was typical, he thought, of the control she displayed over everything in her waking hours, and seemingly she could exercise this same ability even whilst she slept.

He turned over, to face outward, widening the physical space between them even more. He couldn't bear it. He didn't want to be there, in the bed, with his wife – a woman who had virtually become a stranger during the four years of their marriage. He felt no husband's love for her now, if indeed, he ever properly had, simply a concern for her welfare as the mother of his child.

Michael's depth of feeling had never been awakened before Nancy, he could see that all too clearly. Annabel had just happened. It had been *expected* of him. It had all been so very *conventional*. The pressure to end bachelorhood with the dawning of his thirties. The need for an heir. The suggestions for a suitable partner, from an appropriate class of family. The courting, the engagement, the marriage, the wife; and now, a stifling state of lovelessness, arrived at due to their intrinsic incompatibility as a couple. He didn't want to think about it anymore. It depressed him.

Instead, he turned his thoughts to Nancy. She had brought out passion in him, strong emotions and a vibrant sexuality he hadn't realised was possible, in a way no other woman had ever done. With Nancy he did not have to be reserved, nor necessarily polite. She expected no social conventions. What she demanded was for him to be present, in the moment, feeling whatever he felt, speaking his truth, but most of all, being *alive*. He knew without any shadow of a doubt that he loved her deeply, and that she was good for him, and he for her. He *must* not lose her. He would find the courage to do what his heart was telling him. What he needed was a plan – a bridge across these rapids – and soon. He would focus on that in the morning.

He thought of her alone in her bed, guessing she would be lying on her back, her long hair flowing across the pillow. She would be naked under the quilt, as always, abandoned to sleep, her breath condensing in the cold air of the room. He could sense her bodily warmth, and began to visualise her contours; luxurious in their roundness, their firmness. He couldn't stop his penis becoming harder then, with the beginnings of an erection, but it just as quickly subsided, as the overwhelming fear he did not want to face crept over him once more. Annabel.

The routines, the rituals. The keeping up of appearances. Why? For what? He did not have to search hard for an answer.

For Lucinda. I do it for my darling daughter.

It was three more days before Nancy received a telephone call from Michael. Three days spent in a dream-like state, working on autopilot in the lab, wandering around her flat distractedly, touching something here, another thing there, in tears at times, yet also relieved that she had managed, finally, to say what needed to be said between them.

In a different setting, Michael had been coping with similar feelings of distraction. He'd been asked twice by a colleague that day, 'Are you sure you're all right old boy?' and heard himself reply, 'Yes, of course', when what he really wanted to say was, 'No, I'm not at all sure I am, actually.'

He very much wished to talk to someone about his predicament, but whom? *Who would be sufficiently understanding and non-judgemental? Who could possibly be trusted to keep confidence?*

There was only one person he could share this with. He must hope that Robert wasn't currently out of the country.

Nancy's heart was beating fast when she picked up the receiver. When she heard his voice she had to work hard to keep her own steady. He was asking to come over to see her, to talk some more.

'Okay then, let's meet; but not here,' she said. 'Somewhere else. In town is best, I think.'

* *

The table at the back of the café was cosy enough, well-shielded from the cold, wet and windy weather that had now descended upon Edinburgh, washing away the last of the snow. They sat awkwardly, keeping their voices low, hands grasped around steaming mugs of coffee. He looked pale and tired, she thought, somewhat older. Nancy was smoking again, and she didn't care that he saw her lighting up, that he would disapprove. It steadied her nerves. Part of her wanted to reach out to him, grab his hand playfully, but she stopped herself doing it, she must be sensible, so left it glued to the cup, leaden fingers on the pottery.

'I'm missing you,' he said. 'I can't sleep properly. I'm thinking about you constantly.'

'Good,' she said, turning her face away at an angle, blowing smoke out through her lips very slowly, affecting a coolness, 'you do that.' Then, catching his eyes full on, added before she could stop herself, 'I miss you too,' which was enough to melt her icy face and start the tears flowing again.

At this he grabbed her hand and held onto it firmly. She didn't resist him, because it felt comforting, despite the sensation of her skin burning under his touch. He shook his head.

'Nancy, Nancy, Nancy, what on earth shall we do? Look – I'm going to find a way, believe me. I am,' he said with conviction.

'I hope so, Michael. Something's got to happen. I'm so miserable like this. It feels awful, but I can't take back what I said, and I don't want to take it back, because I meant it. I can't carry on as we are.'

'I know you did. And yes, this does feel awful. Abject misery in fact, Nance. Bloody awful. Trust me. I have something to do first, then I'll call you, before next week hopefully, it all depends if I can get it sorted.'

She looked at him closely, attempting, unsuccessfully, to be cool again.

'Don't leave it too long Michael, I'm going away for a while, I'd rather we talked before I went.'

'Where are you going?' he seemed nervous now. 'When will you be back?'

'I'm not sure on either count. I just feel a need to get out into the country for a bit. Home perhaps, or maybe I'll go to visit Lesley in Inverness. Just somewhere. For a week or so. I'll need to negotiate it with the lab first.'

'But you won't leave until next week?'

'No, it'll take a few days to organise, at least.'

'I'll definitely speak to you before you go then,' he said, rising to his feet. 'I'm sorry, but I have to leave, I'm already late for my next meeting.'

They stood outside the café, facing each other self-consciously, not knowing quite how to part; not yet wanting to leave, with so many words unspoken. Then, unexpectedly, Michael gently grasped Nancy's shoulders, leant forward and tenderly kissed the top of her head, before turning away and walking briskly off down the road.

She stood there stunned, watching him striding into the distance.

That seemed a very intimate thing to have done, she thought, *kissing my hair like that* – it was an action only a parent would do to a child, or made between lovers. She could feel the spot on the top of her head still – it seemed to be pulsating. He had done it before, of course, she reminded herself, lots of times, usually after they had made love, when he held her close, her head to his chest, when she luxuriated in the smell of him. But – he had never done it in public before, in fact, she couldn't remember him holding her hand in public, even, certainly not in Edinburgh where there was more than a fair chance he would be recognised.

This realisation produced a wide grin. She wondered if he'd given her a signal. A subtle sign that things were about to change. Or was it simply a rash moment when he'd let his guard down? Nancy didn't like that latter thought very much at all. No, it was more than that, she felt. She would stick with the former interpretation instead and trust in him. He loved her. He'd said so often enough. Then let him show it. She could give him another week for that surely – for after all, what was a week when she was trying to engineer a lifetime?

* *

Robert Lindsey couldn't remember Michael sounding quite so agitated, not since the time he had mislaid the best man's speech on the morning of Robert's wedding seven years before.

Fortunately the speech was found just in time, allowing Michael to regain his normal composure, and deliver it with his usual charm and subtle humour.

They went back a long way, these two, all the way to the first day they'd met, as fresh-faced thirteen-year old schoolboys, sent away as boarders, in time-honoured upper class tradition, and thus finding themselves in the same Gordonstoun boarding house.

A mutual love of rugby and shooting had sustained a long friendship, interrupted only by travails in different universities (Edinburgh for Michael, Oxford for Robert), and then, the demands of married life. Robert was a father to three children, godfather to Lucinda and generally considered by Michael's family to be affable and trustworthy. Now he found himself in the unenviable position of being party to something that Michael was desperate to talk to him about, for which he required urgent help, but that could not possibly be gone into any detail in a telephone call. It sounded as if his friend was in deep trouble of some nature.

'I must see you in person,' Michael was saying, 'and please – could you *not* mention to anyone that you're meeting up with me.'

'Yes, of course,' Robert said emphatically. 'No, no, I won't say anything to Helen, but can't you tell me anything more?'

Michael was uncharacteristically elusive.

'No, I would rather wait until I saw you, Rob. Till Thursday then.'

Michael replaced the receiver gingerly, taking in a sharp breath as he did so. It was becoming more difficult to explain his absences – those 'gaps' in the diary – to his secretary as the week went on. She was giving him some strange looks – as if she didn't believe him – which of course, she didn't. It made him feel even more guilty, as if he wasn't feeling guilty enough already. Lies did not sit easily with Michael, he'd always been uncomfortable with them, and now, here he was, up to his neck big, fat ones, feeling desperate to create a safety net, in case they all came crashing down over his head before his plan was fully formed.

* *

'Good God, Michael! How did you ever let yourself get into this mess?' Robert was peering at him over their drinks, a shocked expression on his face.

'Having a mistress is one thing – no one can deny that the aristocracy have been keeping mistresses for centuries – but it isn't the done thing to go falling in love with them, then abandoning everything just so you can satisfy their need for legality.'

Michael ignored the pompous sentiment behind Robert's words. 'It's too late, Robert. I *have* already fallen, hook line and sinker, and that was my choice. I love her, and I don't want to lose her.'

'But setting an ultimatum like she's done isn't fair, to my mind! Are you certain she's not just after your money?'

Michael snorted at the absurdity of this suggestion. 'Nancy doesn't care about money. Anyway, what's fair in all of this? Is it fair of me to expect a beautiful and gifted young woman to play mistress forever, hanging around waiting for me until her youthfulness is gone and with it the chance of having children of her own? She's got a lot to lose as well by remaining simply a 'mistress', as you put it. As for the money – how much would I really have if you discount my inheritance and the fact that it is my father who owns the major equity share in my house?'

'My point exactly!' replied Robert, slapping his hand down on the table with some force. 'Are you going to risk the wrath of your father over this? You could stand to lose everything if he so chooses.'

His voice was getting rather loud in its earnestness, since he couldn't quite believe what he was hearing from Michael.

'Robert – keep your voice down – I don't want the whole of bloody Edinburgh to hear about this, do I? You must believe me – you of all people – you know me so well – you *know* when I'm being honest and I tell you – I'm being honest now. This isn't easy for me to say but I've been afraid of my father all my life. I've always done what he's wanted. The school, the profession. I married Annabel because it was expected of me. A society wedding between two old county families with a long-standing association. And what did I get? A marriage made in hell! My life's a sham, Rob, and it's taken a sassy girl from a different class to show me that. To teach me what it is to love – to really love

– and to enjoy. Enjoy being with each other – in and out of bed. I *can't* let her go, Rob, and if I don't do something about my situation then I will lose her, there's no doubt of that.'

Then, lowering his voice a little, Michael said, 'I'm doing this for me, and if my father disapproves then so be it; I'll take the consequences.'

Robert raised his eyebrows and sighed heavily. 'Sounds like you're in deep, old chap. Too deep for comfort. Why are you telling me all this, other than because you obviously need to talk to someone about it?'

'Because I know I can trust you Rob, and because I think you can do something practical to help me other than listening to me pouring out my troubles to you.'

Robert looked surprised. 'I can? What would that be?'

Michael sounded weary, over-emotional, Robert thought. He had never before seen him like this.

'The bottom line is that I must ensure I have access to Lucinda. I have no intention of abrogating my duties as a father to her, and neither would I want to. If it wasn't for her this would all be a damn sight easier to manage, because if I tell Annabel that I'm having an affair then all hell will break loose and she will use Lucinda as a pawn, I know she will.'

'But,' said Robert, with the tact of a rhinoceros, 'that is exactly what you're doing.'

'Yes,' replied Michael, 'but she doesn't have to know about Nancy. Couples can, and do, split up without a third party being involved.'

'You're losing me, Michael.' Robert looked puzzled, his round face squeezed up into what might have been mistaken for a grimace.

Michael continued with his line of reasoning. 'If I leave on the grounds that the marriage has broken down, live somewhere on my own for a while, whilst the divorce arrangements proceed, and access is agreed, then it would look better all round, don't you think? And perhaps I will gain some saving grace in the eyes of my family.'

'So you're going to lie to them all?'

'Yes.'

'That's not like you.'

'No, it's not, you're right, but there are three of us here to consider: myself, Lucinda and Nancy. This lie is very necessary, I can assure you.' Michael's voice had now taken on a determined edge.

Robert leaned forward, saying, 'Will that satisfy Nancy?'

'It will have to. It's a temporary step to a long-term solution.'

'Which is?' Robert asked, although he thought he already knew the answer.

'I marry her.'

Robert leaned back against his chair again, took another deep breath and asked, 'so just how, precisely, am I supposed to help you?'

Michael smiled. 'I need a bolthole. A house. A cottage. Anything – for up to a year. You must have room for me on your estate – something to fit the bill. And I'm likely to be in a bit of financial difficulty for a while. I would have to owe you the rent – run up a tally. Like old times.'

He looked expectantly at his friend, smiling weakly.

'I'll pay you back when it gets sorted out, I promise.'

Biting his lip, Robert asked, 'how soon do you need this "bolt-hole"?'

'From the minute I speak to Annabel, I suspect.'

Michael made a feeble attempt at a laugh, which came out slightly strangled.

'I'll speak to the Factor this afternoon. Where can I reach you later?'

'I'll be in the office, working late. Thank you Rob. I knew you'd understand.'

'I'm not sure I do understand,' Robert said, 'but you're clearly determined to follow this course of action so I feel I should help lessen the trauma, if that's at all possible.'

'Anything's possible,' Michael said, almost in a whisper. 'I'd do the same for you, you know that, don't you?'

'Of that, I have no doubt, my dear fellow,' Robert said, smiling for the first time since they'd started this conversation. 'I just hope you never have to.'

In the event, the hastily arranged week's leave proved to be judicious. He hadn't actually expected to feel quite so shaky. The time away from the office meant he could concentrate on settling himself into the changes, rather than putting on a brave face for clients and colleagues. He'd taken Robert's advice and confided in his secretary. Not the whole story, no mention of Nancy, but enough to gain sympathy, and a protective cloak around his whereabouts for the next week.

'Do whatever you have to do to rearrange things,' he'd said, flashing her a smile. 'This number is for emergencies only.'

'But of course,' she'd replied loyally. 'You can be assured of my discretion.'

'I know that Linda, that's why I'm confiding in you.'

'I just wish you'd done it sooner,' Linda said, her voice taking on an informal tone, as she warmed to the role of confidante.

'I've been worried about you for some time, you know. You've not been yourself at all.' She lowered her voice, even though there was no possibility they could have been overheard.

'Maybe I shouldn't say this but I was beginning to wonder if you were having an affair, although obviously that's not the case – you've just had a lot of family matters on your mind.'

'Yes,' Michael almost froze at the mention of the word 'affair', and hoped his face hadn't given the game away. 'Yes, that's exactly right.' He gave a big sigh and shrugged his shoulders for good effect. 'I'll go now, as there's a lot to do, and I'll see you on the 20th. Good luck managing the ship whilst I'm away.' Adding, 'and thank you, Linda, you're a great secretary.'

Her face lit up with pleasure at his compliment, and the thought flitted through her head that he would now be single. Given time, available, even. Her cheeks flushed ever so slightly at this idea, but it was all right, he wouldn't have noticed, he had his back turned, striding out through the office door. She needn't have worried. He had already forgotten her under the weight of other things on his troubled mind.

* *

When he woke early two days later, it was to the sound of songbirds chirruping furiously immediately outside the bedroom window. His initial reaction to this noise was to feel annoyed at being woken up. But as he lay there, letting the sound permeate his consciousness, he could sense the power in their songs, the infectious energy contained in the repetitive rhythm of the notes. He had to admit they sounded really rather joyful. If only he could feel the same. Instead he was disorientated and deeply tired, his body aching as if he'd run a marathon, his mind drained of coherent thought.

He forced himself out of bed, making his way to the very basic and windowless lavatory, where the coldness of the room made him shiver and the whirring of the fan did nothing to help his headache.

One too many, I'll have to watch.

Last night, alone in the cottage, he'd unpacked the suitcase and a few boxes of essential items, then sat down with a bottle of whisky and contemplated the several conversations he'd had that day, and what he must do next. A chill of loneliness passed over him. He wished he'd been able to bring Portia for company, but he wasn't organised enough yet. *Soon, very soon.*

Nancy was the first person he'd phoned after downing the first glass.

'It's done Nancy,' he'd said quietly, 'I'm in the cottage sitting on a tatty old sofa, drinking a glass of whisky at the end of one long and *very* difficult day.'

He'd imagined himself on a number of occasions in the previous weeks saying precisely these words, and feeling elated as he did so, but now he felt only a peculiar kind of relief, mixed with anxiety. Nancy's voice was quiet too; not entirely steady.

'I wish I could be with you there, right now Michael,' she'd said. 'I want to give you a big hug, tell you it's going to be okay. This is going to be the worst bit for you I'm sure. But it'll get better, I know it will.'

He touched on the scene with Annabel, saying just enough to reassure Nancy he had coped. He told her about his phone call to the solicitor, briefly outlining some of the complexities, curtailing her questions with 'I'll tell you the finer details after I've been to see him tomorrow.'

He said nothing about the conversation, if one could call it that, with his father. She didn't ask about arrangements for Lucinda, and he chose not to tell her what Annabel had said. It was all too immediate, too uncertain; besides, if he thought about Lucinda he just might not be able to stop his voice from breaking.

'I love you Michael. I love you so very much,' Nancy had said just before he'd put the receiver down.

'I know,' he'd replied. 'I love you too.' And he'd meant it. Sitting in the stillness of the dimly lit room, drinking the fourth glass, he knew, without a shadow of a doubt, that his love for Nancy was valid enough reason to have thrown his life into utter turmoil, and why he now found himself alone in an old and shabby cottage in the depths of a country estate, to all intents and purposes bereft of the familiar trappings of wealth and luxury. All bar a Range Rover bearing the number plate MR1. It was a sobering thought for a man used to privilege.

* *

What a pity his mother had chosen this very week to arrange a visit to her sister in Banchory. He could have done with her moderating influence this morning during that awful conversation with his father. Michael had thought it better to tell him of the separation immediately, before he found out about it from a third party – more than likely Annabel. It was no wonder he'd needed a few drinks – that part of the day warranted a bottle in itself, he thought.

His father hadn't seemed too pleased to be having his lunch interrupted. After brief greetings had been exchanged, Michael had sat at the opposite side of the table, grasped a glass of water, taken a deep breath and launched straight into it.

'Father, this isn't easy for me to say – I've come to tell you that Annabel and I have separated. As of today I'm living in a cottage on Robert's estate, whilst we work out the terms of the separation, and eventually, the divorce.'

Lord Robertson had been clearly shocked, and not at all amused. He sat up straight, placed his knife down then bellowed back at Michael, 'What's that you said! What bloody news is this? You've only been married for ...' he paused a moment, struggling to recall the number of years before spluttering crumbs out of the corner of his mouth along with the words, 'four years is it? What on earth's brought this on?'

'I don't love Annabel, father. I'm not sure I ever have. I feel stifled in this marriage. She tries to organise my whole life outside work. I …'

The interruption had been shouted, again with a tone of disbelief. 'Stifled? In a house the size of Abercaskie? There's enough room in it for three families! What's wrong with being organised? Annabel seems highly efficient to me. First rate. That house is managed perfectly. You always did need directing.'

Michael's heart had sunk. It was turning into a battle. As usual. His father had the most annoying habit of dismissing anything he did not want to hear, or with which he disagreed. He had tried once more.

'I cannot live with her any longer. I'm finding it too stressful. *I'm* not happy. *She's* not happy with me. The marriage was a big mistake, father. Please understand that. If it wasn't for Lucinda then I would have come to this point sooner.'

This had only served to inflame the situation. With barely disguised fury his father had launched into a tirade, which Michael knew from long and bitter experience would have to run its course before he could manage to get another word in.

'Have you ever stopped to consider the potential scandal? There has *never* been a divorce in the Robertson family and I don't want to hear about one now! You say you're skulking off like a wounded rabbit to some dingy cottage! Why? At the very least you could have come here for a while, kept it quiet until things blew over – where's your sense? Have you taken a mistress? Is that what this is about?'

'No,' Michael had replied, feeling as if that was some horrible denial of Nancy.

'Are there problems with your sexual relations then?'

'Yes.'

'Well, see about it. There are professional people out there who can help aren't there? If all else fails, there are other ways and means to satisfy that side of things, rather than leaving your wife.' He left the words hanging, but his meaning had been clear.

Michael felt sickened. *How deplorable, that this family would condone such double standards for the sake of appearances;* yet he had said nothing, given that he had just, less than a minute ago, lied himself.

'It's more than that, Father. As I said previously, the marriage isn't working, it's never going to work. We are two very different people, and ...'

Back and forth it had continued for a further ten minutes until Michael decided it was hopeless to prolong the meeting. No amount of explanation of the situation or how he felt would have convinced his father that his own behaviour was anything short of lunacy. The arguments were being consigned to a waste bin of dishonour and disrepute. It was an abject failure in his father's eyes, which, despite their small size and the wateriness of old age, now burned with a frightening intensity. Michael had forced himself to meet them for the final lance, which he already guessed was coming.

'You realise the seriousness of this action on your financial position?' Lord Robertson's voice had assumed an air of menacing gravity.

'I've done some preliminary figures,' Michael had answered.

'And do these ... *figures* ... take into account any capital from a disposal of Abercaskie, should it come to that?'

'No, they do not, Father. I am well aware of the terms of the agreement made at the assignation of the property.'

'Ah ...then you will be aware also of the other difficulties that will be ahead of you should you insist on taking a flight back to bachelorhood?' His father rubbed his mouth with his napkin, then rose carefully from the chair and walked slowly and deliberately towards the window.

Michael had chosen not to rise to the taunt. His response could wait for another time. There had been enough talk for one day already.

'Goodbye, Father. I will telephone Mother myself, this afternoon.' This last said to an old man standing straight backed, facing away from the room, gazing out of the enormous bay window to the garden beyond, his hands clasped firmly behind him. It was his customary way of signalling a summary dismissal.

* *

'The legal position is black and white,' Mr Alastair Sneddon of Campbell and Sneddon Solicitors stated. 'The Family Law (Scotland) Act allows for divorce where both parties are still alive on the following grounds only: living apart for a period of two years with your spouse's consent; living apart from your spouse for five years without consent, or on the grounds of adultery, no time limit if both partners agree to divorce. From what you have told me you fall into the second category.'

'Five years?' Michael said incredulously. 'My God,' then stopped himself immediately from saying anything else.

The solicitor looked at his client slightly quizzically over the top of his bifocals, then continued in a monotone that conveyed the impression he had recited the following more times than he could remember.

'Given that you have a child, and property, it would be sensible to have a legally binding Separation Agreement in place as soon as possible. This may include division of capital, sale of the matrimonial home and endowment policies, aliment, periodical allowance, payment of debts and succession to your estate on death. Such an agreement is very useful to settle financial matters since Court proceedings can be protracted and extremely expensive. Should you have to enter into them, then you would both be left with less capital at the end of the day.'

Michael felt weary already. 'What about my daughter and ensuring I have sufficient access to her?' he asked.

'Arrangements for your child confirming where she is to reside and what contact she is to have with the parent with whom she does not reside can be put into the Agreement. These are subject of course to what the Court may rule is in the child's best interest should Court Proceedings be raised. And, if aliment for children is included, then such arrangement is always subject to the child maintenance rules.'

After an hour of this, including clarifying his own financial position, Michael felt quite despondent. Walking back to the car, mulling over it all, his legs became heavier and heavier. Five years simply wasn't acceptable. Nancy would hate it. He would need to talk it through with Annabel, come to a mutually acceptable agreement. Was that possible? He doubted it, given that she refused to believe the marriage had failed irretrievably and had made it crystal clear she would not condone a divorce.

'You've made your bed, now go and lie in it,' his father had said.

Well, so he would then; tonight he would lie in Nancy's bed all night long, for the very first time, and in so doing, gain the strength to see this through.

* *

There is nothing quite like waking up next to the person you love, thought Michael, propping himself up on one arm to get a better look at Nancy, who was still slumbering peacefully next to him, looking he felt, so very beautiful, young and innocent. He took a mental photograph of her to add to the growing album in his head; each image a treasure, to be recalled at will.

Nancy stirred, finally becoming aware that she was being observed. She opened her eyes, yawned lazily, and grinned at him. 'Hello you. Still here then?'

'Indeed I am,' he replied, returning her grin with a broad smile. 'Would Madam like a cup of coffee?'

'Now that would be a treat!'

Nancy stretched, raising her arms languorously above her head. As she did so, the sheet slipped down just enough to expose her bare breasts, a sight that did not escape Michael's attention.

'Mmm – don't do that to me please!' he moaned, 'or I'll never be able to get out of this bed.'

'Sorry,' she laughed. 'I didn't do it on purpose, it just happened.'

'Last night was wonderful,' Michael whispered into her ear. 'Making love like that, falling asleep with you, waking up with you at long last. Can we do it again?'

'Yes, we must,' Nancy whispered back. 'Tomorrow night too soon for you?'

'It is really,' he frowned, 'but put it in your diary anyway.'

She punched him playfully; he grabbed her; they rolled over together and kissed – long and luxuriously, savouring the unhurriedness of the moment.

* *

Within a month Michael had established a routine, which although busy – involving many miles on the road, to and fro three houses, provided him with the independence he'd craved whilst still allowing quality time with Nancy and Lucinda. Friday night he prepared for Saturday, when he picked Lucinda up, brought her back to the cottage and entertained her all day. He would then stay over at Nancy's Saturday night and all day Sunday.

Robert had sent in a team of painters and decorators to freshen up the place. With a few familiar bits and pieces that he'd managed to extract from Annabel, and various objects he'd bought, the cottage was now looking almost homely.

The plan was that Nancy would stay away from the cottage for three months, until the separation was well-established, so she would not be linked to the breakdown of the marriage in any way. It would also allow time to develop a pattern of access to Lucinda, and, Michael hoped, time for the Separation Agreement to be accepted.

But even the best-laid plans go awry. Annabel had acquiesced over the Saturday arrangement (actually, it suited her quite well, she could go shopping, or lunching with friends, unencumbered by a child); she had even encouraged Michael to visit at least once during the week to bath Lucinda and put her to bed, but she had not been so obliging over the details of a Separation Agreement. Four months down the line it still did not exist.

* *

It must have been Robert's gamekeeper, Michael was certain, who had told his father's keeper that he'd seen a woman coming out of the cottage one morning at 7.30am, and driving off in a Mini Cooper.

Given that Keith was the brother of Annabel's cleaning lady at Abercaskie it had taken only two days since Nancy had stayed over at the cottage for the first time before Annabel got to hear about it. Michael was met by a tight-lipped, strung-out wife that Wednesday evening when he arrived to see Lucinda.

'I want to speak to you,' Annabel had said curtly. 'Let's go into the kitchen.'

'What's the matter?' he'd responded, innocently.

'Don't give me that, you know very well *what*, or do I have to spell it out for you?' Annabel's thin face bore a mean expression, her eyes blazing with anger.

'I have no idea what you're talking about, Annabel. Where's Lucinda?' he replied, although he had a sinking feeling he knew what was coming.

'I've left her with Christina for a few hours.'

'But it's Wednesday night – we agreed that would be my time with her.'

'Not tonight,' Annabel replied firmly. 'Tonight, everything changes.'

'I think you'd better stop talking cryptically and explain exactly what's going on here.' Michael braced himself for the inevitable outburst she was clearly struggling to contain.

'What I understand to be going on here, Michael, is that you are having an affair behind my back. Is this true?' Her voice had started to crack, ever so slightly, at the mention of the word 'affair', but her anger was still palpable.

Michael's brain whirled. *How should he answer? A denial? An admission?* In those few seconds of hesitation Annabel saw in his face the proof she was seeking.

'It *is* true, isn't it? I can tell from your guilty expression. Don't lie to me Michael, I have always despised liars.'

The phrase 'innocent until proven guilty' passed slowly through his mind. Should he take that tack?

What's the point, nothing is going to convince her otherwise now.

'I *am* seeing someone, Yes. Someone I met recently (true, depending upon your interpretation of *recently*.) How do you know?'

'The domestic grapevine can always be relied upon. A person of your breeding should have learnt that by now, surely?'

She looked venomous, he thought; her colour high like that, her words being spat out like droplets of poison, of which, he had no doubt, there was an unending supply.

He struggled to find a response that would calm, rather than inflame the situation. 'Ahh,' came out involuntarily. A small word, that had a large, and undesirable effect.

'Is that the best you can say?' Annabel exploded. 'How about saying sorry? How about *I didn't mean to hurt you like this*? You *bastard*, Michael! You bloody *bastard*! Just look at what you've done to our marriage. Made me a laughing stock in the eyes of the servants, for some little tart, no doubt. How could you? How could you have done this to me? Up until now I'd felt that we could have got back together eventually. But *not* now. I don't want you now. You're soiled goods Michael. Your tart is welcome to you.'

She sank down into a chair, sobbing, and put her head in her hands, elbows balanced on the kitchen table.

Michael just stood there, not knowing quite what to do.

'I'm sorry, Annabel. I haven't hurt you intentionally, believe me.'

She lifted her head, looking at him squarely, defiantly now, her moment of angst visibly passed.

'Believe you? Why should I ever believe you about anything again? You've ruined my life, Michael, but I won't let you ruin Lucinda's that's for certain.'

The mention of his daughter's name had the effect of gripping his attention, bringing his mind more clearly into focus.

'This has nothing to do with Lucinda,' he said warily, as calmly as he was able. 'I will always be a good father to her no matter what happens.'

'A good father!' she retorted. 'Do you call screwing around being a good father?'

'Annabel – that's not fair, or true. Let's focus on us, and how we can work out something sensible – arrangements – keep things civil; can we do that please?'

She gave him a withering look.

'You can focus on what the hell you like, Michael. I shall focus on getting as much out of you as possible. From now on you can speak to me through my solicitor.' Her voice rose into a kind of scream. 'I don't want to see you, or have you here in this house. I don't want to even be in the same room as you; in fact, I don't want to be near you at all!'

She was shaking, her fists clenched as firmly as her jaw.

They looked at each other in silence for what seemed an age, before Michael ventured, 'Very well, as you wish. I'll come for Lucinda, Saturday morning, as usual.'

'Fine,' she replied, 'but Wednesdays are out from now on. And take the dog with you right now. All she ever does is whine after you leave. I can't stand it any more. Get out. Just get out.'

It was another summary dismissal. However, this time, one he was very glad to receive.

* *

Portia was happiness personified, smiling her Labrador smile, her long tongue hanging out, her brown eyes gleaming, sitting in the front seat of Michael's car like a black queen, totally oblivious to the scene that had just taken place, and completely unaware of its far-reaching implications.

'All right, old girl?' Michael leaned over and patted her affectionately. 'Just you and me then, like old times. But there's someone I want you to meet properly. You're going to love her, I promise you.'

It was going to be a new life for all of them, starting right that minute.

* *

Annabel was true to her word. There were times when Michael was so weary of the constant interplay of solicitor's letters and meetings that he would have willingly given her his last penny to get a resolution. Nancy, thankfully, was more pragmatic, keeping the long view.

'It's your future, Michael – our future. Give it all to Lucinda if you want, but you don't have to keep your wife for ever. She can work for God's sake, like most other women have to!'

Being named as the 'scarlet woman' in the divorce papers provided Nancy with much amusement.

'Fame at last,' she joked to friends. 'A femme fatale, I am.'

To her family she was more circumspect, until the divorce was finalised.

Following the exposé of the affair, there seemed to be no logical reason for them to live apart. Living together and maintaining only the cottage reduced the financial pressures on Michael a little as well. It was a relatively easy transition to make in a physical sense. Two houses into one via a rented van for a day. Some disposal of items here, an acquisition of others there. Shopping as a couple gave Nancy such a pleasurable glow she felt she was shining outwardly. There was no need to hide from the world anymore. They could walk around in broad daylight holding hands; they could kiss and not worry if anyone saw them. It was such a luxury, and they loved all of it. Gradually they began announcing their presence as a couple to the world and accepting social invitations, and damn those who didn't like it.

* *

Nancy's parents had been charmed by Michael. Concerns about the age gap and his title dissolved with the realisation that he was actually a very good match for their daughter, and so obviously in love with her. She seemed settled and happier than they had ever seen her before.

'I wouldn't be surprised if they'll be trying for family right away, given his age,' Nancy's mum had said to her dad after Nancy and Michael had left. 'Just think of it, us being grandparents! I never thought I'd see the day.'

In contrast, Nancy's brief and tentative encounter with Michael's parents following his divorce and announcement that he and Nancy were to marry confirmed his worst characterisations for her. She couldn't see how she would ever fit into the family. Even if she tried her hardest, would they ever accept her?

And Lucinda? Saturdays were sacrosanct for Lucinda. Sometimes with Michael alone, more often with Nancy too. Nancy's baptism into children via the 'terrible twos' into the even more terrible 'threes' provided an induction into the ways of toddlers and allowed the development of a patience Nancy never knew she had. Lucinda was a strong child who knew her own mind. Dark-haired, long limbed, a face like an angel, babbling away constantly, she was utterly enchanting, but at the same time totally demanding; her visits left Nancy drained of energy.

'Don't even think about it tonight you, I'm too tired and I've got a headache,' she would smile at Michael, as they lay in bed together discussing the day's activities.

'But she's absolutely wonderful, isn't she?' he'd said two months before the wedding. 'You'd surely like one of your own?'

'No, she'd answered,' teasing him, seeing the crestfallen look on his face. 'Not just one, *four*. I want four,' she'd said. 'Then with Lucinda that would make five. Five children between us. The Famous Five they'd be then. Just think of it. It would be absolute chaos! Then we'll see just how good a father you are.'

They'd laughed for ages at that.

'What a good idea. We'd best start soon in that case,' Michael had whispered. 'Neither of us is getting any younger.'

'Right then,' Nancy replied forcefully, pushing him away. 'But only once that ring is on my finger, Lord Robertson, do you have my permission to impregnate me with your children. All four of them!'

'But not,' she added as an afterthought, 'all at once. That would be too much. One at a time is best, I think.'

In the name of love

As well as being 'Diane the watcher' I was also 'Diane the coper'. This had some distinct advantages. You never asked for help, others saw you as strong and capable, and maybe they were a little reticent about criticising you. For me – I was able to organise my own wedding with little interference from my parents.

The day went as well as we might have hoped. It had been a singular brainwave of mine, getting married in Edinburgh. That meant we hadn't had to follow the traditional route of local church filled with distant relatives, a big reception in the Royal Hotel, and all the worry of whether or not the McDonalds would mix with the Stevens. This way Willie and I could organise it ourselves, keep it all very low key, and dispense with speeches, the bridal waltz and silly little tartan favours. That was what I told Willie anyway. In truth it was about not being the centre of a big fuss, and not risking Dad spoiling everything if he was in one of his moods. Disagreements over guest lists, arguments over place settings, hoo-hah over bridesmaids' dresses, the unspoken disapproval of a match beneath 'her station' – it would all have generated high tension in the Steven household. I could cope only if I minimised the emotional triggers.

Mum and Dad might have called Willie 'just an electrician' but what they didn't seem to appreciate was his confidence, ambition, drive, and enthusiasm for life. I knew even then that I could let myself be carried along safely in his wake. Later I would become an adept 'follower' – able to up sticks, relocate and make a new life many times over the years to come. But Willie – he followed no-one – he made his own road.

It hadn't been that which had first attracted me to him when we'd met at the end of second year, in the summer of '74. With one eye on a possible future career in social work, I was working for the summer in Dumfriesshire in a holiday home for children with disabilities. He was on site as an apprentice electrician for his father's company which had been contracted to check and certify the safety of all electrical wiring and appliances in the old renovated school building. With his gift for easy interaction with the teenagers, they, just like me, loved his cheery, cheeky charm. He had an impressively slim, fit body too and I had always been a sucker for blonde hair. But maybe subconsciously I also recognised a highly suitable potential mate.

They gave me only one day off per week – not enough time to go home to Forfar. He asked me out for a pint at the local pub, one evening. Took me for a run in the work's van a week later. Another day we went bird spotting, and I was seriously impressed by his knowledge of wildlife. On our fifth date, and just when his work at the home was almost complete, we went for a long walk. After leaving the village far below and well out of earshot, we lay under a perfect blue sky, listening to the soft sighing of the wind. We laughed, tickled and teased, and then without hurry or worry progressed to an easy lovemaking. He swore that was his first time. Even now I'm not 100% sure if that was true!

We saw each other for the next six weeks, Willie turning up to take me out in the van, smartened up after a day at work – until my summer job came to an end. He made regular visits to see me in Edinburgh over the next year, tying it in with Hibs' home games at Easter Road. We kept the relationship a relative secret from both sets of parents. I knew Mum would be disappointed in my choice. He just wanted to keep things simple until it became necessary to do otherwise.

Very much as I had with Bruce, I found Willie 'safe', strong, uncomplicated, good fun, and totally lacking in introspection and angst. I'm not sure what he saw in me, but whatever it was, he kept coming back for more. It was a few months before I told him that he hadn't been my 'first'.

I'd met Frank at the Freshers' Ball. He was a mature student in Moral Phil. It was love at first sight on my part, although he wasn't my usual type. More of an intellectual and less of a tall blond hunk. *And* he was English. On a cerebral level I fully concurred with his views on virginity or rather why it was an over-rated commodity. On an emotional level the 'breaking free' left me ill at ease with myself and increasingly edgy in his company. He soon found a new fresh face to impress and no doubt *depucelate*, or as we lesser mortals might express it – pop their cherry. I rather wished I'd 'done it' with Bruce after all.

If Willie wasn't my first, he made a career out of being my

most memorable! We were pulled up short when I had a pregnancy scare. The 'what if you'd got pregnant?' prompted us to get engaged and plan for a post-graduation wedding. If my parents weren't too happy, well, I didn't have to face it, being in Edinburgh.

In contrast, Sandy and Margaret welcomed me warmly into the McDonald family, maybe some light relief after three sons.

After the wedding we set up home in a small farm cottage near Dumfries belonging to one of my father-in-law's clients. Willie and his Dad had rewired the 'big hoose' a few months previously. The cottage was basic and *very* cold. We tried our best to make it our own, but it was a serious challenge disguising old and battered furniture and stained carpets. Still, the newness of married life and the everyday closeness that we both valued so much made it all quite bearable.

While I was considering what I might do for my future career, I found a job in a local old folks' home and was soon involved in what I suppose I always did best – taking care of others and making sure everything was well organised. If I didn't own up to having a degree, it was probably so that I could fit in more easily with the local women who had worked there for years.

Most of the time Willie and I were careful, but when we were up in the border hills on days off, listening for the curlews, watching the wispy clouds race by high up in a bright blue sky and feeling relaxed and happy together, it would have spoiled the moment to have taken out the Dutch cap.

So that was how Susan happened, not quite planned.

The girls at the home were all delighted, but I found it very strange to be at the centre of such warmth and consideration.

'Don't do too much now Diane. Watch you don't strain yourself.'

'Make sure you take the weight off your feet at break times.'

'Ginger biscuit with your cuppie – that's good for morning sickness.'

It was as if a pregnancy created a bright and shining counterbalance to the decay, dementia and the occasional despair implicit in the work of the home.

It didn't take me long to get used to the idea of being pregnant. I would lie most nights in the bath, counting and counting again the forty weeks from the date of my last period, to find the expected date of delivery, talking to that new little life inside me, toying with names, imagining her lying in the carrycot. Soon I would have my own family – it was what I was born for, I thought. I could cope with anything now, and by and large I did. But Christmas *was* stressful – too much accommodating so that everyone else was happy, no-one noticing that I badly needed a rest. Fortunately, Nancy visited just after New Year and allowed me to discharge a lot of pent up tension. All that stuff you think and can't say, you swallow it and it fills you up until you can hardly find room to breathe. I didn't need to be a coper around Nancy. What a relief.

By the time my pregnancy had extended to forty one weeks I had 'gone off the notion'. Anticipation had turned to dread, joy to regret, bloom to disintegration. Willie took all phone calls; I couldn't bear another 'You still here then?'

She was finally born on the 10th June 1977, just short of our first anniversary, after a protracted and drug-assisted labour. A scrawny, wee black-haired thing, flaking skin denoting her overdue arrival. The two of us were transferred to the convalescent home for ten days' recovery.

Feeding was to a strict timetable, which also contained a litany of negative reinforcement.

'That's your wee Susan crying again Mrs McDonald. She's a right one. She'll never give you a minute's peace, I'll bet.'

'She's probably too tired to suck now after all that crying. Maybe better give her a bottle, eh?'

'Well, that's only two ounces she's put on – she's not getting enough you know. Make sure you weigh her accurately before and after every feed, and let Sister know.'

'No, no. You try and get a good night's sleep. We'll not wake you if she cries. You look washed out. She can have a bottle for one night.'

Couldn't they see that I had to make a success of breastfeeding? Didn't they know that I had to be able to cope? I had read the books – 'Breast is Best', Dr Spock, and 'Your New Baby' which came in the Bounty Pack with an assortment of goodies promoted by one of the big suppliers. No chocolate bars – so what *did* they know about women struggling to cope with their first child?

Life was marginally easier back in the cottage. And if I fed her after only three and a half hours and not four, who would know? Even then she cried and cried.

The nights were the worst. Willie would kick me in his sleep when he heard her crying for a feed. I could have kicked him right back but what was the point? – I had the milk on tap and he needed his sleep. Mind you, the husband of one friend of mine would get up and make her a cup of cocoa each time she rose to feed the baby. Now, that's love and devotion.

Being a coper means having everything under control, and managing it 'all' on your own. 'All' amounts to a tidy house, home-cooked meals, nappies boiled up in a Baby Burco so that they're always soft and white, a satisfied baby who sleeps well, time for your husband, a warm welcome for visitors, the odd cake baked for a local charity coffee morning – and everything calm.

I started to have irrational fears every time I picked up a kitchen knife, that it would slip and give me a nasty cut. When I walked downstairs carrying Susan, I had no confidence in my balance and visualised myself stumbling and falling. My dreams were all of disasters.

The Health Visitor seemed to do nothing very much when she popped in every couple of weeks. She weighed Susan, had a chat about how she was sleeping – or not, suggested one or two possible tips – apparently gripe water wouldn't do any harm if her tummy was full of wind. But that 'nothing very much' concealed a watchful eye and a list of indicators to mentally tick off.

Then just one question – but it prompted a significant and life-saving response. 'And who is looking after *you*, Diane?'

'You're catering for everyone else, you're doing a great job making sure Willie, Susan, your parents, your in-laws, old Mrs Jenner next door and no doubt Uncle Tom Cobley and all get what they need. But what about you? How are you coping? Who's looking after you?'

It pulled me up short. I spoke before thinking. 'You're right. I never thought of it like that. And I'll be no use to anyone if I crack up, will I? What should I do?'

It wasn't maybe the response she had been looking for. Better that I get things in perspective for my own sake, not so that I would be strong enough to go back to being everything to everyone, but at least we could begin to make some changes so as to halt the downward spiral.

Josie became my lifeline. I didn't think of her as my Health Visitor, more a wise and trusted friend, although I doubt if any friend would take so much care to find the right words every time.

'She's absolutely where she should be for weight now Diane. You've done a brilliant job sticking with the breast-feeding. If you pick a formula that's closest to breast milk, she'll tolerate a bottle feed now and again. Why not have a meal out with Willie and let Granny have her overnight?'

'The latest evidence is that putting baby in her own room from about six months old seems to work well. She's in a sleeping routine now and you'll definitely hear her if she wakes up for a feed. That way you just won't be wakened by every tiny noise she makes in her sleep.'

'My experience of many years is that babies love being out of doors. So just put her out in her pram every morning unless it's foggy, and she'll watch the trees and the birds for a while and then probably fall asleep. You can get your tidying up done then. Or maybe have a bath.'

'You know, she really responds to Willie, doesn't she? It's so important for a child to have a close relationship right from the start with her father.'

And finally, 'Any chance of meeting up with some of your old friends maybe?' And so it was that I was in exactly the right frame of mind when Nancy phoned with a great idea for a night out.

Feels so good

Edinburgh: January 14th 1978

A Classic Night Out – Peffermill Sports Club to be transformed into a Greek Taverna, fancy dress to be worn, much money to be raised for the 1st Eleven Ladies' Hockey Team to go to the world student games in Athens, fun to be had.

Nancy caught me at the right time when she phoned to suggest we go. Patricia was coming through from Dundee and the three of us could stay overnight with the Gibson girls in their flat at Cameron Toll.

Willie said 'Go – and for goodness sake let your hair down and have a good time.'

Patricia had been covering the gods and heroes of Greek mythology with her primary 4s so had loads of ideas for costumes. Apparently, Athena was goddess of the domestic arts, and of crafts. Her symbol was an owl. Aphrodite was the goddess of love and beauty. Men fell hopelessly in love with her when they caught sight of her magic girdle. And Styx, one of the three thousand daughters of Okeanus, was given by Zeus the special obligation of having the young in her keeping. Pouring a pitcher of her water binds the pourer to telling only the truth. Well, that all seemed to fit with us three nicely. Nancy had a black lacy girdle, now to find an owl for me to carry. Patricia brought a few props to embellish our basic costumes of red, blue and green shifts, gold and silver chiffon scarves and garish flip flops. Elaborate gold sprayed card-board necklaces, button-studded wire tiaras, silver belts made out of foil milk bottle tops – we were all set.

It was a typical Edinburgh winter night – damp, cold and windy. Nancy turned the heater full on for the drive from Dolphinton. We had a drink in the flat till it was time to go. It was good to catch up on some of the news.

'Apparently Alix is having a ball in Egypt. That Gerald bloke got her a job teaching English with the British Council in Cairo. She just wrote one sentence on my Christmas card "Whatever you've heard about BCal pilots – double it!" Doesn't take much to imagine what she means,' said Nancy.

'She'd better watch out she doesn't pick up some tropical

disease then,' was Patricia's concern.

'Oh you know Alix; she'd bounce if she was dropped from a great height. Bet the parents don't have a clue,' I mused.

'While I remember,' Patricia cut in, 'talking of parents, Lesley's having problems with hers – and Nick's. She was in tears on the phone to me at New Year. She just wanted someone to understand her dilemma I think. Nick's parents just won't consider any option other than their local Presbyterian church for the wedding and Nick's going along with it to keep his Dad happy. Of course, he'll be taking over his Dad's practice one of these days so he has to keep in with him. Lesley's parents are threatening to boycott the wedding. Lesley is just dithering, torn between supporting Nick and doing the right thing by the church. I couldn't do it if I was her. Just as well Trevor went along with anything I suggested. Turning up was his grand contribution to the planning.'

'Well, probably only you out of the five of us have any idea what she's feeling. All I know is that when you get parents making all the decisions, you never end up with what you want. Willie would have walked away if there'd been a lot of fuss like that.'

'Come on you two old married biddies,' chipped in Nancy. 'Let's change the subject. Now what's everyone drinking tonight? We can always leave the cars here and get a taxi back Patricia.'

'I'll probably just have a half of lager – maybe a couple – and that should do me.'

With 'let yourself go' echoing in my ears, I thought I might just try something different. It had been a long time since I'd had a girls' night out, and it might be long enough till the next one.

You would not have recognised the place. As the clubrooms were due for modernisation, someone must have given permission to give them a makeover for the night. The function room was painted in sky blue with a traditional gold Greek frieze round the walls. Keen archaeologists would have spotted images of the Parthenon, The Temple of Hera at Olympia, the Knossos and the Acropolis. There were plastic vines laden with purple grapes hanging above trestle tables covered in blue and white checked tablecloths. The bar staff were wearing togas. All things Greek, with no respect for chronology or consistency, were incorporated into Yanni's Greek Taverna, open for one night only. But what a night!

We spotted countless Zorbas, a few Helens of Troy, one beautiful bronzed Alexander, Jason complete with golden fleece, and Mary normally at left half but that night appearing as Nana Mouskouri. We assumed that the big plastic triangle wielded by Mary's boyfriend Stan represented his alter ego Pythagoras.

A Greek night is not a Greek night without retsina and ouzo. And they are naturally accompanied by dolmades, calamari, tsatsiki and hummus. A bit of food and a few drinks, several hilarious attempts at Zorba's dance and we were more than ready for a bit of plate smashing. Nancy had loosened up – a lot – by that stage.

'This one's for Michael's wife – smash! And one more for his snooty Mother – smash! And a big smash for his pompous old Father – there you go! And two at a time for Michael and me – one day we *will* be married!'

'And my first one is for dirty nappies – I'm sick of looking at them – *smash*! And another one for cold draughty cottages – take that! And two more for getting a life at last – here's to the future – *smash*, *smash*!!'

It was almost too much to bear for Patricia. The sight of that perfectly functional crockery being wantonly destroyed upset her sense of order and decorum. She had to try hard to resist the temptation to begin clearing up the bits. She declined to take part until she was wrenched off her chair by her fellow Dundonian – Grant Buchan – captain of the University Men's Hockey team.

'Come on Patricia. Shake that wee arse of yours and show these Greeks how to do it.'

The sight of him in a huge white kaftan and a long black beard miming to the latest Demis Roussos record cracked her shell. For once she dropped her reserve and had fun. It was an easy step then to take a couple of drinks and accept getting a taxi home to the flat. She even smashed a couple of plates herself; one for filling in pupil report cards, and another for the pile of papers waiting to be filed.

We danced for ages to all the modern classics – The Bee Gees, The Eagles, Roxy Music, 10CC. We toasted absent friends in retsina, fed grapes to assorted Greek gods and scholars and soaked our aching feet in the wash-hand basins in the ladies' toilet. The costume jewellery disintegrated over the evening and the papier maché owl was last seen adorning the bonnet of an old Austin Maxi containing four very drunk rugby players being chauffeured on to a night club in Princes Street by a long-suffering girl friend.

Fun for its own sake. No expectations. People who know you well. A bittersweet reminder of other days, other places, a time when life was less full of duties and more about experiences.

'Well,' said Willie. 'Good time?'

'Yes, you know Nancy when she's on her game. But yes, I do need to do that more often. It felt like the old me for a while. Did you both miss me?'

'Susan did. She cried for ages when Mum put her down to bed. But I managed to sort her out. Tea in the pot if you want a cup.'

And a bit of fun in bed too later. Hardly an absence to make the heart grow fonder, just one night away. But if it had that effect I thought I would try it a bit more often … and I should have.

Love and Marriage

Wales 1979

Carys had never thought of herself as the marrying kind, somehow. She simply could not imagine going through a ceremony where she felt subjugated to a man by saying she would 'love, honour and obey'. It was so very antiquated.

Neither did she yearn for the cosy domesticity that marriage is thought to bring. It appeared stifling to Carys, as an outsider, this 'cosiness'. Looking in on the marriages of her friends and family it seemed to her that each partner had to ask the other for permission (or at the very least must negotiate) each and every time they wished to do anything on their own.

'Do you mind if I go out with the girls on Friday, darling?'

'Are you okay about me bringing a few of the boys back here to watch the match on the tele Saturday?'

Then there was all the going shopping to check out each other's potential purchases. 'No that doesn't look right on you, try this one instead.'

Compromising on colours to paint the house. Feigning interest in each other's day after work. Having sex when you didn't really feel like it.

And that's just the start of the long, slow rot. Sod that for a bunch of soldiers.

With regard to marriage as an effective environment for bringing up children, she would argue that was poppycock – just an institutional construct encouraged by the government in a vain attempt to keep some social stability and make people accountable for their own children. Every time there had been a debate in the flat, Carys had pulled out the statistics on divorces, remarriages, numbers of single parent families, and all manner of choice facts from her encyclopaedic knowledge of world religions and sociology.

No doubt, had she chosen to do so, she could have propounded a robust counter argument – the case *for* marriage. But she never did. Not even after leaving Edinburgh, when all her friends were 'succumbing to convention' as she so nicely put it, did she waver from her resolve *never* to be 'Mrs Anybody', at anytime. Take on a man's name instead of the beautiful Lloyd-Jones? You must be kidding. As for those women who adopt the title Mrs X (*his* initial) Y (*his* surname) – they were a disgrace to the female gender.

She had seen all five of the others walk down the aisle. Only metaphorically speaking in the case of Alix, who'd got married in a swish registry office in London in 1978 and none of them had been able to go. Sad, but that's how it was.

There'd been Diane's and Patricia's weddings in 1976. She'd gone of course, although found it hard to believe they were getting married so young, so soon after graduating.

At least Lesley had waited until she was 24, when she became Mrs Lesley Mathieson (née O'Donnell) in Ness Bank Church (United Presbyterian), Inverness. That had been a tricky one. How does a Catholic girl get married in a Protestant church and still please her family? Or was pleasing Nick's family more important? No answer. But the surroundings were stunning.

Alix had been 24 as well when she took on the name Mrs Alix Fitzroy (née MacKay) in Cheyne Walk registry office, Chelsea, London. Her parents hid their disappointment at not hosting the event in Aberdeen, but time was of the essence given Gerald's impending move to Singapore. Apparently she was the epitome of style on her wedding day. The Fitzroys eschewed their usual country tweeds for their trip up to town from Shropshire. Polite conversation was the order of the day.

And last but not least, before the end of 1978, Nancy finally captured Michael for a husband to become Mrs Nancy Robertson (née Thorpe). So much for sanctity and sacraments. In contrast to the others, Nancy's travels to the altar had been complicated by Michael's messy divorce, a legal battle over maintenance, financial difficulties and hostile future in-laws.

Now that wedding, Carys thought, had been *really* interesting. A sociological gem. A cornucopia of psychological observations. She wouldn't have missed it for the world.

Despite her personal antipathy to marriage, Carys had done the honourable thing by attending these ceremonies, singing the hymns lustily during the services, and throwing confetti afterwards like it was going out of fashion. *But* she'd made sure she ducked hard when the bride's bouquet was thrown into the crowd of well-wishers. It had been a very near thing when Nancy had thrown hers – Carys could have sworn it had been directly aimed at her, even though Nancy denied it later.

Carys's mother despaired of her. That last visit home had been particularly fraught, with Mam behaving like a dog with a bone it refuses to drop. Somehow or other she had managed to bring almost every conversation around to what she clearly thought was Carys's lack of attention to finding herself a husband. Sometimes this was subtle manoeuvring, at other times it was blatant.

'Your Auntie Non phoned last week. She was asking after you.'

'Oh, right, how is she?'

'Fine, apart from her hip. Waiting to hear from the hospital about going in for a replacement. Shouldn't be too much longer now, she's been waiting a year already. She was asking if you'd met anyone serious in Ireland yet.'

'And what did you say to her?'

'That I didn't think so, but you were coming home this weekend so I'd hear more about your social life then.'

Here we go. More prying, more questions, more innuendos. Roll on Monday morning.

'Not much to tell actually,' Carys offered, attempting to head off the interrogation before it got going. 'I've been working too hard lately to have time for much socialising. Final year approaching and all that. So much to organise and write up. Drafting and redrafting my thesis. I don't want to get distracted. So you can tell Auntie Non: No, there's no-one special.'

'I do worry about you, Carys.' Her mother looked genuinely concerned. 'You work too hard. Surely you don't want to sacrifice the chance of a normal life for the sake of your career? Auntie Non was joking that at 24 you might be in danger of getting left on the shelf, as she put it, remaining a spinster, as we used to call unmarried women.'

'Call them what you like,' Carys said huffily. 'Auntie Non's living in the dark ages.' And just in case 'Auntie Non' (you can't fool me that easily Mam) had thoughts of extending this conversation, she added, for good measure, 'That kind of talk makes me mad, Mam, so best I don't hear any more of it, *please*! I'm perfectly happy being on my own at the moment. You can tell her I have boyfriends, but nothing serious, and that's *just* how I like it, thank you very much.'

It was impossible to please her mother, Carys felt. If she'd have got married young and had three kids by now, like most of her contemporaries in the village, then that would have been wrong. 'Fancy sacrificing a career for motherhood and apple pie' it would have been. Now, here she was at the ripe old age of 24 being consigned to the shelf and criticised for putting her career above finding a husband and procreating. Catch 22. You can't please all of the people all of the time, it's a fact of life. So, she would damn well please herself and live with the consequences. If she ended up old and lonely as a result, so be it.

Thus it was that with more than a slight touch of disbelief, Carys found herself just over one year later wearing a tasteful ivory and white dress, with matching accessories, standing at the head of the aisle in Capel Berth, Tregaron, with Lesley demure in mint green as her Matron of Honour.

After the minister had pronounced them 'man and wife', JJ had turned, held her left hand, with its band of Welsh gold firmly ensconced on her third finger, and kissed her gently on the lips.

Then he'd said, 'There you are, honey, not so bad after all, was it?' wearing the cheekiest grin he could muster, and with his eyes twinkling.

As she'd admitted in the reception afterwards, to Diane and Nancy, it hadn't actually been too bad really, all things considered, although it would have been better had her father still been alive to see it and be by her side.

'He would have been proud of you, Carys,' said Diane, cradling her bouncing six week-old Elizabeth who was suckling noisily underneath a white shawl Diane had draped around herself to be discreet.

Carys tried not to look, since although she knew it was natural, she'd always thought breastfeeding a bit peculiar, not that she'd ever have to worry about it herself. Getting married was as far as it was going. There would be *no* children, she'd made an explicit agreement about that with JJ.

'I'm sure he's looking down on you today.'

'No doubt,' smiled Carys.

Nancy looked enormous. Although her face and legs were normal size, her abdomen was hugely swollen by her seven months pregnancy, pushing out her flowered maternity dress to the maximum. Her boobs were massive, too, Carys noticed.

'You're like a ship in full sail,' her Uncle Idris had bellowed outside the church. 'Magnificent!' Fortunately Nancy hadn't seemed the least bit embarrassed by this banter.

'I'm so glad you could both come,' Carys beamed. 'It's really made my day. I appreciate you making the effort Diane, given you're nursing the baby, and you Nancy, with your imminent arrival.'

'Not too imminent, I hope!' was Nancy's quick response. 'It's going to have to wait a while yet. I'm going over to Skipton first to see my mother, then I've got to drive back to Edinburgh. Otherwise I'll be in trouble!'

'Oh she's got a while to go yet, Carys,' Diane joined in. 'I was much bigger than that at her stage, carrying Susan. Like a stranded whale, I looked, absolutely huge! I put on *three* stone, still haven't shifted it all yet. I'll bet it's a boy you're carrying, Nancy, you being so big like that, all over!'

'Diane, please don't talk about stranded whales! I don't want to get bigger than this, this is bad enough!' Nancy grimaced.

'Well, I'll leave you to your baby talk for a while girls, I have to circulate apparently. Catch up with you later.'

Carys waltzed off happily into the throng of relatives and friends clustered in little groups around the room. They watched her go.

'Never thought I'd ever see the day,' said Nancy. 'Did you?' shaking her head in wonder. 'She does look happy. He's nice that JJ don't you think, Diane? A real hunk. Seems to know how to handle her all right as well from what I've seen so far.'

Diane looked thoughtful. 'Time will tell. I hope it all works out for them. I've never seen Carys so – what's the word? – *enamoured* – yes, that's it! I do believe she's actually in love. Finally, someone got to the ice maiden.'

And as usual, Diane was right. Carys first knew she could fall in love with JJ when she'd woken up in bed, the morning after the conference dinner, with the mother of all hangovers, to find him perched at the bottom watching her anxiously.

'Can I get you anything, Carys? A drink of water, or coffee perhaps? Some toast?' he'd offered.

'What the hell are you doing there? How long have I been here? What time is it?' she'd replied, sounding feeble and quite confused.

He was smiling; then, fixing her with an intent gaze, he took his time replying. 'I'll answer your questions in reverse order. It's 1.45 pm on Saturday afternoon. You have been in there since 2.30am last night. I'm here because someone had to bring you home otherwise you wouldn't have made it on your own. I carried you out of the taxi, and up the stairs. I cleaned the sick off you and took your shoes off before I put you in bed. The taxi driver wasn't best pleased at you puking all over his cab but he'll get over it. I stayed because I was afraid to leave you like that. You were so drunk you could have choked on your own vomit if you'd been sick again, like Janis Joplin did. That would have been a pity, wouldn't it? Carys Lloyd-Jones expiring before she'd got her PhD!'

'Oh my God! What can I say?' Carys mumbled in an uncharacteristically embarrassed tone.

'Try "Thank you, JJ".'

'Thank you, JJ ....'

'A pleasure, Carys.'

'Yeh, right. Why did you bother, JJ, when I'm always so antagonistic towards you? Why didn't you just leave me to some other man, no doubt with lecherous intent?'

He took in a deep breath of air. 'Because I care about you, Carys. I know you don't want to hear me say that, but it's true. I care about you a lot. I care very much what happens to you, even though you don't feel the same way about me.'

She had a grade A hangover, knew she must look like something the cat had dragged in and felt very weak and weedy at that precise moment. Perhaps that is why she let her guard down and heard herself say, before she'd given it consideration, 'You can't say that, JJ. You don't have a clue how I feel about you.'

'Tell me then,' he'd said. 'Tell me the truth, Carys. Be the *real* you now. After two years of us sparring, you've nothing to lose, and neither have I,' he said, in his slow drawl, leaning back against the bed's footrest, looking, Carys thought, seeing him through new eyes, quite desirable, except that she was in no fit state to even think about it.

What she really would like instead, she decided, was a great big hug, and for him to stroke her hair and hold her gently, then tuck her back under the cover until the room stopped swimming.

There were three other PhD students who had started in the Faculty at the same time as Carys and the American, John James Bloomberger II, or JJ to his friends. His thesis (Church History) was in a different area to Carys's research subject (Systematic Theology), but all the postgrads met fortnightly, for peer support, and to challenge each other's work – which led to some interesting analytical arguments, not to mention disagreements, on points of methodology. They found it all absorbing and exciting – cloistered in their own little world.

Carys and JJ had never seemed to hit it off. She'd thought him rather strange, conceited and artificially enthusiastic about Ireland and the Irish people. Admittedly he was tall and definitely handsome, but he looked rather old fashioned with short hair when all the boys were wearing it long. His clothes – jacket and trousers not jeans and tee shirts – were odd too. (His strict mid-west upbringing?) He, however, thought Carys was quite gorgeous, a real little Welsh gem. Her long dark hair and stunning figure were wonderful, something to be lusted after – particularly when she'd worn hot pants and a strappy vest top to one of the meetings. He found her feistiness attractive, and her intellect awesome. By the end of their first year, JJ had fallen in love with her hook, line and sinker despite not so much as a peck on the cheek. Unrequited love is a terrible thing. He tried so hard to impress all the time but she didn't respond to this, rather, it seemed to annoy her, but he didn't know how else to behave. Although, he had received the odd flash of sexual interest, he'd like to think. There again, Carys was good at playing the intellectual femme fatale with all men.

So, JJ had decided to bide his time, be Mr Nice Guy and be there if she needed him. The events of the conference dinner night had proved fortuitous. He wouldn't tell her that he'd muscled in on that sleazy Kevin who would have had her knickers off for sure, drunken stupor or no, shoving him out of the way when the taxi arrived. She'd find out all in good time. Maybe she'd see him as her knight in shining armour. Now that would be romantic.

Carys had her reasons for agreeing to marry JJ. Yes, it was about love, which blossomed gradually over that third year, and yes, it was about showing commitment, but the thought of moving to America to pursue an academic career and becoming a US citizen in her own right was also very attractive. It made financial sense as well. She drew the line at taking his name, however – some beliefs are too deep to change. Hence it was passengers Dr C Lloyd-Jones and Dr JJ Bloomberger, husband and wife, who boarded the Boeing 707 to leave for a new life in America two weeks after their wedding in Tregaron. It was also about shared dreams – of high standards of living, borne from the fruit of successful academic careers, free from the responsibilities of children. They would live for each other, and for their work, they'd both agreed. A promise made six months after Carys first told JJ she had always secretly fancied him, whilst she lay, ashen-faced, in her bed, having her hair stroked gently.

It's all I ever wanted

In June of '79, I had Elizabeth, a plump dark haired wee treasure according to the midwife – I was too tired to speak by the time it was all over. They (some so-called experts) say that having the second one is more of a shock to the system than having the first. I bowed to their superior knowledge early on. With one you might snatch an hour to read the paper or wash your hair. With two – it was constant. But I coped, although I didn't as much as pick up a magazine for years, let alone follow any academic interest in societal development.

My life was still all about caring – I cared for everyone – the babies, the old lady down the street housebound and a bit lonely sometimes, Willie's Granny who liked a pot of home made soup but couldn't be trusted with the cooker since her macular degeneration had developed, and all sorts of other waifs and strays. Willie would jokingly refer to me as the Mother Theresa of Dalmore or wherever we were at the time. But the strange thing was – I didn't *actively* care for Willie. He didn't complain, and he always did his bit – in the traditional sense of putting out the bins, wiring plugs, checking lawnmowers for safety, dealing with all the bills. My parents could come to stay any time and he'd make them welcome. He'd baby-sit while I went to a Toddlers' Group Committee Meeting. But looking back, bit by bit we drifted out of real intimacy into a functional friendship. Maybe it was because he always seemed so confident and in charge of his life – his needs were not as obvious as some.

Funnily enough Willie and I still sustained an active love life although God knows where we found the time. Early mornings some days when I was barely conscious and took so long to respond that it was all but over before I knew it was happening! Once in a while Margaret would come over and give us a couple of hours off. Then we'd head for the hills and act like silly teenagers again.

One weekend when Elizabeth was about two years old, we actually went to a hotel in the Lake District – on our own – for two nights. The first night I had half a bottle of champagne with the gastronomic feast, lay down to let it all settle for half an hour and woke up the next morning with make up still intact, fully clothed.

Willie tried plan two. A warm bath sprinkled with geranium oil, fluffy white bath towels and a box of speciality chocolates to share in the tub. Just as well we had been half thinking about trying for a boy by that time. The cap stayed in the toilet bag in our rush and David was conceived. In the end Willie got his two sons – David and John – in '82 and '84. Both were blonde and healthy like their father. I just got on with it. It was what girls did. And that career? Well motherhood would be it for me – at least for a while. In a way, I thrived on it and was at the hub of it all – two girls at the local school, one boy in the pram and another by the hand. I grew thin and brown with all that walking back and forward to school, toddlers and playgroup. We always had traditional home cooked meals, I still boiled the nappies, Willie grew vegetables for us wherever we were living. It was the storybook version of how to be happily married.

I assumed we were all living it.

Be my baby

Inverness 1981

It should have been a cause for celebration – the 100th baby delivered that year in the maternity unit at Raigmore Hospital. It *was* a cause for celebration for some. She could see the other midwives enjoying a rare moment of relaxation and congratulation over a glass of wine in the staff room before scattering in their rush to get home to the demands of their other lives. But somehow it all seemed rather distant. Lesley smiled in the right places, successfully faked a spirit of bonhomie and managed to stay till the end of the informal event. But her inner reality was far more present than any external gathering could ever be.

Yet again she went over her brief conversation with Nick in the kitchen, in the minutes before they had both left separately for work that morning.

'It's just a few colleagues, Lesley. You don't have to put on a show. How about you nip down to M&S and pick up some party food, finger buffet type of thing? I'll get the wine and the crisps. They'll only be here for a couple of hours before the meeting starts.'

'Maybe next month Nick. I don't feel like being sociable just now. Can one of the others do it this time? John's wife Hilary is good at this kind of thing. She probably wouldn't mind.'

Nick had sighed; a long wistful, drawn out sigh. He pursed his lips, looked briefly up to the pale cream ceiling and replied in a weary voice, 'Lesley, I'm worried about you. You never seem to want to go anywhere or do anything these days. What is it? We need to get to the bottom of this. Let's talk tonight when we're both home.'

Talk? What would that mean?

Questions no doubt ...

'You used to go places with me Lesley, and now you always make an excuse. Is there something wrong?'

Observations surely...

'You seem to be really restless during the night as if you're dreaming a lot. And even when you're reading a book you're fidgeting.'

A few tips maybe ...

'Why don't you try having a relaxing bath before bed and take these nursing journals out of the bedroom? Maybe you've got too much on your mind. Can't leave work behind, that sort of thing.'

If only work was the problem. In some ways it was easier being at work. Plenty to occupy the mind. No time for thinking. Focus on the job in hand.

It was in the quieter moments that the thoughts came flooding back and then circled round and round like a flock of crows over a dead animal. But at least the crows complete their task and move on.

* *

Plain as the nose on your face. Except you can't see your own face, other than in a mirror and then you're looking at someone else looking back. Someone you only vaguely recognise. Someone who looks like you and yet isn't you. Someone who could frighten you with her stare if you didn't avert your eyes. Other people can see it or at least some of the signs. But they struggle to tell you or don't want to risk making a big mistake and falling out of favour with you.

In the end, the mirror wasn't necessary.

The one hundred and first baby was born after a particularly long delivery. Due to complications with the cord, the child which 'had issued forth from its mother after the 28th week of pregnancy and which did not breathe or show any other sign of life' was classed as 'stillborn'.

Lesley wept for that infant, she wept for its bereft parents, she wept for the baby she wanted and couldn't seem to conceive, she wept for her parents and the distance created between them by her non-Catholic wedding, she wept for the times she had been a less-than-perfect wife, friend, nurse, daughter, sister, grand-daughter. And when the tears started, they just wouldn't stop. It was the confirmatory sign that made the diagnosis firm. She was advised to take some time off work and attend her GP.

Ah – attend her GP. Now that wouldn't be easy when your husband was a GP, it was a small community you lived in, and you weren't even of the same race. There were always tensions: Welsh and Scottish, Catholic and Protestant, Nurse and Doctor. And there were always paradoxes: sex and fatigue, delivering babies and being barren.

The locum GP covering for Dr Kay's maternity leave saw her for the last appointment of the day, which was the fated turning point.

'Mrs Mathieson, just take a seat. I'm Dr Gregg. What can I help you with today?'

An oceanful of tears later, Lesley said the unnecessary – 'I just can't stop crying. Everything is a mess.'

The GP was suitably empathetic. 'Now, take your time and tell me what brought all this on. There's no rush.'

They agreed that Lesley would attend once a week, always for the last appointment on a Tuesday evening, when there would be time to unravel the tightly-wound ball of grief and find some solutions for how life could go on. Meanwhile, she would take some anti-depressants and have a quiet time at home for a few weeks.

Nick had been too close to the problem, too pre-occupied with his own work and had already begun to accommodate Lesley's relative withdrawal without noting its significance.

When life did get back to normal, Lesley could recount the build up to her depressive illness in chronological order, starting with the incident with lifeguard Paul and progressing through to the sad event in the maternity ward which had precipitated her collapse. But in the unburdening, the exploring, the confronting and the resolution – the past returned in jumbled stories, flash-backs, dreams, physical pain, and tears.

'I was caught, caught in the middle you see. There was no way Nick's family would even consider having a Catholic wedding and I was just swept along with it all. Nick's father thinks I'm not good enough for him. Just a wee Welsh lassie. His mother's okay though and she knew it was very hard for me, Mam and Dad refusing to come to the wedding and that. But there was nothing she could do about it. So only Maureen and Rose were there from my side and they looked like fishes out of water. Just as well Diane and Nancy looked out for them. They were stars. There was nothing Welsh about the service except my bridesmaid Carys. And it was so cold in that church – I was shivering – you can see it in all the photos. It would be cold there even on a hot day. No pictures, no statues, no stained glass windows; it was nothing like a Catholic church. It didn't seem like a real church to me. I didn't feel properly married at all.'

'Tell me how you met your husband, Lesley.'

'Well, we were both working at Edinburgh Royal. I was in final year of my nursing degree, doing a placement in the gynae ward. I was really nervous and Nick was kind to me. He was quiet like me, and in his final year at med school. We used to meet for coffee at the end of the shift, and go over anything significant that had happened on the ward that day. Have a laugh about all the names people used for parts of the female body. Do you know that there are about 50 different words for 'vagina'? Oh, that's stupid of me isn't it! You probably would know that, being a doctor. Anyway, it just developed from there. We were good pals before anything happened. Thinking of that makes me feel so sad now, because we hardly seem to talk much these days.'

'And you ended up married and living in Inverness?'

'Oh yes, he was very patient Nick was, but eventually we did what everyone else seemed to be doing – having sex, although I was glad the others had gone by that time. I could never have been like Nancy or Alix – they were my flatmates – bringing men home to the flat and waving them off gaily in the morning, relying on those awful condoms. I was so careful about what time of the month it was. I had no idea that getting pregnant could be so hard or maybe I would have enjoyed it a bit more often – or even just enjoyed it full stop.

'And then when I'd finished my matty training and Nick had done his house jobs, it seemed to be just expected that we would get married, and so we did. I wanted to though. Don't think I didn't – don't – love him. Because I did – I do – still. I just can't get all these thoughts out of my mind.'

Some revelations indeed. Dr Gregg recognised a breakthrough when she saw one and was keen for Lesley to continue, even though her patient had gone quiet and was looking down into her lap, fingering her wedding ring nervously.

'What are these thoughts Lesley?' she asked gently.

With a deep sigh Lesley resumed speaking. 'That I'm not good enough for him. That he must be sick of me by now. That I can't keep this up. Why can't I get pregnant? How will my parents ever forgive me? Am I really married?'

Such thoughts continued to circle, but gradually released their hold over Lesley as she talked through the past, and in so doing, gained some perspective on where she was and how she'd got there.

In addition to the talking therapy, the doctor ordered rest, and 'to be kind to yourself' – massages, country walks, that sort of thing – plus regular exercise and a healthy diet.

When the talking was over, what Lesley needed most was a strategy for the future. She had some work to do first, and it would need to revolve around action, rather than constant ruminating. And it would involve honest discussion with Nick. And it would be hard. And she could expect to feel quite anxious at times – that was normal. But it would hopefully establish a pattern which would work then and in the future. It would focus on needs, wants, and managing stress.

Q1 What do you want to be doing with your life?

A I want to have a baby.

Q2 What needs to happen to make this a reality?

A I need to talk seriously with Nick about what we can do to increase the chances of that happening.

Q3 What might be important in that discussion?

A Both of us being healthy, having sex more often maybe, me not being so stressed.

Q4 And how might you become less stressed?

A I need to see Mam and Dad, make things right between us. Maybe I could get a cleaner a few hours a week because that big house is a nightmare to keep on top of. And I need to have Nick on my side

Q6 How might you do that?

A Maybe think more about what he wants from our relationship. I need to talk to him, let him know I still really care about him. I need to ask him how he's feeling. I've been so caught up with my own thoughts that I haven't really paid him much attention for months. No wonder he was getting short with me. We need some time away on our own probably.

It was a start.

* *

By 6pm on Tuesday September 15th, the same year, Lesley and Nick were at opposite ends of the country. Cardiff Central Station was the next and last stop on the long and convoluted train journey from Inverness. Up north, a comfortable lounge in The Golf View Hotel, one hundred metres from the Nairn Golf Club, was the venue for the monthly meeting of The North of Scotland Medical Education Group, chaired that night by Dr Nick Mathieson.

Mrs O'Donnell had cried when she'd ripped open Lesley's letter and read its conciliatory contents. Easier to start the process in writing, time to choose every word carefully, get the tone and the message exactly right, Lesley had reckoned. Dad had been gruff in his response but stood side by side with his wife as they awaited the train's arrival.

Her mother was shaking with excitement. 'Lesley, my lovely. Oh, come here and give us a big hug. It's so good to see you. And you're brown, all those freckles like you used to have every summer down here. How's Nick, how's the job? I hope you're staying for a decent length of time this visit. We miss you such a lot.'

'Hiya Mam, Dad. It's been too long hasn't it? I'm really sorry.'

There had been perfunctory contact over the three years since Lesley's wedding – a card here, a telephone call there, a fleeting visit on the way to some medical conference. Enough to keep the door open, but only by an inch or two. Nothing meaningful, nothing that would resolve the breach, had ever been raised. The chat had always been only of the job, the new house, how Dad's knees were doing, whether or not the Social Club would survive the developers.

Lesley knew that she had to take the active part this time. She had spent most of the train journey rehearsing her 'speech'. Not just the what – but also the how. When would she broach the topic? Where was Dad's soft spot? How could she make up for her 'transgression'? Should she get Mam on side first? In the end it all came tumbling out over a cup of tea in the overcrowded living room in that gap between supper and *Coronation Street* when the two who were still at home were in the kitchen squabbling over who was doing the dishes.

If there were tears, they were not Lesley's. A wobble in the voice, an occasional sharp intake of breath, a minor note of remorse and pleading maybe. In the end, the three agreed on a few very important things:

'It's horrible not being close like we used to be.'

'What's done is done, water under the bridge, isn't it?'

'Let's just say that we'll make the best of it from now on.'

'And there'll be children to think about too. They'll need a Nana and a Bampa, won't they love?'

* *

Nick meanwhile was rested and refreshed after a satisfying eighteen holes and a long hot shower. The meeting would start shortly, after a sandwich tea and the usual spiel from the drug rep. The topic for the evening was 'Depression – forms and recognition.' Hmm.

Nick's three years as a GP, firstly in a junior role in his father's long established practice, and latterly as a full partner, had developed certain necessary aspects of his character – maybe at the expense of others. If you require to be decisive, confident in your diagnoses and decisions, and able to sleep at night without worrying if you've made the right ones – then almost inevitably you develop self belief – or you couldn't do the job. It doesn't come without study and review, without hard work, systematic application of up-to-date knowledge and a willingness to learn from your mistakes. And it is aided by the respect and deference given to you by patients and non-clinical staff. The risk is, however, that self-belief extends into the less desirable trait of arrogance.

He appeared self assured and strong minded and was treated as such. His physical frame broadened; he seemed to Lesley even to have grown a couple of inches since they'd met. A line or two bred of active listening added an attractive maturity to his face. At 31 he showed no signs of losing his hair, although he had noticed a few grey ones in his sideburns.

Had he been actively listening to the presentation on depression he might have gained some insight into how he had allowed Lesley's decline to progress so far without intervening. But his mind was straying, pleasantly relaxed in the comfortable surroundings of the hotel lounge with its huge padded sofas and chintzy armchairs.

I bet she's a go-er.

The reaction came from the part of the brain that engages before conscious thought. The subject – one Dr Wendy Jennings, long limbed, blonde, fair skinned and sharp as a needle. New junior partner in the Culloden Medical Practice.

And I wouldn't mind a bit of that.

This time the thought was under conscious control.

* *

When she returned from Cardiff, Lesley advertised for a cleaner via a box numbered advert in the Inverness Courier. Mrs Milne might have been a little surprised that Mrs Mathieson, the doctor's wife, was rather anxious but put it down to her being a long way from home. She took to bringing in a few bits of home baking from time to time and starting a 'wee bit earlier' if she had nothing on that day. Once Lesley came to terms with the notion that you could simply pay someone to do what your mother had always done for herself and not feel guilty about it, she valued the extra time in her week. Mrs Milne had brushed aside the tentative list of duties Lesley had spent hours devising and redrafting, with a 'Now, I'll just keep this house the way I would my own and don't you worry about it.'

So that was Mam and Dad sorted, more or less anyway, and some help in the house organised. There could be no putting off any longer that discussion with Nick over the future – *their* future.

In the end Nick pre-empted it. He noticed her over a weekend, constantly poring over a blue notepad, scribbling, nibbling the end of her pen, and then scoring out and scribbling some more.

'What're you doing Lesley? Writing a book or something?'

'No … no, actually I'm just getting some thoughts in order.'

'Well, either your head is full of them, or maybe you can't sort them out. You've spent ages over it. Can I help? Here, let me have a look.'

Lesley snatched the book back quickly, but in the friendly

scuffle Nick caught sight of one statement written in big, bold capitals and underlined three times: I WANT A BABY.

He went into the kitchen and returned with a bottle of Cotes du Rhone and two glasses. 'Time we had a chat, don't you think?'

* *

Nick has been a studious younger man, had to study hard just to keep up. He'd not had many girl-friends before Lesley, and none of them serious. If he wasn't studying he was out on the golf course or watching rugby. A crowd of them from the Medical School would meet for a pint, Friday and Saturday nights in Sandy Bell's and maybe go to the baked tattie shop in Bread Street on the way home. He'd gone back home quite regularly to Inverness and kept up with some of his old school pals too.

Lesley had grown on him. He'd allowed her to get close to him over months of an easy friendship based initially on their shared experiences of life on the wards. Not that she wasn't attractive with her reddish hair and creamy skin. He just hadn't thought of her in that way before.

Once their relationship deepened and he found his need for her body surprising and pressing, he had been tentative in pushing the boundaries of their friendship, sensing a fear somewhere deep in Lesley. He took considerable care to make her feel safe and loved before extending, just a little each time, the range of his caresses. It took some control on his part not to let his desire for her take full rein, and only his solitary release of sexual tension later, allowed him to hold back when their bodies were close.

She had been uncharacteristically light hearted and radiant one summer Saturday afternoon when they took a picnic up Arthur's Seat to feel the cooling breeze at the top, and enjoy the panoramic view. They raced each other up the final fifty feet, collapsed laughing at the top and shared a few lingering soft kisses as they lay on the picnic rug. It was the perfect day.

Later, back at Nick's flat, happy and carefree, Lesley allowed herself to participate body and mind in their lovemaking and this time agreed, even welcomed, Nick's breathless request for her to let him 'make her really happy' this time. And after it, she was

– really happy – if a bit sore.

But it was risky. She hadn't worked out the dates.

Nick went into medical mode.

'I've studied the research, Lesley. For most couples this rhythm method just doesn't work. The woman's cycle isn't totally regular or predictable. And then all the spontaneity goes out the window – is it safe today, oh no, better wait – and then you go off the notion or get frustrated. We have problems enough meeting up now, what with our different shifts. I love you Lesley. I want us to share something really special. Why not go on the pill? I'd love kids one day – but not like this, not yet. And what kind of bad example would you be setting – a midwife who gets pregnant by accident and can't finish her training?'

He'd pressed all her buttons with that speech. She had her practical head on when she agreed to see her GP. Later, in a quiet moment she felt compelled to discuss her decision with a higher authority.

I know it's not what the church rules. But even then, they say there's always your own conscience – and I've really thought about this, God. It will be better for everyone if I do it this way. I'll finish my matty, Nick will finish his house jobs, we can plan for a proper future together and then create a lovely home to bring children into. Surely that's better than an unplanned pregnancy which would wreck everything? And my parents would be so disappointed after all the sacrifices they've had to make to get me this far, if I had to give it all up.

Once she went on the pill, Lesley was rarely as relaxed and carefree as she had been that very first time. Maybe it was her conscience, or perhaps the hormones affected her. And even when she stopped taking the pill, two years into their marriage, she held a bit of herself back, without knowing why.

* *

Nick appeared surprised. 'Lesley, is that what all this is about? A baby? I thought we were just waiting to see what happened. It's only been a few months since you came off the pill.'

She looked straight at him, her voice accusatory.

'A year – it's been a year. And still nothing. And you never even mention it!'

She got a defensive response.

'Well, I've been really busy with the practice. I suppose I just haven't given it much thought. Didn't think there was any real urgency anyway.'

Lesley's face crumpled, she was close to tears.

'I'm worried. Surely it should have happened by now. And it just kills me to see all those women who come in. Treat it like shelling peas some of them, you should see them. And all the while I would give anything to be in their shoes.'

She looked up at him earnestly, willing him to understand the depth of her feeling.

'Okay, okay. I get the message. I should have thought. I'm sorry. But you know you never even show much interest in sex these days. Always too tired, or got a headache. Doesn't seem to matter to you whether it's a quickie or whether I really try to help you come.' He smiled. 'Hey – if you want a baby that badly, shouldn't you be grabbing me at every opportunity? Ripping all your clothes off and getting me excited when I walk through the door at night?'

Not the right thing to say it seemed.

'Nick, stop it. It's *not* funny! I know I've been distant but I've been wound up for ages. Anyway, I'm better now and I want to stay that way. So I need to tell you – I was trying to find the right words when you caught me earlier – that I want our marriage to work, I want to get back to where we were a couple of years ago – when we were great pals, when we could talk about anything, anytime. And I want to make getting pregnant a real priority. Yes – I know – I'll have to make more time for you and time for much more sex. And I will – I really will. I'm sure it will be much better now. I've sorted out a lot of things in my head recently, so it's all feeling better. I'm going to have more energy now, I know I will. What do you think?'

He gave her a long stare, searching for the 'right' words this time.

'What I think is that you've obviously been working on all of this in your own quiet way. But okay – it's a deal. And let's set a time limit for you conceiving. We'll try to have more quality time together, make love regularly so as to increase the chances, and then how about we give it another year and if you're not pregnant then we'll go and see old Henry Crichton in Gynae. But I'm sure it won't come to that, now that a lot of the stress has been taken out of the equation.'

Lesley beamed. He sounded like the old Nick again. She still loved him. She wanted his baby. *Really* wanted it. Life suddenly looked a whole lot more hopeful.

* *

And they did try – in their own very different ways. He was more tender towards her. She tried to be more responsive to his touch. They agreed that Friday night would be designated 'stay at home' night, if Nick wasn't on call.

That first Friday Nick arrived home from surgery with a bunch of sweet-smelling freesia and a bottle of Lesley's favourite sparkling wine. She sipped a glass while he cooked his one standard offering – creamy chicken curry. After dinner they watched American Gigolo, a mildly erotic film showcasing a young Richard Gere. Nick stole a glance at her from time to time, hoping to see evidence of some level of arousal. He moved to join her on the brown leather sofa, putting an arm around her shoulders and pulling her closer.

'I bet you wouldn't mind Richard Gere attending to your needs, would you?'

'Nick! Don't be crude. He's not my type anyway. Just watch the film, will you.'

Lesley tried to concentrate on the film while Nick began to 'help her relax'. Turning her head more towards the televisions screen, and undoing the top two buttons of her white shirt, he lightly massaged her neck and shoulders, quietly kissing her from time to time behind the ears. He carefully removed her shoes, and using a handful of lavender and geranium oil, made circular movements with his fingers over the upper part of each foot before addressing each toe individually.

When the film reached its unsatisfactory sweetened conclusion, designed to lift it from the gutter of prostitution and crime, he encouraged her to lie down so that he could massage her lower back. Slowly, slowly.

The first time he made to move down over her buttocks she

stopped him. 'Not yet, Nick. Not just yet.'

After a few more minutes when their breathing began to synchronise, he fetched a warm fleecy blanket to keep her warm and then removed her shirt and skirt. Still he massaged her, making long stroking movements on her legs, smoothing out the creases on her forehead, gently tickling her occasionally. And slowly she thawed and relaxed.

It was as if he chose to postpone or even deny his own gratification for a change, concentrating all his efforts on Lesley.

When he moved his focus to her creamy white breasts, she concentrated on her breathing, willing herself to remain relaxed, trying all the while to enjoy these lightest of massage strokes.

'I do love you, Lesley, and I want to make you happy. Really happy. Let me do it now.'

For a moment she saw the young student boy, from a time before ego and pride changed the very heart of him. And with a shy smile, she opened her arms, and pulled him towards her. He slipped inside her, moving carefully to slow himself down until he could hold back no more. With a sharp intake of breath, and a slight shudder, he experienced a quiet climax. For Lesley, the emotional closeness was all she needed.

* *

Nick's sperm count was within the normal range. He had never doubted that for one minute but had felt obliged to comply with the standard investigations. There was no obvious indication for Lesley's apparent infertility, other than some irregularity in her menstrual cycle which might make ovulation less predictable. Nevertheless, they had been taking no precautions for a total of two and a half years without the desired result.

Well then, thought Lesley, this baby that was wanted so badly might just have to come from someone else.

They decided to consider adoption.

* *

Nancy and I caught up with Lesley at Camilla's christening in the summer of 1987, just a few months after the adoption process was finally completed. The two of us were having a satisfying moan about babies and nappies, and all those sleepless nights. A bit tactless in retrospect, but we hadn't intended to upset Lesley; the moans were natural given our lives breathing, eating and sleeping children.

'All I can say is that you two should count yourselves lucky, you shouldn't moan really you shouldn't. I'd have given anything for a big family. It must be lovely to look at your own children and see your two selves and your ancestors in their eyes or the way they walk.

'I went through every emotion known to man – or woman – during that period of almost three years until we were granted leave to adopt Jonathan. You have no idea the hoops we had to jump through. The ups and downs. The time it all took. Would we be approved as potential adopters? The questions we were asked, the detail they wanted to know. And then that adoption group we had to attend. It was all about questioning our attitudes and beliefs towards children and adoption. The religion thing came up of course. We had to be united on that one. I let the side down again – but I had to do it. We said any child would be brought up Christian, would have exposure to both churches but would attend the local non-denominational school. The home visits were a nightmare. They say it's not about whether or not your house is tidy but I'm sure that's part of it. So I went round like a mad thing putting all the papers and books away, replacing the flowers so that they were always fresh.

'But it's all been so worth it. Don't you think he's just *such* a lovely boy?'

If we could see that Jonathan was a little slow at almost two years of age, we were not going to comment on it, when his mother was radiating such happiness.

Hit the road Jack

Living the dream, that was me. It was all I'd ever wanted I told myself. But gradually, as the years passed, I woke up.

Looking back, the hardest bit for me, during that period of all absorbing motherhood, became the moving about. It seemed like the *only way* to survive, to continue to get up in the morning and make it through the day – was not to think – just to do.

Willie left his Dad's business in 1980 to go down to Kent to work. It was the opportunity he'd been waiting for and a significant year for him – and others. Ronald Reagan became US President, British Airways was privatised, John Lennon shot and killed in New York whilst Willie McDonald landed a promising job with Sir Robert McAlpine.

We moved again in 1982 when Willie was transferred to the combined heat and power plant construction in Birmingham. And again in '84 further north to Washington, Tyneside, for the Nissan Car Manufacturing Plant. His involvement in the early stages of the Coal Clough Wind Farm in Lancashire meant another upheaval in '88. It was all progress – for him. Wider experience, some on-the-job management training, a chance to be in at the design stage for some projects. And for a long time, if he was happy, then I was too. Or so I thought. But then I didn't indulge in too much thinking. Four years of a university education – read, absorb, understand, analyse, synthesise and maybe then even create new knowledge – that mostly went out the window in the day to day round.

Each time I would pack up, promising to sort out *this time* all that stuff we were carting around with us for who knows why – and then end up packing it too as I ran out of hours in the day and the necessary will. Then would come the big top to bottom clean in case whoever came next might think I had been less than perfect as a housewife. All to be reversed at the other end. Occasionally there would be a new neighbour who would ask us over for tea and scones and I would reprise my coper role:

'Oh, it's fine, really. I'm used to it. We've moved about quite a lot with Willie's job. I've got a routine going now!'

Better that they admired me than saw my weariness or weakness. Better to focus on the children, how confident and adaptable they were through it all, than on me – and the risk of exposing that whole hidden creative side of me which was withering from lack of nurture.

The children seemed to adapt amazingly well. These new neighbours might well have noted that Diane worked hard to sustain a happy, lively and loving home environment, while their Father provided well for their physical needs, although he couldn't be at home as much as he might have wished, (and when he was, usually too tired to do much more than read the odd bedtime story or take the boys fishing once in a blue moon).

I took up yoga after one move severely taxed my back. But had to give that up when the crèche closed. I joined PTAs, toddler groups, adult swimming classes – even a 'return to study' course when I feared my mental powers had totally deserted me. That had been during a particularly low period when in exasperation I had rooted out a copy of that old favourite 'Structure, Culture and Function' and cried in frustration when I couldn't concentrate on the complex arguments, let alone make any sense of them.

And yet, there were times when one of the children would say something funny, or another perform 'in tune' on the recorder at the school concert, and Willie and I would exchange private smiles. It was what we had always intended, wasn't it? A comfortable home, our own family, a happy bunch. They were all healthy, they were bright, they mixed well, had friends, brought them home, played in the school football and netball teams, did well in exams, got excellent school reports, grew into tall, attractive, well adjusted children. Surely that was enough.

The idea of a move abroad had been on Willie's mind for some time before he felt able to broach it. Mother-in-law Margaret had come down to Burnley for a week in late '89. The children were 'old enough to be left for a few days' she said as she shooed us off for a weekend on our own in the Lake District. It had rained – buckets of it. The food had been mediocre. But Willie had worked hard to please me – and I had noticed. An appointment pre-booked for a luxury facial, the latest Margaret Forster book left at my side of the bed, a bottle of my favourite port sent up to the room after dinner, slow and sensuous massages. For a change, life was not about *doing* but simply about *being*.

After an early morning love-making session when I had been relaxed enough to properly let go and enjoy a rare wave of excitement and fulfilment, we had watched the rain lash onto the windowpane, laughing at our bad timing, and vowing to spend all day in bed if it didn't clear up. Willie resurrected a game we hadn't played for years – the 'What If' game.

'What if you hadn't met me – who would you have married?' asked Willie.

'Easy,' I replied. 'Kevin Costner of course.'

'Very funny. Well then, what if you'd had to move to the States to live with him. How would you have liked that?'

'No problem for a seasoned re-locater like me!'

'And what if *you* hadn't married *me* – where would you be now?' It was my turn to ask the questions.

'Probably getting ready to move to Saudi Arabia to work on a huge public lighting project in Jeddah' was his reply.

The game stopped right there.

'Are you serious?' I was shaking …

'Yes, seems so. I didn't know how to broach it with you. I know its cost us a lot, all that moving. Losing out on house price booms, you not being able to get any sort of career going, not getting much help with the parents being so far away. But this move really might be the one that boosts our fortunes. And the company make it as easy as possible for the families – nice rent-free house, private schooling, paid trips home twice a year. Give it some thought Di, please.'

That was our carefree weekend over. Of course, he would take the job, and of course I would go with him, uproot the kids again too. There was no debate in my mind.

In a perverse way, that move saved our relationship. Not from divorce or anything remotely as serious. But from mindless routines, carelessness, lack of effort, lack of respect, failure to nourish.

Willie left in the March of 1990 to help set the project up in Jeddah. I made all the arrangements at home to sell the house in Burnley and put the furniture in storage for who knew when we might return. The company organised the visas, flights, information packs, family housing and enrolment at the international school for the four children. You would have thought we were leaving for ever with all the goodbye visits we made. Up to Forfar to Grandparents Steven, back down to Dumfries to the in-laws, via Dolphinton and Nancy. Then Campbell and his wife Jenny met us in Manchester one day for lunch on their way to Tenerife for a holiday. Norma, Maxwell and the baby came up from Stoke the same day to make it a very rare gathering of the Steven clan.

When I was packing, I found 'Structure, Culture and Function' at the back of the bookcase.

Not that one, I don't think! I laughed to myself. But this move might just be an opportunity to get my brain working again – especially since there's a maid thrown in.

Ten weeks we'd been apart by the time all the paperwork was complete and the children and I finally landed in Jeddah in the early hours. The kids were ecstatic at seeing their Dad again. In the sublime joy of our own reunion, Willie and I rued the years we had taken each other for granted, only then realising how deep our bond was and that it never would be broken or damaged – we simply wouldn't let it happen. Like most revelations, its effect diminished over the subsequent weeks, but on the nights when it was too hot and sticky to sleep, or when a stray cockroach had crawled up my arm and left me wide awake, I would relive that joy and feel again the conviction that in spite of it all, I had made a wise choice in marrying Willie.

You can get it if you really want

Patricia, the one who had it all mapped out, the one who thought she had created the perfect future, found the reality to be something quite different from the plan. Real life didn't always unfold in the correct sequence. Others didn't necessarily fit in with her carefully drawn plans. Nature, the Universe, did not always provide.

Her master plan was to graduate in 1976, start her probationary teaching year in her old primary school, St Joseph's, then marry Trevor in the Christmas holidays of the same year. They would plan for a baby after she had a couple of years' teaching under her belt, have another child quite soon, and then when that one was about three, she would get stuck into her career. With any luck, she'd have a boy and a girl. Granny Foley would mind them when she went back to work. That would still make her under 30, giving plenty of time to work her way up to Head Teacher. Meanwhile, Trevor would stay in the Biology Department at Harris Academy to build up a bank of experience before looking out for a promoted post. They'd move from the flat in Scott Street just as soon as they could afford to, so that they could have a garden for the children.

But it seemed life wasn't like that. Too many assumptions made. No account taken of the human side. What about feelings, relationships, family commitments? The trouble was that Patricia had never been much of a listener. Much of the time she was having an internal conversation which largely revolved around planning and checking progress.

Now, if I write up these teaching plans for next week today, I can finish that marking at the weekend.

If I'm organised, I'll have time to pop into Safeway's for some messages on the way home. Then I can put the washing on while I'm making the tea. Trevor's got a golf match tonight so that means he'll need to be out by 6pm. That leaves me time to do a bit of reading up on child development before the case conference on Tuesday.

It was all about the who, what, where, when and the how. The juggling, the managing, the completing. Mastery of the day-to-day would facilitate the achievement of the master plan.

What Patricia didn't realise is that there is no action without reaction, no benefit without cost, no victory without loss. She believed that you just keep trying harder, and harder, to make your plans work.

Claire was born in the October of '79. The timing was perfect. Vindication then for all those who said the rhythm method would never work. Not that she'd used it to prevent pregnancy – too risky all round. But when it came to conceiving, she plotted her temperature chart religiously, made more space than usual in her busy schedule for sex, and even agreed (after much prompting from Trevor) to try one of those marital aids which add '*fun, an enriching part of a satisfying sex life – guaranteed to result in orgasm*' – but only to aid conception.

She finished work at the end of the summer term and spent the next three months getting things in order for the baby. Painting, sewing, knitting, practising the breathing exercises, attending parentcraft classes.

Claire's date of birth might have conformed to the plan, but there it stopped. She slept during the day but not at night. She developed nappy rash from wearing disposables and so had to wear cotton nappies – creating piles of washing. Cow's milk did not suit her. She wouldn't stay with anyone other than her mother. Even Patricia's father – not known to pass judgment on anything to do with children – was vocal in his comments:

'Where did you find *her*, Patricia? She's a nightmare of a child.'

'You're thinner than ever these days – let your Mum take her for the night and give you a decent sleep.'

Talk of a brother or sister was off limits. Sex was even rarer. Trevor took to midweek golf as well as Sundays during the summer months. That was in addition to his Friday nights at the pub and Saturday afternoons at Dens or Tannadice, time out with the lads, although the teams weren't a patch on his beloved Newcastle. He couldn't find a grain of warmth or welcome in his own home. Everything revolved around Patricia's lists and her ticking off every last item on them, regardless of whether she'd been up all night with Claire or elbow deep in soiled nappies for half the day. He couldn't find the words, couldn't create the opportunity to say what was in his head.

Patricia, ease up a bit love. Let's have a night at the pictures. You can leave that washing till tomorrow surely.

No, everything would be fine, if only she kept to the schedule.

* *

With no sign of another pregnancy, and no real desire to pursue it on either side, Patricia went back to work when Claire was three years old. By that time the child was a happy lively little girl, well behaved and a good sleeper, as long they kept her away from cow's milk. But what a relief it was to Patricia to be back amongst attendance lists, teaching packs, lesson plans, pupil reports. Numbers, dates, timetables, records, systems, procedures – all under control, all neat and up to date, all present and correct. Some of her enthusiasm returned for life returned. She went back to running, and joined The Cecilian Choir. Life was back on course.

* *

The talk in Mennie's bar on the Perth Road was a little different from the usual.

'No sign of a promoted post for you then Trevor?'

'Actually Tom, I'd rather not go for one. Don't tell the wife that though. I'm comfortable these days with the job. Ten years I've been at the Harris now. Got a good stock of materials. And there's the odd field trip away – off the leash kind of thing.'

'Patricia still running everywhere?'

'Oh God, you know what's she's like. "A mile a minute" as my Nan used to say. Won't be happy till she's Head Teacher and in total control. She's been back teaching for five years now and she's never drawn breath.'

'She's some girl though. How does she fit it all in – the running, the choir, the family stuff, the church? Bet there's not much time for nookie!'

'Well she certainly fulfils all her duties – that's all I'm saying.'

Maybe it was like Easter duties – all right if you do it once during the Easter season. Or would it be more like Lent – give it up for 40 days and 40 nights? Better if it was a daily obligation, like evening prayer.

I could use that one, thought Trevor. Appeal to the guilt in her. She could do the right thing by everyone else, why not by him?

Up, up and away

Position announcement: Lecturer Pool (Religious Studies 1979)
Religious Studies Department, University of Kansas

It wasn't quite the auspicious start to the fast-track glittering academic career she had in mind, but as an unknown quantity in a foreign country, and in a niche field, it would, at least, be a foot in the door.

Carys put in an immediate letter of application to Professor McKinney, dutifully enclosing her CV (impressive, for her age, given her famous prize), three letters of recommendation (not a problem) and evidence of prior success in teaching (a bit of a stretch of the truth).

Although not a tall man, the Professor had the presence befitting a Head of Department. Stocky, charming, eloquent, decisive, and on paper – academically gifted.

I could work with you, she thought.

The Celtic extraction also appealed.

He got the impression she was a little cocky, definitely career minded, knew her subject undoubtedly – but could she teach it? Despite a few qualms about her relative lack of teaching experience he couldn't pass up the unexpected opportunity to plug the gap left by a heavily pregnant Lecturer who should have gone on maternity leave weeks ago. And this Welsh girl could talk authoritatively, no doubt about that – 'the academic study of religion should acquaint the student with religion as a phenomenon in human experience, examining the forms in which religion has been described, organised and practised throughout history' – had just tripped off her tongue during the interview, with no effort at all.

And so it was that Carys's prompt application was rewarded with the immediate offer of a semester's work teaching undergraduates. Three hours of class contact time per week, plus grading and submission of all relevant course records. Not too arduous, leaving plenty of time to establish the marital home properly, get to know the area, and, more importantly, she felt, produce some papers, work up her applications for research grants, and investigate up and coming posts – here and elsewhere.

But later that afternoon, sitting in her new home looking out over the front lawns to one of the broad streets of suburbia, she experienced a rare wobble. Even for Carys, the academic route map now looked slightly daunting from this angle of part-time Lecturer swimming in a pool. Tenured Lecturer to Associate Professor to Assistant Professor to Professor to Chair (Distinguished Professor) to Head of Department. Six steps on the ladder.

How many papers, books, conference appearances, student contact hours, Masters and PhD supervisions would that take? How many tedious hours bogged down in marking, reportage, meetings?

She rallied her thoughts. *I can do it and I will do it. I'm good enough, aren't I?* She always found a way.

* *

Yesterday was the third day of the school summer holidays. A rare trip to Aberystwyth's 'flea pit', to see *Tarzan the Ape Man.* Mam's treat, a counter to the mounting excitement of the children, anxiously waiting for Dad to finish off in school and take them away for a week's break to the metropolis of Cardiff.

Today they are playing Tarzan in the jungle of Coed y Dderwen. A troop of three, lumbering along the path, bent-over, ape-like, swinging their arms clumsily from side to side. Huw is in front, acting the part of leader in their games, as usual. Because he is the eldest, he says, and the tallest. Dafydd is in the middle and Carys brings up the rear.

'But I am next oldest,' she says. 'I should be in the middle.'

'And I am taller than you,' he replies. 'So you need to be on the end if you're the shortest.'

Carys, for once, doesn't bother to argue further. She would rather get on with playing the game and pick her time for getting her own back.

Huw is a dictatorial leader. He says when they must walk, when to run, when to stop and pick imaginary bananas from the tree, where to sit and eat them. Dafydd grows weary of being bossed around, makes a break for it, shims up a tree, stands tall on a branch and starts to holler as loudly as he can, banging his fists against his chest.

Carys is taken by surprise at the speed of his ascent. She stops on the path, then cranes her neck upwards and watches him acting out his Tarzan role.

'I didn't say you could break rank!'

Huw is angry, he's turned around and is striding back towards them, the gap closing rapidly. She quickly tries to climb up as well, to reach Dafydd, to be another rebellious ape defying the leader, but her spindly little arms are not strong enough to pull her up more than a few feet, then her legs give way, so she ends up sliding down the trunk, landing in a heap on the ground, one hand rubbing her cut and bruised leg, the other pressing against her eyes to stop the tears from spilling out.

The boys laugh. That raucous, unrestrained, slightly forced laughter that almost, but not quite teenage boys have.

'Ah ha ha ha ha,' they say, pointing at her, holding their bellies, precariously in Dafydd's case, ten feet up the tree.

'*Girls* can't climb trees – everyone knows that, Carys!'

She is sore, but it is her pride that hurts the most.

Later she steals a bag of nails and a hammer from the shed, sneaks out, back to the tree, bangs in nails as hard as she can, from the bottom of the trunk to as high as she can reach standing on tip-toe. She tests her theory out. The nails provide enough leverage to get her to the knot in the bark five feet up, and after that she can stretch to the old woodpecker's hole, large enough for a hand or toe of shoe.

She is clumsy, not a natural climber, like Huw, but she stays there practising until she has memorised each move, the best way to reach the branch safely; until it would look, to an observer, that she can climb with relative ease. It takes twenty attempts for her to be satisfied, and then she sits on the branch triumphant in her exhaustion.

They play Tarzan one more time before they go to Cardiff. The troop is passing the tree and now Carys drops back, unnoticed. She climbs up to the branch, sits astride it, legs dangling down for balance, then, fully poised, she fills her lungs with air and shouts loudly, pummelling her chest with bony fists until she cannot hold the pressure any longer.

The boys are stopped dead in their tracks, shocked by the noise. They turn around, looking bewildered. Where is their sister? Carys whoops again, revealing her presence.

'How did you get up there?' they ask.

'Easy, peasy,' she says. 'I flew of course, because girls can't climb trees – *everyone* knows that, don't they?'

* *

Carys doesn't know where the hammer and nails are yet, in this University. She hasn't met the staff. She hasn't sussed out the system. She is too new. She will need to think about it, work on it. But what she does know, with absolute certainty, is that if they are there, then she *will* be able to find them. She has faith in abundance.

The Graduate Director has assumed an air of friendliness, overlaid by an ill concealed attitude of distraction, as if all this is taking her away from the real business, some important paper waiting to be written it seems.

It's obvious they need to get through the meeting quickly, so that she can return to her desk, and eat some more cakes whilst she's at it, I'll bet, thinks Carys, making a mental note never to get as fat as that, and never to wear a dress as hideous as that either.

'Welcome one and all,' Professor Carol Hawkins says, smiling broadly at the two women and two men sitting around the table. 'I think some introductions to start would be useful, don't you? Name, very brief career biog, special academic interest, something like that? Bill, since you're the old hand here, would you go first please?'

Carys kept hers purposefully short, but did throw in a mention of the Selwyn Harold Smith Award, just so they were aware that she might be young but had credentials. It took less than thirty minutes to sort out who would teach what, and her pitch for Celtic Christianity was successful. That meant her notes and slides preparation could be minimal; she knew this subject inside out and would have no trouble padding out the lectures on the day.

'Please call me Carol' then proceeded to gloss over the assessment system, deal with the few questions she received hurriedly, then disappear back to her paperwork, leaving the four of them to 'get to know each other a bit better' and agree a 'peer support system', which was clearly code for 'don't bother me again unless there's an emergency.'

'How on earth do these people get promoted?' Carys asked JJ over supper, recounting the day's events. 'She was ghastly. I did a search on her publications after the meeting – can't see she's produced much of note either.'

'Aw, I don't know. Maybe she was in the right place at the right time. Knowing people higher up helps too. And getting your face recognised on the conference circuit. Being an editor of a prominent journal, all that kind of thing.' He grinned mischievously. 'Maybe she slept with the HoD!'

Carys was genuinely horrified at this suggestion. 'God JJ, surely he's got more taste than that! I *don't* think so. All that stuff you're talking about sounds like playing a game. What ever happened to good old-fashioned reward for ability?'

'Yeh well, that happens, of course, just look at me,' he said cockily, 'but all the other stuff is important too. You're going to have to do it Carys, whether you like it or not, everything except sleep with the HoD though,' he teased.

'I wouldn't dream of it,' she smiled coyly, faking a deep, sexy voice, in an ambiguous tone, just to wind him up.

* *

She is in her element now.

'It was an opportunity I simply couldn't refuse, no matter how much upheaval it caused on the home front,' she'd written in her letter to Lesley back in June '81.

Of course, at first, JJ hadn't been too keen on the idea. After all it was a thousand miles between Lawrence and Walton but he had to admit that it would be the ideal step up for Carys's career. It was really difficult at the start – sometimes they went for a few weeks without seeing each other, but they got used to it eventually. She managed to get a lot of work under her belt with all the extra time she had on her own. And then when JJ did come over or she went back for the weekend then it was worth the wait. In a nudge, nudge, wink, wink, kind of a way.

In the room at Walton with her nameplate bearing the title Assistant Professor, she sits behind her large, wooden desk; hands clasped firmly together, her body inclined forwards, her expression expectant. She is waiting for an answer to the awkward question she has just asked of her sixth PhD student – Eleanor, a tall, chubby, pasty-looking redhead who would dwarf Carys should they stand side by side. But mere stature alone has nothing to do with presence, or authority; in small people these things come from all manner of other characteristics.

Eleanor squirms a little in her seat under her supervisor's enquiring gaze. She is not quite sure how to respond. A blush has started up on her face; she can feel it spreading across her cheeks. She attempts a smile of confidence as a counter, yet the palms of her hands are moistening and her heart quickening. She is used to Carys's theoretical interrogations by now, but despite frequent pep-talks to herself, they still have the same affect on her as they did two years ago.

Only one more to go. the thought passes fleetingly across her mind as she prepares to answer. *Then I will never have to sit here and feel so uncomfortable again.*

'Yes, I agree,' she says deferentially (although in actuality she would like to argue against the Professorial suggestion if only she felt certain she was able to convince Carys otherwise). 'I should expand that chapter to include the early years of the establishment of the Christian Catholic Church in Zion.'

Carys smiles now, yet parts of her face have a slightly frozen appearance, Eleanor notices, thinking how her supervisor looks not unlike her own Mom laying down the law before a teenage night out.

'And you'll tend to the bridging text between chapters that I asked you to do last time – a request I've reinforced today – by our next tutorial?'

'Yes, of course. I'm really sorry I don't have it ready for you just yet. I meant to – it's just that I got awfully bogged down researching Dowie's early life in Edinburgh – before he went to Australia in 1860 – that I ran out of time.' Eleanor rubs her sticky hands together anxiously, hoping this nugget of fact and allusion to initiative will be sufficient to stave off a further reprimand.

It is – but only just. Carys is in a rare generous mood.

'Reading around your subject is imperative, Eleanor, as we've discussed many times before. However – you must be careful not to get sidetracked into realms of literature that are red herrings at this stage to the important task in hand – your writing up of this thesis. We've agreed the structure and content, haven't we?'

She leans even further forward, giving Eleanor a final shot from her piercing blue eyes. 'Best you stick to it then, yes?'

Yes. Upwardly mobile academics do not want to attract failure in any aspect of their remit, especially not in PhD or Masters' students, and Carys has no intention of clocking up any in either category. So far her tally is six Masters, five PhDs. If success requires *firmness*, then so be it. It is all in a good cause she reasons – her career and theirs. She has their best interests at heart, she always tells them, right from the very first interview. She also makes it abundantly clear that she expects diligence, creativity and academic rigour, no exceptions allowed. No wonder then she has developed a reputation as a hard task master, but there is no shortage of students wanting to come under her tutelage, nor for that matter, of invitations from other academics for collaborative projects.

* *

As Lesley read the letter from America, dated 26th June 1981, she could just imagine Carys forcefully convincing JJ of the merits of her departure to Massachusetts, where the hallowed halls of Walton offered an enticing Visiting Scholar appointment.

Lesley offered up a silent prayer that Carys and JJ's marriage was secure enough, in the longer term, to overcome constraints of geography.

I just don't know what to do with myself

April 1990

The kids were just about settled into school and I was beginning to wonder what I would do with myself other than lounge around the compound pool. Before I'd had the chance to ring Alix, I bumped into her quite by chance at a meeting of Jeddah Wives. It wasn't my normal haunt – not that I went anywhere much without Willie, since women were not allowed to drive – but I didn't have the cool elegant clothes, the right husband or the cut glass accent to feel comfortable at its weekly get-togethers. However, they were always looking for demonstrators for their regular activities' afternoon and Meryl, the wife of Willie's boss, knew that I was beginning to paint again. You didn't turn down an invite from Meryl if you knew what was good for your husband's career, hence my 'offer' to give a class in watercolour one Monday afternoon.

Sitting around small tables with the remains of coffee and German cakes in front of them, were the Jeddah Wives – the idle halves of assorted Consuls, Headmasters, oil company executives, trade envoys, military advisors and the like. Flitting about like the proverbial butterfly was Alix – tanned, lithe, impeccably dressed in a pale turquoise silk shift and speaking in an accent indistinguishable from a Home Counties socialite.

She fell on me like a desert wanderer on an oasis.

'Good grief! Diane! Why didn't you phone? I didn't think you'd be here for weeks yet with all that visa business to go through. Where are you living? How's Willie? And the children? Are they at Jeddah Prep? They might have met Timmy and Caroline already.'

I managed to contain her exuberance long enough to give the group a short demonstration of how to capture the subtle colours of the desert sands before we could leave the 'wives' to it, having a go themselves for the next half hour. I sat back and listened – to the 'me, myself and mine' story.

* *

Alix's Xmas cards had been the group's main source of information about her life after university. None of the girls had managed to her wedding, although they had already known about Gerald and his job with the British Council in Moscow from Alix's final year placement. Although it was news to them, the British Council had been set up many years before to promote a wider knowledge of the United Kingdom and the English language abroad, and to develop closer cultural relations between the United Kingdom and other countries.

In '76, Gerald had helped her acquire a job with the British Council in Cairo once she had completed her London-based course in Teaching English as a Foreign Language. They had stayed in touch, he'd arranged flights to the UK for her to meet up with him on his trips to the London office and she was no doubt flattered by the attentions of a well read, well travelled and somewhat smooth 36 year old.

Gerald was public school educated, Home Counties, and a career civil servant, albeit in an interesting and challenging environment. He could be rather reserved, but on the other hand was highly effective in social settings, and also liked a bit of skirt. His last long-standing girl friend had left him somewhat disappointed when she had refused to consider moving to Moscow. However, her tuition on achievement of the female orgasm by 100 different routes had developed his skills in that direction so that by the time she left, his talents in bed ably complemented his aptitude for languages and his knowledge of how to behave anywhere in the four corners of the world.

He found Alix to be a keen pupil. She'd started young, frequenting the Aberdeen Students' Union while still at school, then working her way through assorted Hooray Henrys and lusty locals in Edinburgh before graduating to the Chelsea set in London and the BCal pilots in Egypt. The attraction of Gerald was that he had got over that impetuousness of youth with its timing problems, and was more of a rhythmic match for Alix. She was happy to play the pouting schoolgirl to his strict tutor in order to extend her own repertoire in bed. And he did know how to treat a girl when they ventured out from the bedroom, always knowing the best restaurant for authentic local food or the backstreet jeweller who carried an exciting range of silver and gold pieces.

They shared a love of travel, Alix particularly keen to visit where she could use her Arabic and French. Together they visited Jordan, Syria, The Yemen, Algeria, Morocco – their passage always smoothed by Gerald's local counterpart.

His proposal had been more romantic than she might have expected, with a single line entry highlighted in her itinerary for a trip to Singapore which read,

'18 November 1978, Cheyne Walk Registry Office, Marriage to Mr Gerald Fitzroy, followed by a wedding breakfast at Simpson's-in-the-Strand.'

'Yes?' asked Gerald.

'Why not?' replied Alix.

And why not? A suitable match, time now to make it legal, next step on the journey, passport to travel, approval on all sides.

Singapore was a plum posting for them both. Alix could apply herself to teaching English as a foreign language for sufficient hours in the day to then justify a spot of swimming, a few games of tennis, followed by drinks and dinner at the home of friends. And of course Singapore was the perfect hub for further foreign travel.

Route 76 or maybe it was 81 precipitated a fertilised egg, only three months into their marriage, corroborating yet again the theory that orgasm aids conception. Maybe working their way through a selection of the remaining *pathways to pleasure* had something to do with the subsequent miscarriage too, who could be sure? It must have happened quite early on, in fact just about the same stage as she'd been the last time back in Edinburgh. This time she did cry for the loss, although not for too long. Better just to get on with life again and plan a trip to Thailand maybe. Even Gerald hadn't been there before.

So 1979 passed by with enough of the excitement of the new and the exotic to keep Alix amused and occupied. And 1980 too.

Then they began to try actively for a baby. Gerald didn't want to be an elderly parent and Alix thought *as well now as any other time. Plenty of suitable nanny material out here.* The golden girl was delivered of twins in Foresterhill Hospital Aberdeen on September 27th 1981, having escaped the humidity of Singapore to spend the final two months of her pregnancy at home with Olive and Rab, hiding her cigarettes and toning down her colourful language just as she had in her gymslip days. Caroline Olivia (after Granny) and Timothy Gerald, duly delivered by caesarean section, travelled with her to join their father at the age of six weeks. Just when Mummy's stitches were all healed and she could pick up where she left off.

The comforting presence of Imelda, the nanny, allowed Alix plenty of time for socialising and beauty sleep. Alix and Gerald resumed their joint study and exploration of the human body for the benefit of mutual pleasure.

Nancy, Lesley and Diane had a brief introduction to the twins at their christening in Aberdeen on Gerald's next trip home the following March – sunkissed blonde wee beauties they were, the picture of health in their antique white gowns. They smiled for the minister, slept while their Mother circulated and chatted with friends at the celebratory lunch, and played with their toys at Imelda's feet the rest of the time.

Diane simply couldn't hold it back. 'Hasn't she just got everything? How *does* she do it?'

* *

Apparently, the twins cried when they left Imelda five years later. Fortunately they took to Fatima, her Eritrean successor, with apparent ease. The climate was hotter and drier in Jeddah but there were plenty of new playmates in Arabian Homes, Sierra Village. Daddy was in charge of the Jeddah office – a big promotion.

It can be a hard life when you have nothing to do but lie in the sun, wander round the shops with other wives on a Monday and Wednesday and play the odd game of bridge. It sounds like a dream – but the boredom eventually gets to you. Alix – not best known for embracing the work ethic – found herself actively seeking out potential students for some English tuition, just for something to do. There were 57 different nationalities attending the local international school, their school fees typically funded as part of their father's salary package. English was the language of the curriculum. Fluency was absolutely essential in order to achieve. And these were the offspring of achievers after all.

She set up a little teaching group with Salma from Lebanon,

Lakshmi from India and Marta from Norway. Although mixed classes existed in the international school, it was protocol for women to teach only girls in their own home. In fact, even that's not strictly true. Women were not supposed to work at all, other than in a very few specific situations – in those areas where they could be of direct assistance to other women, as doctors and nurses in female hospital wards, as teachers and support staff in all girls' schools and colleges. Those who were working in the international schools were labelled 'consul employees' to protect them. So Alix dealt purely in cash for obvious reasons and kept quiet about her new venture.

She had bitten her tongue on many occasions since her entry into Saudi life. When the checkout abruptly shut down just as she reached it with a full trolley, and she had to wait, tapping her fingers with impatience, until prayer time ended. When lecherous stall holders in the souk wanted to measure her up, for more than a simple dress it seemed judging by their ever attentive hands. When Gerald absolutely forbade her to go out of the compound alone when all she had wanted was a walk in the evening cool. The surface attractions of constant sunshine, a life of leisure and exposure to a new culture had long paled by the time the twins were nine years old, Gerald was absorbed in his job and all Alix had to keep her brain from turning to mince was a weekly hour with Salma, Lakshmi and Marta.

Finding Diane was like manna from the gods.

* *

Was it fake or was it real? Had we been that close in the flat days and I hadn't been aware of it? More likely I could be of use to her now in some way.

'You and Willie must come over with the children. Where are you living?'

'Saudia City, not too far from that roundabout with the big bicycle.'

'We're in Arabian Homes. Gerald knows his way around so maybe we'll come to you first and then he can prime Willie for a return visit. How about this Friday afternoon? Do you have a pool?'

'Okay, okay. Slow down a bit Alix! Yes, we have a pool. The kids can lark about in there while we catch up. Come about one for a late lunch.'

We made it a regular date, visiting each other's compounds every other week on a Friday afternoon. With no family on hand, your friends become your family in the expat life. Susan and Elizabeth were glad of another girl to play with although Caroline was still a bit of a Barbie fan while my girls had graduated to MTV and non-stop pop music. The three boys led by Timmy went skateboard crazy. Willie and Gerald were hardly peas in a pod, but Willie's new found passion – diving – was one of Gerald's many interests, so they often took off to the reef for the afternoon.

At first I couldn't make my mind up if Alix had become that perfect diplomat's wife or was just playing the part. It took a few weeks before the truth began to emerge – and then only under the influence of a 'light refreshment.'

If you visited the international supermarkets in Jeddah for the first time, you might be bemused at their shelf filling strategy. Sugar, grape juice and plastic dustbins sit side by side for example. Other items seem designed to confuse. Something that looked amazingly like bacon is labelled 'breakfast beef'. The other expats would keep you right. No alcohol on sale? – well, make your own and here are all the ingredients and equipment on the very same shelf. Like a bit of bacon but pork is not allowed? – try breakfast beef and if it tastes amazingly like the real thing – then just eat up and shut up. The mother of invention was hard at work.

Alix and Gerald could access Johnny Walker and Blue Sapphire via the diplomatic circle, but they very much enjoyed Willie's home-made varieties, lovingly known locally as 'siddique' or friend – Sid for short. There was a virtual recipe book of variations of Sid. It was under the influence of very smooth 'Bailey's' that her guard dropped.

'Diane, how do you like it here?'

'You know, I'm really enjoying it now that I've settled in. I've got Amina for the housework – imagine – me with a maid! And then Willie's making sure we want to stay here by being very attentive when he's around. The kids are doing really well at the school. And I've plenty time to paint. It's like I've rediscovered an important part of me that was totally submerged back in the UK. The light here can be amazing, especially in the evenings. I've done some of my best work ever here. How about you?'

She hesitated before replying. 'Oh, I liked it fine at first although I'm used to this sort of climate so the sun is no big deal. But I'm fed up being so restricted – not allowed to drive, no cinemas, no theatres. Truth is – I'm bored stiff. I want to take these smug expat wives, shake them by the shoulders and shout out like a true Aberdonian – *A'm mebbe aaricht, a've got a hoosie, ma bairns and ma man but fer a quine lik me it's no enuff!!*'

I must admit I was a bit shocked.

'But you hide it so well, Alix. What are you thinking of doing?'

'There's talk – about a group that meets sometimes. At Sharbatly Village if you know where that is. Just a social event really, but a bit different.'

'In what way?'

'They're swingers.'

'What? Wife swappers?'

'Yeh. Don't look so surprised, Diane.'

'Here? In Saudi? God – that's risky, isn't it?'

'We manage to keep the drink secret – so why not the sex too?'

'Maybe – but is it worth the risk? You know the penalties.'

'It might be fun – that's all. Don't get on your high horse about it.'

'It's not my idea of fun. And what does Gerald think about it?'

'Not mentioned it yet. Just trying to find the right moment.'

'Alix, for goodness sake, get a grip. Gerald couldn't get involved in that kind of thing in his position. Surely there's something else you could find to do for excitement – learn a new language, take up diving yourself, write a book even on your life as an expat.'

Alix simply shrugged, her mouth turned down like a sulky teenager's. She reached for her black abaya, pulled it over her head to cover up her body, head to toe and leaving the sitting room of the villa, turned to me with, 'You might think I've got everything, Diane. But everything counts as nothing if you're bored, bored, bored. Just wait, you'll see. Stay here long enough and you'll be the same as the rest of us. The envy of all your friends at home, but your spirit shrivelling in the sun like a desert plant, flowering only once or twice a year. I want to flower again. Or life just ain't worth living.'

Moving seamlessly into rescuer mode, I tried to incorporate some activity or distraction into our regular meetings from then on. I badgered Alix to teach me how to play bridge, organised trips to the riding stables in the desert area outside the city and even dragged her along to a St Andrew's night at the school. She seemed to go along with all suggestions and the subject of withering and flowering slipped off the agenda.

By the end of the autumn term I was just about relaxing my vigilance for any hint of the threatened misdemeanour as she took to the stage as a most convincing Laura Jesson in The Off Runway Players winter production of *Brief Encounter*.

That is, until I read the cast list.

Laura Jesson .....played by Alix Fitzroy, Sierra Village

Alex Harvey ......played by Mike Nash, Sharbatly Village.

Back in the old routine

Time, space, money – they all helped to give me back a part of myself during these two years in the land of the Prophet. I could focus on my painting. I had a regular game of bridge in the diary and there was a weekly trip to the downtown souk where I could pick up a few things to furnish the villa or take home to wherever we'd settle when the time came. Crumbs on my table – and just for me. But just like crumbs, the birds can eat them and you lose your way back.

Mum phoned me one February Friday lunchtime when Willie was loading the car to go to the Creek.

'Hello, dear. It's your mother. I know I don't usually phone at this time of the day but I thought I'd catch you now before I go out to the hairdressers. Everything okay with you? Dad and I are just back from a weekend away in Pitlochry. I managed to pick up a lovely suede jacket in MacPherson's. Beautiful shade of blue. And we bumped into the Hendersons. You remember them – Professor Henderson and his wife? She always looks so elegant. Well, they invited us to share their table for dinner at the Hydro. Sally was just remarking how good my skin still is. We've got another weekend away next week with Dad's golfing pals. Really pushing the boat out this time. Turnberry no less. Golf for the men, and a shopping trip to Ayr for the ladies. How're the children doing? Still growing I expect. When was it you said you might be home for a holiday? Better go now, you know how much these calls cost.'

Bump.

All was fine in Forfar then. In fact, all was obviously fine in the whole world. Mum was up. So Dad must be up too.

But what about me? What about my plans for the weekend? What about 'how is life with you?'

And you can't remember when I'm coming home, can you not?

I'm a listening ear. I'm a sympathetic voice. A rock when you're down. A comforter when life's hard. You can always count on me Mum, you know that. Mum, Mum … are you listening? We've got our limits you know – we 'copers'.

I was swamped with feelings. I felt lonely, angry, restless, used.

And that might have been the end of it – a bad day. A rotten week even. But for a string of unconnected events.

Alix phoned after a few weeks' silence. She'd been back to Aberdeen for Christmas and had experienced a 'perfectly ghaaaastly time'. 'Daddy' had wakened one morning and found moving even an eyelid impossible. His dead weight was manhandled into the ambulance and sped through town to Aberdeen Royal. He made a partial recovery from the stroke but remained in intensive care for more than a week until he slept away the very last of his nights. Olive had been distraught, the children were pining for Gerald; it was almost too much to bear, so it seemed. Alix had made arrangements to fly back to Jeddah as soon as the will was read, the family home made winter-safe and 'Mummy' could face packing and leaving Daddy's ashes behind on the hall table.

'But you know it can be a bit of a pain having Mummy here when we have things on. Could you just be a dear and have her for a few days while Gerald and I go to Riyadh to see the children in a school sports competition?'

Oh, no problem. So glad you feel you can ask. Just leave her with me and I'll listen to her endless reminiscing about the early days in the business, and the time when the Queen came to Aberdeen and Robert was presented to her. I'll see she doesn't sit too long in the sun or tip the gateman. You just go – and leave it all to me.

I found myself saying, 'Poor you. Just bring her over when you're leaving for the airport.'

The School was next, just after Easter.

'Mrs MacDonald? Glad to have caught you. We're a bit stuck just now. Mrs Hassan has gone off sick – looks like she'll be off for a while. Any chance you could fill in for her art classes in the meantime?'

Oh sure, no problem. I wasn't 'qualified' when I first approached you for a few hours' work. But suddenly I'm in great demand because you're stuck. And no doubt you won't be able to pay me the full teacher's rate either, as I don't have the necessary bit of paper. Never mind though. You can count on me.

But instead I did my usual, 'I'd be delighted to help. When do you want me to start?'

Then Mrs Ronaldson from villa 25 approached Susan and

Elizabeth one day in the pool and asked if we would maybe take her dog for two weeks while she went on 'a trip of a lifetime' to Jordan.

'A dog? You're not supposed to even *have* a dog on this compound!'

'I know Mum but we thought you wouldn't mind. It's just a wee thing. You can put it in a shopping bag when you have to go out. Anyway, we said we'd check with you but that it would probably be okay.'

Teenie joined the family the next week. The kids were delighted with the gifts Mrs R brought back for them. They would be, especially since they took very little to do with the 'wee thing' when she was pooping and peeing everywhere.

We were planning our trip home for Christmas when Willie dropped the bombshell.

'I'm not going to manage home this time Di. Sorry, but the project is just at a critical stage. You go though – it's all booked and your parents would be very disappointed. And while you're home ... It might be a good idea to start looking at houses.'

I looked at him in total disbelief.

'What did you say? I can't believe I'm hearing this. Surely to God you are winding me up? I'm only just properly settled here and the kids love it. You're not telling me we have to get up and go again?'

Breathing deeply to stay calm, I challenged him once more.

'We've only been here two years and you said it might be four or five. And anyway, when was all this decided?'

'Sorry Di. You know how it is. The job calls and all that. And you always seem to manage.'

I could barely speak. 'Where to this time?'

'Looks like the Edinburgh area. Problems with the rail bridge. Great opportunity for me to get back into the UK market with this experience under my belt. You'll be fine Di. You're such a trouper with these things. Won't be till after the summer though. This would just be a recce.'

Oh yes? And what about talking it through with me first? What about a partnership decision? Where might I like to go? Good old Diane. She'll always be there, trailing behind you like a bloody Labrador.

I can articulate it all now, but back then, while I might have complained at first, in the end I just buried my feelings and got on with the coping. They all needed me. I packed my paints and brushes away. The window had opened just a fraction, but now it was closed again.

We had coffee and cakes at my leaving do in the Wives' Club on the compound. They'd clubbed together to buy me a Spencer Tartt print of the Old Souk. The inside of the farewell card was covered with comments – I should have been touched and gratified.

'Diane – you keep us all RIGHT. Why have you LEFT us now?'

'One of the best – in any language – au revoir, auf weidersein, and good luck'

'A fine Scots lass. Haste ye back!'

'We could always count on you. You'll be sorely missed.'

'D down to earth

'I indestructible

'A a friend to all

'N never lets you down

'E ever caring

'We're so sad to see you go.'

Same old, same old.

The paints stayed in their box along with the brushes for many weeks after our return home. Caring and coping became the only song to sing. Mum phoned me in a panic when I was still deciding where to hang the Spencer Tartt in our new house in Kinross.

'It's your Dad. You're going to have to come right away. He's taken something. He might not live more than a few days. How will I ever manage? I'm scared, Diane, without him.'

Given his job in environmental health, Dad could have selected from a range of deadly poisons. In the event, he must have acted on impulse, taking a large glass of whisky with a generous handful of tranquillisers. Mum's original dire forecast was quickly downgraded by the professionals, his stomach recovered from its forced emptying, and following review by the ward registrar, he was discharged from psychiatric admissions in Dundee, and lived on to reflect briefly and probably with little insight into his actions with the help of a psychiatrist from Sunnyside Hospital, Montrose. Reflect, he might have done a little. Talk about it to his family? – no.

'To find relief from a terrible state of mind' was all the reason he gave. He didn't return to work that year or any other year and at 64, filled his time thereafter walking long distances in the Angus countryside, having once read that physical fitness was hugely important in maintaining mental health.

Mum was a bag of nerves for a while. Rages, tempers, veiled threats had been one thing. Cool, withdrawn, quietly sad – that was different. She didn't know how to behave around him any more. Better to stay busy with the church, take her turn on the meals on wheels and go out most Thursdays with the theatre group. Just as long as his tea was ready at five on the dot and his paper on the coffee table by the fire. She wouldn't take any chances. Then she would prattle on about her day until he put on his specs and began wrestling with the crossword.

An accommodation.

I couldn't find the words to reach him although I would lie awake at night rehearsing openers.

'Still managing that climb up to the Airlie Monument? You really must be quite fit these days, Dad.' I could find those words.

'Can't imagine Jim McLean not being in charge at Tannadice any more now, can you? Golac's got a hard act to follow, don't you think?' Football was a safe topic and you might even get a few sentences in reply.

'How are you finding it, not working now Dad?' That was more likely to be answered sparingly with a 'getting used to it' or 'glad to see the back of that place. Too many changes in the offing – and not for the better either.'

Anything about the future, about where he saw his life going was dismissed as irrelevant – 'I'm retired now. I don't look for things like that, only a quiet life.'

Of feelings, or anything personal, these questions were avoided through close scrutiny of the sports pages or a sudden need to take in Mother's washing, after a lifetime of ignoring the rain ruining her Persil-white efforts.

Seems I could only resume my watching. This time for a real or imagined deepening of the depressive state – and only then through signs and not words. Or for possible triggers and it was difficult to know what these might be.

My other role was as reporter.

'He's much the same, Norma. You know how he tends to be – going off on his own most days. But at least he isn't sitting around getting miserable.'

'Actually he seems a bit brighter these days, Campbell. He came along to sports day to see the boys this year. Never thought I'd see the day really.'

Mum took to phoning me almost every night. Willie and I would take bets if the phone rang at or around 7pm. I would give a sigh, draw on my rapidly depleting caring resources and put on my kind and patient voice.

'Hi Mum. How's things?'

'Fine, fine. He seems quite bright today, but you just don't know, do you? It's such a relief to know you're there Diane. And not too far away if there's another emergency. Your dad always said how reliable you were.'

A house is not a home

1992 Kinross

Routines, patterns, preferences, choices. Conscious, unconscious. Learned, innate. Beneficial or detrimental. To whom or for whom? At the time, you just do – and keep doing. Until you're forced to confront your actions, seek to understand them, maybe change the way you do things. Make it all conscious. Or is that possible?

I read somewhere 'She began her adult life for the fourth time at 45.' Well at 39 I would have dismissed that as smart posturing. Or the result of too much navel-gazing. There was too much to do, the focus was 'out there', not in here.

We had found a brand new house to buy in Kinnesswood, just about six miles or twelve minutes from Kinross. I'd wondered if we were taking a chance – buying. What if the next job was in Baku or Almati? But at 15, 13, 10 and eight it really was time the kids had a settled home and the security of knowing which school they would attend for the foreseeable future. They quickly learned that the locals were not interested in hearing about life in Jeddah, or about their friends from 57 different lands. Skateboards were fine. Forget the Toronto Blue Jays and the Chicago Bulls – it was football, Rangers preferably, not basketball or baseball that counted. Bon Jovi, George Michael and Axl Rose apparently had worldwide appeal, but the turquoise surfing tee-shirts didn't fit with the grunge look. So shopping trips to Edinburgh were a priority. Fitting-in was everything. The kids did it almost effortlessly.

Seasoned campaigner maybe but it still takes time to make a house a home. I busied myself for several months, unpacking, sorting out which clothes would still be wearable and boxing the rest, hanging and then moving pictures when the summer light threatened to bleach them. Set myself projects – sort out all the photos from Jeddah and put them in albums, gather up all the videos and log them in a book so that we know where they are when the kids lend them out. Put the address book onto our newly acquired computer in preparation for Christmas. The question – why? – occasionally raised its head above the parapet of consciousness. But not for long. I was creating or recreating our life so that house McDonald felt like home. So that location was secondary to familiarity, order and warmth.

And of course there were the nightly calls from Mother.

Patricia always had a plan for where she was aiming and how to get there. Alix followed a principle – enjoy life to the max! Carys aimed upwards and wouldn't stop till she reached the top. Nancy knew what she wanted – husband and kids, horses, home and job – and worked hard to have it. Lesley was happy if Jonathan was. I was just always there – for anyone who needed me.

I'd have plenty to share at Nancy's party but by the time of our planned reunion in 1994 my stories about Jeddah might be old hat and I'd have nothing new to add. It wouldn't be enough simply to have organised it all.

Endless Love

Nancy's party December 1993 – 15th wedding anniversary

Nancy caught sight of Angus carrying the big silver tray, laden with full wine glasses, all gleaming red under the conservatory lights. He was striding confidently towards his grandfather, in an elegant style reminiscent of Michael, she thought. The old man was half-slumped in his wheelchair, which his nurse had parked next to the flowering cactus, close enough for him to legitimately be 'in' the party, but far enough away should he start performing.

The hub of conversation dulled around her as she focussed in on the scene unfolding. Angus's face was a picture of concentration, his brown arms bearing the tray strongly. So far, at least, he didn't appear to have spilled any of its contents.

The boy bent over his grandfather, holding the tray out to one side, as if to whisper something in his ear. A gnarled hand reached out for a glass, but had some trouble grasping it, almost knocking it over in the process, had not the boy intervened with the speed of a viper, and saved it. Angus put the tray down at a safe distance from the chair, and together they managed to get the glass to his grandfather's mouth, and tip some of the contents inside, a feat which seemed to please, if the wide grin on the old man's face was anything to go by.

If the nurse sees that she'll flay him! Nancy thought, whilst being under no illusion that Angus had been put up to the job – an earlier request no doubt.

'Be circumspect, Angus; those wretched hawks'll be watching I don't touch the demon drink. Damn women. Bloody doctors and their bloody pills. Pah!'

She could just imagine it. He didn't mellow any with age, nor with sickness either, her father-in-law. He'd go to his grave moaning and cursing – why change the habit of a lifetime? Yet he'd always had a soft spot for Angus, and Angus had managed, more than any of the other grandchildren, to forge a bond between them. She felt swelled with pride, yes, that was it, pride. She was proud of her son; of his ability to lighten up his grandfather, of the way he conducted himself, despite the difficulties of being an age where he straddled childhood and manhood.

Amy ran over then, her long brown hair flaring out behind, her pretty face flushed, her lips in a pout. 'Mummy, Daddy says one glass of champagne is enough for any twelve-year old but I'm okay, I really am, not drunk or anything, not like Grandmother's getting. *Please* can I have another one? Angus has had two, I've seen him, so why can't I have another one as well?'

Nancy smiled wearily. 'If Daddy says no then it's no, and please don't go around making insinuations about your grandmother, better to keep your opinions to yourself.'

'But she *is* drunk honestly, look! She's waving her arms around again and talking ever so loudly, even though nobody's deaf, well, only grandfather, but he's over there and so she's not talking to him.'

Her daughter's lips were set in an act of defiance. Diplomacy was definitely required.

'Look – I tell you what. You can have another glass once people have gone home, okay? I'll save you one, promise. And please be nice to your grandmother, she has a lot to cope with.'

Another flounce and Amy was gone, back into the mingling crowd, to tease and flirt, testing out her attractiveness, craving reactions. Awful. Had Nancy been like that at the same age? She couldn't remember being so, but things were different these days, children seemed to be growing up too soon.

It will be make-up next, then the pursuit of boys, in the time-honoured fashion of teenage girls. Where have they come from – all these children of mine? Where have the years gone?

It is six years since Camilla's birth, she notes, and just what has she done in that time? Angus and Amy – one minute babies, now this – transformed into teenagers; confident yet insecure, demanding yet selfish, polite yet also more than capable of answering back, but they were loving still, each in their own way; and their bodies – sprouting in all kinds of places. In them she constantly saw glimpses of their past childhood, and flashes of the people they might become, and she would wonder. What if she hadn't met Michael? Then they wouldn't exist, any of them, not as they were. But she had met him, and married him after all, hence here they were today, celebrating fifteen years of marriage. 'Please join us on the occasion of our Crystal Anniversary', the invitations to the party had said.

Michael had presented her with a beautiful gemstone necklace that morning, which now hung around her neck. The children had given her matching earrings, which made her look a little overdressed, perhaps, in the middle of the afternoon in the conservatory, but no matter, it was her day and be damned, she would dress up for the occasion and strut her stuff.

'You look gorgeous,' he'd said, kissing her before the guests began to arrive.

'You don't look half bad yourself,' she'd replied. 'Just wait until I get you alone later.'

She was lucky, so lucky to have all this; she sometimes pinched her arms to remind herself it was real. Husband, children, house, horses, dogs, the countryside, the social life. Even her job. She loved it all, every bit of it. Although, if she was to be honest, it *had* seemed as if she had to try harder and harder recently to balance it all, keep all the plates spinning, find the energy to be there for everyone, all the time. Never a quiet moment. But would she want it any other way? No, of course she wouldn't.

'A penny for your thoughts?' her father appeared at her side offering a plate of sandwiches.

'Oh, just thinking how lucky I am, Dad. Michael, the kids, the house, you know, my family around me today, friends too, people making an effort to get here for me. I'm having such a lovely day.'

'Well you deserve it love. You've worked hard for it. And despite any misgivings your mother and I might have had about Michael in the beginning we've none now, none at all, I hope you realise that by now. It's obvious to us how happy you are. Let's drink to the next fifteen years eh?'

A rare speech from her father, a man of few words. Nancy wondered if the champagne had gone to his head a little.

She looked at him fondly, noticing how much he'd aged in recent years and resolved to make an effort to get down to see them more often.

'Yes, let's!' She raised her glass and clinked it against his. 'To the next fifteen years then.'

* *

'Willie, for God's sake, do up your tie!' I looked around to make sure no-one had noticed Willie remove his jacket, drape it over a chair and then begin to undo the knot of his new navy and grey striped silk tie. 'And put your jacket back on,' I urged him.

'What for? I'm overheating here, trussed up like a prize turkey. It must be all the hot air this bunch of toffs is spouting.'

'They're not toffs! They're just county people, well bred, that's all. And lower your voice, please. Everyone'll hear what you're saying.' I couldn't believe he would act in such an objectionable fashion. Maybe it was the champagne. He wasn't used to champagne – a poof's drink he called it.

'Well, they look like toffs and sound like toffs to me. Who else wears Paddington Bear checked trousers that *you* know? And who in our circle has been in the Guards or rides with the hunt?'

'Stop it. That's just mindless stereotyping. They're a perfectly nice bunch of people, if you take the trouble to get to know them. You like Michael all right don't you? He's born and bred county.' I tried to take the heat out of the discussion. It didn't seem right to be squabbling at an anniversary celebration.

'He's okay, I suppose. But then he's got Nancy to keep him right. Although she's becoming a bit of a toff herself these days, a fully paid-up member of the green welly brigade. It's only because of her that I'm here you know, or that I'll stay till the end. I'd rather be back home watching the game on tv. And I'm taking this tie off whether *you* like it or not.'

He removed it with a flourish and stuffed it in his jacket pocket, still hanging over the back of the antique nursing chair, then smirked at me defiantly.

'You're looking a bit flushed yourself. Or is that embarrassment at your working class husband?'

He could be an obstinate pig on occasions. But there was no point in making a scene. I wouldn't win – I never did. So I swallowed my retort and turned to make a fuss of the nearest Labrador, Minty. I could count on *her* adoration.

Then I moved off to find Lesley. If he was going to behave badly, I would pretend he wasn't with me. She'd been collared by Nancy's Mum to give her a bit of advice on her health problems. It didn't matter that Lesley was a midwife. She was married to a doctor and must know all about high blood pressure.

'And I was just saying to my neighbour, these tablets make me right tired, they do. Is that what I should expect, love?'

'I wouldn't like to say Mrs Thorpe. But let me ask my husband when I get home. And I'll give you a ring later. Will that do?'

'Oh you're a fine lass. And where is your husband today? I'd have thought he'd have been with you. A nice day out with old friends.'

Lesley looked at me to intervene and save her from the inquisition.

'Ah Lesley. Jonathan was looking for you. Something about a phone call I think. Sounded like it might be important.'

'You'd better be off then dear. I'll see you later maybe.' Mrs Thorpe moved off to attach herself to some other unsuspecting guest.

Lesley and I made for the remains of the buffet in the dining room, plonked ourselves down at the table, and consoled ourselves with mini profiteroles.

'Where is Nick anyway?' I enquired.

'Another blasted regional meeting. A whole weekend this time. Why he couldn't have given this one a miss I really don't know. He'll not be interested in my news either, when I get home. He always switches off after five minutes, so I don't bother even telling him anymore. And as for anniversaries, my fifteenth passed without mention.'

Her sadness was tangible; I wasn't quite sure how to reply.

'Och he'll just be busy I expect. A doctor's job is never done. But everything's all right at home, Lesley, isn't it?'

'Oh I suppose so. I just feel a bit down seeing Michael and Nancy like a pair of lovebirds over there. Don't you?'

I looked over wistfully.

'Wouldn't it be lovely to have someone look at you like that – all soft and loving? I wonder if there's a magic formula – or did she just land lucky?'

Glad tidings

Each year the Christmas cards come without fail; a mixed bunch, although each sender is easily recognisable by the handwriting, and the postmark on the envelope.

Always first to arrive, at the beginning of December, due to superior organisation and forward planning is Patricia's; written in her neat hand, with the address symmetrically balanced. She always sends charity cards of course, usually supporting Barnardos, or occasionally Help the Aged. Her greeting is the same each year; 'With love and best wishes for a wonderful Christmas and a joyous New Year. God Bless, Patricia, Trevor and Claire.'

Lesley also sends charity cards, most often from the Scottish Society for Prevention of Cruelty to Animals, or the Brooke Hospital for Sick Animals, in Egypt, although she has never been, and is not likely to go, to Egypt. She pens a short update note on each card, in her careful, round handwriting, and includes a personal greeting to each of the other girls. Each year, as she writes her cards, Lesley feels a wave of nostalgia, and is prone to shedding a tear or two. More than a few cards have been spoiled over the years, as the tears splash onto the ink, making small blotches and rendering the words unreadable. She has kept all the girls' cards in a special box. She doesn't know why she does this, but it is perhaps because she can't bear to throw them away, as if by doing that she would be destroying the tie between herself and the others.

Carys's Christmas cards are always expensive-looking. She and JJ design them each year and have a printer produce them. There is usually a photograph of them on the front, and a fancy verse inside, with their contact details printed in smart type. She must have a lot of cards to send each year because she rarely finds time to write anything extra inside them, not even a personalised "To …" If she does write anything it is about the most significant feature of her year in America. Things like: 'Got tenure at Walton!'; 'JJ's new book sold 5,000 copies in first two months!', or 'I learnt to fly this year, working on getting my pilot's licence! – Concorde here we come!' They seem, to the girls, other-worldly somehow, except to Alix, long accustomed to a more exotic existence.

Alix's cards come with brightly coloured postage stamps which are highly prized by Nancy's daughter, Camilla, for her stamp collection. So far Camilla has stamps from Bali, Cyprus, Egypt, Jordan, Saudi Arabia and Singapore. The cards are always interesting, with the greeting in the native language of the country, wherever Alix is currently living or holidaying for the festive season.

The cards that Diane sends are of good quality, taken from a Marks and Spencer box set, or the top range of some other high street retailer. Diane loves Christmas, her greetings are buoyant, full of cheer and hope for the year to come, concluding with 'Until the next time we meet, lots of love, Diane & family xxxxx.'

It is always touch and go whether Nancy will be organised enough to send cards that actually reach the girls *before* New Year. Usually she is working hard right up until Christmas Eve, and puts the cards through the office franking machine to catch the last post before she leaves. They are worth waiting for though, since they include a chatty, funny newsletter of the 'Robertson year', highlighting the ups and downs of her family's lives. As one reads it is hard to imagine how Nancy fits everything in and still manages to stay sane.

Lesley could tell them that there are ninety cards in her 'Dalmeny Girls' Christmas box, and that next year she will need to buy a bigger one. Meanwhile, she savours this year's messages:

'See you soon!!!!'

'Can't wait!!!'

'Why did we leave it so long?'

Let's get together

1994 Edinburgh

A six-bedroomed flat with a fully equipped kitchen, two bathrooms, secure entry, walkable distance from Haymarket and Princes Street, short lets available during off-season at £120 per night.

It was a safe option. There were 18 years, 11 children, three post graduate qualifications, six husbands, some rocky times and an undisclosed number of significant life events to catch up on – or take care to conceal. We would be comfortable back in Edinburgh. We'd be nostalgic, girlish, misty eyed, a bit reckless with the wine maybe. The focus would be on the past and we'd remember only the good bits. Yes – better to play safe.

That was 1994. I was just back from a couple of years living and working in the Middle East – full of something to talk about at last, having emerged from a long episode of half life, moving around with Willie's job, manacled by four young children, vegetating and sinking.

The six of us (Alix, Lesley, Nancy, Carys, Patricia and I) had been in touch with each other over the years in a way you might have predicted back in '76. Patricia and Lesley had met several times at an annual national church event in Carfin, both finding some solace in the traditions of their childhood faith. Carys had always rung Lesley and waxed lyrical for hours, when home on her annual trip from the States. Patricia and I had caught up over a lunch whenever I was home as long as it was during school holidays. Alix and I had picked up our friendship again overseas when she came along to my art class at Jeddah Wives. As for Nancy – over the years she'd become like another sister to me, but almost a stranger to the others.

I couldn't say it fell to me to organise the reunion. The truth is that I wanted to do it. Alix and I had found a new way of being friends in Jeddah. She had looked fantastic – all tanned and groomed and expensively dressed. If *she* had kept a journal she might have written that *Diane is obviously a dedicated mother but seems to have lost herself a bit along the way*. If I had read it, I probably would have agreed. We'd never been close in the flat days, and had probably disapproved of each other in a tight-lipped way. Alix was a social butterfly who fluttered in and out, brought a splash of colour and a scent of excitement, created a party atmosphere with a bottle of cheap wine and a loaf of French bread and held centre circle for as long as it pleased her. I was serious, anxious about putting in the hours to get a decent degree and unable to let myself go. If *we* could meet again as adults, enjoy our shared history as well as our differences and find in each other an easy way of being friends and even confidantes, then why not the others too?

We arranged the date around Carys. Apparently, she came over from the States for Christmas most years, with or without JJ her husband, and would have a few days to spare after seeing in the new year of 1994. Edinburgh was the obvious choice as most of the memories were there and it was reasonably central for all of us.

I had tried my best to make the travel arrangements as easy as possible for everyone – suggesting suitable trains, co-ordinating arrival times, identifying parking places – doing what I had always done – taking unnecessary responsibility for everyone else. They were all perfectly capable of getting to Edinburgh without any help from me. All *I* needed to do was make the short drive from Kinross early enough to arrive at the flat first. Alix would fly up from London, Carys from Wales, Lesley and Patricia would travel by train from Inverness and Dundee, and Nancy by car from Dolphinton. The best I could do was to have a note of all estimated arrival times so that I wouldn't worry about when they would all turn up.

My plan was that we would meet late Saturday afternoon at the flat. Everyone would bring something for a cold buffet, plus a bottle of wine, and then we'd spend the night catching up on all the news. Sunday breakfast would be coffee and croissants as it always was in Dalmeny Street, then we'd go for a walk around our old haunts, ending up in Henderson's for a late lunch before going home.

The letting agent let me check out the flat ahead of time and gave me maps to send out to the girls, accompanied with suggestions of things to bring (photos, a decent towel, warm clothes and a cheque for £20 to cover the rent), and an emergency contact number in case the worst happened. To Patricia's copy I attached a list of possible food and drink to produce, tagged it with a '*complete and pass on*' note. I knew what they'd say about me but I was too nervous to leave anything to chance.

With a few phone calls, I established that some of our old haunts would be open on the 5th January: The University chaplaincy centre, DHT refectory, Ensign Ewart's pub at the top of the High Street and The Purple Onion café. If we ran out of chat, we could always wander down memory lane.

There were a few more items to put in my bag which would increase the chances of a successful weekend – decent wine glasses, Abba tapes, a spare hairdryer and Belgian chocolates. Then I had to think about myself. Willie wasn't much help.

'Who will I be?'

'Don't be daft. Just be yourself.'

'How can I? Alix won't be the only one who looks better than ever.'

'Well, just make the best of yourself then. Get your hair dyed; get a new outfit – something like that black effort you wore to the PTA dance.'

'But I was all bumps and lumps in that.'

'Well, buy one of those Wonderbras and a girdle thing.'

'But should I go casual or smarten up a bit?'

'Christ, I don't know. Give Patricia a phone and see what she's wearing?'

'That's no help. She always wears Markies' stuff or running gear. I'll ask Susan what she thinks.'

My 16 year old daughter had a typical teenager's view of her (almost) 40 year old mother – past it, out of touch, well meaning but a *fashion disaster*. I decided against her suggestion of layered black with big jewellery and splashed out on faux suede trousers with a cream lambswool polo. The Wonderbra helped up top. The cut of the trousers provided an effective, albeit expensive, illusion of sleek below. I dived into the new hairdressers in Perth for a Diacolour before I lost my nerve, and asked the stylist to 'tidy it up a bit.' Willie's face was a picture of either surprise or shock but in any case it was too late to grow it back in, in the space of a week.

There was so much to worry about.

What if we have nothing to talk about? What if they don't like the flat or there isn't enough food?

Who's going to sleep where, and how will we decide? I wonder if Carys will still dominate and Lesley still mother everyone. What am I going to do when Alix ignores the no smoking sign?

Will everyone have changed? Will we still like each other? Will we still care?

Will we still be The Dalmeny Street Girls after all that's gone before?

We're together again

Edinburgh. January, 1994

The keys felt cold in my hand as I opened the locks on the flat door. A tingle of excitement passed through me, followed rapidly by a surge of anxiety.

What if it doesn't go well? Maybe it will all be a big disappointment. Will they blame me if it is?

I quickly pushed these thoughts out of my mind, and, breathing deeply in an effort to relax, I walked through the open door into the hallway, switching on all the lights as I went. The place looked lovely; bright and clean.

This will pass the Patricia test, I thought.

So far, so good; it was going to be fine. I felt better already and started to relax.

I plonked my heavy shopping bags in the kitchen and gazed around, taking it all in again. It was spacious, with a decent cooker and a breakfast bar with three stools down one side.

There'll be no fighting for places at that breakfast bar come the morning. I was conjuring up a picture of first thing the next day: Alix asleep, or having a fly cigarette with a cup of strong, black coffee in her own bedroom, Patricia putting us all to shame running down to Haymarket and back. That left the breakfast bar occupants as Nancy - sat silently nursing a hangover, Lesley – clutching a huge mug of tea, wittering away between slurps, and me. Me – doing what? Half listening, half worrying about how the morning would go no doubt.

All conjecture of course, I reminded herself, suddenly realising that my perceptions of how everyone was likely to behave were based on experiences that were eighteen years out of date. I gave out a big sigh.

I do hope we haven't changed too much; we might not get on as well as we used to.

Oh stop it! I brought my thoughts to an abrupt halt and gave myself a small pep-talk. One thing hadn't changed, for sure – my ability to worry so much and always think the worst was going to happen unless I'd planned every last detail. Willie was right – I really had to stop putting myself through this all the time.

I walked around the remaining rooms, taking in the décor and ambience as I went, with a train of thoughts running through my head.

How will we sort out who's going to sleep where? Should I allocate rooms or let it be a free-for-all?

I couldn't decide, but anyway, it didn't matter because there were more important things to do, like unpacking the bags, getting the wine into the fridge to cool and setting the table. An hour to go. Time was running out.

* *

The luggage carousel in Edinburgh Airport was packed full of bags off the 13.30 BA flight from London. She had been over-eager to grab her suitcase before it disappeared.

Goddamn it! Now what am I going to do?

Alix looked down in dismay at her broken nail, which was indeed ragged, in sore contrast to the perfect appearance of the other nine. There was nothing to be done other than go to the Ladies, file it down and hope no-one would notice.

'Caledonian Crescent please – number 26.' She settled herself into the back of the taxi and lit a cigarette. She was looking forward to seeing the girls again. It was lovely to be getting away from the London social whirl for a few days. She didn't think she'd miss the twins too much. The demands of two twelve-year-olds were so wearing – all that arguing, sulking and backchat – ugh. Gerald wasn't much better with them either.

You'd have thought given his job he'd at least bring home some diplomatic skills he could use on them to keep the peace.

The reality was that he didn't see much of the twins during the week, not by the time he got home from the office each evening. Actually, he didn't get much practice with them at all; secretly much to his relief.

The taxi driver thought she was 'a bit of all right', and tried to engage her in conversation all the way from the airport. Alix really couldn't be bothered with this but the poor driver didn't seem to realise he was failing miserably in his efforts to chat her up and find out what she was doing in Edinburgh, so he just kept up his patter.

The cab braked suddenly, jolting Alix out of her thoughts.

'Hey Jimmy! Get that bloody car out of my road you idiot! Did you see that? I have to put up with that shite all the time. Doctor says it's bad for my blood pressure.' He looked hard at Alix in his mirror, expecting a response. She gave him a half-smile then turned disinterestedly to look out of the window.

Not far to go now if my memory serves me well. Best find some money for this little man. A nice tip might cheer him up.

'Thanks hen, have a nice stay.'

'I will,' she replied, unfolding her long legs carefully and alighting out of the cab, suitcase and handbag in tow. She peered at the door.

Number 26, yes, that's it.

The buzzer made Diane jump. It couldn't be that time already, surely? She rushed to open the door, wondering which friend it would be. Alix glided through, offering her cheek.

'Diane, darling! So good to see you! You look just the same as you were in Jeddah. You haven't changed a bit.'

Diane wondered if that was supposed to be a compliment. Much to her annoyance, and uncharacteristically, she had always been unable to 'read' Alix properly.

'Alix! You look fabulous as usual. Come in, come in, you're the first to arrive. How was your journey?'

'Fine, all went to plan for once. Do you have any coffee? I'm dying for a cup!'

They settled down to chat, mugs in hand. It had been two years since they'd last met in Jeddah and there was a lot of catching up to do.

* *

Nancy was nearly ready now. Clothes, make-up, hair, all sorted. Just one more thing to check. She flicked open the compact and wiped away the excess powder from the mirror, then turned around so that her back was to the wardrobe's full-length mirror and held up the compact to get a good view of her rear.

This was the action she always performed last before going out. She wished she could stop doing it, as the reflection never failed to disappoint. It really didn't matter what she was wearing, her bum *always* looked too big.

A scene flashed into her consciousness. She was back at university, having a somewhat drunken conversation with her flatmate Diane in the toilet of the bar. Which parts of themselves would they change if they could? Say – they were able to have some magical plastic surgery?

'I'd have a nose job!' Diane had said emphatically, 'to get rid of this horrible lumpy bit on the top.'

Nancy had opened the door to the corridor. 'And I'd have my bum lifted and made smaller to get rid of all this fat,' she had said in a loud voice; just as the bloke from the folk club she'd been fancying like mad for months walked past. He'd obviously heard as he gave her a knowing smirk and disappeared rapidly through the gents' door.

Nancy had been mortified. 'Bugger! That's him put off me for good now. If he ever looks at me all he'll think about is my big, fat arse!'

She thought it strange how memories of nearly twenty years ago could surface so quickly and be so vivid. She smiled, contemplating.

Diane never did get the nose job, and I've still got a ruddy big bum. Never mind, my face is lovely, my best feature.

She had always taken great pride in her face. Nancy closed the compact and slowly turned around a half circle to face the wardrobe mirror, at the same time moving closer to it, examining her face critically.

Yes, still pretty, she concluded, although drooping a bit and those little bags under my eyes are a bit worrying …

At thirty-nine I can expect that, she reminded herself.

'Time to go and party!' she sang out-loud, which seemed to have the desired effect of boosting her confidence. She threw the compact into her make-up bag inside her handbag, picked the whole lot up then trotted down the stairs to get the Landrover keys.

'Bye everyone!' She poked her head around the lounge door. 'Don't forget to give the ponies a last hay net each before bed and let the dogs out. I've left all the emergency numbers on a list pinned on the noticeboard in the kitchen.'

'You've already told us that twice Mummy, just go and enjoy yourself, we'll all be fine,' Angus replied confidently.

'I'm going to sort the ponies tonight Mummy,' Amy chipped in, 'and Camilla is going to feed them in the morning.'

'Well Camilla, watch out for Domino's teeth when you give him his bowl, you know what he's like with you,' Nancy warned.

'I will,' chirped Camilla.

Nancy still worried about her youngest daughter being on her own with the ponies. She was a good little rider but at only six years old she didn't have much savvy with them on the ground and they often took advantage of her, causing all manner of knocks and bruises. Camilla didn't seem to mind though, always going back for more. She was a tough child, *just like I was*, Nancy thought affectionately.

'It would be better if Amy went with you, you know,' she tried another angle.

'No way,' Amy whined. 'I'm not doing them tonight *and* in the morning as well; that's just not fair.'

Nancy could see that if she wasn't careful she would start them all arguing and that would make her feel even more anxious about going out.

'Right then, you all just sort it out to suit yourselves. I'll phone you tomorrow morning sometime to check everything is okay. Mind you tell your father when he comes in that supper is all prepared in the fridge. You just have to pop it in the oven.'

'You've told us that twice as well,' Angus said wearily. 'Bye-bye.' He got up and gave his Mother a big hug. 'Go have fun! – you need to get out more!'

Nancy kissed Amy and Camilla goodbye, although they seemed to be more interested in the horse racing on Grandstand than their mother's departure. She experienced a strange feeling of being superfluous. That hadn't happened before.

Best I leave now whilst the going is good, she decided.

The roads were quiet. Nancy's thoughts started to focus on the evening ahead.

Just as well I know where I'm going, but I can't remember the exact street where this flat is supposed to be. I'll just have to drive around a bit when I get close to it. Probably nowhere to park either.

She was feeling a little tired and hoped it would pass off once she arrived. This weary feeling appeared every Friday night, just after returning home from work. It really annoyed her, as usually all she was good for then was a few glasses of wine, a take-away and a slump in front of the television. Fortunately she'd managed to pick herself up this morning. She swung onto the dual carriageway that would lead towards Edinburgh city centre.

Not far now. I'm really looking forward to this; it's been so long since I've seen Alix, and I'm even looking forward to seeing Patricia again.

She smiled. A parking space materialised just a street away from where she was going. As she walked to the flat her heart felt as if it were beating just a little bit quicker than normal. She needed a large glass of wine, and a big comfy chair to collapse into.

The door was yanked open with a flourish.

'Nancy!' Alix's face was beaming at her excitedly. 'Come in, your wine is chilled and ready for you darling!'

They embraced and Alix danced Nancy down the hallway to the kitchen, where Diane was taking pizza out of wrappers and putting them onto baking tins.

'Nancy!' Diane stopped what she was doing to give Nancy a hug. 'It's great to see you again so soon. All still well?'

'Okay the last time I saw them,' Nancy grinned. 'They seemed to be glad to get rid of me actually. Angus told me to "go have fun"; oh, and "that I ought to get out more". So I'm not going to worry about them this weekend, Michael can hold fort for once, it won't hurt him.'

'Quite right,' Alix joined in. 'We girls need to have a breather every now and again, and anyway, our men will appreciate us more on our return. By the time I get back after seeing my mother in Aberdeen as well next week, Gerald will be gagging for it!'

'Some things don't change then, Alix!' Nancy smiled. 'Where's that glass of wine you promised me on my way in?'

* *

As the train left Inverness, Lesley caught a glimpse of her reflection in the carriage window. It wasn't worth lingering over, she felt, so quickly turned away, pulling her novel from her bag and opening it at the inserted marker. Chapter 2, Endangered Species.

I should have brought a lighter one as well. This books threatens to be a little bit dark.

But she hadn't, because it had been a push to get ready as it was by the time she'd packed Jonathan's bag and taken him over to Nick's parents. *And* she'd had to turn back half way there because he'd forgotten his teddy. That's why she had left her hair appointment to the last minute, and ended up with the most junior stylist of 'Luscious Locks', who was the only one available that morning.

Her new 'look' had not turned out quite how she'd envisaged, and yet again, she was disappointed in the outcome. It didn't make her look younger, or more sophisticated, and there were some uneven bits on one side. She should have said something to the girl, but she knew she was too much of a coward to complain.

So she had said 'Yes, it looks lovely, thanks,' when the girl had held up the mirror to show the back of her hair, swinging it around both sides to get the views there as well. Lesley had hoped her face didn't register her dismay, as the girl was so sweet and friendly, telling Lesley all about her family and boyfriend troubles as she busily washed, snipped and dried. It didn't sound as if she needed any more upset in her life.

Lesley had handed over the money at the till, and then given the girl a handsome tip.

Why did I do that? God, I am such a wimp! All I had to say was it doesn't look quite right here, could you just even it up a bit, and I couldn't even say that!

She was prone to having dialogues with herself. Whatever the salon, whoever the stylist, it always seemed to be the same story, replayed almost word-perfect, time after time, she reflected. She imagined telling this story to the girls that evening and hoped that if she did, they would think it was funny.

'So they ask you, "What are you having done today?" You answer, describing the hairstyle you want to have, and show them the picture in the stylebook that's closest to the image you have in your head of how you want your hair to look. Then they say "Okay, I can do that, but you'll need to blow dry it / scrunch it / straighten it / roller it to give it height / put gel on it", or whichever one applies to the style you're still pointing at in the book, as your heart begins to sink a bit, and you wonder whether you'll ever be able to get it to look like that yourself the next time you wash it. Well, of course, the answer is no – you won't. But they never tell you that, do they?

'So then the hair cutting starts, at which point the girl will say, "It's quite fine isn't it?", and you reply, "Yes, it's always been a bit difficult." At the blow-drying stage the girl will follow up with "Oh, it's got a natural wave hasn't it?" as she puts some more gel on it. If she has to reach for the curling tongs to finish it off then you know you're really in trouble and you'll have no chance of getting it to look anything like the picture ever again. It will be back to the elastic band and two slides.'

Lesley had brought these items with her, just in case she needed them after she washed her hair the following morning …

One of her dreams was to be able to find a hairdresser who could make her hair look *exactly* like the picture. Now that would be a real find.

Did such a paragon of tresses exist, she wondered?

Probably not, since she had yet to come across one in all her 39 years. Her hair had started to go grey on the sides now, compounding the problem of trying to keep it looking nice. Not that anyone cared much about it, she felt, except herself, that was. Nick hadn't even made a comment when she'd kissed him goodbye.

Had he even noticed?

It was hard to tell these days if he noticed anything about her.

Trying not to dwell on those thoughts, Lesley returned to her book and started to read, immersing herself in a world of other people's lives, instead of her own. She was hoping she could keep cheerful over the weekend, and get into the spirit of it all. It was too late to back out now, although part of her wanted to get off and catch the next train heading north.

Sitting opposite was an old lady, smartly dressed, with various bags dispersed about her person. She had placed a flask and cup in the small amount of space left over on the table, and had opened a copy of *The Scots Magazine* in front of her. Now she looked as if she wanted to start up a conversation with someone, peering over her glasses and smiling at Lesley, and other passengers around her.

Don't pick me, prayed Lesley. I've had enough of making polite conversation with strangers for one day; actually, enough for a lifetime after this week on the wards.

By the time they reached Aviemore station the page of *The Scots Magazine* had still to be turned and there had been three separate attempts at engaging Lesley in talk.

'How far are you going, dear? I'm going to Edinburgh to stay with my daughter for the weekend, she's just moved house so she's going to need a bit of help to sort it all out. That's what mothers are for, isn't it? Helping out when needed.'

'Yes, of course.'

'Would you like a cup of my tea? I've got a spare cup in my bag. The prices they charge on the train are ridiculous, don't you think? Always best to come prepared, so I have. I've some cake too, made it myself. Would you like a slice?'

'No thank-you, although that's very kind of you to offer.'

(She'd actually been looking forward to a cup of coffee, but now she could hardly buy one off the trolley having refused the tea, could she?)

'Do you live in Inverness? I've lived there for the last thirty years, moved up from Cumbria to run a B&B when my husband had to retire early through ill-health. He's dead these last ten years now, God bless him, but we had some lovely times. I sold up after he died; "Cairnforth" it was, have you heard of it? We had two stars! Clean as a new pin, everywhere! But I didn't want to carry on after Bill died, so I bought a lovely bungalow instead. Two bedrooms, so my family can come and stay. It's got a small garden, which I can manage myself, and lovely neighbours.'

'That's nice you're so happy there.'

Lesley rose and went to the toilet; she didn't actually need to go, but she *did* feel a need to get some peace. She took her time, and then went to the buffet car to sneak a coffee and a sandwich. Thankfully it was further on down the train; she didn't have to pass her own seat to get to it. All the time she held the hope that the old woman would have latched onto someone else by the time she returned .

By the time they reached Edinburgh Lesley was feeling very sorry for the woman's daughter, whoever she might be. A whole weekend of that would drive even a saint to distraction. She would look *very* carefully at the passengers on the return journey on Sunday before choosing her seat. Old ladies and mothers with young children were most definitely to be avoided. Another woman her age might be a safe bet, or a man would do, just as long as they left her alone.

* *

The doorbell went again.

'Next!' shouted Alix, 'Who's going to open it?'

'I'll go,' Diane volunteered. 'How about you carry on sorting out the food?'

'Bummer,' Alix laughed, 'That's the servant's job where I come from!'

Diane was in her element. It was all going to plan, and she couldn't sense any tension or awkwardness to dampen the proceedings. She opened the door to find Lesley standing outside.

'Hi Diane! I made it! You look great! Who's here already, tell me!'

'Oh, it's good to see you Lesley. Alix and Nancy are in there, we're still waiting for Patricia – she's coming by train too. Then it will nearly be the *Dalmeny Street Girls* all together again, just like the old days!'

Alix and Nancy appeared from the kitchen and met Lesley half way down the hall.

'Who shall I hug first?' Lesley giggled.

'Both of us!' Alix replied, throwing her arms around Lesley, with Nancy quickly following suit.

Diane felt rather emotional and turned back towards the kitchen to pour a glass of wine for the newcomer and one for herself. The spread on the kitchen table was shaping up a treat, and the breakfast bar was now fully occupied.

'Look at us, started drinking already and it's only 5 o'clock!' Nancy laughed.

'That never bothered you before Nancy!' Alix teased. 'Please don't tell me you've become a fuddy-duddy now you've joined the landed gentry!'

'She doesn't look fuddy-duddy to me,' Lesley remarked. 'I'm wondering just how you've managed to stay looking so fit and toned, Nancy, when some of us have been fighting off the pounds over the years and not entirely successfully.'

Some of us? She must mean me as well.

Diane's colour rose and inside she felt a wave of embarrassment, or was it anger? She tried not to dwell on it. Lesley couldn't possibly have meant to be hurtful about her size, that wasn't in her nature, it was just a careless remark, surely. Nancy made a good job of trying to change the topic quickly.

'Oh, it's all the country air, mucking out and dog walking that keeps me fit. I also use some lovely organic skincare products that Michael gets from a business contact. I'll show them to you afterwards if you like.'

Alix as always, had an opinion on all things to do with beautification.

'I don't think you can beat Clinique actually, and a good professional facial and massage at least once a month.'

'That's all right if you have the time and money,' popped out of Diane's mouth. She instantly regretted the remark. But she needn't have worried; Alix didn't take offence easily.

* *

Meanwhile Patricia was having a dreadful train journey from Dundee. Trevor had insisted he drive her to the station. It wasn't often he volunteered to be so helpful, so Patricia wondered why he was wanting to make so sure she was safely ensconced on the train. She was lucky to have caught it in the first place what with the road works outside the station and the apparently brainless ticket clerk who just couldn't seem to operate the ticket machine properly. His inefficiency was really irritating Patricia and she had to try hard to stop herself going into Headteacher mode and telling him what he should do.

The clerk had just extracted the ticket as the tannoy announced 'the 16 hundred hours train from Aberdeen to Edinburgh Waverley is now standing at platform 2, calling at Leuchars, Kirkcaldy, Inverkeithing, Haymarket and Edinburgh Waverley.'

She grabbed the ticket out of his hand, picked up her suitcase and sprinted easily down the stairs, managing to leap onto the train just before the doors closed.

It was very crowded and there seemed to be no empty seats. She groaned inwardly.

Looks like I'm going to have to stand all the way to Edinburgh. Why on earth didn't I ask Trevor to drive me all the way?

She knew she would need to calm down to get into the right frame of mind for the weekend. Stop this temper rising. She was aware she wasn't good when things started to go out of control, as they frequently did in the world outside her own school. The railways, however, were particularly annoying; journeys never seemed to go smoothly. She looked across at another woman who had put her suitcase down on the floor, using it as a makeshift seat and who was now calmly reading her newspaper.

Why don't other people seem to be fazed by all this inconvenience?

'Next stop Leuchars,' the guard announced merrily over the tannoy.

Oh Heavens, she moaned under her breath, thinking, just look at the platform – it's full of St Andrews University students, all going south. They can't possibly all squeeze onto this train, it's bound to be in breach of the rules. Surely some people will get off here to make way for the new ones getting on?

'Henry! Shove over a bit – I need more space for the guitar,' a plummy male voice rang out.

'I can't love,' Henry replied, 'there's nowhere to shove myself over to. You'll just have to sit on me – again.'

'Aren't you ever satisfied Henry?' the first student retorted.

Oh no. Patricia could feel a creeping dread starting up inside her stomach. The group of students had clearly been drinking and some of them must have 'come out' a long time ago. She knew she was going to struggle with all this – she had never been comfortable in the company of gay men.

I hope to God Claire doesn't turn out like these arrogant yobs. I couldn't bear to have a daughter like that.

Maybe she should try and find somewhere else on the train to stand, but there probably wasn't a space anywhere. If the situation didn't improve by Kirkcaldy, *then* she would move.

* *

The lively conversation in the flat was suddenly interrupted by the doorbell ringing again.

'My turn to get it!' Nancy jumped up. 'Now look lively girls, ship shape and Bristol fashion, here comes Patricia!'

Take it back

It took only half an hour before they felt the years rolling back. All eighteen of them, then the old group familiarities could descend once more.

Five women. Catching up eagerly with each other's life events. The satisfying chink of glasses, the clatter of knives and forks on plates. Easy conversation, punctuated by bubbly laughter and the odd raucous shriek, as is the want of women getting together for a good time, especially when the booze is plentiful.

Diane's Belgian chocolates melting in smiling, lipsticked mouths; sticky fingers popping in and out of the chocolate box. Purr-like murmurs of contentment at the rich, extravagant flavours. Photographs passed back and forth in no apparent order – husbands, children, parents, pets, houses, gardens, holidays. Questions asked, answers given. Stories of family successes, incidents, hints of difficulties.

All ground-clearing for the reminiscences that were to come.

At least – that would be the interpretation of the earlier part of the reunion if one were wearing rose-tinted spectacles.

Whilst elements of this cosy picture were undoubtedly true, it is also fair to say that there were significant undercurrents, whose originators were attempting, for the sake of geniality, to keep well-controlled.

With proceedings underway, Diane's organisational anxiety had been supplanted by a renewed surge of embarrassment – or was it resentment – over her appearance. The faux suede trousers and cream lambswool polo over which she had long agonised were now doing nothing for her confidence given the stark realisation that she was at least one dress size larger than the curvaceous Lesley, *two* bigger than athletic Nancy and svelte Alix, and all of *three* more than tin-ribs Patricia. She felt huge – staid and frumpy; plus, now she'd drunk a few glasses in quick succession, another form of discomfort had arrived; she was becoming hot and sticky. She should have gone for the layered black with big jewellery, just as Susan had suggested, shouldn't she?

Why do I always get it wrong? And whose fault is it, if I'm being honest, that I'm the size I am?

Alix had got nicely into her stride from the off. She really and truly had been looking forward to this girlie weekend, such a rare event in her calendar, and a welcome interlude to the tour of duty in London. Now she was here she was damn well going to make the most of it – and so would they all – she'd make sure of that. Her first sip of alcohol was accompanied by an habitual involuntary reflex – the stretch for her handbag and its most important contents – after the purse and make-up bag – her treasured cigarette case; gold, initialled A.E.F, and matching lighter. The case was always almost full, replenished furtively from the packet of Benson and Hedges stowed away in an inner compartment of her handbag. Flicking it open with her left hand, Alix took a cigarette deftly from the middle with her right hand, placed it carefully between her lips, then substituted the case with the lighter. One more second, a quick snap of the clasp and the flame would bring the cigarette to life.

'Sorry, Alix,' Diane intervened. 'This is a no-smoking apartment, and I've signed the contract on behalf of us all to say we'll uphold that.'

'Diane – you cannot be serious.' Alix looked genuinely shocked, her hands suspended in mid action, the lighter poised three inches from her face. She turned to Nancy – her old smoking buddy, fag-scrounger par excellence, hoping for back-up. 'Nancy – did you know that?'

Nancy cleverly ignored the question.

'I think she is serious,' she said firmly. 'But that's okay for me – I gave up ten years ago, never touched one since.'

Lesley was, by now, feeling and looking acutely embarrassed, praying that someone would sort this out and not get her involved, whilst Patricia, who hated smoking with a vengeance, and had been worried about how she'd cope with it over the weekend, was quick to spring to Diane's aid.

'I don't think we can risk losing the deposit, Alix. There's already extra money for each of us to pay with Carys dropping out at the last minute. For once, it looks like we'll all have to obey the rules.'

Alix could have sworn this was said with some smugness, but what the hell, no point starting something she'd only regret later.

'God! Looks like I'm well and truly outnumbered here, so if nobody minds I'll just go outside to smoke this.'

She fluttered her eyelashes rapidly in an expression of annoyance, jumped to her feet and flounced off towards the doorway, stopping just long enough to turn her head around over her shoulder, to shout, with an affected prissiness, 'If that's not breaking the rules of course. So you just carry on without me for five.'

Patricia, having recovered from the irritation of her journey, was now, at the mention of Carys, reminded of another source of annoyance, her no-show. She asked Diane to confirm how much extra they'd need to pay, and how she'd like the money, then launched into,

'So why couldn't she have let us know sooner that she had to drop out? This whole weekend was planned around when she could be available. There were plenty of other dates that would have suited me better, with all the marking I've got to finish by this coming Monday.'

It was probably the pressure of this, rather than any intended bitchiness toward Carys that prompted Patricia's remark, but the damage had been done, in Lesley's eyes.

Quick to nip this one in the bud, Diane suggested that now was as good a time as any to watch the video Carys had sent via Lesley, hoping it would resurrect some sisterly feelings to their absent number.

The video. An offering from Carys in lieu of a personal appearance. A way of making her presence felt whilst giving a brief taster of highlights of her life in America.

With Alix back in the fold, Nancy topped up the glasses whilst Diane loaded the machine and they all settled back in the sofas.

* *

'Hiya girls!' boomed the figure in the floor-length black dress. 'This is Professor Carys Lloyd-Jones, yes, I did say Professor! Sending love and greetings from the U ... S ... of A.'

[pan out to include background of Walton buildings and lawns]

'Sorry I can't be there for you all. If there was any way I could have managed it then I would have come, you know that, but there are greater powers than me in this hallowed institution and they've been invoked from on high, commanding me to be here for the Faculty review, or face dire consequences.'

[hands raised above head, head and eyes tilted upwards to the sky]

Diane hardly heard a word Carys was saying. Instead she was transfixed on the figure-hugging black dress, Carys's ample bosom and most definite midriff bulge. *She must be a size 16 if ever I saw one*, Diane thought, sensing a surge of satisfaction, then feeling ashamed at the recognition of it.

'Doesn't she sound American!' ventured Nancy, not wanting to comment on what they had all obviously noticed. 'But the Welsh lilt is still in there. Her accent sounds really strange now, don't you think?'

The next camera shot was of Carys's office, starting from the professorial nameplate, then panning around the luxurious room, finally alighting on the bookcase, and the numerous volumes written by Carys and JJ.

[close up of book spines, then pan to Carys sitting at desk]

'So, as you can see – all the hard work over the years has brought me fame and fortune *[throaty laugh]* well, not quite fortune, but we're working on it I'll have you know!'

[change of location to house, large colonial type, wide lawn, triple garage, in through front door to large living room, Carys standing in front of fireplace, wearing jeans, cowboy boots and voluminous flowing shirt down to her thighs]

'Why don't you come and see us soon? You're always welcome – anytime – just phone first to make sure we're not off gadding about to a conference. It's a great place for a holiday.

[pan to swimming pool, then tennis court in the back garden]

'New York's not far away, and we've a small cabin up country in the reserve. JJ says Hi! JJ, say Hi to the girls!'

[JJ's voice in background "Hiya girls! How're yah all doing?"]

'Here's someone you'd like to meet, Lesley!'

[shot of cat walking across kitchen unit]

And so it went on for another 10 minutes, ending with:

'So – until we meet again, I love you all, remember to keep in touch, now. And have a *wonderful* time in Edinburgh. To the Dalmeny Street Girls!'

[shot of Carys in trouser suit raising glass of wine. The End.]

It might have been cheesy but Lesley loved it. Her old pal made good. Up the Welsh! Seeing Carys all happy like that had made her feel tearful. Never mind that Carys had got a bit fat.

'Well!' exclaimed Patricia, 'she certainly seems happy. Hasn't she done well for herself?'

'Just like the cat that's got the cream,' said Nancy, laughing. 'OTT of course, but that's her, isn't it?'

'She seems to me to have got everything she ever wanted. Professor indeed,' snorted Alix. 'You have to hand it to her – she was always the bright one.'

Diane had laughed along with the rest of them, enjoying the scenes, despite thinking that it seemed all a bit 'other-worldly'. She stood up with the intention of turning off the video and putting on an Abba tape.

'Now – here's a question for us girls.' Alix had assumed an aura of largesse, as if she had something eminently precious to bestow. 'What about us then? Have *we* got everything we ever wanted?'

A very good question, but not, given the ensuing silence, one that the others would necessarily like to answer.

Diane walked over to the TV, bent down to change the video, turned her head back towards them smiling.

'Oh Alix, that's rather deep – you'll have to give us time to think about that one. Ask us again later. Let's get some Abba first.'

'Oh I will!' came the reply, 'you can depend on that. More drinks anyone? Is *Dancing Queen* on that tape Diane? You know that's my favourite.'

* *

The view of the incident would have varied depending on who was asked, but there could be no denying it happened, and, like spilt milk, useless to try to put it back in the bottle.

After Abba, the conversation had turned to sex. Or rather, if one was being strictly correct, Alix had relentlessly *manipulated* it towards her favourite topic.

'I'm hoping to pick up some sexy silk underwear while we're out tomorrow. It's getting harder to turn Gerald on these days. I'm missing out on my 'rations' most weeks! Any tips girls for keeping the man in your life interested?'

Whilst Nancy had been quite open about the fact that sex with Michael was 'as good as ever' although 'down to three times a week now!' the others had been more circumspect.

Diane had gulped down a glass of wine and mumbled something about 'Well, you know how it is when you're tired a lot of the time, even with the best of intentions ...'

Patricia, glancing sideways at Lesley, had assumed a scowl of disapproval at Alix, and made valiant attempts to change the topic, to no avail. Alix had got into full swing, swigging back the wine with gusto, and laughing loudly at her own brilliant conversational swipes. She was unstoppable.

'Oh *come on*, Patricia, surely at nearly forty you're not still as sanitised as you were at twenty-one for God's sake, when any man would have needed to dip his dick in Dettol to get within a yard of you!'

But surely she was, even at this age now, she was.

'That's not fair, Alix, and you know it.' Said with a teacher's scolding attitude writ large on her face, but to her credit, with composure maintained through her retort. 'But being just a simple heathen, how could you be expected to understand a Catholic's attitudes to sex?'

And if that wasn't enough damage for one night, poor Lesley came under scrutiny a little later on when the rather dog-eared Book of Bastards was brought out with a flourish.

'You know Lesley, you don't have an entry in here at all! I'm just wondering if there's anyone you'd like to put in now as an update, nudge nudge, wink wink, eh? Come on, you can tell Auntie Alix if you've been a good girl or a naughty one, can't she girls?'

If Lesley had been able to answer, who knows what she might have said, but she didn't get the chance; Patricia jumped up quickly, and made to grab the Book from Alix's hand. But Alix was too quick for her.

'Get your hands off it, you po-faced party pooper!'

'Oh grow up Alix. It was a stupid idea then and it's even more juvenile now. Most of us have grown out of parties by now. It's about time you did something more useful with your life.'

'Fuck off Patricia. You're nothing but a sanctimonious prig. God help Trevor.'

Diane was pink with embarrassment by this stage.

'Right, that's enough you two. Too much drink I think. Now just apologise – both of you – and let's forget it ever happened. We're supposed to be enjoying ourselves, not bickering.'

'Forget it Diane. I'm off to bed. She can apologise all she likes but it will be to the blank wall.' Patricia grabbed her shoulder bag, checked that she hadn't left anything of hers in the room and made for the door.

Lesley brokered a truce the following morning, catching Alix drawing deeply on her first cigarette of the day out of the lounge window, and then Patricia removing her running shoes at the front door. A few tears proved the catalyst.

'Please Patricia. It was just the drink, you know that. I couldn't bear it if you two didn't make up; I've looked forward so long to this weekend. She wasn't very nice to me either but I can let it go for the sake of our friendship. We've all got our faults.'

'Alix, Patricia was really hurt by what you said last night. I know you didn't mean it, not really. She's a decent person you know, even if she is a bit straight-laced. How about you offer the olive branch? Please.'

Alix took a gamble, playing the religious card.

'Mea culpa, mea culpa. Forgive me sister because I have sinned. I promise to make good any hurt I have caused you and ask that you accept my sincere apology.'

Diane was looking over Patricia's shoulder as her friend read Alix's note, placed on the table mat in front of her with a single carnation from the artificial display in the hallway.

Maybe the run to the Castle and back had defused some of her inner tension; Diane kept her fingers crossed for a suitable response.

'You daft besom. All right. Okay. Just burn that stupid book will you? I never want to see it again.'

The air visibly cleared, the mood lightened and the talk moved on to what they might have for lunch in Henderson's. They would walk there, and reminisce at every street corner no doubt about favourite pubs, parties in top floor flats, and hot pies from late night bakeries.

Patricia, forgive? Yes. Forget? Unlikely.

Too short

Was that really it then? Relieved that the flat was suitable and the food worked out. Delighted to see everyone again and catch up. Amazed at the detail of our memories of Dalmeny Street. A bit annoyed about Alix and the way she'd turned on Patricia and Lesley. I was pleased that I'd been able to smooth things over and blame it on the generous size of the wine glasses. Gratified that the girls had acknowledged my pivotal role in finally bringing us back together in the same place at the same time, after all those years. And now … left with an empty feeling as I saw them all off back home before handing in the keys to the flat. Time together gone in a flash.

I now had no more stories to tell of life in Jeddah. Another time I would need to have done something else with my life or I really would be fixed in the singular role of good listener. There is only so much you can say about your children and husband, your lovely home or your latest good buy, before someone wants to know what you're *doing* with your life. And they don't mean as a housewife or homemaker either.

When I got home, Willie's interest in my weekend away was time-limited by the start of *Star Trek* Deep Space Nine. So the exchange took off at speed.

'How're the girls then?'

'Great really. Carys couldn't make it you remember but she sent this cheesy video of herself. Priceless it was.'

'Plenty drink?'

'We had a few right enough. Alix overdid it and blotted her copybook, but we got over that. Nancy's a bit more restrained these days. Never did take much for Lesley to go giggly, she's just the same now.'

'Patricia go out for a run?'

'Oh yes, never misses a day. She looks very fit though. Still in the same size of clothes – maybe even a smaller size.'

'And how was your outfit?'

'Mmm. Maybe I should have listened to Susan after all. But I managed to make sure my spare tyre was hidden when we took photos.'

'Well, that diet business – *you* know what you have to do, Di. Anyway – good to have you back. The stew you left was brilliant by the way. Any nibbles in the cupboard? Put the kettle on would you when you go through. Deep Space Nine's about to start and I know you won't want to watch that!'

Nancy popped in a few weeks later when she was at a conference at the Green Hotel. Over a leisurely coffee, we relived the highlights of the weekend and agreed on our summary.

'Patricia is too thin and just as uptight as ever. The tiffin she brought, on the other hand, was truly scrumptious and utterly sinful. She didn't mention much about Trevor. I wonder if everything is all right there. I can't imagine she'll have any more children now. It's just as well Claire grew out of being such a difficult baby; the two of them seem to be very close. She never lightens up does she? And she's got her headship now. You'd think maybe she could slip the reins a bit now and then. Too ingrained, all that planning, order, and standards stuff.'

I had taken small comfort when I'd looked at Alix showing the signs of too much sun on her fair skin, when my own was still relatively unlined.

'Alix puts us all in the shade with her understated elegance and classy clothes. Wonder how she'll cope moving back up here from London next year, when Gerald retires? Can't see her settling down to parochial domesticity, that's for sure. She was bad enough in Jeddah, and she had one or two distractions there I know. Her twins are just stunning, aren't they? Blonde, tall, athletic, musical, good all-rounders apparently. Got the best of both their parents. No worries about *their* future I wouldn't think, particularly now they're going to a posh boarding school not far from here.'

'Lesley's quiet, I noticed. Jonathan's maybe a bit of a worry?' Nancy raised her eyebrows as we exchanged looks. 'He gets learning support at school, she said. A little behind with his reading. Everything seems to be fine between her and the parents, thank goodness. It's just that you always feel she's vulnerable somehow.'

I sighed knowingly, as she continued with her observations.

'And Nick's fairly gone up in the world, hasn't he? He sounds a bit puffed up to me. I think she struggles to keep up socially.

She's not really the type – all those formal medical functions, the national events he has to go to, her tagging along behind when she can't get out of going. I bet he's glad to leave her at home half the time.

'It just shows you, Di – the boy of 18 you once knew was only half way to being the man he would become. Whereas we seemed to be established in character and personality even when we first met. Don't you agree my old pal? And what about that video of Carys? I shouldn't have been surprised, but that really took the biscuit. Maybe it's the American influence. But it was all 'look at me' and 'haven't I done well?' And as for 'why don't y'all pay us a visit?' My God! Is there room for more than their two big egos in the place I wonder?'

'Ah, the green eyed monster, Nancy. Have a bit shortbread and calm down!'

'I know, I know. We always did niggle each other in the flat. I'm pleased for her, really. She always worked hard and wasn't deflected by the male of the species as I was. Anyway …life begins at 40 they say. So I'd better get out there. You too. No-one's going to lead you by the hand. What are you up to this year?'

'I need to get into something now that the house is settled and the kids are out all the time. And there's the diet of course!'

'Yes, it gets harder as you get older. Get a horse. That keeps me fit.'

'No thanks. Animals never were my thing although lame ducks and lost lambs – they all find *me* almost by magic. But I've had about enough of that type of person. Maybe I'll have something new to report next time we meet. Say Hi to Michael for me. And love to the kids.'

Back home to *The Bridges of Madison County*. I read it in one sitting. Francesca took her chance when it wandered in. Mind you, if it had been Clint Eastwood, I would have done the same – I think …

Life imitating art

There was a boxroom upstairs in the house, with a large velux window in the roof. Elizabeth had pleaded for it. Sick she was, of sharing with Susan and all that make-up gunge everywhere. But I had my eye on it for a studio. I needed quiet, private space in order to be creative, and the boys at twelve and ten were still careering around the rest of the house as Superman, Spiderman and various Musketeers. So, for once, I asserted myself and claimed it.

I did my best thinking when the studio door was shut and the house was quiet. It was as if my mind entered another state where I could see things much more clearly and come up with innovative ideas and solutions.

Shortly after the reunion, Patricia had sent me an advert for the Dundee Art Society in Roseangle with its regular classes and exhibitions for local artists. I could tie in Tuesday evening painting classes with visits to Forfar. Maybe even meet Patricia for a drink afterwards. A sensible use of my time. And I could still fit in all that ferrying back and forward – to karate (Kinross, Monday nights, David and John), life drawing (Glenrothes, Wednesday after school, Susan), piano (Kinross, Wednesday evening, Elizabeth), swimming (Kinross, Thursday evening, David and John), scout football (Kinross, Saturday morning, John), and skating (Perth, Saturday afternoon, Elizabeth). Willie and I kept sacrosanct our Friday night take-away and bottle of Merlot. Just the one bottle; I had to drive next morning.

I worked away at home and in the classes on my landscapes, always watercolour. Oils just didn't suit my style. And I never could muster enthusiasm for still life or portrait painting, much as I maybe should have branched out.

The society awarded a new prize in 1995 at their annual spring members' exhibition – the Discovery Art Prize. The criteria were simple and few – a painting of a foreign scene by a new member of the society. I submitted a watercolour of the desert as seen from the riding stables on the outskirts of Jeddah, summarised under the title 'Desert Diamonds'. I had spent many a Thursday evening there waiting for Susan and Elizabeth. It seemed to please the judges. 'Desert Diamonds' brought me a stylish glass trophy to display for the next twelve months. And now I had something to say when asked 'and what do **you** do, Diane?'

'I'm an artist actually – well, sort of.'

Alix bought my painting of Desert Diamonds! She didn't breathe a word. Just showed me round her new home (mansion more like) outside Auchterarder, commenting on this old wooden Jeddah door made into a coffee table, that Persian wall hanging which brought warmth and colour to the square hallway, the wonderful Egyptian bronze cat which had been Gerald's leaving gift from the Cairo office and now stared enigmatically from the drawing room window ledge and the beautiful watercolour of the desert near Jeddah by a talented local artist! It was strategically placed to enliven a rather neutral palette in the dining room. We did a wee celebratory dance around the huge dining table.

'I just didn't twig. How did you sign the cheque? Surely I would have noticed Alexandra Fitzroy?'

'Ah well now. A girl needs a little stash of her own, does she not? I have a business account these days – Rubislaw Treasures. I've been buying and selling a few bits and pieces. Useful for this house of course, but there's the future too. I've a few ideas for when I get bored with all this.' She made a grand gesture to take in the size and scope of Dalfruan Grange. 'And of course I just couldn't resist the title. Desert Diamond was Mike's pet name for me. You remember Mike, don't you?'

'Mike?'

'Yes, Mike Nash. Sharbatly Village. My acting partner in Brief Encounter. We had a thing going for a while.'

'You are *some* girl Alix. I thought you'd got over that notion. I thought you'd seen sense. Jeopardising Gerald's career and all that. You didn't mention *that* in Edinburgh.'

'Oh, come on Diane. With Patricia there? And Nancy still gooey about Michael. Although God knows why. Especially with all those kids and animals to contend with. It was enough for me to blot my copybook over the Book of Bastards – and that was all *history*. Imagine the reaction if I'd brought up Mike. Mind you, he'd have to go in a totally different category!' She lowered her voice and purred like Eartha Kitt. 'How about the File of Fabulous Fucks?'

She was outrageous. You had to hand it to her.

'Well I hope you've left all that behind with the sand and the sun. You'd never get away with that around here. Too small a playground this part of the world.'

'Mmm, we'll see. Don't shut your mind to it Diane. It didn't harm my relationship with Gerald – he doesn't know a thing about it. And in fact it stopped me going off my head completely. All those boring wives' meetings, that round of consular events, the long days with nothing to do. Not being allowed to drive for God's sake! If I hadn't had Mike and access to some good whisky who knows what I might have done just to prove I was still alive!

'Don't worry yourself though. I've plenty to keep me going here for a while. And of course Gerald is around much more these days. I need to push him out the door sometimes to get a bit of time to myself. He thinks this is 'our time' now. We can go golfing together, make trips to the theatre, have friends to stay from London. The children are boarding and I'm here to keep him company in his retirement. Christ, I'm only 41, not 61. I'm working on finding him a new absorbing interest so that I can live a little.'

Francesca did it – found a brief and exciting life in Madison County, albeit for four short days, with Robert Kincaid. Alix had spiced up her life for a few months with the fabulous Mike. It wasn't that I'd never been tempted, I had. But I just couldn't bring myself to hurt Willie like that, not for a bit of short lived excitement.

And anyway, what words of comfort would Francesca and Alix have offered to Lesley for example? Or Patricia … when the time came.

Reflections of my mind

Lesley was glad she'd made the effort to get to Edinburgh, even though parts of the reunion had been unsettling. In many ways the girls were just the same; yet, there was also much that had changed. It had been silly of her to expect otherwise.

The talk of children, schools, houses, gardens, the photos they'd passed around – all of that had been comforting. She'd joined in enthusiastically, showing off her carefully chosen pictures of Jonathan.

But when the conversational emphasis shifted to the state of marriages, husbands, and sex, she had become all squeamish inside. Embarrassed to listen, yet not wanting to appear so. Feeling like an outsider, in fact, not wishing to engage, or volunteer any vaguely intimate information and rather afraid of being probed for it, most of all by Alix who seemed hell-bent on a mission to uncover their secrets of what went on behind closed doors.

Patricia had been canny, slipping out under a cloak of pretence about 'making room in the kitchen', 'replenishing glasses', 'sorting out some more nibbles'. She hadn't needed any help, thank you. How mean of her – surely she might have sympathised with Lesley's plight?

So there had been nowhere to hide, other than the toilet, for as much time as seemed reasonable. She'd made frequent trips all evening.

They'd heard how Nancy was still so very much in love with Michael. Her soulmate, her perfect man. And they made love at least three times a week, sometimes more, if they weren't too tired. And it was just as good as always, better even, 'like a fine wine you know,' Nancy'd said. 'Matures with age'.

Three times a week! Was that normal? Lesley had wondered. Maybe not, given Diane's response, but maybe it was, given Alix's.

What about once a month, on a good month? Try every three months, more like. Was that normal then? Sex aside – what was normal for a marriage of sixteen years?

If she thought about it, *really* thought about it, then in comparison to the others, hers didn't fare well at all.

In the weeks after the trip Lesley kept remembering disjointed snippets of conversation. They flitted briefly, and most disconcertingly, across her mind.

'But how do you *know* he's never been unfaithful?'

'We're still great pals, best friends I'd say.'

'Of course, we've had our ups and downs over the years, doesn't everybody? But nothing really serious.'

'A wife in the kitchen and a whore in the bedroom, that's me!'

And then she'd get a headache, and have to shake herself out of it, praying all the while it wouldn't turn into a migraine attack.

Seeds of doubt. Sown and sprouting. Growing inwards, down deeper and deeper. Even when she shut her eyes and lay on her bed in the darkened bedroom they were there.

She seemed powerless to stop the growth. Inwards, then outwards, wider and wider in ever-increasing circles. She became more vigilant then, beginning to observe his movements more closely, paying more attention to how he dressed, when he came home, when he went out, when he looked at her, when he didn't, but should have. All the while she said nothing to him, just felt a peculiar gnawing in her stomach, a tightening around her head, a pain deep in her lower back, which came and went. Sometimes it arrived on cue, from a look he would give her; sometimes seemingly out of the blue.

Then one morning when he left for yet another two days 'on College business in Edinburgh' it dawned on her – the cause of the problem, the reason, the truth of it all. They might share a house, a son, a marriage, but it was in name only; they inhabited different spaces, they actually led separate lives, bound together by tenuous threads: quick pecks on the cheek, messages hurriedly relayed in passing, shouted goodbyes, scrawled notes, phone calls to alert a delay in arrival. Even the occasional call from one of the practice receptionists to say 'Dr. Mathieson has been called away and asked me to tell you he'll be a few hours late.'

Sex was relegated to the perfunctorily, wine-fuelled act of releasing tension, rather than passion.

The obvious questions are burning inside her.

Where is the love in this? Where is it? Where did it go? When?

Yet of Nick she asks not a single one.

It would, she thinks, be painful even to try.

Christmas 1995 is more of an effort than ever, for both of them, she senses. At least Jonathan is happy, no trouble, as always content with his games and toys, the television, for hours on end.

'I think we should get out the house for a bit,' Nick says, 'get some fresh air in our lungs; it'll be good for us after all the food we've stuffed over the last few days.'

Her back is playing up but she doesn't try to dissuade him. He's bored sitting at home; she can see that all too clearly, he's not making a very good job of hiding it.

This is a rare family outing. The doctor, his wife and son on a drive out to Arderseir. All together again. They agree that the beach looks inviting. It is cold, but dry, the wind has seen to that. As they get onto the beach a sudden gust picks up Jonathan's helium balloon and whisks it off towards the sea, with him shouting and laughing in hot pursuit of the trailing string.

So it is just the two of them now, walking along the sands, with the sun bright, although low in the sky because it is winter, and they are wrapped up well against the cold, wearing heavy jackets, hats, scarves and gloves. As they walk they are side-by-side, not touching, and there is an uneasy atmosphere between them. They do not speak. He picks up a bottle from near the tide line within minutes of leaving the car, saying he will carry it back to the bin. Yet they won't reach the bin until the end of their walk, since it is in the opposite direction from where they started, back in the car park.

Why couldn't he have left it there and picked it up on the way back?

With a chill of realisation she knows that he is doing this in order to avoid holding her hand.

She goes around to his other side but finds his other hand too is out of reach; lodged firmly in his coat pocket. She is left with the option of pushing her arm through his, which she does feebly, almost apologetically, sensing a coldness as she does so. She cannot bring herself to ask him to hold her hand if he doesn't offer it willingly. She feels she will not be able to ask him for any part of himself ever again. His hand is out of reach; now, and forever it seems. It is the last time they ever go for a walk together.

In the ensuing months the distance between them grows

cavernous. She can't explain why - there have been no arguments. They are speaking as usual - politely, accommodatingly. But she knows he is only half-listening, and that hurts. It really hurts. To be so uninteresting that your own husband only listens when he feels like it, and doesn't think she even notices. Still she will not say how she feels; she will not weep, but she knows it's coming to a head, this situation. This marriage. What marriage?

Any fool could tell – and she has been a fool. She berates herself hard now for her stupidity. A trail has been laid, the clues obvious if one happened to be searching. Even if not, eventually a clue will reveal itself, as if it can't keep a secret any longer. It's the way of the world.

Not lipstick on his collar. Too obvious, too plebeian. Something much more subtle…

She hadn't meant to pry, not really. Looking through the papers on his desk for a stapler was an excuse she'd made to herself – she could have stapled her own papers in work quite easily the next day. Then suddenly there it was, turning up under a pile of documents. Neat, flowing handwriting on a yellow post-it sticker, attached to a faculty flyer, advertising the next set of lectures in the postgraduate centre.

'You were simply brilliant last week. And I don't mean just your presentation either! Can't wait for the next time.'

W x

W. One letter, saying more than a thousand words. Lesley has found what she was looking for and her world closes in around her.

When Nick arrives home late that evening expecting to find her in bed asleep, she is instead sitting at the table motionless, empty teacup in hand, hair distressed.

'You should have come with me,' he says, 'it's always great food at that hotel and as much drink as anyone could possibly want, all laid on by the reps.'

Lesley can hardly summon up the energy to reply and it hurts her head to do so.

'You didn't ask me.'

'Didn't I?' He's taken aback, goes on the defensive. 'If I didn't, it was because you always say no. So I've given up asking you.'

'Given up asking, or given up on me?' she throws back at him, rising up from the chair, forcing her legs to move in the direction of the door.

'No! Don't run away Lesley!' he says firmly, raising his voice to her. 'You can't come out with a statement like that and then pretend you haven't said it and run away!' His voice is getting louder, uncharacteristically loud for Nick.

'Can't I?' She doesn't even turn around as she speaks, so doesn't see his eyes flash with anger, the colour rush red into his cheeks.

'No, you can't, not this time. Why don't you *ever* say how you feel? For God's sake, it's like living with a dummy at times. Look at you! You look a state! All messed-up. So bloody miserable! What I can't understand is why. How can you possibly be so damn miserable and not tell me why?'

If she was capable of telling him then she would, but the words won't come. They are stuck in her throat. She is *so* tired, all she wants to do is crawl away, find a safe place to hide, pretend this isn't happening.

He's like a dog with a bone, and he's not going to give it up, not this time. She's not the only weary one.

He stands there running his hand through his hair, breathing hard to force the words out. If he has to go and grab her, push her into a chair, make her sit down and talk then he will. 'We have to sort this out, Lesley. Now. Right now. Don't you see? It will be better for us both if we do.'

She turns around to face him, but no, she does not see. She is blind to his words, blind with her eyes, with her mind also. She can form no vision from his words. It is as if they come from another dimension, not belonging to this world, to this moment. This is not Nick speaking, she feels, but a hologram of him, his voice sounds like his, but it cannot be him.

'You must listen to me,' he implores her.

She does not want to listen. Every fibre of her body is telling her to run away, get under the bedclothes, be in the dark, until he wakes her with a cup of tea, and the day can begin again. She feels giddy, and has to sit down on a chair.

'Lesley, we have to talk, and this time you must listen; I can't put this off any longer. I can't go on like this. I'm not happy. This marriage has gone stale, and it seems like there is nothing we can do to make it better. You're not happy either, I know that; it's obvious you've not been for a very long time, so there's no point us pretending that we are. We need to work out what we can do so we can sort this out, get on with our lives, do what's best for Jonathan.'

She tries to form a response, but her mouth will not work. There is only a feeling of helplessness, weakness throughout her whole body. Tears are streaming down her face, which is crumpling up, as if it were about to implode. She collapses in the middle, puts her face into her hands, holds her head up to support the weight of it. She has a severe pain across her temples, behind her eyes. A migraine is beginning.

'I'm sorry Lesley, I'm really sorry. I don't want to hurt you, I really don't.'

'But you have Nick.' The words come now, from somewhere deep inside. Through her tears a wobbly voice blurts out. 'You've been hurting me for years, haven't you? I know. I know about her.'

He is visibly taken aback, not sure how to reply. This wasn't the response he'd been expecting.

Now what should he say? Come clean about Wendy? Pretend he doesn't know what his wife's talking about?

He needs time, time to devise a strategy. But there is no time. They are here, in the present, and this dialogue is playing out as if in slow motion, where they are caught in a loop. Lesley holds her head up and looks at him directly. She is angry, he can tell; she is almost spitting the words out.

'Don't lie to me any more, Nick. There have been enough lies. Don't lie to me anymore; no more, *no more* lies please!' Her voice is sounding hysterical. Can she calm it? She tries. The words keep coming, her silence has been finally broken.

'You're having an affair, I know that, so don't try to deny it. I don't know who she is, and I don't need to know. Just tell me the truth, Nick. Can you do that for once?'

He feels hurt that she seems to be accusing him of being a perennial liar. Thinks *that's not fair*, but wisely doesn't say it. However there is no point in denial, he will tell her the truth, simply and honestly. He tries to be gentle, adopting his consultation manner.

'Yes. Yes, I am having an affair.'

'How long for, how long has this been going on?'

'It doesn't matter, Lesley, right now is all that matters.'

'I want to know! I have a right to know!' She is screaming at him now, she can't help herself, she feels out of control.

'All right then, three years on and off.'

'Three years? You've been screwing her for three years? Oh my God, Oh-My-God. You bastard Nick. You selfish, selfish bastard!'

'Lesley, I'm not proud of this, please don't make it worse for me.'

'Worse for you? What's this got to do with *you*?'

She cannot talk anymore. Her head is going to explode she thinks. She stumbles to the cupboard, reaches for her migraine tablets, and swallows them whole before turning to walk out of the kitchen. She knows she needs to lie down before she falls down.

'Lesley, don't walk away from me; we need to talk about this some more. We might as well do it now we've got this far,' he shouts after her. 'Come back Lesley, please; don't just keep walking away from difficult issues.'

She doesn't bother to reply because she cannot; she must stay focussed on getting to the bedroom. As she reaches the top of the stairs, nausea floods her body, and forces her to divert to the bathroom. She is going to throw up; it is all too familiar a pattern.

Hearing her retching, he accepts the conversation is over for the time being. Best he leaves and comes back to see her later. He must get some sense out of her as to a course of action, before she attempts something stupid. He wouldn't put it past her.

'I'm going to check the surgery phone, Lesley. I'll be back in an hour.' Pulling on his coat he wonders if he should go up and say anything else to her, but decides against it. *What would he say if he did go up?* He cannot think of anything appropriate, in the circumstances.

Black is black

Brown might have been the new black in 1996, or maybe it was grey. Whatever it was – I wore my black suit with the velvet lapels to all the funerals – struggling to fasten the bottom button on the jacket after more sausage rolls and cakes than I should have eaten at the teas, and wrung out with the effort of offering sympathy and some small crumbs of comfort to the bereaved.

'At least he didn't suffer, Nancy. It was all so quick. Better that than what happened to Alix's Dad. Lying for a week unable to move, the tears trickling down his face and everyone waiting at his bed for the worst to happen.'

'I know, I know. It's just such a shock when it happens. And Mum is all over the place. She doesn't seem to have taken it in properly and still looks for him sometimes. The kids are devastated. This is the first death they've had to face and I'm not much use to them.'

'Leave it to Michael. He'll see to them just now while you cope with your Mum. You can't be strong for everyone else when this happens; you've got your own grief to deal with. Give yourself a bit of time. Get off that relentless merry-go-round for a week or so. You need to take care of yourself. It's not possible to just put your coat on and get back out there determined to keep the whole show on the road.'

'Easy for you to say, Di, although I appreciate your concern. There's the horses and the dogs to think about – they don't take a week off. And work is so busy just now – for me *and* Michael. I'll be fine, honest I will, I know it. I just need to get today over with and then focus back on normal life.'

'Just take it easy. Please Nancy. You push yourself at the best of times.'

* *

'She's at peace now Alix. She's never been the same since your Dad died. You said it yourself – and that's more than five years. You need to think of her and how much she wanted to be with him again.'

'Fine for you to say, believer and all that. I'm not sure we *do* meet up with anyone after we die. I think it's just a never ending blackness. Nothingness. She's gone and that's it. She drove me nuts, you know Diane. Over and over, all those stories. I could recite them word for word.

'Do you remember the time the Queen came to Aberdeen and your Dad was presented to her? He was thrilled to bits. And what a great photie there was in the P&J'.

'But that's it now. No more stories. There's only me left. I hate to think I'm the older generation now. God … Forty three … I'm too young yet to be all sober and serious.'

'You'll never be that, Alix. Come on. We count on you for a bit of light relief. It just takes a bit of getting used to. This change of status.'

Platitudes – easy to say, bringing a momentary comfort. Spoken with a desire to show caring, but with no *real* understanding.

Words like those, many of them, well meant, carefully chosen, written in cards, attached to wreaths, whispered in awkward embraces – and bringing no measure of relief when the shadow crossed my own life.

This time he left no room for discovery or treatment.

Paraquat is a quick- acting, non-selective herbicide, which destroys green plant tissue on contact and by translocation within the plant. Absorbed paraquat is distributed via the bloodstream to practically all areas of the body. Multiorgan failure with circulatory collapse is a major cause of early death within 3 days of paraquat ingestion.

Mother was on a theatre group outing to London. Willie and I were helping out at scout camp in Douglaswood for the weekend, agonisingly close to Forfar yet temporarily out of our radar. Dad had a golf tournament on, he said.

'Don't bother phoning while your Mum's away. I'll probably be out most of the time. We'll see you next Tuesday as usual.'

And then a strange thing. 'You're a great lass Diane.'

We had to wait for the post-mortem report and procurator fiscal's decision before we could have the funeral. *He* was most awfully sorry. However, there was no need for an enquiry given Dad's ongoing problem with depression, his medical history and the notes that he left behind for us all.

Norma and Campbell looked to me to organise everything,

being on the spot as I was, and expectations being as they always were.

* *

Lesley still had both parents alive and well. But the grief she expressed at Dad's funeral would have marked her as one of the bereaved. Her grey trouser suit hung off her slightly bowed frame. When she walked, you could detect a slight limp. Her eyes were hollow and red with weeping. We were all shocked at the change in her. According to Patricia it was all down to her bad back. Not that she was ever the most perceptive of us.

In her Christmas card that year, Lesley sent a brief note to each of us with her new address.

I am sorry to let you know that Nick and I have separated for good. We just couldn't make our marriage work any longer. It is the best thing for the three of us. He has bought this small bungalow for Jonathan and me. It's near to Ninewells Hospital where I start my new job after New Year. Ken McPhee, my old boss from Raigmore, is in Dundee now and is keen for me to work with him. I just hope this old back of mine holds up. Will be in touch again soon.

Love Lesley (now O'Donnell)

Lost and found

Reframing they call it. Choosing to view the same thing from more than one perspective. Life is not black and white after all.

I'd never heard of it before, nor of its potential – for good *and* bad.

As the days passed and became weeks, and as I struggled to find the necessary inspiration and calm in order to paint, I engaged in hours of displacement activity thinly disguised in my own mind as 'coming to terms with Dad's death.'

I would play and replay recent events, trying to view them from different angles, and work out what had really happened. Take his last words to me 'you're a great lass Diane.' Was that really 'I'm going to let you know how I feel about you because this is the last time we'll speak?' Or was it just that Mum was away and he felt more relaxed without her ear-wigging on the conversation?

Did he know what paraquat would do to him? Don't be silly, he was an environmental health officer – of course he did. But was it a cry for help or did he really mean to do it this time? I couldn't deny the obvious.

But where it hit me full in the face was when I asked myself why.

Why did he put us through so much all those years? Why did he inflict his moods on us and make us all jumpy and on edge?

When reframed as – what did we do to help *him*? how could we have made his life *happier*, worked with him on his problems, whatever they were? – I had to face a second wave of grief. To see my own role in it all as so inadequate and so misguided that my very sense of myself was shaken and split into fragments.

Our family life had revolved around Dad's moods – avoiding him when he was in a trough. Or keeping him happy in the minor details of meals on time and children kept quiet during the six o'clock news. Avoid, contain, prevent, protect, ignore, hide, suppress – all negative and defensive routines and traditions. Because the focus was on what *his* behaviour did to *us*.

As a family, we colluded with each other. We placed mother in the centre as the one in need of support. We did nothing to show him that he was safe in our love for *him*, in our concern for *his* happiness and wellbeing. We never thought to encourage him to share with us the roots and maintenance system of his depression.

He suffered, and then must have suffered again when we effectively rejected him. His human failing was his inability to express his innermost feelings; our failing was to withdraw and keep ourselves safe from him. We had so let him down. And now it was too late.

It took Francka to reframe it all again for me some time later, when deeply relaxed in the reclining leather chair, with the fleece blanket over my legs. Meanwhile, my shattered self image was being battered by a force nine closer to home.

Susan and Elizabeth were sharing a flat in Fountainhall Road by this time, roughly equidistant between the Edinburgh College of Art and Kings Buildings. I had gone back to my old trade as a care worker in a residential home for the elderly in Perth, working a couple of night shifts every week to help pay for the girls' paintbrushes and scientific manuals. It also took my mind off Dad and how we had failed him; allowing me to make it up to him in a strange way by being extra kind to some poor old soul reduced to a narrow life in a high backed PVC covered chair, with a fellow guest list of the deaf, the defeated and the almost dead.

Willie and I were just pleased the two girls got on well enough to live together in relative harmony after years squabbling over wall space for posters, shelf space for CDs and personal space for boyfriends.

I noticed the stud in Susan's tongue just before we sat down for Christmas dinner, that first Christmas without Dad, when we were all trying to keep Granny from crying. It didn't seem the right time to address it but she knew that I'd seen it, and wore a rather thin smile any time there was anything worth smiling about that festive season. Lips pressed together. So no-one else would notice.

I cornered her after our Boxing Day visit from Campbell and his family. Susan had always enjoyed a teasing relationship with him – wrestling and giggling. She'd been offhand and rather nasty in her exchanges with him that day, and it had obviously hurt him. I snapped at her. 'What's got into you these days? That stud affecting your normal good humour?'

'Oh very funny. What's it to you anyway? Lots of girls at college have them. It's no big deal.'

'You never used to go in for that kind of thing, Susan. Pierced ears and all that. In fact Elizabeth had hers done long before you did. I trust you haven't got a tattoo as well.'

'And why not? I'm an artist, after all. What do you expect – twinset and pearls? As a matter of fact ...'

And she lifted her long skirt to display a small green turtle just above her right ankle.

'I'm thinking of getting another one on my shoulder. A moon this time. Jason already has the sun, and a dragon on his left bum cheek.'

'Jason?'

'Yeh, you know ... Jason. We've been kind of seeing each other these last few weeks. We've decided I'm Yin to his Yang.'

'Yin?'

'Feminine, dark, receptive, soft – the very opposite of Yang. It's masculine, bright, active, hard. Surely to God you've heard of Yin-Yang, Mum?'

'Okay, yes of course. Well, I'm not happy about the piercing or the tattoos. Just don't tell me you're pregnant or taking drugs, please. And what was all that about with Campbell? You usually love it when he visits.'

'Oh, he just doesn't accept that I'm grown up these days. Always treats me like a stupid kid. I hate that. He wouldn't take the hint either.'

'I hadn't noticed.'

'No, you never do, do you? Always too busy running after everyone, putting yourself here, there and everywhere. And what's going on under your nose? – you're just oblivious to that.'

A sob escaped before she ran out the door and slammed it behind her. I had to think this through before acting.

Was there something going on here? What had I missed? Why hadn't she come to me?

The house was empty the next day. Rangers were kicking off against Dundee United at Ibrox. By 4.45 it would be the old story re-run. Rangers 4 Dundee United 1, goals by Laudrup, Cleland and Negri (2). No-one was interested in the consolation effort by the other side.

While the boys were cheering on their team, I was hearing a very new story from Susan.

I picked my moment. Made a cup of tea for both of us, and served it with a joke about mince pies and how much I knew she hated them. And then I broached the subject.

'Susan?'

'Yep?'

'Is everything okay with you?'

'Oh fine. What do you mean anyway?'

'I noticed you were a bit upset yesterday.'

'That was just me missing Grandad. Funny thing is that I used to wish he didn't have to come for Christmas sometimes – grumpy old git that he was. But then when I realised he wouldn't ever be here again, that upset me. Things never stay the same.'

'And that thing you said about me – that I never notice anything. What exactly did that refer to?'

'Oh Mum. Give it a rest. It was nothing much.'

'No, really. I would like to know. I lay awake half the night wondering what you meant.'

'Okay, then. Here's a few things for starters if you really must. John is being bullied at school. You know he's still small for his age and the boys at the big school are just taking the mickey out of him – short arse, Mummy's boy, poisoned dwarf – that kind of thing. He won't tell you because he knows you're still upset about Grandad. But any idiot could see he's worried about something. You just don't seem to notice.'

'And ...'

'Well, David is bunking off school to go skateboarding on a regular basis. Forges notes from you. Doesn't do it often enough to look suspicious. But he must be falling behind in his work. He swore me not to tell so you'd better not say how you found out.'

'Anything else I should know?'

'Dad is spending a lot of time out of the house these days. Fixing motorbikes he says. I think he's fed up of you never being around – always at work, or over at Granny's, or up in that so-called studio of yours. You should hang on to him. He's a top guy.'

'And you – Susan. How am I letting you down?'

'Hang on a bit. I didn't say you were letting people down. I just said you rush about too much and don't notice things like you should. You don't need to worry about me. I'll be fine. The student health doctor gave me some blue pills. He said they would just keep my mood stable, that it would take a bit of time to come to terms with Grandad dying. It doesn't mean that this is inherited. Most people go down a bit with a bereavement.'

Depression. Family history. Three generations affected. More than one possible explanation?

Diane, a fine lass. Always there for everyone. But ultimately lets them all down.

Reframe that if you can.

We don't talk any more

Willie – never in? I gave it some thought over the early months of '98. Right enough, he was spending ages out in the workshop on that motor bike. And then there was the bikers' club too. I used to joke about all the fat middle-aged men with their bulging leathers, growing their hair a bit longer and using new found nicknames for each other – Big B, Chopper, Python, Tramp, Chief. Maybe he found their company more welcoming than mine. He spent most Sundays with them.

Maybe he was having a mid life crisis? But the facts didn't quite add up. At least not according to *Ask Anna* in a recent edition of the Woman's Own. Apparently it usually happens when the children have flown the nest and you've reached your maximum earning potential, (surely not yet?) You're feeling newly discontented with your lifestyle, doubting decisions you've made about your life, feeling bored with things and people, questioning the meaning and value of your existence and confused about who you are, or where your life is going. He hadn't said a word to suggest any of that was going on. Come to think of it, though, we probably hadn't had a decent conversation in weeks.

'How're you feeling today?'

'Not bad, Willie. I'm getting there.'

'Busy week this week?'

'Just the usual – working Monday, Wednesday and Thursday nights at the home. Mum's on Tuesday, then art class. Then Perth on Saturday for the shopping. How about you?'

'I'm working in Glasgow this week supervising that station refurbishment. So we'll be like ships as usual. I'll be away on that bike run on Sunday to Oban with the club, remember. Catch up Friday maybe?'

Before I'd developed a strategy of any kind, Patricia planted another more disturbing seed.

The two of us met up one Saturday in Perth for lunch. Littlejohn's was packed, so we ended up in the Station Hotel in the big lounge having home-made lentil soup and smoked ham salad sandwiches. Patricia almost licked the soup plate clean but just picked at the sandwiches.

I went into Mother mode. 'Come on you. All that running you do. You'll be wasting away to nothing if you don't eat. Get that lot finished and then we'll have a coffee so that we can chat for a while without anyone moving us on.'

Patricia sighed deeply. 'I'm a bit off my food these days. I can't face a full meal any more. My appetite seems to have diminished. Maybe I need a holiday.'

I began to wonder if she was ill. 'What's been going on?'

'Just the usual, but we've introduced a new maths system into the school and all the staff have been complaining. I'm a bit sick of it actually.'

'They can never leave well alone, can they? The famous 'they'. Has that meant a lot of extra work for you then?'

She laughed bitterly. 'You bet. Not that I was forced into it, but I thought we'd manage it best if I set up a rolling programme of protected training time for the staff. So I've been taking classes myself every Wednesday and Friday afternoon since Christmas to let the teachers work on it. And that's on top of everything else I have to do.' She sighed again. 'There seems to be no end to it. I only finished that project for the leadership training programme just before the October holidays. I'm wiped out.'

That's okay then, I thought. Tiredness, not cancer or anything sinister.

'What's the family saying about it? I bet you're never at home.'

She had to think for a moment. 'Well, I do manage to fit in a couple of things with Claire. We still go to the Runners together on a Wednesday night, although she's at Abertay now and has her own life. And sometimes we go to the pictures on a Sunday afternoon when Trevor is at the golf. Otherwise it's work, work, work.'

'Sounds rough. And Trevor?'

'Honestly, Diane. I hardly see him. He's got school stuff too and then its golf, football, out with the boys.'

'I know what you mean. It sounds a bit like Willie and me. Any chance of you two getting away then for a few days over Easter?'

She pursed her lips. 'No, no chance. School trip to Germany to the twin town – Wurzburg Festival of Sport. Trevor is supervising the second eleven football team. Or so he tells me, but I bet there's a fair amount of German beer to be sampled once the kids have gone to bed.'

Another hint of bitterness.

I wondered if I should probe a bit. But Patricia had always been reticent when the conversation strayed on to personal issues.

'Maybe it's just a phase we're all going through,' I suggested. 'Busy with jobs, got more responsibility now, need to do extra training to keep up, lacking energy, burnt out even.'

She nodded in agreement, her very posture echoing the words – burnt out.

I should have stopped there. Instead I prattled on, trying to jolly her up a bit.

'Just as well he's not chasing skirt as they say!' I meant it as a joke, but by the look on her face, I had struck a raw nerve.

'Well, I've sometimes wondered,' she retorted. 'I found photos from the Harris staff Christmas night out in Trevor's sock drawer. The new PE teacher is a bit of all right and she was draped all over him in a few of them.'

I began to wonder if this was the real reason for her lack of appetite. Surely not Trevor?

'Oh that's just the drink. Trevor wouldn't do anything like that. Don't worry yourself.'

'It's not just the men that instigate things, Diane. Some of these younger females would make your hair stand on end. Even at my school – and we're a Catholic primary. I've had to enforce a standard for staff workwear this year. It was *not* popular I can tell you. But I just don't go with cleavage on show, or short midriffs, or big dangly ear-rings. What kind of example is that to set?'

I couldn't disagree. 'I suppose you're right.'

'So I just don't know. I've got to get back on track with him, Diane. I won't be able to function if things go badly between us.'

Later, I watched her leave, the usual spring in her step sadly missing.

* *

The following Friday I made a big effort. Hairdresser's in the afternoon to top up the rinse. New black trousers which performed miracles of concealment and a pink top which showed off just a bit more cleavage than I would normally risk. I had a Spanish stew in the slow cooker, bruschetta to start, and Willie's old favourite Apple Crumble for dessert. The boys were out at a Scout sleepover at the local hall, the house was tidy, the wine chilling nicely, my speech rehearsed.

'What's going on here then? Something cooking? Smells great.'

'I thought we'd have a nice home cooked meal instead of take-away this Friday. And I've put a new Motown revival CD on. Have your shower, then sit down and we'll have a drink first.'

'This makes a nice change. How did you fit it into your busy schedule?'

'That's the point really. I'm re-prioritising. Patricia brought it home to me, without knowing it. She's running around daft and never sees Trevor. He's possibly playing away from home, and she doesn't know *what* to do. I'd hate if you did that Willie. So I'm trying to create some quality space for us.'

'Well, well. If you keep this up, I might need to change my biking name then. Hot Rod maybe! You know we've got everything we need now and the kids are doing fine. I just wish you'd take life a bit less seriously Di so we can have a bit more fun now and again. It's not all about being responsible and seeing to everyone. Surely you want that too, don't you? Come here.'

A few kind words, a soft and caring tone, open arms, that familiar warm embrace. The speech went out of my head. I started to sob.

'Start prioritising yourself, Di. You don't need to be doing things for other people all the time to be a decent person, surely. You deserve a life too. We do. Together. I don't want to feel bottom of a long list every time I want to spend time with my wife. And I don't mean you doing things for me, either. Just having fun together. Doing what we fancy. Having less family responsibility and being a couple again. I haven't strayed. You know that. But maybe I *could* be vulnerable, who knows. I'm getting a bit of a paunch. I'm going grey. I can't kick a ball as far as I used to, or even catch as many fish.'

'I can't help it Willie. I've spent a lifetime watching out for others, coping alone when I should have asked for help, being a survivor. I thought it was the way to be. There have been people in my life who might have gone under without my help – Mum for one. Or had no-one to show them some caring and love – like some of the old dears at the home. They depend on me. I don't know who I am if I don't do that.'

'Di, that's a right daft thing to say. You're an artist for one thing. You got the chance to take a class at the art club. Too busy with other things you said. What was that all about?'

'I didn't think I was good enough to do that. And it would have meant extra time preparing. I couldn't see where I would fit it in.'

'But it's about choices, Di. You can choose for you, what you really want to do. And of course you're good enough. They wouldn't have asked otherwise, would they?'

'I don't know what I want, Willie. All I know is that it's very hard for me to see someone needing help or support and not give them it. And sometimes that all gets a bit too much.'

Willie sighed. 'This is beyond me. I just want my wife back. Maybe you need to think about getting professional help with this. Anyway, let's leave it for now and start having some of that quality time you promised. What about that stew? I'm starving.'

He pulled me in close to him and squeezed me tight.

'Come on old girl. You know, you'll always be my girl. You always were.'

His words set me off again. This would not do. I was at risk of ruining the whole evening. I sniffed loudly, wiped my eyes on my sleeve and stood up to check the dinner.

I wanted to say, You're not perfect yourself you know. You're never here for one thing. So who else is going to do everything?

But that really would have been the end of a lovely evening. So I humoured him, an art at which I was truly competent.

'I'll give it some thought, Willie. Now I must dish up that bruschetta before it's ruined. Pour the wine will you?'

In the heat of the night

I rummaged through my wardrobes and drawers for clothes to take to the church jumble sale. There was to be a 'good as new' table as well as the usual racks of 'well-worn' and 'better in the bin'.

I found skirts I'd owned for years, waiting for me to finally come out of trousers. There were trousers almost unworn, waiting for me to lose those extra two stone. Under protective covers were several sadly dated velvet and sparkly items for those rare formal events we used to attend, most of which I had avoided in recent years, too fat to feel sociable. And at the back of my underwear drawer I unearthed two sets of 'alluring items for the fuller figure', one black, one red, still packaged. Gifts from Willie. Accepted with an 'Oh Willie, you know I look a fright in that kind of thing.' Put away with no intention of ever allowing them the light of day.

That matronly look ran in the family Mum said. 'Your Dad's family that is.' There was a long line of tall, rather serious looking, grey haired women. '*Stout*, you might call them.'

I hated that word, especially when it came from my mother.

About a year after Dad's death, Mum began to act and dress like a much younger woman. No-one would have said 'mutton' since she didn't look common, or wear anything other than expensive and well made. Just fashionable really. Not Forfar fashion of course. More the kind of thing you might see in 'She' magazine. There was plenty of choice if you were a size 12, regardless of your age. A group of these 'She' women went gadding about on a Merry Widow day trip every other week. The theatre in Edinburgh. The Burrell Collection in Glasgow. Shopping in Perth. Even a cheap flight to Rome.

Against the usual odds, I would have to *improve* with age to have any chance of looking so well when I got to their stage in life.

I had tried numerous diets – they all had their drawbacks. Cabbage soup and wind. Boiled eggs and constipation. Low fat and total loss of concentration. Any diet – and deprivation.

The benefits of deprivation never came quickly enough nor

lasted long enough to make it worth feeling that anxiety in the pit of my stomach, and then not soothing it, calming it, making it better with a bar of chocolate or a piece of cake. And there was so much to feel anxious about.

That summer, Susan had gone off for three months on the back of a frighteningly fast motor bike to tour Europe, holding on to a tattooed vision in black leather. It wasn't Yang; he'd dumped her for the real thing – a tiny Chinese girl named Lee Kim. This was Sam. He was given to transplanting cows' eyes into sheep's heads to symbolise different perspectives on life. Susan was in awe.

Elizabeth had refused a 19th birthday party in favour of sponsorship to cycle across India for charity, setting off with bags of sweets in her luggage for the child beggars she might meet on the road. She had researched the route, the food, the 'basic' accommodation and the weather. Now she thought that all she had to do was keep her legs moving and the bike would take her from one end to the other. The innocence of youth.

John and David were hitch-hiking to a pop festival in Germany with three words of German between them, none of which would help if they got lost, unless that happened to be in a beer keller. Their rucksacks contained only the essentials – a few spare tee-shirts establishing their pedigree as followers of Status Quo and Queen, a couple of pairs of boxer shorts (probably for emergencies only), a sleeping bag, a toilet roll and a pack of black bin liners. Any empty space was for 'refreshments Mum.'

And Willie was hardly around. I had too much time on my own when the panic would rise unchecked.

How can I keep them all safe when they're so far away, surrounded and followed by all manner of danger?

I kept catching sight of myself in shop windows and doing a double take at the middle-aged frumpish woman with the worried expression, who was undoubtedly me, yet seemed like a stranger.

My hair dresser suggested going for a permanent tint rather than semi-permanent.

'We're having a hard job covering up the grey these days, Mrs McDonald. But don't worry, I've loads of women your age on the "hard stuff"!'

And then there was the sleeping. Or lack of it. If Willie was away, I would put on the light at 02:06 or 03:14 and read for a couple of hours, rather than lie in the dark trying every sort of relaxation or visualisation technique to get back to sleep. One night I'd relived a fortnight's holiday to France, flights, hotel, days out, meals and conversations waiting for that elusive state to descend on me. Sometimes a biscuit and a drink of milk would help. Night starvation they call it, apparently. Must have been the only time anyone mentioned Diane and starvation in the same breath.

It was worse when my memory started to deteriorate. I'd lie very still and focus really hard on what I had done the previous week, struggling like mad to distinguish one day from another and then promise myself to keep a diary from that very day onwards.

Then that furnace which suddenly sparked into life and heated me up to 1000 degrees in the space of seconds would fire up several times a night and leave me dripping with sweat.

'Menopause, The Natural Way' described it all in fine detail – and explained what was happening in biological terms. I skipped over the science in my hunt for remedies.

Red clover, sage, gingko biloba, black cohosh. I wasn't sure where to start and how far to go with it. There was something for every depressing symptom – loss of confidence, loss of libido, thinning hair, anxiety, sleep problems, persistent low mood, weight gain, continence problems. Maybe I'd just 'take the gas', I used to joke. 'A lot cheaper and quicker'.

Francka still advertised in The Courier.

Want to stop smoking and can't? Worried and anxious and don't know why? Phobias preventing you enjoying life? Try hypnotherapy. A pain-free alternative treatment by a fully qualified professional.

She took me along windswept beaches, up thickly wooded hillsides, through beautiful gardens and into warm inviting sitting rooms – all while sitting relaxed and comfortable in that leather recliner. Eventually I could take myself there too.

For a while her words would replace my usual inner chatter. I would hear her in the background of my mind:

'See yourself strong and happy. Feel the warmth in your stomach. Know that you can handle life's problems. Eat only when you're hungry and enjoy a healthy diet.'

And do you know, it worked for a while. As long as I kept playing the tapes regularly and reminding myself that the anxious little girl who was once Diane, was now happy and safe.

Then I saw Bruce by sheer chance at a training day for care staff on 'Managing Medication.' He was giving a short presentation on 'common drugs for common conditions'. Still blonde, still with a full head of hair, still slim and fit looking. Surely not. Maybe it was his son. Yes, of course, that was it. He couldn't possibly look almost exactly as I'd last seen him almost 30 years ago. Not when I had aged so much.

The chairman introduced him to the group, fortunately forty or more in number. I could remain out of direct sight.

'I am delighted to ask Bruce Patterson to give us a short presentation today from his perspective as a pharmacist in a local community. He took over his father's business in Forfar some fifteen years ago and since then has been instrumental in improving communications between GP surgeries, care homes and local pharmacies. He is currently involved in a multi-centre study in seven European countries to improve the well-being of elderly patients via community pharmacy-based provision of pharmaceutical care. Bruce …'

It was my Bruce all right.

* *

'Go and introduce yourself Diane. He's having coffee now with the tutor. I bet he'd be delighted to see you.'

'I couldn't, Mary. I just couldn't. For a start he might not recognise me, I've aged so much. And I don't want him to see me like this. Flabby, floppy, greying hair, wrinkles, support tights. Not when he still looks in his prime.'

Willie just laughed when I recounted the event later. Didn't take my despair seriously.

'Come on Diane. None of us looks the same by the time we get to this stage. Go and put the kettle on and we'll have one of your Paris buns. Old Bruce whatshisname would probably die for one of those.'

I never felt more alone in my life.

I heard the news today, oh boy

Carys would want to make very sure that her old friends knew the truth. Not what was in the confidential memo sent to her on the Monday of the last week of the Spring term, 1999. Not that ridiculous suggestion, that slur on her reputation.

The University Academic Freedom and Tenure Committee, after detailed analysis of the evidence and consideration of all relevant issues, has concluded that while Professor Carys Lloyd-Jones may have failed to give due credit to her some time co-author Conrad Hayden in her publication 'Meredith, Gwladys and Tathan,' this 'lapse' does not amount to plagiarism. The Committee recommends that Professor Lloyd-Jones takes a sabbatical, preferably overseas, in order to make the necessary amendments to the text and begin research on her proposed follow-up publication.

All right then. Let them find someone else for a year to provide leadership for the department, sit on all those boring committees, chivvy along lazy, self indulgent, spoiled daddy's girls and mummy's boys who want a doctorate without the hard work. I'll go back where they know a world-wide authority and a superior brain when they see one, where hard work and dedication still count and where you have to earn your stripes, not gift a new library in order to get a professorship.

Not that she used those exact words in her 'chat' with the Faculty Head.

'I've turned down a number of invitations from the UK over the past few years, as you know. Maybe this is the time to accept one of them. Go back to Belfast possibly. And as you rightly point out, I'm long overdue a sabbatical.'

'Very wise, Carys. We all benefit from a bit of time and space for reflection, particularly after a period of upset. It lets the dust settle. You might find it a relief to be free of managerial responsibility for a while. Free to concentrate on what you love and do best. You might even find you don't want to return once you've immersed yourself in the research. Let's see how it goes. We'll manage without you, I imagine. And I'm sure you'll thoroughly enjoy the change of scene.'

There was no going away party, not that she would have

wanted it. Staff had drifted off at the end of term and learned of her absence only by email. She packed her bags in a fury, barely exchanged two words with JJ and arrived to spend a week or two with Huw in Cardiff, still fuming over the whole business.

* *

Her letter to me was brief and along the lines of 'so sorry I missed seeing you all at the last reunion. Five years have passed. Surely you're planning another one? I'm in the country now. This one I will move hell and high water to attend. Please see what you can do.'

Did we owe it to her? Did we want one?

I tested the ground with a quick call to each of the girls.

'Nancy? Hi, it's me. Yes, I know. I meant to phone you back last week. How's life?'

'You know me Diane. Not much gets me down but I'm struggling a bit just now. In fact I've struggled a lot since Mum got more confused. It must be reaction to all that running back and forward to Yorkshire these last few months.'

'You could do with a good rest, I bet. How does a weekend away sound? I've had a note from Carys asking me to organise another reunion. Seems she's coming back to her Alma Mater for a year's sabbatical and would like to catch up with us all before she goes to Belfast.'

'Well, I could maybe manage something next month. Where were you thinking?'

'I hadn't got that far. Just testing interest and availability at this stage. Leave it with me and I'll speak to the others.'

Lesley was on sick leave with an aggravated back problem. She was going stir crazy stuck in that small house in Dundee, eating tea with Jonathan the only high spot in her day. She'd manage it if someone could drive her and it wasn't too far.

Alix was strangely hesitant. Gerald was a bit under par and didn't like her going out for any length of time. She would work on him and hopefully get away overnight if it was somewhere reasonably local. Patricia was snowed under with work, winding up the school year. Maybe a meal out but she couldn't commit to a whole weekend.

Oh well. The omens weren't favourable, but I felt we owed it to Carys to try.

I struggled to find anywhere reasonably priced and accessible which would accommodate us for only one night. Even then I couldn't be sure how many would stay over and how we would share the costs. In the end Willie suggested I invite them to stay with us. I would provide dinner on the Saturday evening and those who wanted to stay and had the time, could do.

'Willie will pick you up Lesley. No need to bring a thing. I'll rustle up dinner.'

'Why not stay over, Patricia, so that you can have a drink. No, the boys are away that weekend camping. As long as you don't mind the boxroom. You won't need to share.'

'That's great Alix. Okay, bring some wine since you're coming by car. You can decide on the day whether or not to stay. I hadn't realised Gerald was no better.'

'No late night, I promise Nancy. And you can leave straight after breakfast if you must. Please try and make it.'

I invited Carys to come on the Friday night and stay till the Sunday if she was free. She was delighted.

So, three weeks to get ready. Food, drink, jobs to be done.

Cold buffet or hot meal?

What kind of wine? Obviously we weren't celebrating.

Pudding? Diets could go for one weekend surely.

Willie had little patience with my ruminations.

'Christ Diane. They're only coming for a short visit. Surely the company is more important than the food and drink?'

'Well do you think you could paint the girls' bedroom before then? You've been promising to do it for months.'

'No, I don't think I could, as it happens. I'd rather leave it till after the summer. Anyway, it's not all that bad.'

'You're not much help are you?'

'If it was my friends they'd take me as they found me.'

'If it was your friends they'd know you never bother your arse.'

'You're getting beyond a joke Di. Take a look at yourself. Stressing out over a few friends coming for a meal and a bed. These are supposed to be your oldest pals. The ones who saw the real you when you were all together in the flat. You don't need to prove your worth to them. It's not about you anyway. And it doesn't need to be perfect in every last detail.'

Typical. It wasn't about him either and that, no doubt, would be what was bothering him. Give him the quiet life. Have the meals on the table, the washing done and everything under control and he was happy. Don't demand. Don't nag. Be there for him. Deal with the kids and all their arrangements. And *then* he was easy to live with. Kind. Generous. Loving even.

It didn't surprise me when a fishing trip came up for him 'unexpectedly' that very same weekend. Maybe Patricia could bring Lesley.

Carys phoned me from Wales.

'Diane, lovely. Thank you so much for organising everyone. It will be wonderful to see you all again. No video this time, I promise!'

Alix was the first to call off, two weeks before the event. 'He's really not too well, Diane. We're just waiting for some test results. I don't know what it is but for once I feel I'd better be a good wife in case it turns out to be something serious. Come over and see me when you can and I'll maybe have some news then. Tell Carys I'll catch up with her next time.'

Patricia was 'up to her eyes' in preparation for a school inspection. Parents were being asked for their views and she was spending a lot of time on PR type activities. It went against the grain; but a poor report would be too damaging. That night there was to be a summer disco for P5, 6 and 7. She would normally leave that to her deputy but this year she felt she had to attend, as there would be a captive audience of parents there, dropping off and picking up all the little Lisas and Stevens. Another opportunity to talk up the school.

When Nancy phoned with a weariness in her voice and a variety of reasons why it might be difficult, I stopped her mid sentence.

'Let's cancel it. Everything is working against it. There will be another time. I'll phone Carys and explain. She let us down last time so what can she say? We'll try again when everyone is better placed. Maybe next year.'

It was obvious that Carys was decidedly disappointed.

'Diane, I was counting on you. I was sure you could fix it. And

I've been so looking forward to seeing you all again. You won't know, but I've been through a difficult time recently and all I wanted was to be with my old pals who know me and what I'm worth.'

'I'm really sorry, Carys. If you want, come and stay with me for a couple of nights anyway. You can tell me what's been happening. Then maybe you can head up to Lesley's for a few more days.'

She could have the spare bedroom; it was in reasonable shape. And maybe we'd just go out for a meal on the Saturday night. In some ways it was a big relief.

* *

'And he was a womaniser, a lazy sod; he was always missing deadlines. So in the end I told him I'd write the damn book myself. He just walked away without another word. Until the final proofs were ready for printing. And then the shit hit the fan. He wanted his name on it. Proper recognition of his contribution, he said. I told him to bog off back to that doe-eyed student who was acting as his latest muse. The rest is history, as they say. I just can't believe the University would take that line – accusing me of plagiarism! They couldn't make it stick of course, but it's damaged my reputation nevertheless. I haven't worked all those years, reached the top of my profession and established an international reputation for it all to go down the pan.'

She was utterly convincing. Strong, determined, fired up, indignant.

'That sounds so unfair, Carys. What's JJ saying about it?'

'That's another thing. "Trying to see both sides" he said. Can you believe it? His own wife and he still sees the need to balance the evidence! He should have been out fighting for me and with me, every step of the way. Of course he has a professional reputation to protect too. Relations have been somewhat strained of late, if you know what I mean.'

'Is he coming to Belfast?'

'No. Not yet anyway. Maybe not at all. I don't know.'

There was no point in trying to change the subject or shift the focus, until she had talked herself hoarse. Then as something of an afterthought she looked at me and came straight out with it.

'Don't tell me you're still working in that old people's home? I bet you're not even in charge. You had so much promise Diane. Such a good balance between intellect and social conscience. Surely to goodness you could have found something more suitable by now.'

I'd had no intention of breaking down. It was the word 'promise' that set me off.

'It's what I've spent my life doing and now I don't know what else to do. I'm not fit for anything that needs brain power any more. And I can't commit to anything full time because there's still so much to do around here. Anyway, they all like me in there. It makes me feel I'm worth something.'

'There's a word for that somewhere, Diane. And I don't think it's a compliment either. You can't keep choosing to sacrifice yourself so that other people feel better. Where's the status? Where's the reward? Where's the recognition? You should be at least running the service if you want to stay in that line of work. Are you going to see out the century like this? Are you going to see out your life underachieving, cleaning up after all and sundry? I'm fighting to hang on to what I've achieved. You've given up the fight before ever taking up arms. And you had so much promise. Is this what you really want?'

I blamed the tears on the bourbon she brought, the flu I'd had recently, my hormones – anything but the truth.

Everybody needs somebody sometime

You Care? Then We Care!

Writ large on the poster, blue-tacked to the staff notice-board in the home. Another initiative. Another short-term grant funded project. The difference this time was that it was actually for staff benefit.

Go in private for help with personal problems. Professionally trained counsellors offer a confidential service – completely free to employees of Millbank Care Homes. Make that call. You owe it to yourself. You won't regret it. Millbank UK. A caring employer.

I took a note of the number.

Following Carys's visit, the house of cards had slowly tumbled around my ears. Carys had removed the first card with her 'Is this life what you *really* want?'

Willie had inadvertently pulled out another supporting diamond with a 'isn't it about time you got yourself a proper job now that John's about to leave school?'

Mother had demolished a whole floor with a 'Maisie was asking how your painting is doing these days. I just told her we'd seen nothing of it for years and weren't likely to. You're past all that now.'

And John had knocked the whole roof off in his Standard Grade essay on 'The Role of Women in Society'. He had used his own family as an example of what was becoming anachronistic in family life – a mother who reprised the traditional female role and whose achievements in life tended to be experienced vicariously through her children's successes.

Once I confirmed my understanding of 'vicarious', I tested out my perceptions with Susan on one of her rare weekends at home.

'If John is anything to go by, it seems none of you here thinks much of what I do for you all.'

'Now I wouldn't go that far, Mum. I suspect it's more that you're like a piece of furniture. You know… Only noticed when you're not in your usual place.' She tried to give me a hug.

'No wait.' I pushed her away. 'What have I been doing all these years?'

'Don't get on your high horse about it. I didn't say you hadn't done a good job. It's just that you've always been here, beavering away in the background but not exactly inspirational or innovative. Take it as a compliment – of a kind. We don't notice you till something goes wrong and you're not here to fix it. Metaphorically speaking that is.'

'And what do other mothers do? Your friends' mothers.'

'I don't know really. Jenni's Mum is into Yoga and healthy eating and all that stuff. Judy's Mum's writing a cookery book. Kerry's Mum's gone back to college to study archaeology. Clare's Mother is a bit more like you. She has a wee job in the Spar in Peebles but otherwise is a bit of a home bird. Makes wonderful toffee. That kind of thing.'

'And what do you think mothers *should* do?'

'Don't ask me. I don't intend to have any children. I'm gonna be too busy doing my own thing. Enjoying life. Travelling. You won't find me up to my ears in soap suds and dirty nappies. Women don't need children nowadays to be fulfilled. It's all about choice, and I won't be choosing that.'

* *

Choice. What do I choose? You can choose you know.

I'd always chosen to care. I'd always chosen to make everything right for everyone. But maybe it hadn't been an active choice. Not a real considered option. More like a compulsion. A 'what would happen if I didn't?'

Now it seemed, some people might have been better off if I hadn't.

I didn't take advantage of *You Care? Then We Care!* But I did go back to Francka. She knew much of my story already. I thought she could help me with this compulsion.

* *

'Remember we did the inner child work when you came here before? We tried to get rid of that knot in your stomach so that you didn't need food to calm it down. I think we'll do some more of that and work on responsibility this time.'

I really tried.

Focus on every bone, one by one.

Consciously let go of any tension.

Let yourself sink right into the chair.

Still your mind.

Let any stray thoughts come and just as easily go.

Remember a day when you felt carefree. Picture where you were, what you were wearing. Feel that wonderful feeling again. Walk through that scene, paying attention to the colours … the sounds … the smells.

It was all very well at the time. But the triggers were stronger.

* *

'Diane. It's your Mother speaking. You'll never guess what's happened. The chimney went on fire and I had to call the fire brigade. The mess … you wouldn't believe it. The young man in charge gave me a real ticking off for not having the chimney swept more often. Your Dad always saw to all of that of course. You'll come over and give me a hand? Oh that *is* good of you. How about this afternoon then?'

I couldn't just up and go, however.

'Willie, is that you? Just to let you know I'm away to Forfar this afternoon. I'll probably have to go straight to work from there. But I've left a casserole in the slow cooker. One of the boys can put on potatoes. Yes, it's Mum. Her house is a total tip after a chimney fire, apparently. No, I'm not forgetting you need your blue shirt for tomorrow. I'll iron it before I go out.'

Norma phoned me later.

'How's Mum? What was the damage?'

'Oh, not as bad as you might think. I cleaned it all up in a couple of hours. You know what she's like about getting her hands dirty.'

'Just as well you're near enough to help. By the way, I was wondering if you might be able to have Roddy and Erin for two nights next month. Max and I have been invited to a company do at Dunblane Hydro. You're not far from there are you?'

And then the charge nurse at the home collared me.

'Would you mind doing a couple of extra nights next week,

Diane? School holidays you know and everyone wants time off as usual. I'll make it up to you later.'

Everyone was in my debt but no-one was repaying.

'Mum, I said the boys could come back here on Saturday after the game to watch Liverpool on the tele and have some pizza and stuff. I knew you wouldn't mind. Can you pick up a selection of goodies at Safeways when you do your shopping?'

Willie was his usual sympathetic self. 'For God's sake Diane. Just how many headaches can you have in a month? Oh sorry, headaches *and* heavy bleeding. And then there's *too tired* because you're not sleeping properly. What does a man have to do around here to get his rations?'

Demands, demands. Pulling me this way and that. Filling every waking moment. Chasing me into fitful sleep. Draining my energy so that life became one ever-revolving merry-go-round, with the fun removed.

And someone said you can choose?

* *

The choice was made for me one sunny June afternoon. I had been at work the previous night at the home, spending several hours with a terminal patient, sitting with her through the long dark hours when she could neither sleep not find a comfortable resting position. I arrived home after picking up some groceries to find the kitchen full of dirty dishes and the washing basket overflowing again – of once-used bath towels. Tired and weary I certainly was, but I couldn't leave the place like that.

Sleep took ages to come and when it did, was full of dreams. Dad eating poison out of a mouse trap. Mum's house going up in flames. David and John in a football stadium crush. Susan falling off a motorbike into a quarry. Willie touching a live wire half-way up a pylon. I was running, running, running – running from one to another. Seeing it happen and not getting there in time. Cleaning gaping wounds, shouting for help, trying to phone an ambulance but never managing to hit three nines in a row.

When I finally woke I found a couldn't move a muscle. Paralysed. I felt raw terror.

Oh my God. I must have had a stroke.

It was the only explanation I could think of.

How can I get help? I can't move.

In Newfoundland it is known as the 'old hag'.

Dr Kent was mildly sympathetic.

'Sleep paralysis we call it. Maybe it should be waking paralysis. If you did a survey, you'd probably find 30% of the population have experienced something like it at some stage. It's the result of premature mind-body disconnection as one is about to enter into (or exit from) REM sleep. You can also experience it on falling asleep. I wouldn't worry too much about it. It really is relatively common.'

Well, that's bloody reassuring, I thought.

'You're probably doing too much, and not sleeping well either. That combined with the usual pre-menopausal changes. I see a lot of women like you and they usually find a course of anti-depressants and maybe a holiday in the sun help. Take these tablets for a minimum of six months anyway, but come and see me in a month's time and we'll check how you're getting on.'

I didn't like the sound of that. Six months on medication. 'What about any possible side effects Doctor?'

'You might experience dry mouth and constipation. Occasionally we see a bit of weight gain. And just for the first couple of weeks you might well have problems sleeping at night – restlessness and feelings of anxiety mostly. But stick with it because these will disappear quite quickly as the medicine kicks in.

'Now, are there also some changes you can make so that life is a bit easier for you? What do you do for relaxation or fun?'

I looked at him blankly.

What indeed?

Bad Moon Rising

The Campbells were coming! Judy and Pete had been acquaintances of ours in Saudi through our shared connection with Alix and Gerald. They'd left The Kingdom in the early 90s and settled in Perth Australia. Now it seems they were brushing the dust from their canvas covered address book with its familiar Saudi symbol of a date palm tree and two crossed swords, and looking up ex-pat friends and acquaintances. Of particular interest were those likely to offer them free B&B, while on their grand tour of the old country. The Mitchells, ex Jeddah Prep, had offered them use of their Cardiff flat for a few days while they were on a school trip to the Dordogne. The Kennedys took time off from the hard graft of self sufficiency in Devon to show them the south west, albeit on bicycles. John Mackie had given up his golf for a whole weekend to act as tour guide in the Lake District. And now they were staying with Alix and Gerald for a couple of nights before heading up to Argyll and the site of Pete's ancestors' most infamous act.

Alix was breathless on the end of the phone, as if a major panic was in full flow.

'Diane, thank God you're in. I need a big favour from you. Next Saturday, here at my place, you and Willie, lunch. The Campbells are coming. You remember – Judy and Pete, from Arabian Homes. Bring any photos or cine films you might have of Jeddah. I can't imagine how we're going to fill the time. They were never the most scintillating of couples.'

Alix's dining room was a study in gracious living. Too perfect for the messy business of eating. My 'Desert Diamonds' had been joined by a number of Spencer Tartt originals of Old Jeddah. A beautiful Persian rug in creams and reds complemented the original oak flooring. The table was set with Spode Brocato china, the glasses were of course of crystal. In that elegant serene setting, the casual clobber of the Campbells jarred on the eye. I was glad I'd selected the Country Casuals shirtdress from my small range of safe and reasonably slimming. For once, I felt slightly superior.

We survived smoked haddock pâté on oatcakes, followed by Aberdeen Angus roast rib of beef with sauté potatoes, broccoli and green beans, by covering '*whatever happened to old whatshisname*?' During crannachan, Alix moved on to the '*do you remember the time when* …?' With sighs and smiles, we relived the one day it rained in Jeddah, the parent-teacher football match at the Conti that ended in a brawl, and the day the Saudi Government announced a rise in taxation and all the Westerners downed tools and threatened to leave the country. But by the time the coffee was drunk and the port was poured, the conversation was drying up.

'Willie, be a dear and help Gerald set up the projector will you? It's years since we had it out and I bet it won't be working. We've loads of old films from Jeddah days. I'm sure Pete and Judy would like a comfy seat and a trip down memory lane.'

* *

I helped Alix carry the dirty dishes through to the dishwasher, the pair of us whispering in case the guests could hear us, dissecting their clothes, their accents, their travel plans; I am rarely bitchy but for once I took some delight in it.

'What do you make of them then, Diane? It seems to me like they're just using old friends to save on hotel bills. I had forgotten quite how awfully boring they were. Just as well Gerald has had a lifetime's experience in acting as a host to foreign nationals! It's taking his mind off his illness too, for a few hours.'

It seemed like an invitation to probe a little.

'What exactly is wrong with him, Alix? I noticed he seemed to be limping. That's ages now he's been under the weather.'

'It's not good news Diane …'

Gerald popped his head round the dining room door.

'Come on you two. There are a couple of young lads on this film I want you to see. Good looking, fit, tanned. Might just be your cup of tea!'

'Okay Gerald. They wouldn't be you and Willie at the Creek I suppose?'

'Later, I'll tell you more later, Diane' was all she managed before he dragged us off to the den for the film show.

On our way home I quizzed Willie about Gerald.

'How did you think Gerald looked?'

'Okay to me. A bit slower – but then he is a few years older than the rest of us. Must be pushing sixty now. He didn't mention anything in particular.'

I'd have to wait until Alix could meet me in Perth for coffee. Apparently, that would be dependent on how Gerald felt about her going out for the afternoon. Changed days when a man could dictate to Alix.

* *

'Black, no sugar please. Have a cake Diane if you want. I'm not hungry.'

I dithered and then opted for a less fattening digestive biscuit – a chocolate one.

Was it best that *I* broach the subject of Gerald or leave it to Alix?

The way it happened, Alix wasted little time on how the kids were before launching into a medical description of Gerald's problem.

'There's no point in glossing over it, Diane. He's got cancer. Malignant melanoma. And it's already stage 3.'

I knew enough to recognise that diagnosis as bad news.

'How did you find out?' I asked. 'Is he getting treatment for it? Where is it – on his face or on his body?' I couldn't stop the questions spilling out.

Over the previous winter, Gerald had been going for several weeks to the podiatrist for treatment for an in-growing toe nail. She had noticed a dark brown mole on his lower left leg, irregular round the edges, uneven in colour and measuring bigger than the end of a pencil eraser. Her advice had been to show it to his GP. Gerald took no notice. He had several moles on his body and had done for years. Nothing to worry about.

Only when it started to itch and bleed did he think it might be worth checking out. Tests and biopsies confirmed the consultant opinion. Malignant melanoma, probably as a result of growing up in Africa and then living in the Middle East. We all need vitamin D, but 20 minutes a day in the sun will suffice apparently.

'I'll beat this thing, don't you worry,' he'd told Alix.

The surgeon excised the mole and later removed lymph nodes in his groin. A recent MRI scan had shown metastasis in his bones. Chemotherapy would begin the following week.

'We had no idea he was really ill. He's been off colour for a few months and to be honest, getting on my nerves not wanting to go anywhere or do anything. I had to literally drag him off to India to look for new stock for the business. Since I went public with Rubislaw Treasures he's really enjoyed our trips to antique sales and I was so pleased – and relieved – that he'd found something to occupy his time. He would catalogue everything, make up invoices, keep the books. It let me off the hook a bit too. I could go out for the day and he'd be happy working away in the study. That's all changed now. He doesn't want me out of his sight.'

I looked her straight in the eye. 'You never were one to be held back Alix. Remember how you struggled with the restrictions in Saudi.'

'And remember how I managed to cope? Brief Encounter and all that.'

'Let's not go into that. So, how *are* you coping with this?'

'I'm struggling, Diane, I really am.' Her voice wobbled.

'I'm not going to pretend ours was ever the great love match. Oh we enjoyed the sex right enough, but that doesn't last forever. But I suppose you could say we were a partnership. He had his role and I had mine, and we both benefited from the proceeds. We travelled together and enjoyed that. We have two beautiful and talented children who bring us great joy. And if we've had the odd dalliance, well we've been discreet and made sure it didn't compromise our relationship. I know for a fact there was a secretary in the London office who provided more that shorthand and typing. But this dependency – that's not me, Diane. I feel caged, and drained by it. And I don't know what the outcome is going to be.'

I thought for a moment. 'Have you contacted the Macmillan nurses? They've got a base in Perth.'

'He's not ready to accept them yet. Still denying the situation really. Or frightened that once he names it, it becomes real. He seems to cope if I'm here and we lead a quiet life.'

'So, where does that leave you?'

'The consultant in Edinburgh is very good. Private of course, so he has time. He suggested a book which has helped me understand Gerald's reactions, and what I can maybe expect. It seems we have a few more stages to go through before he resigns himself to the truth about his condition. He'll get angry, depressed, maybe deny it all again until eventually he might come round to accepting it. And until we can be reasonably sure of the outcome, he prefers not to even talk about it.'

'That must be hard for you, Alix.'

'I'm trying to carry on as normal, although you'll have noticed we've a sign for the business outside the house now. Viewing is by private arrangement and we've set aside two rooms, one for furniture and the other for jewellery and collectibles. That way I can arrange viewings around hospital trips, and the business still survives. I might need it more in the future.'

'And what about finding new stock? Are you still getting out to auctions and sales?'

'Only locally now. Especially after that last trip to the Borders. Diane, can I tell you something? Something really serious?'

I was quick to respond. 'Of course you can Alix. What on earth is it?'

'I did a very silly thing on that last trip and I just hate myself now. I don't trust my own judgement any more.' Her hand shook as she lit a cigarette and asked, 'Do you mind?'

'Of course not, go on.'

'You see I hadn't been away for weeks and the stock was getting a bit low. So when Gerald's sister was visiting for a few days, he suggested I went to an estate sale in the Galashiels area. It was to last for two days, which meant only one night away. I took the van so that I could bring back any small items – paintings, china, the kind of thing that sells well on a day-to-day basis.

'I had the CD player on all the way down, the windows open to let the smoke out and the fresh air in, and I was singing at the top of my voice, feeling a sense of freedom at last.

'It was a very good sale. I recognised loads of people I knew from the trade and several of us were staying in the same small hotel just outside the town. We gathered in the bar before dinner, arguing the toss over who paid what and whether or not it was worth it, and then I was introduced to a couple of guys from the North of England. I took them to be gay to be honest. Charming, well dressed, full of the chat, you know the type. One of them flirted all evening with the waitress who didn't know where to look she was so embarrassed, the wee soul. And the other one, well … he flirted with me.'

I raised my eyebrows.

'I've met his kind before, usually all talk and no action when it comes down to it. So I enjoyed a bit of repartee you might say. A few gins, a few cigarettes, a few more gins. And when the bar closed we went up to his room for a nightcap. Bad move. The rest is history, I suppose you might say.'

There was no easy answer. Or justification.

'Goodness. Was it the drink then?'

'I'm telling myself it was. But my conscience won't accept that so easily. I did a terrible thing, Diane. My husband is dying and at the first opportunity, I betray him like that. Am I just a bad bitch? Am I? Don't answer. I don't need kind words or understanding. I don't deserve that. But please don't tell anyone else, will you Diane? I feel so ashamed.'

I felt the pain in two places – in my gut and in my heart.

I wished I'd never known.

Look what thoughts can do

Gerald's sudden notion to visit the Kenya of his boyhood to celebrate his 60th birthday served as a useful diversion - from thinking about his death. Whether his immersion in flight time-tables, safari schedules and insider guides was another indicator of his denial of the inevitable, or conversely an acceptance that time was short, was unclear. In the end it was also immaterial. He died just two days before his October birthday and two months before the date of the proposed trip. His last six months had been trial by chemotherapy.

Black didn't suit Alix one little bit. It drained her already pale colouring. We Dalmeny Street Girls (minus Carys) all looked cold, pinched and tearful, the day of the funeral. I couldn't rid myself of the frightening realisation that this was just the start of bad times for us all.

As usual, Willie was less than helpful in his comments.

'So we're all getting older. What's new? You start dying the day you're born, don't you?'

'But this is too soon Willie. Alix is only 46 and that's her a widow already,' I replied.

'She should have married someone younger then, shouldn't she?'

'Oh for goodness sake, life's not like that and you know it.'

'Well, he gave her a great life when he was here, and no doubt left her well set up too. You know Alix. She can be pretty philosophical about life. Don't let it get *you* down Di.'

True to form, over the next few weeks and months Alix grieved but never lost sight of the future. Whereas I ruminated over what it all meant and could see only doom and gloom. I struggled to look ahead with any optimism.

* *

The catalogue said that if daffodil bulbs are planted by late October, then by March there will be a lovely display of yellow trumpets, all fresh and hopeful, announcing Spring's arrival, whilst adding much needed colour to the garden at this time of year. The picture showing the daffodil scene was indeed beautiful. There they stood, pointy green leaves around strong green stems bearing yellow trumpets, poking up in clumps through a large, green lawn. I resolved to buy some the next time I was near B&Q. The bulbs would go alongside the hedge, which went the length of the lawn on the left hand side of the garden. I would plant them to provide a daffodil accompaniment whenever I walked down the path the following March. That would be a lovely sight, and something to look forward to, I had thought.

The new hand trowel and fifty bulbs, still in the brown paper bag, ended up sitting on top of a kitchen unit, the one nearest the back door. They looked at me, and I looked at them, every time I passed to go out. I knew the bulbs needed be out in the garden, under the soil where they belonged, not sitting in a bag in a warm kitchen, in limbo. Yet the thought of going out there and digging the garden was completely overwhelming. I simply couldn't muster the energy or the enthusiasm.

My lack of action became the stick with which to beat myself.

You're hopeless. Can't even get your act together to plant a bag of daffies. Look at Alix. She's coping with being a young widow. And you – you're always anxious about something, tired all the time, and struggling to keep up. And life won't get any better for any of us. Alix is only the first. What about Patricia? Trevor's up to something. She'll be the next to be on her own. And Carys? She's out of a job now – and probably out of a marriage next. Lesley's back problems are ageing her in front of our eyes. And Nancy is far from well. She could hardly make it through the funeral service before having to lie down. This is just the first big hiccough. How are you going to cope when the rest happens? How are you going to be of any help to anyone?

At my review appointment, Dr Kent started where he had left off.

'So – what about the fun? Finding the tablets suiting you now, giving you a bit more energy?'

'Not really Doctor. I'm still so tired most of the time. Maybe it's because there's a lot of bad stuff going on around me just now. It's wearing me out worrying about everyone and how they're going to manage through it all,' I answered.

'Are these all family members Diane?'

I had to admit they weren't. But that family members were yet another constant source of anxiety. Mum getting older, Susan and Elizabeth finding decent jobs, David passing enough Highers to get into University, mother-in-law becoming forgetful and a bit of a danger to herself on occasions. Then there were the old dears in the home. I was dreading losing one or two of them who'd been there for years.

'Sounds like there's little room left for fun, then. How do you see that changing over time?'

I thought it could only get worse.

'I'd like to suggest something to you Diane which might help. We all fear the future at times. Most of us have days when we berate ourselves over mistakes we've made. But I think your preoccupation with doom and gloom and your own high standards are putting a strain on your mental wellbeing. With your permission, I'm going to refer you to a psychologist who uses an approach called cognitive behaviour therapy. It focuses on helping you change your thoughts.'

Change my thoughts? If only.

* *

All that winter, from the weakening of daylight in the second week of October, I had craved the sun, longed for spring, ached for warmth. But when it came, it seemed to arrive too quickly, before I was ready for it. Under the influence of a few bright days in early April, the trees turned green seemingly overnight. A clever female blackbird had surreptitiously made her nest in the ivy and hatched her eggs to reveal three chirping gaping mouths on the constant lookout for sustenance. The noise irritated me day and night. The green shoots of the winter wheat were showing an obvious surge upwards towards the sun. Everything was growing, blossoming, bursting into new life.

I couldn't bear the contrast with what was happening inside. My mood sank to new depths, my desire to stay under the duvet was almost overpowering. I shut my eyes to the brightness, pulled my cardigan tighter around my body to keep out the energy. My face echoed my inner feelings – weak, tired, despairing.

The family didn't know what to do.

Willie kept his distance, thinking I preferred to be left alone, when all I wanted from him, but couldn't bring myself to ask, was some tender loving care. A pair of strong comforting arms to hold and stroke me.

Susan and Elizabeth invited me to a girls' day out in Edinburgh.

'A bit of pampering. We could all do with it,' they said.

I pleaded a bit of a cold and not wanting to spread the virus.

John tried to give me a hug, then slinked away embarrassed at my tears.

Even Mother, not usually the most observant or demonstrative, expressed her concern.

'What about a wee holiday Diane? I know a lovely place in Strathpeffer. And it will be looking at its best with all the spring flowers. Would you like me to send you the details?'

No, I wouldn't, didn't, couldn't – whatever it was, whatever they suggested.

I might have ignored the appointment card too had Willie not seen it. It was six months since Dr Kent had referred me. Six months to go right off the idea. Six months to sink further into the pit from where any movement was almost too much of an effort.

'Please Di. Try it, please. You're really not well, you know. This is more than a bit of winter blues. Go and see what's on offer. We're all really worried about you.'

* *

We spent the first hour just getting to know each other. In fact, even that's not true. It was him getting to know me. I must have looked jaded and totally miserable when I flopped into the well-worn easy chair in his office at Tayside Mental Health Community Centre.

Dr Michaels (doctor of psychology) seemed to suss me out without too much bother.

'Typical eldest child of an abusive parent (*I hope you don't mind me using that term, he'd said*). Wants to make everything right for everyone. Tries not to cause any trouble for the other parent. Takes on responsibility for younger members of the family. Has perfectionist tendencies.

'I see people like you all the time. You have the cares of the world on your shoulders. Others turn to you for support and guidance. But you have great difficulty in balancing your needs with those of others.'

Yes, well, maybe that *was* me.

Over the following six weeks he asked several pointed questions which still reverberate in my mind.

'What might you be preventing your children learning by trying to shield them from life's dangers and hardships?'

'What would really happen if you said no to your mother?'

'Why do you make allowances for everyone else's human failings and yet deny yourself the right to be less than perfect?'

'Who will look after you, when you've worn yourself out looking after everyone else?'

This wasn't a 12 step programme. The questions weren't typed on to a shiny pocket-sized card to carry around. He probably didn't even ask them in that order. And the asking of them wasn't sufficient to effect a miracle change in my thinking.

But week by week, with time to reflect on my life in a structured and safe process and aided by a little homework, a few lights started to twinkle in the darkness. I couldn't change the past, wipe out the effects of growing up in fear, or have the time over again to live a different type of life. But he *could* help me break free from my habitual ways of thinking and acting. Save me from myself I suppose.

With his encouragement, I tried replying to Mother's regular requests for help with a 'thanks for asking me Mum. Let me just check what I have on, and get back to you.' And sometimes I'd do whatever it was, and sometimes I had 'something else on that night.' I found it really hard to do. But when I did it, I found that the world didn't end.

He suggested that I explore my fears and come up with strategies for coping if and when one of them actually came to pass.

Susan can't get a decent job? I suppose she can work in Burger King for a while so that at least she can support herself. Then maybe she can think about a post-grad qualification if that makes her more employable. A degree in Art was her choice and she knew the employment prospects when she started. She must have thought it still worth doing.

Mrs McDonald is losing some of her marbles? There are community services out there to help. And Willie's two brothers live relatively close by. We'll share the load. And it might well just be part of the ageing process. Nothing so far to suggest that it is Alzheimer's.

Patricia is miserable, her marriage looks shaky? You don't know what goes on behind closed doors. Patricia has a rigid approach to life. You can be there if she needs to talk, but she will have her own way of dealing with things. You can't make everything right for her.

And as for 'who will look after me?' – that was when the truth of my situation dawned bright and clear. a) I wouldn't expect anyone to take that on, and b) I had to start taking responsibility for my own health so that it wouldn't be necessary (and if I was honest, so that I would still be around to help others out).

Together we evolved a way of challenging these negative and energy sapping thoughts.

Where is the evidence to support my negative thought?

Is there another way to make sense of the situation?

Am I applying a double standard, expecting myself to be perfect, concentrating on my weaknesses and forgetting my strengths?

How does my thinking help me or hinder me from living the kind of life I choose?

It still left the burning question 'what do I choose?' but at least I recognised my right to choose – and to choose for me, for fun, for light, for living. Maybe I'd plant those bulbs next Autumn. And maybe I wouldn't. But it would be my choice. And I'd feel good about myself, if only for choosing.

'Okay then – what do you think of it so far? Let's have your initial reactions and any ideas for improvement. Robin – do you want to kick off?'

What do I think of it? What on earth was she going to say when it came to her turn? To suggest that Nancy's mind hadn't been fully focussed on Daniel's presentation of the 1999 Sales Plan was an understatement. For the last thirty minutes it had been anywhere but in the conference room, mainly wandering between Dolphinton and Skipton, flitting back and forth in no precise order; a hundred and one thoughts surfacing and ebbing away – tasks to be done, words said, words needing to be said, problems, more problems, but few solutions.

Her current situation might almost have been described by the summary on the final slide – if she replaced the variables with her own, which she then did, smiling away to herself at the private joke.

Objectives: To get through the day
Methods: Just keep on going, one foot after the other
Resources:
a) patience (running out fast as far as Mother was concerned)
b) money (never enough given the school fees and horses)
c) time (into negative equity here)
d) husband (can't always be relied upon when needed)
e) children (a constant drain on resources)
Outcomes: God knows how this will all end up.
Risk factors: My sanity, I think.

'Nancy – do you want to go next? You must be quite pleased with it by the way you're smiling!'

Daniel's voice pierced her vision of the final slide and brought her up short.

'Ah, yes, of course,' she replied, buying time to drag up something eminently sensible from the automatic pilot bit of her brain. 'I think it has a lot of merit, definitely an improvement on last year's plan I feel. But – I'd like to see the objectives translated into a more pragmatic and detailed implementation plan than the outline methods you've described.'

'I thought you might say that,' Daniel smirked. 'Because that task, Nancy, is the very next one I'm allocating to you.' A remark which made all fifteen of the Scottish and Northern sales team fall about laughing.

A challenge to be relished, or a chore? Back in her office Nancy contemplated over a cup of strong, black coffee. There was a time in the not too distant past when she would have been right 'in there' at such a meeting. Wholly present, formulating the next clever question ahead of the others, flagging up problems and proffering solutions. She would have been enthusiastic, motivated, pleased to be clocking up her sales figures and those of her team; doggedly chasing the next bonus or promotion. But not now. She was, she felt, simply coasting. Had been for the last couple of years or more, ever since her father died suddenly, and ever since seemingly unable to shake herself out of it.

Not by choice, she rationalised, but forced by circumstances.

There is only so much energy and time to go around and she was already squeezing as much out of each day as it was humanely possible to do. Michael, Angus, Amy, Camilla, Mother, work, horses, dogs, school, shopping, Mother, Mother and more bloody Mother – sinking deeper into dementia, right in the heart of Skipton. Which reminded her – she'd have to go back down again this weekend and check up after that neighbour's phone call saying she hadn't seen mother go out of the house for three days. That would make it twice she'd been down in the last month. 166 miles, and four hours on the road each way – as if she wasn't already driving enough with her job – and it wasn't exactly a bundle of fun once she was down there either. Arguing about the most menial things with a stubborn old lady who wouldn't see sense wasn't anybody's definition of fun, surely?

Mother's flat refusal to deal with anything to do with money was driving Nancy insane. Every time she visited they ended up like two bulls, horns locked in battle with neither emerging the winner.

'Come on Mother, you can learn to write a cheque, it's not difficult.' Despite all Nancy's efforts to persuade, cajole, coax, bribe even – it was like trying to get blood out of a stone.

'I can't! I just can't do it! Your father always handled the money side of things. I can't take it in Nancy, and that's that.'

Can't or won't? Her daughter's angry thought.

Then Nancy felt guilty as she looked at her mother's stricken face with its pink watery eyes, and the old veiny hands shaking in her lap, clasped tightly together so she wouldn't have to pick up the biro.

There'd been almost no food in the fridge either.

'When did you go shopping last, Mother?'

'Yesterday,' had been the emphatic reply.

'What did you buy then, I can't see much in here.'

'Cheese, eggs, bacon, milk and bread, same as I always do on a Wednesday.'

Yesterday had been Friday, but no matter.

'Where've they all gone then?' asked Nancy perplexed.

'I ate them all.'

When there were no wrappers in the bin? Liar.

And she knows she's lying.

But it wouldn't have helped to say it, so instead Nancy suggested they take a trip to the supermarket 'right now', so there would be enough provisions for a few more days, and so 'I'll know for certain you've got plenty once I leave.'

'No.' Her Mother's thin lips were tightly pursed. 'I can't afford to go shopping again this week.'

'Yes you can! We've been through this lots of times before. Dad left you more than enough to see you through. You can spend £50 a week on food if you want to and *still* have enough to pay the bills and buy a few luxuries for yourself.'

'Where's this £50 coming from then, you just tell me that, Nancy, because *I* can't see it.'

Nancy shut her eyes and sighed hard. 'It's in the bank. All you have to do is go there and get it out with a cheque.'

'I can't do that, I've told you, I can't write them, it's too hard.'

And there they were, back full circle, back to where it started.

Nancy found it exhausting. All of it. Her mother. The driving. The worry. The alternative – to have her mother come live with them in Dolphinton – was too awful to contemplate. Somehow or other she was going to have to seek help, and find a way to get her mother to accept it.

**

No one could have said when, for certain, it had all begun.

The year she'd had several bouts of 'flu, the consultant suspected. At the time, she'd thought it was just bad luck – a case of being in too many stuffy, over-heated offices that winter, and a plethora of virulent bugs from Melrose to Meldrum. She'd been knocked off her feet each time, but a few days in bed had mostly sorted it, then she'd managed to get herself back to work and into the swing of it again.

She remembered too, about the opening meet, 1999 when the hounds, fresh from their summer lay-off, keen and able, had provided such good sport – a long, hard-riding day, with plenty of galloping for miles, and adrenalin rushes gained from soaring over fences and high hedges. When the hunting was over, there'd been the long hack back to the lorry, riding into the sun sinking into the afternoon sky, a light dampness descending on them, horses and riders alike.

She'd lain in the bath later, aching from head to foot, much more than usual, and put it down to getting older, not being as fit as she used to be. And then, the following year there'd been so many of those awful journeys – up and down a quarter of Britain to see her mother. The overwhelming fatigue that usually developed on the homeward run. How she had struggled to stay awake, the things she used to do to force herself to keep driving: winding the window down, having a fly cigarette, turning the radio up and singing along. Even sometimes pulling off the motorway miles before she'd actually intended to stop, in order to shut her eyes for a moment, lean back against the seat and headrest of the car, take a deep breath and pretend she was somewhere entirely different, instead of feeling like a thin piece of out-of-date ham sandwiched between two thick layers of bread – her mother on top, her children below.

Even if the start of her illness couldn't be pinpointed, the incident which precipitated her eventual collapse was easy to identify. The memories were still etched in her brain; vivid, horrible – the day, the time, the place, pitiful images of her mother. She wondered if they would ever leave her.

'It will likely be a bit of a shock for you, to see her as she is,' the nurse had warned, 'but she's comfortable now, and I can assure you she's not in any pain – the drugs will see to that. She might be able to hear you, but she won't be able to respond. I'm so very sorry. If you need anything, don't hesitate to buzz me.'

Nancy's first glimpse into the room made her feel sick to the pit of her stomach. She had some difficulty lowering herself into the bedside chair since her legs and her arms had seemingly turned to jelly, and her heart was racing along, jumping into her throat all the while.

Only recognisable by the face, which looked severely black and blue under the oxygen mask was her mother's prostrate body, looking quite like an Egyptian mummy. Nancy couldn't see whether the grey hair was still there, since the bandages were swathed all over, from the eyes up, and then round the neck and chest. The tips of her mother's fingers were showing on top of the blanket – they were gnarly, reddish black, not quite human. She didn't dare lift up the bedcovers to see any more.

Apart from the noise of the gas moving in and out of the mask, and the machine's bleeping sounds as it drew a graph of green peaks and troughs across the screen next to the bed, Nancy might easily have thought her mother was already dead. But no, she couldn't be – if she were truly dead then the screen would draw a horizontal line, wouldn't it? And the bleeping sound would turn into a long drone. That's what happened on the TV, she'd seen it often enough in those hospital dramas. This was different. This was much more frightening. This was her own real-life and death drama, and there was nothing for it but to stay, and watch and wait, until her mother was finally gone, even though all she wanted to do was to run a million miles away.

The night was too long. She'd remained in the chair, anxious, staring, occasionally managing to speak a few words to the immobile body in front of her. Not the words she really wanted to say, yet couldn't bring herself to do so when she tried to form them, but others, small words of comfort, just in case they could be heard.

The darkness brought guilt-ridden, serious questions, which begged answers, but she couldn't have answered them with any certainty at all. Still they came.

Could the accident have been prevented? Why had she left it so long to visit since the last time? Why hadn't she had the courage to bring her mother to live with them in Dolphinton? Wouldn't it have been better for her mother to die at the scene? How had she survived at all?

Only later was the story pieced together. It wasn't unique. It is possible to read something similar, on occasion, taking up a third page column in the local paper, with a picture of the deceased from happier times. Elderly lady, determined to hang onto her independence, despite a failing memory, forgets to turn the gas off before retiring to bed. On first light she pads through to the old scullery with only one thing on her mind – to make that lovely cup of tea. She fills the kettle, puts it on the cooker ring, reaches for the matches and strikes one before pressing the pilot light.

It is the last action she'll ever take, if she's lucky.

Peter arrived the next morning, an hour too late. In some ways Nancy thought it was worse for him, because he hadn't had chance to say anything at all to Mother, let alone goodbye.

She'd got through the funeral by pushing herself, a step at a time, whilst feeling the most peculiar sensations all over. As if frozen somehow, or made of wood, still moving but at a different speed to everyone else. They appeared to be acting out some elaborate ritual all around her.

When the funeral director had passed her a red rose to throw onto the coffin after it had been lowered into the grave, she'd meekly complied, even though it had seemed an artificial act, another scene in the play she had paid him to produce. She recalled the single rose – plucked from one of the wreaths – an unfortunate choice on his behalf, but how could he have been expected to know any differently? Red roses had been her mother's least favoured flower, on account of their romantic connotations. Just as well then her mother hadn't been around the see the bill for the funeral, since it would surely have upset her frugal sensibilities.

That weird, distanced feeling never left Nancy in the following months. She didn't tell anyone about it, thinking that if she worked her way through it then it would eventually pass. But it didn't go away; it worsened, until the day she collapsed in her office, heart racing, blood coursing, giddy, lying on the floor in a crumpled heap, unable to move, hardly able to speak.

The aftermath had been frightening, painful. And she'd had no energy to do anything other than comply with doctor's orders to rest, forget about work, care for herself. She'd had a lucky escape, they'd told her. Something was bound to happen, sooner or later the way she'd been driving her body over the years. It could have been cancer, or a stroke, or a heart attack. But it wasn't.

Some days she would have said that what had happened to her was even worse.

Tired of waiting

On February 13th 2001 Nancy opened her diary for the first time in weeks and stared at all the blank pages over the last three months. They looked very strange, with the clean, white paper gleaming up at her, instead of the usual cluttered, scribbled entries, with lines through some of them, copious little notes perched at the top, or bottom of the pages, and yellow highlighter over the most important bits to be achieved each day.

The contrast of pre-November 19th to post November 19th was stunning.

How could I possibly have managed all of that intense activity every day of the week?

She felt weary simply looking at the diary, but couldn't resist reading through some of the days, trying to remember what had happened at a given meeting, thinking about the hundreds of miles she'd driven a week, and feeling guilty about all the work suddenly cancelled when she's fallen ill.

She also felt very odd. Disjointed. Far away, somehow, as if looking through a filter at the world. The recurring headaches were depressingly bad, although she tried to ignore them as best she could. The last three months had been one long round of lying in bed feeling awful, or getting up and trying to do 'normal' household things whilst aching all over and having giddy spells. Some days it was difficult to eat but she forced herself to swallow, then often wished she hadn't, when raging indigestion kicked in shortly afterwards. To break the monotony there had been numerous GP consultations and hospital appointments in various clinics, culminating with a referral for a brain scan, for which the waiting was worse than the eventual result.

She'd had enough blood taken from her arms to fill a petrol tank she reckoned. Yet all the tests had been negative. Initially she'd wished they'd find something, anything, just so she could be given an explanation for why she felt so ill. This whole period seemed to have been about nothing other than getting through the day, getting through the week, getting through the months. It felt like purgatory, as Nancy imagined it, most particularly when she overdid it, and then the soles of her feet felt as if they had hot rods of pointed metal sticking in them, sending waves of burning through her whole body. She sometimes wondered what she had done to deserve all the pain.

You must have been a very bad girl in a previous life, she joked to herself occasionally.

But there weren't too many jokes she could think of to cheer herself up, because actually, life like this wasn't funny at all.

The GP had convinced her that she didn't have anything terminal, but no-one yet had told her for definite exactly *why* she was feeling so horrible, *what* this actually was, and neither had they suggested *when* she could expect to feel better, which of course, was what she really wanted to know. To be fair to him, her GP had suggested that she was suffering from 'ME', aka 'yuppie flu' which could, apparently, only be confirmed by 'a diagnosis of exclusion'. That is when every logical test is negative but all the symptoms are present, then the patient is deemed, by default, to have it. This dreadful disease. He'd been putting 'Viral Illness' on her sick lines, and telling her she was 'burnt out' and needed a *long* rest, and that she must also reduce all her stresses as far as possible.

Daniel was pressurising her (subtly) to return to work; telephoning every week to enquire about her progress, asking if she was bored yet, and telling her how the company was struggling without her. The initial response to her collapse had been overwhelming; everyone had rallied round and she'd received the best of care from her family and friends in the early weeks. There had been lots of cards, flowers, phone calls, emails, even from people she was surprised knew about it, or even cared. But now, three months on, everything had gone very quiet. She had an idea that people thought she ought be getting better by now, maybe making more of an effort.

'You're looking better than the last time I saw you,' they'd say, almost without exception.

And it was true, she *was* looking better than the last time she'd seen them, but she wasn't looking like the person she expected to see in the mirror, and she didn't feel a whole lot better either. The children were back to their normal 'I am the centre of my world' selves, and they expected her to be back to normal, which as far as they were concerned, meant putting their needs first.

'I won't know until the day, I'm sorry, but that's how it is,' she'd screamed at Camilla yesterday, when asked for the umpteenth time that week whether she'd be able to drive them to the special pony club hunt next Saturday.

'Just because you *think* I look okay doesn't mean I *feel* okay,' she'd added, instantly wishing she hadn't jumped down Camilla's throat like that. She felt permanently on a short fuse these days, with little energy or enthusiasm for going out doing things, since she knew that if she did, then she'd pay for it the next day when the symptoms surged again.

It was incredibly frustrating. She cried every day when no-one was looking. When she woke up, there was a brief, wonderful instant when she thought she was 'normal' again, but each time the weird feeling returned within seconds, just the same as it had been when she'd fallen to sleep earlier. Sometimes she felt so lonely; no-one seemed to appreciate how lousy she was feeling, not even Michael. She needed a firm diagnosis, a label of some sort, a justification for all of the symptoms and pain. Then people might have more understanding of what she was going through, she thought – or would they? She'd never in her entire life experienced anything like this, so unless other people had, how could they possibly be expected to understand how it felt?

* *

Crrrunchhh, Splosh!; Crrrunchhh, Splosh!; Crrrunchhh, Splosh!

The sound of the ice crunching in the puddles as she walked was very satisfying. Then '*tinkle, tinkle, tinkle, tinkle!*', the noise receding slowly as the shard of ice that had flown up on the last footstep bounced several times and landed a few feet away.

Nancy looked down and saw she was wearing Amy's Joules wellies, which were lime green with bright yellow, orange and pink flowers patterned all over. They must have been the pair nearest to the door when she'd remembered that unless she put the bin out right then, the refuse collection would have done its rounds and missed the Robertson household for the second week running.

One of the few benefits about having a twenty year-old daughter still living at home, Nancy mused, was that it was possible to borrow some of her clothes, providing you were both the same size, which in this particular case, Nancy and Amy were. A neat and athletic size 12. This was not a reciprocal arrangement of course. *Nothing*, that Nancy owned, other than equestrian gear, could be remotely considered for wearing as far as Amy was concerned, even though Nancy felt Amy would have looked rather fetching in the pink silk jumper she'd offered her for a drinks party last month. She'd decided she had gone past offering items now, and neither did they go clothes shopping together anymore, since whenever Nancy saw something that she felt would look good on Amy she couldn't resist selecting out the hanger from the rail. And then the rebuff would begin.

It was the same old performance every time.

'No, Mum, don't bother, it's not what I'm looking for.'

'You could just try it, Amy, I *know* it would look nice on you,' (holding the item aloft for dramatic effect).

'No! I've said, I'll just find my own stuff, thank you.'

They only ended up getting more and more frustrated with each other, every time. Nancy used to think Amy was being difficult, but now she'd come to understand that Amy was simply exercising her independence, as most teenagers will naturally do, cultivating her own style, even if it didn't actually make the most of her.

She had now reached the end of the drive with the heavy bin, and manoeuvred it into position, handles facing out to the roadside, as the bin-men liked to see it. It made their job easier, they could finish the round sooner if everyone took care to position the bin correctly, one of the men had told her ages ago. Since then she had obliged, but doubted if anybody else in the household did, given some of the strange positions she had noticed it in when she'd driven past.

Walking back up the drive Nancy felt a sense of achievement. That was the first time she had taken the bin down since she'd got sick. Hopefully she wouldn't pay for it tomorrow with a flare-up of symptoms. Even if she did, she thought, it was worth it to have felt so strong for ten minutes. That bin had been damn heavy – full to the brim with two weeks worth of non-recyclable rubbish.

The long and winding road

When Diane phoned in early June to ask if she could come and visit, Nancy's first reaction was to make some excuse, in case she was having a 'tired' day on the date Diane was due to come. Then she decided that was silly and pessimistic, she must at least try to be positive. If the worst came to the worst she could cancel at short notice. Diane would understand, she knew that.

In the hour before Diane was due to arrive, Nancy sat at the computer, wanting to check her emails, and powered it up. It was desperately slow as usual. She had been in the habit of getting up and starting something else after pressing the buttons on, whilst the machine trundled and whirred away like this, taking itself step by step through the lengthy boot-up process, then opening *Windows*, until it stabilised into the desk-top background, which was a lovely picture of her sat on a well-groomed Harvey at the Fife show in 1999. Anything would suffice in order for her to feel she was multi-tasking; she could always find something needing to be done, which ensured she didn't waste time just sat there waiting. Perhaps it was making a cup of coffee, loading the washing machine, drying the dishes, cleaning a pair of shoes, putting the rubbish out, making a phone call. There were lots of activities that could be squeezed into two minutes.

Today, however, the keyboard caught her eye, and held her transfixed. It was dirty. Very dirty. Absolutely filthy in fact. Almost every key was covered by a film of grey grease. The back-space, Caps Lock, Control, Enter Keys, the group of six keys from Insert to Pg Dn and *all* the number keys were actually more black than grey.

'My God! I wonder how long they've been like this?' Nancy said out-loud.

Then she remembered how old the computer was – it had been purchased two years ago, but she couldn't remember ever cleaning the keys since she brought it home.

It's disgusting! I'm disgusting! This family is disgusting! This keyboard's been here all this time and no-one has taken the time to clean it!

She then grabbed each end of the whole board, inclining it

towards her as she did so, and peered down the cracks between the keys. Exclaiming *bloody hell, this is a health hazard*, she turned the keyboard upside down and shook its murky contents onto the carpet next to the computer, which, as it happened, she was intending to vacuum quickly before Diane arrived.

The pile of crumbs was large enough to warrant fetching the brush and dustpan immediately, because she couldn't bear to sit there checking her emails whilst there was sufficient food for ten mice right next to her foot. Once that was cleared up, Nancy went back out the kitchen for a cloth, and some washing up liquid, compelled to make the keyboard sparkle before anyone risked catching an infection from the germs it must be carrying.

She applied the cleaner methodically, top left, to top right, a key at a time, first to the upper surface of each key, and then down all the sides of each as she went along. Her progression was logical, on to the next row down, using the same actions, then the next, until she had finished the Control key row, except that she stopped when she noticed with some surprise that it had one key on it that was already clean. She'd never been aware of that one before; it had a symbol for what looked like a lined page, with an arrow pointing to it. Making a mental note to press it next time she was Word-processing to see what happened, she carried on rubbing and wiping the keys.

Then she tackled the number pad, wrinkling her nose up as she worked her way over it, since it was just *so* dirty. Finally, she cleaned all the borders around the keys, and then, in a final flourish, turned the keyboard over and gave it a wipe on its belly, even though that wasn't dirty at all.

Beautiful! and it's only taken me fifteen minutes to make it look like new. Why haven't I ever done that before? Because I would never have had fifteen minutes to spend on something as menial as cleaning my keyboard before now.

The answer came easily.

Nancy had been cleaning for months. Just short bursts, so she didn't get too tired. Bit by bit, the house had become cleaner and tidier. Little nooks and crannies had been inspected, one at a time, and their contents sorted, put away or binned.

Binning is very cathartic, she thought.

She recalled how last week she had filled a whole black bin bag with old papers from her filing cabinet in the study. That had felt good, very good indeed.

The house was definitely becoming cleaner each day, and, Nancy reflected, there was a parallel cleansing process going on inside her at the same time. It was as if she was literally cleaning up her whole life, a piece at a time, addressing the parts that had been neglected for so long whilst she had been immersed in *busy-ness*; busy with work, busy with family, busy with the animals, busy *doing* for other people. And as a consequence, too busy to take the time to notice what was literally under her nose. Things were very different now. Fleetingly, a thought passed through her mind that she could possibly come to enjoy having the time to be still, and wait, calmly, whilst her computer booted up.

* *

They sat at the kitchen table drinking peppermint tea after going through the necessary 'catching up with the families' part of the conversation. Diane's question 'How are you feeling now Nancy?' precipitated a deep response, more than Diane was expecting, which took her a bit by surprise.

'I can't tell a lie Diane, not great actually. I feel weak and weedy. A bit down, fed up with it all. I've had a real shock you know. It's made me to take stock and have a good, hard look at my whole life, and myself, in a way that nothing has ever done to me before. You know me, I'd always believed I was invincible. I suppose everybody thinks that about themselves. Then, after I collapsed last November and could hardly do anything for myself for weeks afterwards, I realised I wasn't invincible at all, and I had to rely on other people to do things for me, still must, to some extent. So much for that life-long belief,' she grimaced.

'Oh Nancy, don't be so hard on yourself,' Diane said softly. 'Not many people would have managed to do as much as you've done over the last few years and kept going for as long as you did.' She put an arm round her friend's bony shoulder.

'You've had an enormous amount of stress, no wonder you ended up keeling over – it was bound to happen at some point! God, just look back over the last few years. The car crash, the riding accident, your Dad's death, your Mum's dementia, Amy's illness, all that management stuff at work. Bodies are not machines you know. They can only take so much, and they need to rest as well.'

Diane held her Nancy while she sobbed quietly, her own eyes filling up.

'What did you *ever* do to relax? And did you ever really deal with all the grief?'

Nancy sniffed and blew her nose.

'I did nothing. And yes, I know now I should have. The strangest thing is, I didn't actually recognise my life as being stressful at the time. People at work, and friends used to say things like, "How do you do it all? It makes me tired just watching you." And I used to smile, and think how strong I was, how energetic, how *good* I was. Smug bitch.'

She gave a teary smile.

'I have to admit it made me feel a bit superior, accomplishing so much when most of them seemed to do little more than potter through the day, go shopping on the weekends, and take a foreign holiday once a year.'

'Well you did accomplish a lot. Don't play it all down.'

'Yes, but now look at me – they're still going strong and it's me who's barely doing more than "getting through the day". It's so frustrating. If I push myself – which is what I'm used to doing – it only makes it worse and I'm banged up for days afterwards. I have no idea how long this will last and the doctors can't tell me that either.

'All the symptoms I get – they're horrible, and I'm absolutely sick of them, quite literally. If it's not one thing I'm having it's another. It's like they take turns to torment me, I'm not joking! I keep getting told "M.E. often takes 2 – 5 years to get better, sometimes longer". I don't want to believe that, but it's been nearly seven months already and I don't seem to be making enough progress, I'm nowhere near normal. Some days it feels like a life sentence for me Diane, just waiting, and waiting to feel better.'

By now Nancy was trying hard not to cry again, but she couldn't prevent the tears welling up in her eyes, and as they squeezed out in the corners and spilled down her nose she brushed them away quickly with the tip of her ring finger as if she didn't want them to been seen. It was the first time in all the years they had know each other that Diane had ever seen Nancy look so frail and vulnerable. She wasn't quite sure what to say, so gave Nancy more space to talk, sensing that she needed to offload to someone who was still prepared to listen.

'They've told me that 'type A' high achievers like me are prime candidates for M.E. That I've probably had it low grade for years – all those cold and fluey type illnesses over every winter – they were warning signs apparently, my body trying to tell me to slow down, take care of it, and I ignored them all. I remember my mother each Sunday when she phoned asking "How are you this week?" and I'd answer "Okay, just a bit tired though"; and she'd say "You're always tired, you can't be getting enough rest", and I'd tell her to stop worrying, that everything was fine, when actually it wasn't, I was just pretending it was.'

'We all do that sort of thing with our mothers,' Diane laughed. 'Tell them what they want to hear so they don't worry about us. No doubt our own kids use that trick with us as well, without us realising it!'

Nancy raised a smile. Yes, that was probably quite true.

'Do you think it's a woman thing, Diane? Keeping going that is, sublimating our own needs all the time for everyone else's?'

'Of course,' Diane said emphatically. 'Especially for women in their forties, like us. Sandwiched between children, husband, jobs, parents etc. Not much time for us as individuals at all is there? I sometimes wonder who I am these days. If it wasn't for my painting, I could think sometimes that 'Diane' has almost disappeared altogether.'

Nancy looked thoughtful. 'You know these last seven months, I've had more time to myself than I've had in the last fifteen years. Time to think, time to feel. I know exactly what you mean. I've looked in the mirror each day and not recognised myself, in that I know it's me of course – I look the same only thinner, a bit pale and pasty, but at the same time, it's *not* me somehow. I don't see *me* when I stare at my eyes. God, this sounds so weird, Diane! Don't you go telling people "Nancy's lost it, she's away with the fairies now!"'

'And since when would you care about what people thought of you Nancy? That would be a first – Nancy Robertson, "shrinking violet". Besides, it's okay to get a bit eccentric as you get older!

'Nancy, what have the doctors said about returning to work?'

'Basically they've advised me not to even try. As I said, I've been doing a lot of thinking. It's become clear to me, and the doctors have told me as much, that I won't be able to go back to doing my job, in its current form. On the one hand that makes me feel very sad, because I've built up such a good sales team, we were the top region for the two years before I got sick, and I've got some wonderful staff. I had plans for further expansion, which of course are now all on the shelf. I don't think I could consider going back part time, or to a lesser position, my pride wouldn't let me, yet these are exactly the sorts of options that the Human Resources Department are talking about now. On the other hand, financial considerations aside – because that's a whole other ball game – this gives me an opportunity to think about what else I could do even though I have this bloody, bloody, *bloody* M.E.'

'So what have you come up with then?' Diane was listening intently.

'Nothing for definite yet, but I'm exploring some options. I've figured that I have to steer clear of the things that make the symptoms worse; like computer work, being in busy, noisy places, artificial lights – all the typical things that are found in any office building. I wouldn't be able to do much driving either as that's really difficult for me if it lasts more than an hour; I just get a terrible headache and feel giddy. So that doesn't leave me with any options that I can see which involve *being* employed. Looks like I'm going to have to be radical. You might be surprised at this, but I'm considering becoming some kind of therapist, working one-to-one with people. God knows I've seen enough of them this year to pick up a good working knowledge of how they operate.'

Nancy began pointing to the palm of her left hand, counting the therapists off one at a time, starting with her little finger and working towards her thumb. She punched her right forefinger into each digit with gusto.

'The osteopath, the hypnotherapist, the acupuncturist, the Reiki lady; guess what, Diane – without exception they are *all* calm, they don't look, or sound stressed, and they appear wonderfully healthy and content with their lot!'

'Yes – I think you're right there. Francka, my hypnotherapist, was like that too. Nothing seemed to faze her.'

'I've looked into a few training courses. I think I could cope with hypnotherapy – it's offered in Glasgow, by The Institute of Hypnotherapy, a two-year course, a lot of it self study. Maybe next year. Also, it's more mainstream than the others, accepted more by the medical profession I mean. It was my GP who suggested I try it in the first place when I couldn't sleep properly and refused the prescription he offered me for Temazepam.'

'Have you talked this through with Michael?'

'Not yet. That's a tricky one. He's said he'd be happy for me to just give up work altogether, and be a housewife again, take it easy. That we don't need the extra money my wage brings in anymore now the mortgage is paid off. In some ways that would be the sensible option, given my lack of energy, I know. But, and this is a big *but* – I think after working all my life I'd go mad if that was all I had to look forward to. It would just be the same old routine, lots of drudge. Housework's not exactly creative is it?'

'I've never found it to be, more like something that has to be got out of the way before any fun starts,' Diane agreed.

'I've got a real urge to find my own niche again, something that I can call my own, that gives me a sense of worth. Being around here all the time being simply my children's mother and Michael's wife sure as hell doesn't do that for me.'

'Well, you must do whatever you feel is best. Go for it if it feels right. None of us is getting any younger, and I've come to the conclusion that if we don't do something we want to do now, we may never have another chance later. I'd be really interested to know how it all pans out.'

'While we're on the subject of the future, what do you want to do with the rest of your life then Diane. What do you really, really, want to do?'

Diane suddenly became unusually animated. With her large brown eyes bright and sparkling, a wide grin filling out her face and both her arms raised with fists tightly closed seemingly capturing something in mid air, she exclaimed, 'I've just had a mad idea! – you remember how we always used to look up our horoscopes in the newspaper every day in Dalmeny Street? Well, why don't we pay a visit to a real astrologer and get a reading on what's in store for us over the next year?

'I saw an advert for one who's in Edinburgh only last week, in a magazine I bought from Tesco's – "Spirit and Destiny" it was – I bought it because it was advertising an article called "Organic Food Makes You Slim" on the cover, but it turned out to have all sorts of interesting things in it, including the advert for the astrologer. We could find out what our destinies are supposed to be, and if they're what we've been thinking about then that would be validation for us to take the appropriate action wouldn't it?'

'Now that *is* a mad idea Diane,' Nancy giggled, 'but it sounds like a lot of fun. I'm well up for it. Let's just do it, and not tell anyone about it – until afterwards!'

Taking a chance on life

Astrological guidance for the year to come: a private consultation with Melanie. To 'Guide You' through the coming year. (1½ to 2 hrs). Group consultations or consultations by post also available! £35.00

Melanie the Astrologer was slim, friendly and vivacious, with mid-length brown wavy hair. She was wearing a pretty dress and stiletto heels, not quite what they were expecting at all. She ushered the two friends into her living room, which was quite ordinary, although it did have pink stars on the ceiling and various New Age type ornaments and decorations. They made polite chit-chat about the journey and finding the house, then she asked who would like to have their reading first. As they'd already decided it would be Nancy, she followed Melanie up the stairs to a small bedroom, which was used as the consultation room. The bookcase along one wall was a prominent feature, with shelves heavily laden with heaps of astrology books and almanacs, bearing titles such as *A History of Western Astrology*, *The Betz Table of Houses (Placidus) for Northern Latitudes* and *Raphael's Astrological and Predictive Almanac*. Some looked very old and well-worn, others had bits of post-its in various pages.

Pictures of stars and planets adorned the walls, and in the middle of the room was a little round table, covered by a floor-length white cloth, with a large white candle offset to one side. Melanie showed Nancy her chair then sat down herself, arranging her dress demurely, and wrapping the shawl that had been draped on the back of the chair around herself. With a deft strike of the match she lit the candle, then leaned over to pick up a pile of papers from the floor, before checking that the tape machine was recording properly.

Her voice was calm and confident. 'This is Melanie Folds, Astrological Consultant and this is "The Year to Come" for Nancy Robertson, October 2001 to October 2002'.

Nancy's astrological report was placed on the table in front of her, and Melanie began to talk animatedly, at the same time pointing to the symbols and divisions ('houses', she called them) on the first chart, telling Nancy to ask if she needed anything explaining in more depth. The chart looked very complicated to Nancy's novice eyes, so she tried hard to concentrate on Melanie's words as she tried to make sense of what was shown. There were large groupings of symbols in some houses, whilst others were virtually empty. A load of squares and triangles filled up the inner circle in the middle, these were troublesome, apparently. Nancy recognised the symbol for Scorpio on the right hand side, and could see that most of the planets were found in that area of the chart, along with a symbol she hadn't come across before, which Melanie explained was a 'Vertex – a fated event'.

'And yours is in Libra, 23° 32', in the 6th house. This links up with the heart and with relating, so health issues may link up with not getting the balance right in relating. Libra represents the heart chakra. If you feel hemmed in at all (in work or relationships), if you don't feel you've got your freedom, then health problems can arise. When you get the balance in your heart area then things settle down.'

That sounded spot on to Nancy. She drew closer, listening intently.

* *

Nancy's feedback would take up to two hours, so I could take a trip to Tesco's and put that to good use. I caught myself just in time. *No – wait a minute, why not sit in this comfortable lounge, browse Melanie's magazines and enjoy a bit of me-time?*

I sipped my camomile tea and let my mind wander. Thoughts flitted in and out of my mind in no particular order.

Maybe she'll suggest I go and join a hippy commune.

Wonder if she'll mention Dad?

Hope she doesn't tell me something bad is going to happen to one of the kids. I couldn't bear that.

Best not to talk too much. She might be in a kind of trance when she gives the reading.

Wonder if it's okay to ask about specific people. I might mention Campbell. A brother's bound to be significant'

It'll be a joke if she tells me I married the wrong man. Too late now to do anything about that.

I read through a pile of Mind, Body and Spirit magazines,

filling in blanks on the half finished crosswords someone had started earlier, before Nancy finally appeared.

She gave me the thumbs up.

'Go for it, girl. You'll be amazed. But make a few notes if you can. I've already forgotten half of it. There's so much to take in.'

I dug deep into my shoulder bag for a little black notebook, the kind policemen always carry, with an elastic band around the current page. It was rather dog-eared, with smudges of Cadbury's Flake on several pages, and streaks of burgundy coloured lipstick on the cover, from the one with the missing top. There were a few cleanish pages between various shopping and to-do lists.

I found it easier just to listen for the key messages than concentrate on the charts. A strategy that proved useful as afterwards my tape would kick around the back of my bedside drawer for weeks before I ever got round to writing it all down verbatim.

'Diane, your life is about service to others.'

God, no. That was the one thing I didn't want or expect to hear.

'Yes, you're here to care, to be of service. That's your life purpose. But almost equally strong in your chart is a creativity of some kind. Of an artistic nature. Maybe music or painting?'

That was more like it.

'And what I can see is that currently you're not finding the right balance between these two aspects. This has been a problem for quite a number of years I suggest. And where the balance is tipped – I can see that it would be more in the caring element – you become blocked. There's a weight bearing down on you. You feel worn out, depleted, despondent even. Does this make some kind of sense to you?'

How spooky, I thought. Whatever's coming next?

'However, you are currently going through a period of reflection, of taking stock, making sense of things. This began a year or so ago, although you tried to address it at two previous stages in your life. It has been quite painful but this time you will achieve a successful outcome. There's some way to go yet, although the worst should have passed.

'In terms of your natal chart, I see issues with a parent – your father. I think he is passed over now.' She looked at me for confirmation.

'Yes,' I said feebly, 'yes he is.'

'Mmm. You have much to forgive before you can put certain negative features of your relationship with him, into the past, where they belong.'

I wasn't ready for that. Not here. Not with a stranger. I bit my lip and struggled to hold on.

* *

The natal chart describes where the planets were at the exact time of your birth and how that has influenced your personality and potential. Being Taurean, ie having the sun in Taurus on my day of birth, was only the start. Apparently I had a lot of Cancer in my chart, explaining my love of home and family. But then again, some Arian fire gave me the get up and go to take on new challenges, and organise others.

Having recognised myself from Melanie's accurate interpretation of my natal and progressed charts, I was keen to hear what the future held - at least the next 18 months of it.

'I see a large sum of money here. Probably next spring. An inheritance maybe. Legal matters also. Paperwork, official documents. At the same time there is an emphasis on creativity and new beginnings. I'm not sure how these will be linked, or if they will. But the impact should see you set up for the next fifteen years or so. Now that's good news, isn't it?

'Your health is due to improve too. A period of energy and increased motivation is showing up in the months ahead and that should be good for several years.

'Family wise, I assume you are still married and I can see children of both sexes.'

Once more she gave me that quizzical look. How *did* she know?

'A move for your third offspring associated with education and learning. Possibly a joint venture for your husband and youngest child. It might be on a voluntary basis as there's no sign of any particular wealth attached to that. And looking a bit further ahead, an opportunity for you and your husband to become involved in a new development, both in your relationship and in your provision for the future.'

There was more. But in what I would later communicate, I chose to emphasise the need to pay more attention to my creative side, and the possibility of a large sum of money. The caring stuff? Why fight it? But no need to invite any more demands!

I enjoyed telling the story to those I thought would understand it and not shake their heads and pronounce it all a waste of time and money. And occasionally I would lie awake at night fantasising about how I would spend that big sum of money if it ever came.

When it did, my horoscope for the day, courtesy of the Dundee Courier, only hinted at what lay ahead.

A surprise item in the mail sets you thinking. Don't be constrained this time.

I got a letter from the postman

'Sinclair Wallace, Solicitors' was franked on the outside of the buff envelope. That meant nothing to me. The postmark was London and it was addressed to me, by my full title. I used a bronze letter opener to save damaging the mysterious contents.

Dear Mrs McDonald, it read, would you please contact this office at your earliest convenience with reference to the estate of your aunt, Miss Marguerite Steven.

Aunt Marguerite, Dad's second cousin. I didn't even know she was dead. We hadn't seen her for ages, probably not since Dad's funeral, and before that not for several years. She used to visit us when we were kids, making the trip up from Worcester every other summer. Mum and Marguerite were like chalk and cheese so she didn't ever stay long. We used to think she was a bit odd with her heavy blue eye shadow and overly defined red lips. She smoked untipped cigarettes, enjoyed a single malt and had a penchant for French writers. 'Bohemian' Dad said. By Forfar standards, certainly. She must have been ancient by the time she died.

She had never married, although Mum used to say, with a rather pinched look on her face, that 'your dear aunt won't die not knowing.' Good for her, although I didn't have a clue what that meant at the time.

Whatever the truth might be, and it was too late now to find out, the old Aunt had remembered dear Kenneth's children in her will. Norma, Campbell and I were to share the £240,000 proceeds from the sale of her home. The rest of her estate was to go to various charities associated with the armed forces. Her fiancé had died in the latter stages of the second world war serving in the Far East.

So – there was that big sum of money. However, it came with a few strings.

And to Diane, a third share of the proceeds of Wellbank House, with the proviso that she invests in her own future, choosing a vehicle for her artistic development and enjoyment.

Campbell and Norma were instructed similarly – Campbell to engage in foreign travel, in particular to trace the routes of the famous railways of the world, and Norma to fund her training in beauty therapy and her own salon.

In earlier years, I would have been pulled and pushed in all directions about how to spend this money. A new car, a caravan, a round the world trip for all the family, a bigger house, a flat for the kids. There would have been weeks of excitement and action, before life as we knew it would settle back into its familiar routine. Not what Aunt M had in mind. Now I could choose for myself if it suited me. And certainly that was her wish.

Inheritance, energy, motivation, a new development. It was all in the stars.

I wasn't sure where to start or which direction to choose. There were art courses at college. Maybe I would take a sabbatical (the first ever care worker in an old folks' home to have that privilege!), and do a fine arts degree. Or be a bit more hedonistic and sign up for an art appreciation course which included visits to Italy and Spain. Then again, I could collect a few nice pieces – paintings, sculptures – for the house. Maybe even build on a new room to hold my collection.

My thoughts were all over the place. Nancy helped me to process it logically over a walk with the dogs.

'What do you really want? Is it a life change or a hobby?'

'Do you want to make money out of it, or just dabble?'

'Are you giving up the care home work? If so, how much money will you need to earn from any new venture?'

'Would you move house or are you staying where you are?'

'Hang on a minute,' I laughed. 'Remember it's only 80 grand!'

In the end, we thrashed out and wrote down my existing attributes and skills, my likes and dislikes, my values and beliefs and my hopes for the future to come up with a set of criteria in order to narrow my world of options down from an ocean of ideas to a single sparkling droplet.

Then after all that, Nancy suggested letting the right brain take over.

'We've done all the logical thinking. How about you just relax for a few days or weeks now? Don't put pressure on yourself to make any decisions. Just let ideas come and go. That's what I would do.

'One day it will all become clear as crystal, you'll see. Look out for the omens! They'll guide you. Trust in the universe!'

She was twirling round now, raising her arms to the skies, dancing like a madwoman. We did have a laugh.

The kids had no patience. 'What are you going to do with all that money Mum? Surely you've come up with something by now. I could spend it all in a week given half a chance.'

Even Willie wouldn't let the subject drop. 'Have you seen a white light yet Di? Had any premonitions? What are the stars saying this week?'

I was on a day out in the community bus with some of the residents from the home when the first omen appeared, although at the time it registered only in my peripheral vision.

'Diane, look over there,' said Mabel. 'That's where I used to live when I first got married. Fifteen **Wellbank** Street. Dunkeld was a quiet wee place then. You were more likely to see a horse and cart than a car. It's full of antiques shops now. The visitors come by the busload at the weekend to browse around.'

Then a card appeared in the post with a jazzy-looking, pop art design on the front. I thought it was an advert for something I neither needed nor wanted and was in the act of binning it, when Susan grabbed it from me.

'Don't do that Mum. It's an invite to the final year art show at Duncan of Jordanstone. Jasmine from across the road has a few pieces in it. I said we would go and that you might buy something.'

Yet another suggestion for how *I* might spend *my* money.

We went together, spending several hours in the various rooms. I was drawn as always to the watercolours, few in number in the show. Susan took pains to educate me when the multi media creations were beyond my understanding. I didn't buy any of Jasmine's boxes, which contained echoes of nightmarish situations – headless babies, ghostly apparitions and lost souls. However, I was rather taken with a small moving sculpture entitled 'In the stars'. It was made of copper wire with small semi-precious stones judiciously placed to represent elements of the universe.

'I might think about that one, and come back tomorrow,' I said to Susan.

'For goodness sake Mum! If you like it, buy it. And think how you'll be supporting one struggling artist to get started on her career. You might be her first ever purchaser. The one who gives her confidence to keep at it. Diane McDonald, patron of the young artist. Doesn't that sound good?'

£200 wouldn't make a huge dent in the inheritance. And I really did love the piece.

The artist, M Kennedy, had made a special box for each of her sculptures. She placed 'In the stars' in its temporary home with a sigh.

'I do hope it brings you pleasure Mrs McDonald. I'm finding it hard to part with. And remember, if you would like to see any more of my pieces, just give me a ring. The number is on the card. Ask for Margy. I never use my full name. Too much of a mouthful, **Marguerite**. And not exactly trendy these days is it!'

Willie took to referring to me as 'Patron of the Arts' if he was trying to attract my attention. He thought it was all a big joke.

When the same phrase appeared in the property pages of the Courier it immediately caught my eye.

*Dunkeld, **Wellbank Street**, a small single storey building, currently used as a workshop, for sale or lease. Might suit a working artist or a **patron of the arts** requiring display space.*

The omens were lining up.

It would need to be painted throughout, all white, with lightly polished wooden floors. Then I'd require a small office space with somewhere to make myself a cup of tea. Correct lighting would be vital to enhance the display. (Willie could help with that.) I could have two walls for paintings and a versatile shelved area for pottery or small sculptures. Oh, I could visualise it all. See myself there showing customers round. Explaining a bit of the background of each of the young artists – I'd already decided it would be a showcase for new graduates. I felt excitement, enthusiasm and energy, for the first time in years.

The second time around

Auchterarder 2001

The party girl, the fun-lover, the flirt. It had all seemed so much more exciting in the days when she'd had a husband by her side. Now that she was widowed, opportunity and desire had all but disappeared. Other women followed Alix with their eyes, intercepting her progress if they suspected she was interested in their partners. Her name was left off the guest list at several events where obviously Gerald had been the attraction. Some of their circle even stopped inviting her for dinner when it was all couples and she was apparently 'on the loose.' Her few close female friends were all still married, not necessarily happily, but nevertheless absorbed in their families and associated duties. Not free nor particularly interested in helping her find a new direction in life. She wasn't looking for a new man – not actively, not really – but a girl needs a bit of a social life or she'll shrivel up and die for God's sake.

At first a social life had been the least of her concerns. It had taken months to sort out Gerald's estate. All that paperwork to deal with. The lawyer had been wonderful, guiding her through the maze, suggesting how to ensure the children's inheritance, but it had used every last ounce of motivation to finalise all the formalities. Then there had been coming to terms with Gerald's sudden sharp decline. She'd thought they had months, even years, to do some of the things they'd always promised themselves. That planned return to Kenya for one thing. And then a trip to Chiva Som Spa in Thailand which might well have improved his quality of life, had he made it until the following January. Once the legal business was complete, she took up the offer of a final visit to Gerald's consultant to discuss any lingering doubts or questions about his illness and treatment and so achieve a kind of closure. He was very kind (at £300 a visit he could afford to be) and his parting words stuck with her,

'I suggest you get involved in a hobby or interest. Not too much pressure but something that you feel an enthusiasm for. It's important to feel an enthusiasm for something in life, after such a difficult time.'

It was with little enthusiasm but more a sense of the need to tidy up the remaining loose ends, that six months after Gerald's death Alix felt able to look through all his possessions with a more dispassionate eye and so make decisions about how to dispose of them.

'Charity shop for these clothes. The Cyrenians can have all ten bags. They'll be the only old winos wearing Burberry!' she thought with a wry smile on her face.

'Timmy can have the pick of Gerald's books. Apart from his biographies of prime ministers which I'll keep for guests. Perfect for curing insomnia.'

'I'm holding on to his CDs. Caroline will probably want the 60's vinyls. It seems they're right back in fashion now.'

At the back of his bureau in the study she found an envelope containing about a dozen faded black and white photographs, obviously taken in Africa given the presence of black servants and flame trees. She could just read the faded pencil inscription on the back of some of them.

John and Cristabel, May 1935

The babies, Gerald and Richard, July 1941.

A picnic at (indecipherable) April 1943

It set her thinking.

She had worried about how the children would cope with their father's death, keeping in daily touch with them after the funeral. Encouraging them to come home regularly, meeting up in Glasgow and Dundee where they were studying. Arranging for the cousins from down south to come up for that first Christmas so that there was some life and humour in the house to deflect their thoughts.

Naturally they would never forget their father, but a record of his life in photographs would be something to share with their own children in years to come. Alix had stored boxes and boxes of pictures in the attic, originally intended for that day in the future when she and Gerald, by then less inclined to go out, would have the time to sift through them, choosing the most memorable for a new family album. No real point in waiting any longer. It was now a lonely task, but comforting in a bittersweet way.

Childhood in Africa, boarding school in Hampshire, University in Oxford, early days with the British Council in their London office, postings to Paris, Beirut, Moscow, Cairo, Singapore and Jeddah. Girls in striped shirtwaisters, youths with short slick-backed hair, honeymoon photographs from the Far East with Alix slightly pink from too much sun and Gerald lean and relaxed in his casual clothes, the twins as babies in Imelda's arms. Some surprises – how young he'd looked on his first posting, how love-struck he seemed with his long term girlfriend Victoria, how alike the two brothers Gerald and Richard were as children.

The photographs were all shapes and sizes, some in colour, many in black and white. The older ones tended to be faded. Several were rather dog-eared. Often there was only one of a certain important event. These albums, one for Timmy and one for Caroline – they should be a work of art. It would be her tribute to Gerald. The raw materials would need some improvement work first, however. Maybe she could manage that herself with a bit of help. It might be a new hobby for her.

Diane pointed out an evening class at Perth College – Digital Photography Made Simple. Copy, crop, sharpen, soften, resize, rotate, lighten, brighten, remove red eye, display in montage. Make your old photographs look like new.

She was noticeably overdressed on that first evening in her Max Mara pale blue trousers and matching cashmere V-neck. She didn't speak the technical language either. However, new situations, new challenges had never fazed her. Her usual strategy worked brilliantly.

'Mr Kerr. I'm Alix Fitzroy. Lovely to meet you. I hope you'll bear with me while I muddle through (*flutter eyelashes at this point*). I'm something of a novice at all this. But I'm a very quick learner (*big smile here*). I might just need to call on your help a bit more than some of the others in the class. I do hope that won't be a problem?' (*hold his gaze slightly longer than normal.)*

Mr Kerr would be delighted to help in any way he could.

After five Monday evenings getting to grips with the software, he suggested to the class that a project would be a useful focus for their new skills, beginning after the midterm break.

It was the first time they had left their individual workstations and sat as group. Mr Kerr encouraged them to introduce themselves in the following way: *Your name, where you live, one interesting fact about yourself, and your initial project idea.*

So, there was John Dalziel, Forgandenny, theatregoer, who wants to record and document the production of a new sculpture for Perth City Centre.

Mabel Brown, Luncarty, volunteers for Age Concern, hopes to put together a montage of faces from her local drop-in centre.

Carol Kiddie, Perth, a keen gardener, plans to frame flower studies to decorate her new sitting room.

And then, James Nixon, assistant manager Glen Devon Hotel, has travelled widely in his job with The Small World Group, and would like to create a photo-diary of his experiences.

Mr Kerr suggested a degree of collaboration where appropriate. 'Maybe you and James could work together Alix? It seems you might have a lot in common.'

James – about five foot ten, tendency to apple shape, bald spot on the crown of his head, smart but conservative in his dress (wears a cravat on occasions), rather lined (too much sun in the tropics?) and a smoker. Polite, shows or feigns interest when others are talking, tends to keep himself slightly apart otherwise. Always rushes straight off at the end of the class.

Well, why not? It was only a photographic project. Just as well she'd been honest.

Alix Fitzroy, Auchterarder, antiques dealer, would like to create stylish and meaningful photograph albums of her late husband's life for their two teenage children.

James came to the house over the midterm break so that they could browse their respective photographs in a leisurely fashion on the expanse of her dining room table. He suggested some techniques for improving the old snaps; she had creative ideas for the juxtaposition of his photographs and text. And they discovered some shared history from Singapore. It was possible they might even have attended the same party one night in 1981 after the races, when old JB after far too many gins, fell into the pool and had to be hauled out fully clothed to the accompaniment of 'For he's a jolly wet fellow ...'

They laughed over memories of the expat life and divulged just a little personal history along the way. James had never married. He'd enjoyed the travel with his job and had obviously taken full advantage of local hospitality judging by the familiarity displayed by a bevy of Eastern beauties in his photographs.

'Very friendly, a lot of the local girls. Just their way of being welcoming.'

Mmmm. I bet, thought Alix.

Over a couple of gins and a few cigarettes, they relaxed and kicked off their shoes. Good old Mr Kerr.

After five more weeks at the Monday class, James had made considerable progress with his photo diary, bringing his documented record almost up to his move back to the UK in 1986, and Alix had completed her selection, enhancement and arrangement of about sixty photographs each for the twins' albums. The course ended, but both were keen to see the other's finished article. The festive season and work commitments would intervene.

James would be going abroad at the end of January for his company's annual winter conference, that year in Dubai.

'James, you could do me a small favour when you're in Dubai, if you wouldn't mind,' said Alix with her best smile.

'Well, spit it out and we'll see.'

'If you're out and about in Dubai, which I'm sure you will be, would you pop into the textile souk and see if there are any of these black and white napkins? I bought some there on our last trip to the Middle East and they've sold really well. I could take a dozen sets of four. Don't pay any more than 20 dirhams a set or it won't be worth my while. They won't take up much room in your luggage.'

'I'll see what I can do. It's customary to offer a tip you know!

'How about dinner when you get back? Then we can see what work still has to be done on our projects.'

* *

In a quite unexpected way, and only once the usual Christmas rush was over, Alix began to miss seeing James on Monday nights.

'It's so unusual for me just to have a man as a friend. With no other agenda if you know what I mean. Maybe I'm getting old.'

'I doubt that, Alix. More likely your hormone levels are dropping to the level of the rest of us,' laughed Diane. 'But let's see what a few weeks apart does to you both, shall we? You will phone and let me know?'

'Don't be silly. I don't fancy James one little bit; he's not my type. And anyway, he never makes a move to suggest he's even remotely attracted to me. So I'm obviously not his type either. It's nice to have a man around the place now and again. Surely a man and a woman can just be good friends, can't they?'

People who need people

It was a month after his return from Dubai when James finally made it over to see Alix at Dalfruan Grange with her twelve sets of napkins and a nicely chilled bottle of Chablis.

'At last, at last. Just as well my livelihood doesn't depend on selling these napkins! Come in and make yourself at home. I'll just check the slow cooker before we catch up.'

James kicked off his shoes and sank into the large squashy cushions of the massive cream sofa in the family sitting room. He had time to appreciate yet again Alix's fine taste in furnishings and her judicious placing of interesting finishing touches which helped define her distinctive style of quality with a creative twist.

'This house really is beautiful, you know Alix.'

'Well thank you kind sir. It's always been important to me to live in comfortable surroundings. And some of the places I've been, it was all there was to do – searching the markets, looking for two or three unusual items to personalise our rented home. Maybe I have a good eye for it. Or else I'm just a lucky besom!'

'Oh don't sell yourself short. You have an eye all right. And a business brain that can negotiate a favourable price. It seems to me you're in the right trade. And a bit of charm goes a long way too,' he added with a mischievous smile.

'Ah, now then. I've always been able to turn that on at will. It comes from the need to escape my roots in the frozen north and build the kind of life I've always wanted. Mind you, it's got me into a few scrapes too. Just as well I've destroyed the photographic evidence!

'And what about you? I'll be interested to read the dark side of your photo diary when you finally finish it.'

'Stop fishing and check that dinner. I'm starving!'

Over the crème bruleé James entertained her with snippets of gossip from the conference, exaggerating for effect to make her laugh out loud, or prompt him for more with wide-eyed interest.

'And when we all had to come up with our plans for "an enhanced customer experience" I had an absolute brainwave. We could furnish one small intimate dining room at Glen Devon with select pieces from a local antiques dealer, and offer luxury private dining for special occasions, to be followed at the customer's convenience, by a personal tour of the antiques shop with 10% discount on any purchases. What do you think?'

'Sounds great to me. How did it go down with your Manager?'

'He was fine about it, as long as I do all the donkey work – and you're in agreement.'

'Me?'

'Well who else would furnish The Dalfruan Room?'

Effective teams are built on joint projects, say the experts. And so for the second time in her life, Alix found herself in a working partnership, based this time on friendship and mutual respect.

Their first year was slow to take off until the PR budget for the hotel was given over to an advertorial entry in Scotland on Sunday, heavily disguised as an article on '*Hidden gems for that once in a lifetime occasion.*' After that the Dalfruan room was regularly hired for graduation lunches, anniversary dinners, retirement presentations and maybe even secret assignations. The spin off for Rubislaw Treasures was steady and growing, particularly popular with overseas guests who just laaaved all that royal commemorative chinaaah.

James would sometimes accompany Alix on a buying trip if it was reasonably local. She added his name to the insurance policy for the van and enjoyed sitting back with cigarette in hand while he drove to Stirling, Perth or Montrose. They might bicker a bit over the best route but otherwise in companionable silence or easy conversation would pass a pleasant morning or evening rooting for bits and pieces amongst the house clearances or choosing larger items of furniture at the specialised antique sales.

A flashpoint occurred without warning one Monday evening in Blairgowrie.

Alix was never off duty when it came to her appearance. That night she was her usual carefully co-ordinated, beautifully groomed self. She had chosen a cream silk blouse to wear which echoed the highlights in her blonde hair and teamed it with a beige trouser suit, a Burberry rain jacket and tan suede boots. Amongst her male counterparts, many of whom looked more like rag and bone men than antiques dealers, she sparkled and shone like a polished piece of quartz on a pebbly beach.

Jack Smeaton caught her eye and smiled. She returned it with a 'Hi, and how are you these days?'

Frank Law put an arm around her shoulders, 'Hey there Alix. Long time no see. You're looking well.'

Stan Wilson followed up his wolf whistle with a 'Where have you been my Rubislaw treasure? We've missed you.'

John McMaster clasped her in a bear hug and asked when she was going to invite him over to see her art collection.

To all of this and more Alix laughed, flirted and played the familiar harmless game. Centre stage and perfectly at home.

Before the end of the sale, James grabbed her by the arm and pulled her outside.

'What are you playing at? There's no need for all of that. You're just cheapening yourself. Playing games like that.'

'Don't tell me what to do James. There's no harm in it whatsoever. I've known these guys for years. Besides it makes us all feel good. It's a laugh. I could trust them with my life.'

'Well it doesn't look like that to me. I wouldn't trust any one of them up a dark alley with you. And what do they think I'm doing here with you?'

'Being the business partner that you are, I imagine. You'd better get used to it, because that's how it is.'

The silence was anything but companionable on the drive home.

Alix drummed her fingers on the dashboard to some internal melody. James chain smoked. Neither spoke.

James helped her unload at the Grange, still without a word exchanged, before jumping into his blue Golf, with an 'I'll be in touch' flung over his shoulder as he drove off.

Be like that then. And see if I care, thought Alix.

Neither was prepared to call a truce. Alix thought him ridiculous. He considered her flighty. The stand-off might have lasted for weeks.

* *

Gerald had always been ultra safety-conscious. Alix had reluctantly followed his dictates while he was alive.

'Always switch off electrical appliances before going to bed.

'Never go out and leave the dishwasher or tumble drier on.

'Have electric blankets checked by the electrician every year before use.

'Level the gravel on the path regularly so as to avoid trips and tumbles.

'Don't leave any bags visible in the car when you go shopping; put them in the boot.'

Most of the habits became ingrained in her over the years they were together. But that one about the dishwasher – well, what harm would it do once in a while to let it finish its cycle rather than stopping it half way through to go to town?

The council use retained firemen in the rural areas; men (and occasionally women) who have other jobs locally but can respond instantly to a request to man the service. The handyman at Glen Devon hotel answered the call that October afternoon, flying out of the drive on his motorbike for Auchterarder substation.

'Fire at Dalfruan Grange, James. I'll need to rush.'

* *

James tried Alix's mobile every five minutes for the next half an hour until eventually she replied.

'James. So you've thawed out have you? Not before time.'

'Alix, jump in the car and come straight home. There's a problem at the house. Drive carefully though. I'll explain more when you get here.'

* *

No doubt a man and woman can be just friends. Had they eventually made up again, maybe Alix and James would have remained in that comfortable state without the sudden jolt to the heart initiated by the fire.

As they sipped a calming malt a few hours later they traced the transformation, trying to put the mystical into everyday language.

'I thought you were becoming a real boring old fart, James. No fun in you at all.'

'It made me boiling mad to see all those guys being so familiar with you, when I couldn't.'

'But you never once showed any interest in me, so what do you mean?'

'I thought I wouldn't have a chance with someone as beautiful as you. You didn't give me any encouragement either.'

'To be honest James, you're not my usual type and I was very sure I wasn't yours, so I had pretty much ruled it out.'

'And what changed your opinion then?'

'When I got back from town to see the fire in the kitchen, you were so concerned for me. So kind and caring. And the way you took charge of all the arrangements – well! I didn't expect that. And probably I didn't deserve it either. I just reacted without thinking when I gave you that kiss. You did the rest.'

They didn't go to bed together that night. Or for the next few nights. They agreed that they both wanted to treasure this new development, to polish it with love and care and to share in the fullness of its beauty only when the time and conditions were right. No need to rush it. That's what they told each other.

* *

James arrived the following Sunday evening bringing champagne and smoked salmon for supper. Alix had already changed into some rather alluring leisure wear, flowing turquoise silk culottes and matching camisole with a swirly pattern reminiscent of ocean waves. The colour and texture accentuated the pink glow of excitement in her skin. She dabbed a little Diorissimo in her cleavage, just as his car turned into the drive.

Their first kiss was soft and light.

'Mmm. What's cooking?'

'Just a chicken recipe I picked up in Thailand. You do like a little spice, don't you James?'

'You bet!' He held her glance.

'Put some music on, while I organise the papaya salad.'

She was conscious of him watching her as she swayed her hips just a little more than usual on her way through to the kitchen.

He took out a tape from his top pocket. The cover was wrinkled and faded, the picture was of two young lovers, arms intertwined. 'Modern Love Songs' and in very small type on the reverse 'compilation produced in The Philippines.'

'You remember this one?' he asked, as he placed the cassette into her Regency style music centre, turning the volume up so that she could hear it.

'Long time since I heard Lionel Ritchie. That song was a big hit while we were in Saudi.'

She came back into the room with champagne glasses.

'Let me see what else is on that tape, while you open the champers.'

'Oh James. Where on earth did you unearth this one from? It takes me right back to the souk in Jeddah.' She laughed.

'All these shops with their racks and racks of pirate cassettes. Cliff Richard on the cover but Phil Collins singing on the tape! And the spelling – here you are, here's a typical one. *Another one bits the dust!*'

'Well, forget the spelling for now and listen to the words instead.'

He opened his arms in an invitation to dance and they smooched their way around the sitting room, blending their voices with the familiar lyrics.

'Cause you know just what to say and you know just what to do
And I want to tell you so much, I love you.'

Slowly and gently he kissed her ears, the side of her long smooth neck, the indentation above her clavicle and the sweet smelling vee of the cleft between her soft breasts.

Then with the help of Lionel Ritchie, he whispered 'Tell me how to win your heart for I haven't got a clue, but let me start by saying, I love you.'

'You old romantic, you. You're doing well so far.'

While Stevie Wonder took over the microphone, James slipped off her shoulder straps to expose the smooth skin of her small, slightly sagging breasts. He continued to place soft, gentle kisses on her, watching her face for any sign of reserve or distaste. As he brushed her erect nipple with his mouth, she closed her eyes and gasped quickly.

'Is that okay?'

'It's been so long, that's all.'

With her upper body exposed, she now shivered a little.

'I can warm you up, Alix. I would really love to warm you up.'

By way of reply, she began to unbutton his shirt, kissing each inch of chest as she went, until she could nestle against his bare skin, feeling his warmth.

'It's been a long time for me too,' he said with a twinkle in his eye. 'But I think I can remember what to do.'

With a laugh and a toss of her golden hair, she led him by the hand upstairs to one of the guest bedrooms.

There would be time later for exploring the secrets of the Orient. Tonight would be about the sheer joy of skin on warm skin, the comfort of a pair of strong arms and a safe place to show her ageing body to someone who really cared.

'Do you like this?' he said as he lightly stroked her thighs.

'And this?' as he traced a line from her navel to her pubic bone.

'And how about this?' as he buried his face in her still blonde pubic hair.

Each time, she would laughingly reply, 'Mmm. Yes. You know I do. What next?'

Until he carefully opened her secret lips, and exposed that most private of parts. Her breathing quickened, she arched her lower back and offered herself to him and his teasing fingers. He watched her every step of the way, bringing her closer and closer to that long awaited moment of excitement.

And when it was finally over, and she lay smiling and slightly breathless in his arms, he nibbled her ear and whispered,

'And now it's my turn. This is a partnership, remember!'

Keep on running

Dundee 2002

Patricia studied the Inspector's report, muttering to herself her own responses to the politically correct expressions, the euphemisms and the fudges, all designed to convey praise and (or) criticism in a type of code, specifically intended to reassure parents, whilst being totally transparent to those on the inside.

Support for weaker pupils – good provision, regular review ... blah blah blah – I would hope so.

Liaison with parents – regular newsletter, well planned programme of meetings, effectively communicated in advance ...... yes, yes, fine, fine, we know all that.

Curriculum planning – effective for Maths and English, more focus needed on Environmental Studies – blast, I thought we'd done enough on that one. But it's Maths and English that are really important, everyone knows that.

Resources and facilities – the multi purpose school hall, while versatile as a shared space, allows for limited provision of sports activities owing to its shape, and the somewhat restricted changing facilities. I knew they'd pick up on the gym hall, but that's the council's responsibility, not mine.

Management and leadership – What?! The head teacher could delegate more? The management style tends towards the autocratic and could be more inclusive and developmental with regards to younger members of staff???!

They have got to be kidding. Do they know what a shower some of these young teachers are? Do they know how hard I work to bring them up to scratch? And delegate more? Staff just want to do the day's work, go home at four, and if you're lucky do a bit of marking for half an hour in the evening. How can you delegate to people with that attitude?

'Trevor? Trevor! Come and see this utter nonsense they've written.'

'Let me look. Oh come on, that's not too bad. You know they've got to find something to pick on. Everything can't be brilliant.'

'I know that, but they've asked for a plan for improvement and will review the situation in two years' time. What a disgrace. I don't know whether to scream or cry.'

'Don't let it get to you. Strong leaders always generate opposition. Just give them some blurb on a new system of staff consultation and mentoring or something like that. Play the game. That's what everyone else does.'

'Trevor, this is *no* game.'

She looked at him, eyes wide, cheeks flushed, fists tightly clenched in frustration.

'I worked hard for years to get this head teacher post. And since I arrived at the school, we've seen an obvious improvement in the kids' attainment levels, they're all wearing school uniform, and we do well in the Music Festival, among a hundred other things. It's been work, work, work for me – all day every day. I'm proud of the place, proud of my achievements. And now this. Autocratic they say? I call it strong and focussed.'

'And as for young teachers,' – she raised her eyes to the ceiling – 'they can serve their time just as I did and then their day will come too. It's all about commitment, extra training, toeing the line, setting an example to the children. Nothing's changed in that respect. I don't see what I can do any differently. It must be that I haven't convinced all of the staff, haven't got the message over sufficiently clearly. *That's* what I will have to concentrate on. I'd better work up a plan.'

'That sounds like a really good idea. You show them girl!'

Anything to bring down her blood pressure.

* *

The inspectorate were satisfied with her strategy for improvement – on paper. They would revisit in two years' time in May 2004 to see the outcome. That would be something to look forward to, along with her 50th birthday, a slower speed in the Dundee half marathon and no doubt a head full of grey hair.

Trevor offered a bright suggestion.

'How about shadowing one of your mates for a few days. You know that girl in Fintry you went to school with – Theresa Whatsit? See what she might be doing differently.'

One day was enough.

Staff calling the head 'Theresa' instead of Mrs McGuire – such a lack of respect. An open door policy – how on earth do you get any work done with all those interruptions? And a rotating chair for staff meetings? Heavens above, who's in charge here?

Nevertheless, she formulated a schedule of staff meetings designed to facilitate the production of the next school development plan. If nothing else, it might mean she wouldn't have to spend the whole of the Easter holidays writing it herself, when the rest of the staff were traipsing off to Majorca or Center Parcs.

I'd better aim for inclusion if that's what they want, so we'll ask all the teaching assistants and admin staff along too. And if its delegation they want, well maybe some small groups can work on different aspects. But I'll have to retain the final say, otherwise the whole thing could be a shambles.

On the first Wednesday of every month (apart from during school holidays), at four pm, the full staff complement – minus those whose Grannies had died, or who had a dental appointment – would squeeze into the staff room, books balanced on knees, coffee cups placed ominously close to tapping feet, attitudes mirrored in their faces.

The theory, as explained by Mrs Baker (and not yet Patricia), was as follows:

'Effective teams have a shared understanding of the task.

'Everyone is clear about their role and what is expected of them.

'Each person commits to the work involved.

'All contributions are respected.

'Values are shared and discussed, particularly when the work is hard going.'

'Hell's teeth. What management book has she swallowed?' whispered Jean Fraser to Mandy McKay.

'We might all share an understanding of the task, but it's her version that she rams down our throats,' was Mandy's reply.

'Shared values? The ten commandments and a load of other Do Nots as far as I can see,' from another.

Patricia had indeed read the book (How to Facilitate Effective Meetings) and thought she *was* modifying her style, soliciting a round of opinion here, splitting the roomful up for small group discussion there, hearing and recording feedback on the chart where possible. Asking for comment before pronouncing agreement on action.

Group task techniques she might have learned and applied, but appropriate attitudes to encourage and support the process – not much change was evident there.

'An environmental study day trip to The Angus Glens? I don't think so Mabel. If you were aware of all the risk assessment factors which come into play here you wouldn't be suggesting that. Thank you anyway. Next? '

'If you'd been in the job as long as I have, I rather think you would be more likely to stick with the tried and tested, Peter.'

'I appreciate your offer Kate. Of course the final responsibility does always lie with the Head Teacher. Nevertheless, let me know what you're thinking and we'll see if we can fit it in somewhere.'

'No, absolutely not. I must use my veto on that one. I've worked so hard to bring everyone up to speed on that particular Maths programme. We're simply not going to change it now. Sorry.'

Leopards and spots. Old dogs and new tricks. Or did she really know best?

Over the next while, Trevor further honed his already well developed skills of simulated active listening while reading the daily paper.

'They've started to make excuses now for not coming to the planning meeting. I'm sure it's all invented appointments or children's illness.'

'Yes dear. Young folk today, I ask you.'

'Well, I'll stick it out if only to prove the inspectors wrong.'

'You do that dear.'

'I've ended up writing that development plan myself anyway. But they can't say I haven't tried, can they?'

'Of course not. Of course they can't.'

* *

The review visit was considerably shorter than the full inspection. Patricia had run an extra five miles the previous evening to rehearse and perfect her presentation to the inspectors. She had all the statistics to hand.

Since the initial inspection she had held 13 full staff meetings, each with an average of 85% attendance (thank goodness the first four or five had been well supported); had reviewed both in plenary and in appropriate small groups the delivery of the curriculum in every subject against the recommended standards of achievement; had facilitated a team based development plan with one, two and five year targets and had appointed a sub group to identify subject leaders amongst the staff. Surely that would suffice.

The staff were well able to interpret the report speak:

'A modified leadership style has encouraged wider staff participation in planning and review. Staff have expressed general satisfaction with this development and look forward to further actual devolvement of authority and responsibility as the new system beds in.'

They could always live in hope.

Homeward Bound

Dundee 2004

There is nothing to keep me in Scotland. Not any more. No husband, no job, no ties. Providing Jonathan will come with me, of course.

It was a startling revelation that had come to Lesley that morning, seemingly out of the blue. There she'd been, sitting at the dining table, relaxing quietly after a lazy breakfast. Looking out over the garden at the sparrows on the fence, she couldn't remember thinking about anything in particular whilst she swirled her cup around dreamily, moving it first one way and then the other, the dregs of coffee sloshing against the sides with each rotation.

The words had entered her head all of a sudden, as clear as could be, almost making her jump with their intensity: *there is nothing to keep me in Scotland …*

She stopped swirling the cup immediately and sat up straight in her chair with a puzzled look on her face. She'd felt quite odd; slightly shocked perhaps, in that she hadn't expected to have a thought like that, but not actually uncomfortable with it.

Where did that come from? she asked herself, starting one of her typical internal dialogues. What should I do about it? Ignore it? Speak with someone about it?

Before Lesley could get any further with this line of questioning she noticed the clock and remembered about her dental appointment. She'd need to hurry now if she wasn't to be late.

Back home, with a frozen lip that was tingling as it gradually came back to life she attempted to drink a glass of water, only to spill some down the front of her new jumper, exclaiming *Damn! That's it then, I'm just going to have to wait for my biscuits until this lip's back to normal.*

It appeared that the surprise thought of the morning was not going to go away easily. It had revisited her several times, in various guises, during the course of the morning, driving back and forth to the dental surgery, accompanied by a whole conversation going on in her head. Sometimes Lesley wondered if she was a little mad when this happened.

If so, then I've been mad all my life.

Why do I stay here?

Well, I've got a nice little house, some good friends.

What else?

I like the area, there's plenty to do here.

Like what?

Swimming, walking, shopping.

You could do those anywhere couldn't you?

Well I suppose I could if I wanted to. Yes, I could.

It's very cold up here isn't it? Seems to get colder every winter doesn't it ? The heating's so expensive. Well yes, it is, but I've got enough money now I'm retired haven't I? Wouldn't you like to spend it on things other than fuel bills? Holidays maybe?

And so it went on. Lesley began to think hard about future possibilities. Where did she really want to live, now that she was free to live anywhere she chose? Where was home? Was it still Wales, after all these years? Thirty to be precise. But she'd lived in Scotland more than half her life so was it Scotland now? What about Europe? No – that was too far away from family and friends, besides, she'd never been good at languages.

One thing was absolutely certain; she wanted a cat. Two cats, maybe. Now she wasn't working she had time for one, but the road outside was a problem. It wasn't safe with people speeding up and down to the park entrance. Her neighbour's cat had been run down last year, the poor thing. It had been a real shame for old Mrs Beattie; she'd loved that cat and had been distraught for a week. Lesley had offered to take the old dear to the cats' home to get another one but that idea was totally dismissed. The episode had aged Mrs Beattie virtually overnight.

She looks quite frail now. I couldn't have a cat here, I know that. I would have to live somewhere else. Where do I really want to be? What do I want to be doing with my life when I'm there other than having a cat to look after? Oh God, I don't know. That's it, isn't it? I really don't know.

And the truth of it was that she didn't. It had been a very long time since Lesley had thought about what she wanted for herself, so she was out of practice. It was going to take her some work and a lot more soul-searching questions to find the answers.

* *

By chance, or was it fate? She saw the advertisement in the Dundee Courier a fortnight later. 'The Nor'East of Scotland Cat Club Championship Show in the Caird Hall, Saturday, 13th May. Spectators welcome.' How could she possibly resist? Lesley joined the throng milling up the steps and queued to get in. Inside it was a hive of activity. Row after row of cages containing all manner of pedigree cats, and a few moggies as well, people in white coats lifting cats in and out of cages and scribbling in notebooks – the judges and stewards, she discovered, and stalls selling every kind of feline paraphernalia. There must have been at least 300 cats there, she reckoned, counting the rows.

She glanced down the programme categories: Persians, Semi-Longhairs, British Shorthairs, Oriental and Foreign varieties; where on earth would she start? Remembering China the Siamese cat from her childhood she made her way to the Siamese rows and peeked inside the cages. How proud they looked – so sleek and refined with those intense blue eyes. Some of the cats seemed pleased to see the crowds, putting their paws through the bars playfully, or rubbing up against them. Others were disinterested in the proceedings. Some looked nervous. No wonder, Lesley thought, with all this noise going on. There was a constant hubbub of voices in the background, a few meows and yowls and the occasional announcement on the tannoy. She wandered up and down the rows, past the Persians with their long flowing hair, so beautifully groomed, some of them having the final touches of titillation to their coats by their brush-wielding owners.

No, not one of those, too much work, beautiful as they are.

There were some breeds there that she'd never seen before, other than in a book. Two huge Rag Dolls, that filled their cages. A Cornish Rex with a coat of short curly hair and an ugly face. A Havana, that looked like a chocolate Siamese but with green eyes instead of blue ones.

She continued to wander down the Foreign Varieties rows, stopping to look at any cats that caught her eye. Then she saw them, and was utterly transfixed. The most beautiful cats she had ever seen in her whole life. The woman fussing around the cages was more than happy to talk to Lesley about her prize possessions, two Red Abyssinians.

'They've got the silhouette of the cats of the ancient Egyptians;

very regal don't you think? Their names are Zarif and Phoebe. They're the Red variety, it's only been recognised as a separate breed since 1963 and they're still fairly rare up here.'

'Do they make good pets?' Lesley asked.

'They're very affectionate and *so* intelligent. They love attention. But you can't keep them contained in the house easily, they prefer to roam around. These two are neutered so I can let them do that, I've got a safe garden, but of course, the breeders can't do that with entire cats.'

'No, I suppose not. So you don't breed them then?' Lesley asked.

'No, I don't. I just show for fun. They've won a lot, these two, over the years.'

'I can see!' The cages had a red card each on the bars, first prize in class.

'Could I possibly pat one?' Lesley was, by now, desperate to get her hands on the cats, imagining the feel of their fur, wishing to gaze into their fabulous copper coloured eyes. She especially loved their little white chins and their brick-red leather noses outlined in black.

Their owner seemed keen to encourage Lesley's interest. 'Yes, I'll get Zarif out for you now, he loves a fuss from anyone, but I'll hang onto him while you pat him – I don't want him escaping here.'

One touch of the close-textured red fur and Lesley was smitten, hook, line and sinker. She smoothed the cat on his head, down his neck and along his back, eliciting a big purr from him.

'He is just so gorgeous!' she cooed. 'I've been wanting a cat for years and years, and now I'm in a position to have one because I've retired early and got plenty of time. I always thought I would get a Siamese, but now I've seen your Abyssinians I've changed my mind. How difficult is it to find one? Do you know anyone breeding them?'

'A red Abyssinian would be a good match for you – it would go with your red hair!' the woman laughed. 'The breeder in Birmingham I bought these two from has since died, but the GCCF would have a list.'

'The GCCF?'

'The Governing Council of the Cat Fancy. It's like the Kennel

Club, only for cats. The Show Secretary would be able to give you the number, she's at a table near the entrance.'

'Thank you, thank you so very much. Your cats have made my day. Sorry! I mean – you've made my day! I won't hold you up anymore.' Lesley smiled and gave the cat one last stroke.

'You're welcome my dear. Any new fanciers of Abbies are always welcome. Good luck in your search.'

Reluctantly Lesley dragged herself away to see the remainder of the show, but before she left she made her way to the Secretary's table and obtained the number of the GCCF.

Just in case, she told herself, even though deep down she'd already made her mind up.

Jonathan was tucking into his fish supper with gusto.

'You could have brought one for me,' Lesley moaned. 'There's nothing here, I'm going to have to nip down to Tesco.'

'Sorry Mum, I only had enough money for one. Pay day's not until tomorrow.'

'Only teasing, lovely. You enjoy it.'

Her son was turning out all right after all. The Nationwide car repair apprenticeship suited him down to the ground; regular hours, not too much stress, and it had brought out a latent talent for car mechanics, which his workmates had recognised. He was finding a sense of self-esteem that had completely eluded him at school. Only three months to go and then he'd be fully qualified.

Now might be a good time to broach the possibility of moving, Lesley reckoned.

Up where I belong

New York 2004

'Ten minutes please, ten minutes Miss Lloyd-Jones.'

'Professor please!'

'Sorry, Professor Lloyd-Jones. Ten minutes.'

'Clear the set please everyone, ten minutes to action.'

Time for one last look in the mirror, a deep breath, a quiet moment and then she would stride with confidence into the studio, wait in the wings for her cue and take her seat opposite chat show host Rod Casey. Wardrobe had wanted her to change her navy wool suit for something less formal. But she'd pulled herself up to her full height, put on her most serious tone and reminded them that she was an academic and should display the necessary gravitas.

'You might know me as a TV personality, but my influence comes from my international academic reputation, which is not enhanced by a celebrity-style outfit from Rodeo Drive.'

They had to be satisfied with the addition of a piece of traditional Welsh jewellery, an 18ct rare Welsh gold Cariad Heart Pendant.

'Welcome all those at home to the first programme in our new series *Women of a Certain Age* when we interview those household names who are willing to own up to being 50 – and many don't. I just can't think why!

'We want to find out their secrets, how they got where they are today. Tonight we are delighted to introduce Professor Carys Lloyd-Jones, fresh from her latest series of *Our Celtic Ancestors*. Professor ...'

'Noswaith dda. Good evening.'

'Thank you Professor Lloyd-Jones. Please sit down. May I call you Carys?'

'We are in America I suppose, so yes that will be allowed.'

'Once a professor, always a professor I take it?'

'I like to think so, yes. It's a hard earned title, at least where I come from.'

'Ah, do I detect a veiled criticism of our little ol' country?'

'You might, yes. But I'd rather focus on what's good about the country tonight if you don't mind.'

'And that is … ?'

'The Celtic influence of course!'

'So tell me how you first came to our TV screens and put that Celtic spell on us.'

'Well, you can thank Johnny O'Brien for that. He and I met up at a rather disappointing conference dinner in Chicago in 2001 I think it was, where we spent several hours over a bottle of Old Bushmills swapping Celtic myths. Then he asked me if I would act as professional advisor on a new series he was planning.'

'That would be "*Our Celtic Ancestors*" I suppose. How did you find working with Johnny? Some say he's a drunken womaniser in his spare time!'

'Ah, that's where you Americans get it all wrong. A little charm, the warming glow of a single malt, a few words of an ancient Celtic tongue and most women are doing the chasing. Johnny's a good pal of mine now. We've worked together on three series and are planning a fourth.'

'Remind our viewers how you made the move from advisor to presenter?

'Series one Johnny used me to verify the facts, or at least what is accepted as such by those who study the history and religion of the Welsh and Irish. Series two he invited me to talk on camera about the roots of the Welsh language, and recite a short poem in Welsh. The Welsh exiles loved it and asked for more apparently. So when he was planning series three, he included a regular slot on the Celtic languages. I was the voice of Wales and we also had an Irish and a Scottish voice.'

'But Kathleen Brady and Mary McLeod haven't seen their stars rise as yours has. What would you say has been your appeal?'

'You're very kind, but I think you would have to ask others that question.'

'Don't be modest, Carys. People magazine called you "*that diminutive powerhouse of facts and authority with the sparkling eyes and the sharp wit. A pint sized modern day St Clare*." That's St Clare – Patron Saint of television – for the benefit of our viewers.'

'Yes, they did seem to like me. But you know, I'm just myself whenever I'm on. Yes, I'm confident, yes I'm very knowledgeable. The rest is the result of good genes and a sense of nostalgia on the part of the many exiles here in US of A.'

'No makeovers?'

'Certainly not. I don't need that. My sense of self comes from my knowledge and intellect. That only grows with every year I am on this earth.'

'And yet, my spies tell me that you did suffer a loss of confidence a few years back. Maybe you'd share with our viewers what happened on your return from Ireland.'

'I wouldn't call it a loss of confidence. Not on my part anyway. I returned to the States just before Independence Day 2001 after more than a year in Ireland researching a new book on the Saints Brigid, Bronagh and Moninna. I had expected to return to Walton to resume my academic career there but found no enthusiasm in that quarter for my latest research, despite earlier indications. And some ridiculous question mark over my performance as departmental head was mentioned. I didn't have (she indicated speech marks with her fingers) "the complete confidence of all staff members." It was suggested to me that I take some further time out to consider my position.

'So I threw myself into preparing a number of conference presentations on my latest work on the Irish saints and toured the States wherever there was an interest in ancient Celtic spirituality, giving lectures and presenting papers. You'd be amazed at some of the places I ended up. I met Johnny as I said in Chicago. And a few months later my life took a completely new direction.'

'So, are you giving the finger to Walton?'

'Now, Rod, twt a lol. You're talking nonsense. I'm sure they view my new career with great interest, and of course I keep in touch with several of my old colleagues. I don't rule out a return to academia sometime in the future.'

'Where do you see your television career going next Carys?'

'I'm very keen to go back to Wales to tell the people at home about the enthusiasm and interest for the Welsh language, culture and history that I find in this country, in contrast to what is happening there.

'The global teenager is alive and well in Wales, you know. And very much influenced by the international cultural icons rather than his or her own local history. I'd like to help regenerate a love of all things Welsh. So I'm in talks with Bryn Morgan at ITV

Wales at the moment. Can't say more than that at this stage.'

'I wonder if I detect a hint of hiraeth?' said with a smirk and a wink to the audience.

'Homesickness for all things Welsh? Maybe. But you ain't seen the last of me here, yet. Don't forget my new book which is coming out next month. It's based on the last series of *Our Celtic Ancestors*. I'll be visiting a Borders bookshop near you very soon.'

'Ladies and gentleman, we haven't seen the last of this woman of a certain age. Thank you, Professor Lloyd-Jones.'

'It's been a pleasure. Diolch. Thank you.'

'And now for someone who has had several makeovers and professes never to have read a book in her adult life – Marybel Kuttner.'

* *

Carys emailed me.

'Have you got Sky TV? Look out for *Women of a Certain Age* on CBS. Someone you know is on the first programme of the series.'

'Have you got Sky Nancy,' I phoned to ask.

'Don't be daft, Di. The landed gentry don't have Sky. That's far too common. Why do you ask?'

'I think Carys might be on a chat show in the States. I'll record it if I can find the programme in the listings. You never know she might mention us!'

'That's the nearest we'll ever get to being famous, then. Let me know how you get on. The interviewer will be in for a tough ride. I hope he's done his homework.'

Women of a certain age. Euphemism. Soft soap.

The Perfect Place

December 2005

The BMWs, Audis and Volvos were lined up outside the castle, waiting for their daily complimentary wash by the young porter. Diane gave a wry smile as she parked her Fiat Punto round the corner.

The entrance to the Newton Castle Spa Resort was through a centuries old massive wooden door which opened into a sunlit, glass-domed hallway. A variety of ages and sizes were sitting or lounging about, reading *Vogue* and *New Woman* and sipping fruit juice. Their white wraparound dressing gowns, blue cotton mules and newly cleansed faces rendered them an amorphous group. Of ladies that is, not women - at £150 per night. (Or £99 if you shared and came in the low season, as Diane and Nancy had). There was one though, who wore a mint green chenille dressing gown – obviously she had brought her own and was too important a client to be given the quiet word. Probably staying in the Canmore Suite; all old stone and heavy silk. Around her pale creamy neck was a gold necklace forming her name, one assumed, in Arabic. That explained it then, new money.

Diane checked in – 'McDonald's the name; just the one night, yes – my friend Nancy Robertson is on her way.' Then she looked out for Nancy's Discovery to appear. Nancy's was old money of course.

Nancy arrived with a whoosh of gravel, pulling up the hand-brake and grabbing her handbag in almost one action. Diane caught a glimpse of an athletic woman with bobbing shoulder length dark blonde hair striding energetically across the car-park. She made a double take to be sure, expecting to see a brunette, but yes, it definitely was Nancy. She moved quickly towards the front door in greeting.

'Nancy, hi there!'

'Diane, you're looking great!' Nancy gave Diane a big hug, thinking how much her friend's new look really suited her; she just seemed to get better with each passing year. The functional style of old had now gone; replaced with a understated sophistication that gave Diane an overall air of mature confidence. She looked completely comfortable in her own skin.

'Thanks, Nance! I feel great, and it's good to see you looking so well. The hair – a bit of a surprise – but it suits you! In a rush as usual. I hope you're still taking time to look after yourself properly?'

'But of course! Sorry I'm late, blame the horses. I really miss the girls now to share the load a bit and I just can't bring myself to get rid of Domino even though he's too old and arthritic to ride any more. Have you done the business?'

'Yes, we're in the Stirling room. All the rooms are called after castles in this wing apparently. I'll get someone to take our bags up.'

'Thanks. Used to be I could manage yours, mine and hers over there too. But these days I have to pace myself. Fingers crossed it keeps me well. Now where are we going to work?'

'Take it easy Nance. Let's have a swim first and a relax in the steam room. We'll have plenty of time later. It's only a weekend we're organising, not the Queen's state visit. Mind you the Queen of Sheba *will* put in an appearance at it! Or maybe that's being unfair. Alix has a more business-like approach to life these days. She's just as likely to use this 'me-time' to negotiate a concession for her collectables.'

'Hate to say it, but that might be no bad thing. She got totally out of order that last time in Edinburgh, '94 wasn't it? Do you remember how pissed off Patricia was about her, and the rest of us too?'

'How could I ever forget?' Diane grimaced. 'But let's unpack first and then throw around a few ideas while relaxing in the spa. Have you seen the ozone pool? It's fantastic.'

For a watercolour artist like Diane, the lighting in the pool area was a balm for the soul, echoing a pale aqua sea on a pink toned summer evening. The £50 swimsuit with its built in stomach support enhanced her mature figure and it was with an air of rare abandon that she dived into the inviting water and swam an effortless 20 lengths before joining Nancy in the crystal steam room. The steam would clear the sinuses. The crystal was probably having no effect whatsoever, given the grubby fissures in the massive piece of quartz. Nancy made a mental note to mention it to reception as well as let them know how to clean it.

'You never know, they might give us a free bottle of wine for that tip.'

Monday nights were quiet at Newton Castle, the weekenders having left after a light lunch around 2pm. Surprisingly, 22nd December was one of the 'white dates' when the special offer applied. Maybe everyone was too busy getting wound up over Christmas preparations to find time to wind down at the spa hotel. Hopefully that would mean a quiet atmosphere for the two friends to devise their master-plan. The only given about this proposed second reunion was the dates – 1st and 2nd July 2006 – thirty years to the day since the six of them had shut the door on flat 6, 26 Dalmeny Street, Edinburgh for the very last time.

Refreshed and relaxed, they sat sipping some herbal tea in the resident's lounge, taking a breather before their first treatment – nails for Nancy, massage for Diane.

'So – how's Willie then?' asked Nancy, 'still on the cooking kick? Can't believe he's turning into a new man.'

'I wouldn't go that far! He just fancies himself as a bit of a Gordon Ramsay since he met him that time up in Lewis when the locals were catching the baby guga for Gordon to cook. It started with him frying up any poor fish that he caught on his day trips and now he'll throw the odd steak in a pan, add a dash of red wine and a few shallots and think he's some kind of miracle worker! Pity he hadn't been so keen when the kids were around. He's fine though. Goes to work in a suit these days and acts as an advisor to the Hydro Board. Far cry from his Dad's wee van and a bag of tools when I first met him. How about Michael? Last time I saw you he was thinking about early retirement.'

'That was last year! This year he did the sums and discovered that his pension pot could benefit from a few extra grand in it so he's carrying on meantime. I do worry about him though, his health isn't 100 per cent.'

'Why? What's wrong? Nothing serious, I hope.'

Nancy looked concerned as she spoke, 'Just a bit of angina, the GP says. He's got to keep his stress levels down, watch his diet and take a daily pill. Apparently it won't necessarily deteriorate, but I still can't help worrying.'

'Well, at least we're both still married. That's something to celebrate nowadays – I think.'

'Carys never mentions JJ these days, and I'm sure Patricia is kidding herself over this trial separation from Trevor. She just doesn't want to accept the inevitable. Lesley and Nick are long split of course.'

An edge crept into Nancy's voice, 'Here's hoping Nick isn't chair of the BMA in Scotland by now, although nothing is beyond belief in the medical world is it? If it's Highland's turn, then the local boy from Inverness gets the post, regardless, so it seems.'

'I don't think Lesley cares what happens to him any more,' Diane said calmly. 'Living away down in Wales now she's unlikely ever to come across him again.'

'How was Patricia when you last saw her?'

'I thought she was looking quite a bit older, thinner again, and she seemed pretty stressed to me, going on about how school's hectic with some new maths system being introduced. I watched her reorganise the contents of her handbag three times during a half hour in the coffee shop.'

'Oh oh. Not the old obsessive behaviour again?'

'Seems like it,' Diane confirmed. 'But - while I remember, she said she'd helped Lesley with her packing to go to Wales, and Lesley was full of it, happier than Patricia had seen her for years and years. Her back was actually much better since she'd stopped working, no more lifting patients, on her feet all day and so on.'

'I'm so pleased for Lesley. I hope she does make it back up here for the reunion.'

'I emailed everyone, and they all said the July dates were fine, I can't do any more than that at this stage.'

'No, you're right, Diane. What about Alix? Have you seen her or heard from her? I've not, not since the last Christmas card.'

'I got a phone call a few months ago when she had the latest supply of furniture in. I'd asked her to let me know when it arrived – thought I would see about a special chair for a bare corner of the gallery. I did buy it, not cheap though, even with a discount 'for special friends'. As you might expect, Alix seems to be getting on with life – and how. A working partnership she has with James, she says. But given the wink which followed it's not all work.'

Nancy smiled ruefully. 'Leopards and spots, Diane. I can't believe it's actually 12 years since the last time in that so-called luxury apartment in Edinburgh – and all those promises about how we would stay in touch, and try to get together as a group every year. I guess that was never going to work with Carys living in the States anyway. The pity of it all is that the last time most of us were in the same room was at Gerald's funeral.'

'And that was five years ago, you know, Nancy. Where has the time gone? Where *does* it go? Scary, don't you think? I'm 52 next birthday, rapidly reaching the old crone stage, as Germaine Greer says.'

'Sod Germaine Greer, you look better now than you did five years ago. Much happier, and it shows in your face, I think you definitely look younger!' Nancy said emphatically.

'Must be the HRT then!' laughed Diane.

'Lucky you, some of us have had to go through this crappy menopause naturally with only a few herbal potions and tea bags to help us. Naturally, it's called! What's *natural* about it when it makes you look and feel so awful? I'll be glad to see the back of it.'

Diane looked hard at Nancy, trying to appear as positive as possible. She was searching for a few words of support. Difficult, since she couldn't deny the difference in Nancy now. She had developed several deep lines on her face in recent years, particularly the ones on each side of her nose which ran all the way down to the corners of her mouth - and her chin was starting to sag. She'd always been trim, but her illness had resulted in a weight loss from which she'd never really recovered. That fresh-faced country look had given way to a somewhat drawn appearance.

'Well I don't know about being lucky, at least you don't have to worry about getting fat, when some of us have a constant struggle to keep the pounds off,' Diane eventually managed.

'I'm hardly likely to get fat am I with my restricted diet?' moaned Nancy.

'What? Still no dairy or wheat? What about alcohol?'

'I can tolerate wheat occasionally, but definitely not dairy. So – take out the cheese, eggs, the ice-cream, the chocolate, the …'

'And then there's nothing fattening left to eat is there!' Diane laughed.

'No! and it's not funny either!' Nancy leaned forward in her seat and pulled a mock grumpy face at Diane. 'Fortunately, I can manage the odd glass of wine now without any ill effects, but if the girls think they're going to see the old Nancy drink them under the table as usual then they're in for a shock.'

'We'll get onto planning the reunion tonight, after dinner, then you can work out how to cope with your requirements if we choose this venue. Right now, we'd best get those treatments in, don't you think? Are you sure you don't want to come and have a massage with me?'

'Yes, positive. How could I pass up the opportunity to have full manicure and polish? You know all about my nail fetish!' Nancy held her hands out to show Diane. Still the long nails, goodness knows how with the country life she led, but no longer the red, black or startling combination colours of her student days. They were a delicate pink.

'I still try, Diane, although the old skin's not as nice as it used to be. Just look at these age spots! You can tell a woman's age by her hands; I read that Gerry Hall wears a pile of cream on hers under cotton gloves when she goes to bed, to keep them looking younger. I wouldn't go that far, but I think I'll get a nifty French manicure today. I can't do that on myself, it takes too much faffing around.'

'You and your nails. Some things don't change I'm pleased to see.'

Diane gave Nancy an affectionate look.

'We always envied you your hands.'

'Mrs McDonald? Would you like to follow me up to the treatment area now? I'm Lisa. I'm your therapist today.'

Nancy was called seconds later. Obviously a well-run ship this place.

'Mrs Robertson, I'm Donna, nice to meet you. Just through here to the nail bar. Weather's still not too cold, is it, given the time of year? Is this your first time here?'

Diane looked at these wafer-thin, tanned and smooth skinned young girls and experienced a momentary pang of nostalgia for her own youth but that was quickly forgotten in the effort to disrobe and engineer her rear end into the paper panties. Thank goodness for subdued lighting.

The two met up again for a quick drink before dinner – Nancy's nails buffed to perfection, Diane's cellulite visibly reduced – at least for now.

'After dinner, once we've decided if the food is up to scratch, we can make a list of the questions we need to ask at the front desk and then if they can satisfy all our needs, we'll make a provisional booking before we leave. I'll draft up an email to go out to the rest of the girls and run it past you before I send it out. How does that sound?' asked Diane.

'Uh, my brain is in reverse now, Di. Ask me again at dinner. Think I'll have to lie down first, for a bit of a rest.'

It was a real treat to have dinner cooked and put onto the table in front of them without either having to lift a finger. Nancy's special dietary requirements had been met without any trouble.

'That confirms it for me, Diane. I think we should definitely hold the reunion here. It's plush, the staff are accommodating, there's plenty of treatments to choose from, and the grounds are lovely to walk in,'

'or run in if you're Patricia,' interrupted Diane,

'Yes, well, she's welcome to that,' retorted Nancy. 'I shall be strolling. *And* it's not too expensive. I think it will be perfect.'

'Other than getting here, perhaps, particularly for Carys and Lesley – they'll be flying up.'

'Some one will just have to get them from Edinburgh airport; we can organise that, surely? What do you think then? Here? Or not?'

'Oh yes, here,' Diane said without hesitation.

The discussion about the reunion parked for the meantime, they caught up on all the family news over dinner before moving on to the bigger questions of life over a nightcap in their room.

'Oh I'm just so relieved to have my old pal back, more or less intact!' Diane gave Nancy a bear hug.

'Yes, life can be a right bitch, so it can. You never know what's ahead of you. Even though I'm over the worst of that illness, I'm not and probably never will be one hundred per cent again.' There was a wry twist to Nancy's mouth.

'Ah come on, things are looking up now. There's me and my art gallery and you and your hypnosis training. Fingers crossed it's all for the best, even if it's not what we thought we wanted. All those high falutin' plans you had! And me thinking I'd be happy as Larry being a wife and mother.'

'You're right, Di. Nothing stays the same for ever. But at least

I'm more at peace with myself now than I've ever been, and if I can do some good my for clients then I'll be happy.'

'And it only cost you £40 to see the way ahead! Here's to Melanie!'

Diane lifted her glass in a mock toast to the astrologer.

You make me feel brand new

Newton Castle Spa 1 July 2006

No doubt some researcher, somewhere, has studied email addresses and how they give clues to character.

My contact list for the Dalmeny Street girls read:

theproprietrix@rubislawtreasures.co.uk;

nancy@changeyourlife.co.uk;

pbakerheadteacher@stpeters.pkc.sch.uk;

profclloydjones@cbs.com;

lesleyodonnell@catfancy.demon.co.uk;

and of course me on djmcdonald@hotmail.co.uk.

The Dalmeny Street Girls had gone electronic – in their own way.

And thank goodness.

Maps, menus, treatment booking forms – we did it all online and by email, and it was so easy. Mobile phones allowed us to stay in touch on the day of arrival at Newton Castle Spa Resort. I sat in reception, suitcase at my feet, practising my breathing while waiting for Nancy and the others to arrive.

Breathe in calm, breathe out tension. Breathe in calm, breathe out tension. Tension? Surely not? Meeting your old friends for a catch up, a fond look back over the years, plus a bit of pampering. You're looking good. You have much to report of a positive nature. Why the tension? Is it too hard to let go of that worry about being too …? Too what…? Too fat? Too old? Why should that still matter? Stop it for heaven's sake.

They all arrived within one mad half hour with their 'Gosh *you're* looking well! What's this about cat fancy? And who's the new blonde member of the group? Why on earth have we left it this long? And Gawd, I need a cuppa caffee!'

Alix had brought champagne, Lesley some of her famous chocolate cake, Carys five copies of the book to accompany the series (well, what did you expect?), Nancy some samples of herbal hangover cures and Patricia a pack of mediwipes for each of us. You can never be too confident that all the gym equipment has been cleaned after each use, apparently. I produced a couple of disposable cameras with instructions to 'keep snapping. But don't show my back view in a swimming costume please!'

Over the afternoon, with everyone in various stages of undress, swimming, lounging after treatments, sitting alone chilling out or engrossed in sharing news, I made a few idle observations which may or may not represent universal truths.

One – if you're too thin your face becomes very lined as you get older. So maybe it pays to carry a few extra pounds.

Two – even those who stay fit experience the slide south of all movable body parts.

Three – we all end up looking like our mothers.

And four – old habits die hard.

However, there *were* a few surprises.

Alix sported a ring on her wedding finger – 1ct of beautiful, breathtaking, ocean blue aquamarines set in 18ct gold.

'James went down on one knee, would you believe! But it *is* time he made a decent woman out of me. You're all invited to the wedding at Dalfruan in September. We're having a marquee in the garden.'

Patricia, in contrast, had removed her wedding ring.

'I'll always be married to Trevor, in my mind and in the eyes of the church. There will never be anyone else. But he wants his "freedom" as he calls it. So that's that. Nothing else to be said unless you want the fine detail (yes we do actually). Now how about a run round the grounds?'

Go on yourself Patricia. We're enjoying not running for one weekend.

Lesley's new outfit, hung up to let the creases drop, revealed a size 16 label.

'Oh I know, I know,' she said quickly. ' I *have* put on a few pounds and maybe I *should* go on a diet. But I'm enjoying having no pressure on me these days. I'm not even thinking about what I'm actually going to do with my life.'

And in a surprising way, the little bit of extra roundness suited her nicely. She exuded womanhood in a soft, feline way.

Next to Lesley, Carys sounded strangely manic.

'I've soooo many stories to tell you. Now, did I mention that I met Anthony Hopkins at the studios? He's Welsh too of course. We had sooooo much in common. And there was the night at the Emmy awards – Hugh Lawrie had his arm around me when the cameras panned on to him. He's a huge hit in the States now.'

On and on without stopping for breath. Although the wistful look in her eyes when the spotlight had moved seemed to suggest another story.

The others were disbelieving when Nancy refused a pre-dinner drink.

'Come on Nancy. Where's that madcap girl of old? Think you're one of the landed gentry now do you? Most of them take a good drink anyway. You used to match me one for one.'

'Times change Alix. You know that. I look after myself these days. No longer Superwoman. That role nearly finished me off. So have one for me and I'll save myself for dinner.'

And as for me – they already knew about the gallery, and they'd had the digital photos attached to the emailed Christmas letter so maybe there was less scope for surprises. What *was* different was that the effort of organising the event and bringing it to fruition on the day had not left me exhausted, as in the past. When it came to the after-dinner chat, and with the benefit of a warming glass of vintage port to round off the meal, I took charge of events.

* *

Replete, relaxed, comfortable. Sipping coffee, real or substitute, no desire to move. At ease with each other. Thankful it was a private dining room. It could only last for so long before someone made a suggestion.

I tapped my crystal wine glass three or four times with my silver teaspoon.

'Ladies – I propose a toast. To Alix! Our sparkling jewel. Congratulations on your engagement!'

'Thank you Diane. And to Diane – for organising us so well. Where would we be without her!'

'To Diane.'

I blushed like a teenager as they raised their glasses.

'To all of us – the Dalmeny Street Gurrls!' delivered in Carys's best Scots accent.

'To us – but less of the *girls*' said Patricia. 'More like old crones these days.'

'Speak for yourself skinny,' laughed Lesley.

'Well – to us – whoever we are!' from Nancy.

Glasses clinked all round and were drained of their sparkling contents.

'Just who are we then?' I demanded. 'The sum of our actions? Nature edited by nurture? The product of our times? The outcome of our plans? I don't know. All I do know is that I regret not finding *me* years ago.'

'But you've achieved so much, Diane. A lovely family, a good marriage, a successful new business. What is there to regret?' from a puzzled Lesley.

I was fired up now.

'I've spent my entire life obsessed with making things safe and happy for everyone else, thinking that was my role, believing it was a valued and necessary job. All the time I was ignoring my own needs – for fun, for creativity, for personal fulfilment. Thank God for Aunt Marguerite and her money. The gallery's been a life saver for me. Rescued me from that impossible load. And you know what? The family are actually happier now without me fussing around them. They're making their own mistakes and surviving. They don't have to worry about me and my state of mind any more. And now I'm a positive, instead of a negative, role model for my girls. Life is good. But it could have been so much better for all those years.'

I was surprised at the strength of my own outburst. It was definitely time to see what the others had to say.

'Hark at me! The good listener hogs the floor for a change! Over to you Lesley since you asked the question. What are your achievements and your regrets? How does your garden grow?'

Lesley took time to think, looking upwards as if reviewing events, smiling gently to herself.

'Well I'm just the same old me that you always knew. No, that's not exactly true. I was looking out some old photographs for this weekend and I could see the strain on my face in many of them. It was the worry that I wouldn't measure up to everyone's expectations. To be that supportive daughter; that wonderful nurse. Or to produce the 2.2 children to complete our ideal family.'

Nancy reached over and squeezed Lesley's hand.

'If I've achieved anything at all it's been Jonathan. He's a lovely boy, very kind and caring. And I brought him up more or less on my own. But in terms of *me* – I think I've found myself now, back in Wales.' She smiled broadly.

' I was sad to give up my job in some ways, but it was a relief when I got ill health retirement. Now I'm leading the quiet life, and I'm not worrying *any more* about what people think. I just wish I'd been more assertive all those years, but that's always been hard for me – to be like that. And it is still is – a bit.'

Alix stood up.

'Christ Diane. Let's liven this up a bit! Who's for Name That Tune? I've brought the Trivial Pursuit version with me for a laugh.'

I wasn't going to be diverted just as easily as that.

'That'll be great Alix, but only once you've spilled the beans on *your* achievements and regrets. That's if you have any regrets of course.'

'You know me. Onwards and upwards. Game for anything in the pursuit of pleasure.'

The familiar tone, the upbeat message. Then she showed a rare contemplative side.

'I'm quietly pleased though that I've built up the business to what it is today, that I kept it going through Gerald's illness and death and that I was lucky enough to have found lurve through it too. Given some of the things I've done in my time, maybe I didn't deserve that. The kids are wonderful, they love James, they're doing so well in their careers. All is well. All is great actually.

'But' – she gave out a deep sigh – 'sometimes I wonder what the baby I lost would have been like. That is one regret I do have.' Her expression softened into wistfulness. 'I've sailed through most things but maybe that was payback time.'

I froze. I hadn't been expecting this.

Patricia leaned forward, her face bearing a puzzled expression.

'Payback for what exactly?'

'The abortion Patricia. You remember? Final year, Dalmeny Street.'

'The what?'

'The termination, the abortion. I haven't spoken about it for years, didn't at the time either, but you all found out anyway.'

Not quite.

'*I* didn't know! Why did no-one tell *me*? This is awful finding out now, like this, all these years later. How could you do such a thing Alix? When there are people like me who would have loved more children and couldn't.'

Patricia was white faced and crestfallen.

The young waitress with the striped hair popped her head round the door.

'More coffee ladies? Or will I take an order for drinks?'

Patricia squeezed past her, head down and hands clenched, aiming for the Ladies. With a backward glance that said 'leave this to me' I followed her out.

Slamming the cubicle door, she subjected me to a prolonged wait.

Leaning close in to the door, talking in exaggerated whispers, I tried to reason with her.

'Patricia. Come on out *please*. We need to talk about this. It all happened a long, long time ago and we don't want it to spoil the weekend.'

Her voice came soaring over the top of the cubicle, clipped, loud, angry now rather than shocked.

'How many other things did you keep from me? Just how many? I was a Dalmeny Street Girl too you know. I was one of you. Or so I thought. And now it seems there were five of you, and me somewhere on the outside.'

'That's nonsense, Patricia. You were our cornerstone, the one that kept us in line. We relied on you to keep the place in order, to keep us from straying too far from the path. Surely you know that?'

She flushed the toilet, pulled open the door with a flourish and marched over to the washbasin.

'Well it doesn't look like that from where I'm standing.'

I tried to keep my voice calm, steady; I'd never before seen her so rattled.

'This abortion thing. We *did* keep it from you, but only out of respect for your beliefs, which were pretty fixed, you must agree. And in fact after we found out, it was never mentioned again – by any of us. Believe me, please, this was a one-off. You were never excluded on any other occasion.'

I was pleading now.

She stopped the vigorous rubbing of her hands under the water and turned around to face me, hands dripping. Her eyes were moist, her face flushed.

'If you say so, Diane. I don't want to cause a fuss. It seems I'm not flavour of the month in many places just now. Trevor complained that I was too inflexible and totally lacking in spontaneity. I should never have married outside the faith, that was a mistake. Then the inspectors judged me too autocratic with staff. I don't know what to think these days.'

And with a sharp intake of breath, 'the only thing that keeps me going is the numbers of parents who want to send their kids to my school – for a traditional approach they say. I just keep working away, trying harder.'

She was gulping back tears by then.

I wanted to hug her but knew she would have felt awkward had I tried, so I simply followed her out of the Ladies, searching my brain for something soothing to say, but I was too late. She turned around briefly before taking off at a brisk trot.

'I think I'll go up early. This abortion business has come as a shock to me and I need time to think about it. I'll see you at breakfast once I've done my run. Make my apologies to the others will you please?'

I watched her climb the stairs till she disappeared into her room.

* *

'God, *she's* touchy,' said Alix. 'I hope that wasn't my fault.'

I was back in peacemaker role. 'Let's just try hard to make her feel wanted tomorrow, okay? We'd never be the same without her, daft old fogey that she is.'

Nancy was next to gather up her things and made to sign off with a 'Well *I* always wished I'd ridden at Badminton, but no chance of that now, not ever. Too old, not fit enough.'

I put out a foot to stop her, wanting her to hear what Carys had to say.

'Not yet Nancy. We didn't get a chance to ask about the life and times of Professor Lloyd-Jones. Carys – the short version please. And now that Patricia has retired to bed, you won't need to censor it!'

'I thought you'd never ask, Diane! My achievements are listed in my latest book of course, or some of them at least. But I suppose I'm most proud of the fact that I'm the first academic historian – and female at that – who has written and presented her own networked series on American television. I'm a household name over there now. I just wish Dad had been here to see me do it.'

Lesley nodded in sympathy.

'But don't you miss home Carys? I'm so glad to be back living there again.'

'Well actually I've spent quite a bit of time there in recent months. There are plans for a new series for BBC Wales – Saints and Sinners is the working title. So I expect I'll be flitting back and forth quite a bit. Funny thing is, in Wales they think I'm a Yank, and in the States they call me Taffy. I'm not sure where I fit these days, especially with the old family home sold off and the boys at opposite ends of the country.'

'And JJ?'

'Ah well. That's another story, for another day. Let's just say we've disappointed each other a bit over the years. But we're still friends, of a kind. Who knows how that will all work out?'

I raised an eyebrow in Nancy's direction.

'Maybe Nancy can help you with that question. What do you think Nancy?'

Alix made to laugh. 'Don't tell me you're reading the tea leaves now, you old hippie!'

Nancy hesitated and shot me a look as if to say 'Will I or won't I?'

'Let's go for it,' I said. 'You see girls, Nancy here' and I bowed to her in mock admiration, 'is not content with conquering illness, striding off in a new direction with her work and enjoying marital relations three times a week. She's now reading the tarot. Roll up here for a consultation with Madame Nancia!'

She gave my foot a hefty kick.

'Keep your voice down, Di! No need to tell the world just yet. But yes, girls, if you must know, I *am* indeed learning the mysteries of the tarot. I'd hoped to keep it quiet until the next time we met, so that I could have been a bit more proficient before exposing myself to you lot - my harshest critics. However, now that it's out, I suppose I might consider giving one reading before I go up to bed, but only one mind.'

'Bags me then,' shouted Carys. 'It might be long enough till I see you all again. We celebrities are in constant demand all over the world, you know!'

* *

Nancy removed the 78 Tarot cards from their midnight blue velvet pouch and shuffled them several times before fanning them out in a semi-circle, face down, on the table in front of Carys.

'Now, as you know, I'm a relative beginner at all this. One day I'll start charging but meanwhile you won't mind will you if I consult my Tarot handbook on occasion, if I need to check out my intuition. This is a lifetime study apparently and I've started rather late!

'Right - before I begin, just let me explain that there are two different types of card in the set. Twenty two of them form the Major Arcana. Here's an example in the book – The Empress.' She showed us the richly illustrated picture.

'This card and the other 21 represent individuals who each personify a particular quality that permeates humanity, both collectively and individually. "The Empress", and I quote, "represents abundance, creativity and fertility".

'Then the rest – all fifty six of them to be precise – form the Minor Arcana and they represent events, people, behaviour and activities that go on in our lives. So, the Nine of Wands, just to pick one at random, indicates that whatever you have been through, emotional pain or bad relationship for example, you're now ready to move on. That's the brief version of course. There's a lot more to it than that. As I said, it's a lifetime's study.

'Okay then, Carys. How about we try a simple Past, Present and Future spread? That way we'll get to bed before midnight!'

'I'm intrigued. Let's go for it then. What do I have to do?'

Following Nancy's step-by-step instruction, Carys selected three cards at random (or was it really random?) from the array. She placed them in a row – still face down, the first for Past on the left, with Present in the middle and Future on the right. And then she turned them over one at a time, repositioning the middle one round to face the same way as the other two.

With me, Lesley and Alix peering over her shoulder, trying to decipher the upside down names of the cards, Nancy began to study and interpret the spread.

'Well well, in the Past position we have the Magician. *Very* interesting. This is the "go out and get it" card. The ultimate high achiever who can work miracles. Whose unconscious desires filter through and influence conscious action. Mmmh. Let's see what's showing in the Present.'

She turned her attention to the Two of Swords, a picture of a woman who has raised a barrier round her heart, and is blindfolded.

'*She* tells us of the way we deny we have feelings. How we avoid our emotions and refuse to feed them. And in the Present position, she challenges us to ask if we are blind to our current situation through choice or by necessity.'

Carys leaned in closer, having crossed the barrier from lighthearted interest to genuine engagement.

'And in the Future position, we have the Eight of Cups.'

The card showed a set of eight cups, all full and stacked up neatly on the shore. A wistful figure of a woman looked on as a beautiful swan, garlanded with a crown of flowers, swam in circles, close to the water's edge, while her feathered partner flew off into the blue yonder towards a hazy mountain range.

She quoted again from her book.

"There is a general sense of dissatisfaction arising from a realisation that things we have fought and struggled to attain may not be as satisfying as we had hoped they would be. What was true is no longer true".

Nancy took a few moments to contemplate the spread. Checking her book. Closing her eyes. Seeming to weigh up possibilities judging by her facial expressions. Then she breathed in deeply before beginning her interpretation.

'What the cards seem to be saying Carys, is that you've achieved much in your life. You've been driven by internal forces to work hard, use masculine energies even and reach heights denied to others. You've made wise choices in order to work confidently with your skills and knowledge. However, your success may have been at the expense of your emotions. You may have denied certain feelings, you may even be raging inside and not allowing that to come out.' She paused to allow Carys time to take it all in.

'But it seems you are approaching a crossroads. You may begin to ponder whether all that you thought important, all those ambitions to which you attached great energy, have been achieved at a cost to yourself. You're possibly being given the opportunity to rise above your habitual or instinctive response patterns. And if you make a conscious effort to do that, they will lose their grip on you, and free you up to seek a more spiritual way, to fly away (metaphorically speaking of course) on a journey of discovery.'

Nancy closed her book triumphantly and looked to Carys for a response.

'What do you think?' she asked. 'Anywhere near the mark?'

Carys attempted to make light of it all.

'Heavens to Murgatroyd. The spirits have possessed her! Who'd have thought it? Watch your back Mystic Meg.'

'No, come on Carys,' I urged. 'Take it seriously, as it was intended.'

'Oh dear, sorry, Nancy. I didn't mean to offend. Let me have another look and a think.

'Achievements, miracles? You got that bit right. Denying feelings – I don't think so. Not much anyway. Maybe about my Dad, but that was years ago. And – what was it? – ready to begin on a journey of discovery? There might be something in that. I do feel a bit rootless these days. So watch this space – or rather – watch my series on CBS. No doubt you'll see where I end up.'

Nancy shared a knowing look with me and shrugged her shoulders as if to say, 'we might have guessed.'

'Let's wait and see then. You can email me if you have any further thoughts. Now I really must go up and get my full quota of sleep. No point in learning life's lessons and then ignoring them!' She gave me a wink. 'See you all for breakfast.'

* *

I looked for Patricia in vain next morning. Her car was gone.

She hadn't paid an early morning visit to the gym, no-one had spotted her running round the grounds, the reception staff had seen no sign of her leaving.

Claire contacted me at the hotel about 11am. It seems Patricia had phoned her in tears the previous evening, and said she would be leaving for home first thing in the morning. Something about stomach pains.

* *

At breakfast, Carys didn't mention the cards or their possible meaning.

But Lesley, as we were saying our goodbyes, whispered to me, 'that's really been our story – all our stories – hasn't it? You know – rising above our usual ways of reacting, breaking old habits. Thinking differently. I wonder if maybe Carys will see it that way once she's gone back home?'

Maybe I thought, just maybe. There again, knowing Carys, maybe not.

Swan song

On meeting Diane Steven I was immediately drawn by her great enthusiasm for her work. Despite her busy schedule, she could not have been more welcoming as she invited me into the striking environment that is "Shasta", situated in a quiet lane off Dunkeld's busy village square. The area's newest and currently most successful gallery owner (over £150,000 turnover in 2006, visitor figures 5,000) was "ecstatic" on learning she had been awarded the Scottish Arts Council's prestigious Lennox prize for Patronage of the Arts in Scotland.

"It was a complete surprise," Diane told me, beaming broadly, her deep brown eyes lighting up with pleasure. She is taller than I had imagined from photographs, and with her clear skin and thick dark hair looks far younger than her 53 years. Cutting a striking figure in a flattering green silk trouser suit ("handmade by a wonderful tailor in Bangkok – that's my husband Willie's, favourite holiday destination") she moved purposefully around the gallery, describing the current collection with knowledgeable flair, interspersed with amusing anecdotes about the young artists under her patronage.

Even though she seems to be almost girlish at times in her unassuming manner, lacking the pretensions of a number of her contemporaries in the art world, Diane has no misconceptions about the vagaries of the business. One gets the feeling that underneath is a dedicated businesswoman, who has worked hard to get where she is today and has no intention of losing her market leader position.

I asked her what, in such a competitive market where others come and go with predictable regularity, was the secret of her success.

"It's quite simple I think. It might sound trite - a bit new-agey perhaps – but finally, I've found myself. I'm really happy with my life and this work. It's taken me a long time to reach this point, but all the experiences I've had along the way have helped equip me for the job, and I've had lots of support from my family and friends in recent years which has given me the confidence to branch out."

* *

And so it went on, ending up with a rather over-the-top pronouncement that "if Diane Steven continues in this vein, with her uncanny nose for what the art-loving public of Scotland and beyond seek, then the Shasta Gallery has the potential to become an internationally recognised centre of cultural excellence."

I read the article in the Scottish Field at least twice before I stopped blushing. It was obvious now that the reporter had lulled me into letting my guard down a bit, and she'd taken some artistic licence with the 'quotes'. The photograph wasn't great either – I looked at least 58, not 53. Just who, exactly, was she trying to kid? I knew I should have gone on that course Alix had recommended about dealing with the media. It was too late to swallow them now, all my gushy words that were on display this week in book-stands everywhere from Tesco's to railway stations.

'Stop worrying for Christ's sake, Diane. It's fine,' Willie said. 'You come over as a lovely person – someone who's made good and deserves to be successful. And the photo is you to a tee. That's just how you look. Accept it and enjoy it.'

By midday I'd already had fifteen congratulatory phone calls for getting into the magazine so was feeling quite a bit better about my newfound fame.

'Darling! You've arrived at last!' Alix had screamed predictably down the line. 'Thank you *so* much for mentioning my chair and squeezing it into the photo! I owe you big style. And maybe I'll be next. Did you give them my card? Look - I'm coming down right now to crack open the bubbly with you and don't say No!'

A fabulous bunch of flowers courtesy of 'Borders Blooms Direct' arrived at the gallery just before lunch-time. I didn't have to look at the card to know that Nancy had sent it. I phoned her straightaway, catching her in the middle of preparing lunch for eight.

'You shouldn't have Nance,' I scolded, 'they're absolutely beautiful though, and there's loads of lilies – my favourites.'

'Good. Glad it's nice. And shut up about "shouldn'ts", Di!' she retorted. 'It's not every day my best friend gets her mug in the Scottish Field is it? See it as an excuse to celebrate. I'm drinking one for you here – Chablis – nice and chilled. I hope Willie's going to treat you to something later. Is he?'

'Yes he is, as a matter of fact,' I replied, 'and it won't be what you're thinking either! He's booked a table for two, but he's not saying where, just that I have to be ready by eight.'

'Enjoy yourselves then. Bask in it. I know I would if it were me splashed prominently over two colour pages, but the only thing I'm splashing in right now is plum sauce for the venison. Going to have to go, Di or I'll lose the plot here and burn the bloody lot. I'll phone you on the weekend for a longer chat okay?'

I smiled at the vision of her in that vast kitchen, pinny on, spattered with stains. Glass of wine in hand, dogs at feet, surrounded by what others would conceive as absolute chaos, but from which she would conjure, as always, the perfect meal for family plus various hangers-on.

Alix burst in with a flourish, a bottle of Tattinger in one hand, two glasses in the other, putting on a toastmaster's voice.

'To Diane Steven, Scottish Arts Council prize winner, famous Patron of the Arts'; and then, parodying the Scottish Field, ' she who cuts a striking figure, the one with a girlish manner but *do not* be deceived – underneath it all she's really a hard business woman, a market leader no less!'

I locked the gallery door and put up the "Closed for Lunch" sign.

'Oh stop it, Alix,' I sighed, pretending to protest, whilst secretly enjoying the fuss. Her excitement was contagious; we ended up dancing around the gallery before popping the cork and raising our glasses in succession to "Diane" "Alix" "the Gallery" "Rubislaw Treasures" and finally "the future". Thank goodness there were no potential customers to see us.

'Girlish indeed,' I laughed. 'We're not girls. We are women of a certain age. Fifty-three to be precise. I can't say the same of you but most of *my* womanly bits are sagging rather, moving steadily downwards, more and more each year. But I don't care. I'm free. Free as a bird.' I raised my arms to shoulder height and smiled at her as I started to flap them gently up and down.

'Not just any old bird though, I'm like the beautiful majestic swan in that print over there – look – the one taking off from the lake into the blue sky – I'm the one in the lead.'

I flapped my arms more energetically then, as I got into my stride, whilst she just sat there looking slightly bemused.

'That bubbly's gone to your head,' she said. 'You'd better get a taxi home!'

I took another swig from my glass.

'I don't need any taxi,' I snorted. '*I'm* going to fly home! I have the air under my wings; I am powerful, thrusting upwards gracefully, steadily, and I know *exactly* where I'm going; towards the sun, that's where; into the light.'

She pulled out her gold cigarette case, signalling an urgent need for a smoke, putting an end to my little performance.

'That's a nice picture Diane,' she said, 'how much are you selling it for?'

'Please don't ask me if you can buy it,' I cautioned, 'because I won't sell it, not at any price. Never again will I give up the things that make me happy. Not for you, not for anyone, not even for Willie. Not ever.'

She raised her eyebrows, feigning shock, pursing her lips in a silent 'oooh'.

I'd surprised even myself with the intensity of my words, yet my voice continued, as if on automatic pilot.

'It hasn't been easy, this change you know. That first reunion's got a lot to answer for. Twelve years, remember? And a whole lot of heartache along the way. I only wish I'd done it sooner, but I didn't know how to. Now I see I'd been asleep in my own life for a hell of a long time. Strange how things have worked out for me; well, for all of us really, don't you think?'

'Yes,' she said, looking a bit agitated, most likely desperate for that cigarette now. 'Very odd in one sense, but in another, not strange at all, if you know what I mean.'

Coming from her that was probably the deepest I was going to get for the time being.

'I know exactly what you mean,' I replied. 'Exactly. Now go and have that cigarette.'

By the time Alix returned, looking much calmer, I'd made us a cup of coffee.

'Thank you sweetie,' she purred. 'That's just what a girl needs after a ciggie and a mid-afternoon glass of champers.'

She suddenly looked uncharacteristically thoughtful. 'But you were wrong about one thing, Diane. It's not twelve years since we all met up in Edinburgh, it's thirteen.'

ACKNOWLEDGEMENTS

The authors would like to thank the following friends and colleagues for their insightful comments and suggestions on various drafts of the manuscript:

Arlene Napier, Doris Watt, Mary Thomas, Lisa Prudom, Caroline Campbell, Morna McKiernan, Jennifer Clark, Sasha Railton, Judy Lever, Jackie Robertson, Kate Robertson, Gillian Wightman, Gillian Gordon and Maureen Jenner.

The detailed critique generously provided by Dr Simon Jenner gave the authors the necessary push to take the novel to publication.

Antony Troon kindly copy edited the text.
Graham Starmore gave invaluable typesetting advice.
Crad Griffin designed the publisher's logo.

Bernard Duffy provided the impetus without which this book would never have been started, and continued to support its genesis from start to finish.

The Outer Hebrides was an inspirational location during much of the writing of this book, as was the picturesque East Neuk of Fife. The authors would like to thank the Tigh Dearg Hotel, Lochmaddy, North Uist and the Castlebay Hotel, Barra for facilitating a writing corner.

Marion would like to thank Elaine for the constant supply of food which oiled the creative process, and Elaine would like to thank Marion for managing the plethora of documents that were generated.

Introducing the authors

Marion Duffy

Born
Broughty Ferry, Dundee

Education
University of Edinburgh (BSc Social Sciences)
College of Commerce, Edinburgh (Dip. Grad. Sec.)
The Robert Gordon University, Aberdeen (CTLCM)

Previous careers
Lecturer
Researcher
Medical practice manager
Primary care facilitator

Homelife
Married with three grown up children and one grandchild

Hobbies and interests
Yoga
Walking
Reading
Travelling

Future plans
To complete Mirren Jones' second novel
To achieve perfect balance in life!

One thing that might surprise you
Marion is a life long Elvis fan and one of her happiest days ever was her visit to Graceland

Elaine Atkins

Born
Cardiff, Glamorgan

Education
University of London (BSc)
University of Wales (PGCEFE)
University of Wales (MSc)
University of Strathclyde (EdD)

Previous careers
Scientific Researcher
Academic
Organisational Consultant
Senior Manager NHS

Homelife
Three grown-up children and a dog

Hobbies and interests
Natural horsemanship and classical riding
Music
Reading

Future plans
To complete Mirren Jones' second novel
To compete in dressage again with my stallions

One thing that might surprise you
Over the years Elaine has been mistaken regularly for firstly Mary Hopkin and latterly Helen Mirren